'est has ...e grandchildren. Her various jobs have included working as a qualified nurse and a civil servant in the Prison Service. When her children were young she successfully completed an Open University B.A. degree studying psychology and sociology. She was a member of the Romantic Novelists' Association for four years and is now a member of ALLi (the Alliance of Independent Authors) and Goodreads.

As well as writing she loves country walks and travelling abroad (she adores bus stations, railway stations, airports and ferry ports – any place where people are on the move).

Contact the author by email at
Julia@JuliaBellRomanticFiction.co.uk

or visit her website at
www.JuliaBellRomanticFiction.co.uk

ACKNOWLEDGEMENTS

I would like to thank:

Amanda Lillywhite for the excellent work she did creating the front cover. Amanda can be contacted via her website at www.AJLIllustration.talktalk.net.

Rob White for all his technical know-how, moral support and encouragement for which I am very grateful.

Hazel Garner. Her wonderful proof reading kept me on track and her sensible advice was invaluable.

Cover re-engineered for paperback by Rob White.

A SPECIAL NOTE FROM THE AUTHOR

In the time in which this story is written there was actually no state of Germany, as we know it. It was more a collection of smaller countries of which the biggest were Prussia and Bavaria. However, for the sake of clarity, I have decided to stay with Germany and I hope my readers will forgive my 'authors' licence' to do this.

For my granddaughter, Jessica

BROKEN BLOSSOMS

by

Julia Bell

I do hope you
enjoy this story

Julia Bell
27/7/2019

PROLOGUE

The young girl eased herself into the corner of the speeding coach and turned her face away from the man sitting on the opposite seat. Even though she wore a blindfold of a red silk handkerchief, she found comfort in pressing her cheek against the soft upholstery. It had been raining, causing the wheels to squelch in every rut as the coach lurched from side to side. She knew the driver must be bent in his seat, urging the horses faster; she could hear the crack of the whip. Fear gripped her as the coach came to a halt and she realised they had reached their destination.

For ten seconds nothing happened until the door swung open and the man stepped out. He was swathed in a coat and scarf, his hat hiding his face. Only his eyes shone from beneath the brim, deep brown eyes that seemed to be everywhere as he scanned the countryside. The sun was just below the horizon; the landscape cast in the indistinct light that comes before dawn. The pastures were bathed in a thin mist that floated across in eerie wisps. There were no labourers at work in the fields yet and only the sheep were witnesses to the man who looked about him.

Satisfied, he reached inside the coach. "Come, give me your hand. Remember there are two steps down," he said in a muffled voice.

The young girl stretched out her hand and allowed him to guide her through the door and down the steep steps to the ground. She groped bewildered, her lips parted as she gasped for air. Stumbling forward, her lightly shod feet scraped against his boots. He grasped her arm and led her over to the stone wall.

Turning her round so that she faced the meadow, he said, "I want you to stay there until you can no longer hear the coach. Remember I will have a pistol pointed at your head and I'll not hesitate to use it if I see you move so much as an inch. Do you understand me?" The girl nodded. "Only then may you remove the blindfold."

There came the squeak of wood and leather as he climbed up next to the driver, followed by the snap of the reins and a sharp command for the horses to 'walk on'. For a few seconds the sound of rumbling wheels filled her ears as the coach turned, passed her and then the noise faded into the distance.

She kept still for a long time after that, gathering her courage and trying to control her constant shaking. A gentle breeze fanned her face and caressed the untidy blonde curls that hung limply from beneath the hood of her cloak. The sun rose above the horizon, warming her. She untied the handkerchief and snatched it away from her eyes, blinking at the bright light that filled the landscape with colour and dazzled her after a day and a night in darkness. Then she heard another noise; the sound of a creaking rope.

She turned round and saw the gibbet, the body of a highwayman still encased in the metal cage. Shuddering, she hurried to the far side of the crossroads to study the signpost. The village of Lenchwick was only six miles away and she breathed a sigh of relief that she knew where she was. If she walked steadily she would be back at the Hall in less than two hours.

Her thoughts firmly fixed on her family and her longing to be with them again, she wrapped her cloak more tightly round her and set off up the long and winding road that would take her home.

CHAPTER ONE

The hooves thundered along the road, drumming on the hard surface and sending up clouds of suffocating dust. It had been a hot summer that year and even in September the heat was oppressive. Katherine was ahead of her cousin and working hard to keep her lead, but Philippa was gaining on her.

"You're going to have to ride faster than that if you want to get the better of me," shouted Katherine.

"You've not won yet," Philippa shouted back, urging her horse faster.

Katherine reached the brow of the hill and waited for her cousin to catch up.

Philippa trotted to her side a short time later, grinning from ear to ear. "One day I might beat you, dear Kate." She nodded over her shoulder. "But at least I've outdone Millet. Poor man. Do you think him equal to the task?"

Katherine turned in the saddle to study the elderly groom, his battered tricorne hat on the back of his head, his cheeks puffed out pink as though he was doing the cantering instead of the chestnut mare he rode.

"Well, I do believe he dreads it when we come out riding." She sniffed in contempt. "It's ridiculous that we should need a groom to accompany us as though we can't look out for ourselves."

Philippa brushed the clinging particles of dirt from her riding habit and gave her cousin a mischievous glance. "Tell the truth and shame the devil. I know that you sneak out of the house and go riding on your own, even though Papa has forbidden it."

"But it will soon be the nineteenth century for goodness sake! With all the promise that brings including the hope of more freedom for womankind."

Philippa didn't wish to argue with her cousin's independent ways and instead smiled as the groom finally caught them up.

Millet touched the brim of his hat. "Miss Philippa, Miss Widcombe, you really shouldn't speed off so. What would Sir George say if I lost you?"

"Probably that you were very careless and should be dismissed immediately," said Katherine, trying to stop her lips twitching. "And we would have to beg him on bended knee to keep you on for the sake of your wife and children."

"Nay, lass, my young ones are fully-grown and I've seven grandchildren to call my own."

Katherine inclined her head in acknowledgement. Millet had been with the family since before she was born and she knew his family well. She also knew that as an elderly retainer he was more indulged than the younger members of staff and addressing her as 'lass' was his privilege alone.

The cousins made their way down the hill.

Stretched before them were the beautiful valley and woodlands and situated right in the middle was Widcombe Hall, surrounded by the estates, now burnished with the gold and oranges of early autumn. Behind them was the glory of the Cotswolds, just starting to hide the setting sun.

Katherine smiled as she surveyed her home. "I love autumn. I think there's something special about this time of year, something magical.

"Perhaps it's because winter can be so harsh," Philippa grimaced.

Katherine shook her head at her cousin's dolefulness and scrutinised Widcombe Hall remembering what she had been told about its origins. It had been a ramshackle seventeenth century manor house when Queen Anne had rewarded her great-great-grandfather with the estate for his bravery against the French at the Battle of Blenheim. Added to this was a baronetcy and her ancestor had immediately set about the task of pulling down the old house and employing the fashionable Scottish-born architect Colen Campbell to build a Palladian structure. Once completed with a grand portico and colonnades, the Hall now befitted the family's position in society.

Leading up to the house was a long, sweeping drive that curved round to the stables at the rear and Katherine shaded her eyes and scanned the driveway.

"I think we have an important visitor," she said, smiling.

"It's the Earl of Croston's coach," Philippa said in surprise. "I thought he was visiting tomorrow."

"Perhaps he discovered it was inconvenient to come tomorrow or," she tried to hold back her laughter and failed, "he's very eager to make you his wife." Philippa gave her a withering look that made Katherine blush slightly. "Forgive me, I was having fun at your expense. But you are happy that Lord Croston asked for your hand in marriage? He seems a nice enough young man."

Philippa nodded. "I'm very satisfied with the arrangement, although he is almost twice my age."

Katherine glanced sideways at the girl riding next to her.

"Well, I suppose thirty does seem old when you're only seventeen. But it doesn't seem so when you reach your twenty-first year, I assure you."

"I want to marry well and Papa says it's a good match. I just don't want to leave Widcombe Hall."

Katherine threw back her head and laughed. "You're only going to the other side of the hills. Croston Court is but twenty miles away. We'll be able to visit each other often."

Philippa wasn't convinced. "Twenty miles can be a long way, if the weather is inclement and the coach gets bogged down. Sometimes it can take the entire day to travel that distance, especially in winter. If it snows, we can be completely cut off from each other." Her voice had risen somewhat and Katherine felt alarmed.

She tried to reassure her. "Don't fret so. Let's face these problems one at a time."

"If only Lord Croston would come and live here with us. How happy that would make me."

"What nonsense you speak. A wife goes to her husband's house, as you well know. I understand it will be strange to leave home but many young ladies achieve it without any undue harm and I'm sure you will also have no trouble in settling down to your new life." She gave a bright smile. "Well, let's go down and see what arrangements have been made for you."

They made their way down the hill and along the drive.

As they approached the front of the Hall, Philippa bit her lip and said quietly, "I think you should wed as soon as possible, dearest Kate." She knew she was on rocky ground broaching such a subject, but separation from those she loved was drawing ever closer and the knowledge caused her such pain.

"And why is that, pray?"

"Then we can visit each other as married ladies. We'll be able to discuss the trials and tribulations of running a household and caring for our husbands."

"I will look forward to that day," said Katherine, glancing away for a moment.

"Will you? Then you'll have to accept a marriage proposal first and since you keep turning every one down, we might have to wait some time."

Katherine grimaced. "I've turned down fops and gentlemen of shallow character and weak intellect. No, dear cousin, I'll not marry a man I cannot respect and hopefully grow to love in time." She paused, thinking. "If I could be in love right from the beginning, then that would be wonderful. And if he should love me..."

Philippa shook her head in exasperation and Katherine waited for the inevitable rebuke.

"But you are so particular. How can a gentleman fall in love with you if you dismiss him out of hand? Thank goodness I didn't behave like that with Lord Croston."

Philippa had been bubbling with the news when she had arrived back from Worcester after a summer visit to Aunt Charlotte, her mother's younger sister. She had met the earl in the bookshop and he had simply inclined his head and said 'Good morning'. But when meeting Philippa again at a ball hosted by Lady Sarah, his aunt, they had been formally introduced and he had asked her to dance. By the time she had left Worcester, he had stated his intentions with a promise that he would call at Widcombe Hall and ask her papa for her hand in marriage. And this he had done, quite promptly.

Sir George Widcombe had been delighted that his only daughter had attracted the attention of Conrad Fitzwilliam, the fifth Earl of Croston and had given his permission wholeheartedly. Philippa and the earl officially announced their betrothal and Philippa began to prepare her trousseau although a date had not yet been set for the wedding.

Katherine had never met her cousin's betrothed, since through the summer she had been visiting her aunt in Bristol. But she had listened for hours as Philippa had listed his virtues; his elegant bearing, his light brown hair and dazzling violet eyes. Not to mention his impeccable fashion sense since he was always dressed in the finest clothes. Katherine looked forward to meeting this paragon of style and beauty, but wondered at his personal qualities. In all their conversations, Philippa had never mentioned them. And Katherine wanted to know if he had charm and portrayed good humour. Was he kind and did he show sensitivity? Katherine's queries were met with a shrug of the shoulders and she had sighed at Philippa's lack of interest in what Katherine believed was the most important aspect of a man, his character.

The cousins reached the front of the house and left the horses in the care of Millet before passing through the large entrance and into the coolness of Widcombe Hall. They were greeted by Katherine's aunt in voluminous skirts and a lace cap perched on dark curls.

"Where have you been?" Philippa's mother complained. "We've been waiting over fifteen minutes for you. Katherine, take your cousin upstairs and make her look presentable and do it quickly."

She turned and made her way back to the drawing room, her silk gown swishing as she walked.

Laughing, they ran upstairs to Philippa's bedchamber. In ten minutes, they were back downstairs, where Katherine pushed the younger girl towards the drawing room. As she entered, Katherine caught a glimpse of Lord Croston rising to his feet and coming forward to kiss Philippa's hand. Then the door was closed and she could see and hear no more.

She ran back upstairs to her own room, changed out of her riding habit, washed the dust from her face and brushed her hair. As she sat in front of the mirror, she contemplated the conversation she had had with Philippa. She hoped her cousin would be happy, but as for her own uncertain future, she dare not reflect too much on it. She studied the small silver-framed portraits of her parents, deep in thought. Only her grandmama knew her secret, since it was only she who had had the strength of character to prise it out of her in the first place. Katherine had told her everything and after it had all been said, she had put her head on the old lady's knee and wept.

Shaking off her disturbing thoughts, Katherine picked up a book and crossed the landing to the top of the stairs. She spent a minute or two trying to listen over the banister, but not a sound could be heard through the solid oak door, so she made her way to a couch placed in a window bay and settled herself comfortably. She intended to be within earshot when the proceedings downstairs came to their conclusion and her book *The Pilgrim's Progress*, did not keep her attention as it had done the day before.

A door opened further along the corridor and Sebastian came towards her. Katherine smiled at her cousin, who immediately leaned over the banister as if trying to listen to what was going on downstairs.

"I've tried that, but it doesn't work," she told him with a grimace. He nodded in agreement and sighed. He came to sit next to her.

"I suppose my sister will marry soon and go off to his lordship's gloomy ancestral pile."

It was more of a statement than a question, but Katherine decided to accept it as a question. "Yes, he's here today to finalise the arrangements."

He puffed out a breath. "I'll miss her."

"So will we all."

Sebastian sank against the plush velvet coverings and gave Katherine a studious look. "We'll have to find you a husband next, Cousin Kate. Although how we will do that I've no idea."

"I like the way you say 'we'. And what do you mean, you have no idea how they are going to find me a husband? Am I that plain and undesirable?"

"Actually, I find you rather handsome."

"Oh, thank you, kind sir." Katherine stood up and made a mock curtsey to her rather pretentious younger cousin. She resumed her seat as he continued his wooing.

"Of course I must finish school first, then there will be Oxford and my tour of the Continent. But I think I should be ready to marry you by the time I'm twenty-five."

"Now let me see," said Katherine, her expression impassive. "You are now fourteen, so that makes eleven years before you reach the age of twenty-five. I'm now twenty-one, so I will be thirty-two before we can wed." She gave an exaggerated sigh and clutched her hands dramatically to her breast. "But I will pine away waiting for you."

The door to the drawing room opened and voices floated up from the hallway interrupting their declarations of love. The two cousins jumped from the seat to lean over the banister where they could get a good view of what was taking place below.

Beneath them they saw Lord Croston, Philippa at his side, walking to the entrance where the footman was ready with his hat and cloak. Once dressed, he turned to Philippa, but their conversation was too muffled for Katherine to hear clearly. Finally, he raised Philippa's hand to his lips and kissed it politely. And then he was through the door and gone.

Katherine made her way to the middle of the staircase and was relieved to see the happiness on her cousin's face.

"Goodness, it's all arranged," said Philippa, breathlessly. "We've decided to marry in just four weeks before the winter sets in. Come and give me a kiss, dear, dear Kate."

The fact that her aunt had pre-empted the date of the wedding and had already commissioned seamstresses and chefs alike on the preparations, did not surprise Katherine one bit. Aunt Beatrice was the queen of organisation and both she and her husband would want to give their only daughter a grand send-off. This would be accomplished by a week of celebrations before the actual ceremony, comprising of lavish dinners, receptions and culminating in a grand ball two days before the wedding.

When the architect Campbell had restructured Widcombe Hall, he had not neglected the interior. The private elegance of the five main rooms, decorated with pilasters and friezes and enhanced with paintings by Stubbs and furniture by Chippendale, simply faded into insignificance compared to the Grand Saloon that sported a Sienna marble fireplace. And it was in this saloon, its pillars wreathed in garlands of silk flowers and ribbons, that the celebrations would take place. Any occasion was an excuse to show off one's home to society and a wedding was the apex of a social event.

It was the night of the ball and Katherine was sitting next to the Dowager Lady Widcombe, her grandmother, enjoying a moment of rest after dancing most of the evening.

Philippa's bridegroom crossed the floor towards her and gave a polite bow. "May I have the pleasure of this dance, Miss Widcombe?"

Katherine rose from her seat and curtsied. "I would be delighted, sir," she smiled and took his outstretched hand. He led her into the formation for the quadrille.

The music started and the dancers made their first movements, the ladies circling their partners.

"I suppose we will be cousins soon," he said, his eyes sweeping over her gown of blue silk, trimmed with royal blue ribbons, the soft golden curls of her hair styled into ringlets and festooned with silk flowers.

"Well, cousins-in-law, I should think," she said, laughing.

"Indeed. But I hope you'll come to the Court and visit as often as you can. Philippa is very young and I've tended to surround myself with mostly male companions. I fear she may get lonely."

"Thank you for your invitation. I'll certainly consider it."

Their brief conversation came to an abrupt halt as they separated to move down the room and take the next person in line. They didn't speak again, even when reunited and finally the dance ended with a bow and a curtsey.

"Would you care for some punch?" the earl asked. Katherine nodded and took his hand as he guided her over to the punchbowl sitting majestically on a side table. "So, dear Cousin-in-Law, are you enjoying the festivities?"

Katherine gave a radiant smile. "Yes, my lord and it will be a wonderful wedding the day after tomorrow. I know your bride will look beautiful." A footman passed her a glass of punch.

"As will her bridesmaid, I wager."

Katherine started at the thought he was flirting with her. "You're very kind, sir." She took a sip of her drink to hide her worried expression. "Do you think the war will last much longer. I mean, it has been five…" She stopped abruptly seeing him raise his eyebrows.

"Goodness me, a young lady interested in politics. You're certainly a rare breed, Miss Widcombe." She could have bitten out her tongue! Trying to make polite conversation was one thing, but politics was not a subject to discuss with a gentleman at a ball. Seeing her crimson cheeks, he nodded. "Well, I was delighted to hear that Nelson had defeated the French fleet in Egypt and sent Bonaparte scurrying back to France, minus his army thankfully. But who can say when a war will end? Victory and defeat share the same bed." He gave her a quizzical glance. "Am I to understand that you have a beau fighting the French and you're concerned for his wellbeing?" His eyes twinkled.

"No, sir. I have no beau either here in England or fighting Napoleon."

"Just making conversation, eh?" He tilted his head. "Tell me, Miss Widcombe, why is it only this last week that I've had the opportunity to get to know you? And why were you not in Worcester with your aunt and cousin?"

"I was visiting my aunt in Bristol over the summer. The sister of my late mother."

"Ah, yes. Philippa told me that your father was a sea captain and you were orphancd when just a baby." She couldn't prevent the blush from spreading into her cheeks once more. He noticed and frowned. "I do beg your pardon. I seem to have disconcerted you."

"No indeed, sir. It just came as a surprise that my cousin should speak of me. And you should be interested."

"And why shouldn't I be interested?"

"I've been told that you returned from Germany in the spring. How long were you away?"

He smiled, intrigued at her sharp change in conversation. "I too, was visiting my late mother's family in Hamburg. Three cousins, to be exact. I stayed for six months and was delighted to be a guest at the wedding of my youngest cousin and the christening of the firstborn son of my eldest cousin."

"What about your middle cousin?" she said, laughing.

"Oh, she's been married years and already has four rascals."

"You come from a large family, then?"

"On my mother's side, yes."

"I have never been to the Continent."

"Then perhaps you would like to accompany Philippa and me to Germany next year? You would certainly be very welcome." Pausing slightly he added, "Of course, you could be married yourself by then."

"I think not, sir." She opened her fan and looked away.

Katherine followed her uncle and cousin up the aisle. They were in their private chapel, attached to the side of Widcombe Hall. It was a modest building, not large, its interior plain, the woodwork sculptured into pure, clean lines that harmonised with the simple structure. Flowers filled every niche and the sunlight on that brilliant October day cascaded through the stained glass windows, warming the congregation and sending shafts of golden light rebounding off the marble bust of the first baronet. The pews were filled with the family, friends and neighbours who had been invited to the ceremony.

Katherine concentrated on her duty as bridesmaid and smiled with approval. Philippa looked beautiful in her gown of cream silk decorated with tiny gold and silver embroidered stars. She had insisted that the dressmaker fashion it in the new style of a straight, flowing garment gathered high under her bosom, persuading her mother that revealing more of herself did not make her indecent and in fact, she would be the envy of every young woman at the wedding. She was right as the gown caressed her body as she walked, enhancing her small, neat figure. Her thick brown hair was coiled under a profusion of silk flowers and she carried a small posy of pansies. Katherine couldn't remember seeing her cousin look so lovely and even Sebastian had given a cheer as his sister had elegantly descended the stairs at the Hall.

The bridal party walked slowly towards the altar where Lord Croston turned to meet his future wife. Katherine's heart skipped a beat when she caught his glance that swept over the amazing vision of the bride and induced an appreciative smile.

Her duties completed, she slipped into the family pew next to her grandmother who passed her a small leather bound book already open for the first hymn. The organ started up and jubilant voices rose to the rafters scattering the doves sitting on the roof tiles.

The congregation eventually took their seats. It was comforting to sit beside the old lady who smelt of jasmine, and Katherine reached out to squeeze the wrinkled old hand. Her grandmother was dressed in one of her best gowns, but a gown that would not have been out of place fifty years ago. The full skirt and half sleeves swathed in frills set off the large wig placed precariously on her small head. Katherine smiled as she watched the ceremony at the altar.

"Dearly beloved," the vicar droned, "we are gathered here in the sight of God, and in the face of this congregation, to join together this man and this woman in holy matrimony…"

Katherine had listened to these words before, as a bridesmaid and a guest, but none of those occasions were as important as this one. Philippa and Conrad exchanged vows and the ring was blessed before he placed it on the bride's finger. A few more prayers and then the final hymn followed. There was nothing left but the blessing before Conrad took his bride's hand and led her to a small table covered with a white cloth. They signed the register with their witnesses.

"Never signed a register when I married," said Katherine's grandmother. "A lot of nonsense, I say."

Katherine shook her head. "Oh no, Grandmama. The Marriage Act prevents clandestine weddings." She turned blue eyes on her grandmother.

Her grandmother patted her hand. "What do you know about clandestine marriages, child?"

The newly married couple had finished the business at the small table and turned to walk down the aisle as man and wife. Katherine passed the posy back to Philippa and took her place behind them, slipping her hand through Sebastian's arm.

The wedding breakfast at the Hall was enjoyable, although rather noisy. By mid-afternoon the banqueting table was in some disorder and many of the younger male guests were a little worse for drink. Aunt Beatrice sighed in dismay at the sugar sculpture of pink and red roses entwined around trelliswork that had made a wonderful centrepiece. She had hoped to preserve it and keep it in her glass cabinet, but now she saw that some of the roses had been snapped off and nutshells had been pushed through the trellis. Turning away she decided that it was time for the bride to withdraw and be dressed for her departure to Croston Court. She smiled when she saw Katherine in conversation with her grandmother and crossed the floor to ask her to assist her cousin.

In her bedchamber, Katherine helped Philippa to remove her bridal gown and put on her travelling clothes. When all was complete, the cousins held each other close, the younger girl struggling to keep back her tears.

"Oh, Kate, I'm happy to be married, but I will miss you all so much."

"Hush now. Remember that your loving family is only a short distance away. You will write as soon as you can?"

Philippa nodded sadly.

Holding hands, they went downstairs where Lord Croston came to escort his wife out to the coach that would take them the twenty miles to the bride's new home. The hot summer had made the roads bone dry and the journey of two hours would make Philippa mistress of her own home before nightfall.

The coach disappeared down the drive and Katherine allowed herself the luxury of a few tears to spill onto her cheeks. With Uncle George's arm round her shoulders, she made her way back into the Hall.

The next four weeks were lonely for Katherine and to make matters worse, Sebastian had returned to school and wouldn't be home until Christmas. How empty and quiet the Hall seemed. But then she became concerned over the letters that came at regular intervals from Croston Court. They were so despondent, it was obvious that Philippa was lonely too. One afternoon, a particularly poignant letter arrived and Katherine read it to her grandmother, while sitting on a low stool at her knee.

After reading it, Katherine folded the letter and looked at her grandmother who shook her head sadly. "So, she is surrounded by men talking politics. I really hoped that Lord Croston would not neglect his wife."

Katherine felt the need to come to his defence. "I don't think he's neglecting her, Grandmama. He confessed that he's a man who feels more comfortable in male company. He will need time to adjust to married life, as will Philippa. All will be well soon, wait and see."

Her grandmother patted her hand. "I believe, my dear child, that your visit to Croston Court might be sooner than intended."

"Do you think so, Grandmama? I'll certainly go if Uncle George wishes it." Her eyes sparkled with delight.

But nothing more was said about the visit for a further week.

Katherine had been out riding and since she only intended riding round the estate, her uncle had given his consent for her to ride out alone. The morning was cold and there was a hint of snow in the air, although it was only the end of November. She had thoroughly enjoyed galloping her horse across the meadow, urging him on as fast as he would go. It wasn't the same as racing with Philippa, but it had still been exhilarating. She entered the Hall and was informed that her uncle needed to speak with her.

She went straight to the drawing room. Her grandmother was seated by the fire as usual, Aunt Beatrice perched serenely on the couch, with Uncle George standing by the mantelpiece, holding a letter.

She got the distinct impression they had been talking about her, since their conversation faded the minute she came into the room and they could be talking about only one thing. Philippa had written to invite her to Croston Court.

Three pairs of eyes turned in her direction.

"You've come back from your ride at last, Kate," said her uncle, clearing his throat.

"Did you wish to speak with me, Uncle?"

He took in a large breath. "Sit down, my dear." Katherine sank into the nearest chair. "Do you remember Sir Herbert Fox?"

"Sir Herbert Fox?" Katherine rolled the name round her tongue, thinking where she had heard it before. Suddenly she remembered. "Oh, isn't he that portly gentleman living near Cheltenham? I was introduced to him last spring when we attended the races."

Her uncle nodded. "Yes, and he has written asking for your hand in marriage."

Katherine felt puzzled. "But I only met him on a few occasions. Why should he be interested in me?"

"Why are you so surprised?" said her aunt. "You're a beautiful woman and it's not as though this is your first offer."

"Yes, Aunt. But he's old. Nearly fifty, I think."

Her uncle frowned. "It's a large age gap, true, but he says he's quite happy with the three hundred pounds I've settled on you when you marry and we must take that into consideration if we are to see you well matched." He cleared his throat in embarrassment. "I wish I could settle more on you, my dear, but I must think of my own children first."

Katherine remained silent, thinking. Was she a burden to her uncle and aunt? They had never suggested that she should marry, but there again they could have been waiting for Philippa to be settled before broaching the subject. Marriage! She couldn't contemplate the idea and her aunt had no inkling of what she had endured. Would they suggest marriage if they knew the truth? She doubted it.

It was her grandmother who broke the silence, rapping her cane sharply on the floor. "No, this will not do! I'll not have my girl married off to a man old enough to be her father and I might add, has already seen two wives buried."

Katherine surveyed the concerned faces of her family. "Even if you could settle a fortune on me, I don't think I will ever marry. I believe my destiny is to remain a spinster and live in the Hall caring for you all. And I shall be content in that."

Her grandmother chuckled, the husky noise coming up from the very depths of her throat. "There you have it, George. Your niece wants to look after you when you are old and infirm." The dowager sighed softly. "I know it's a vexation to you, but please remember your brother and his lovely wife. They left their child in our capable hands and it's only right that we consider Katherine's future carefully."

Aunt Beatrice smiled at her niece. "It seems to me that you have a heart as big as the sea that claimed your dear parents." She held up a second letter. "This also arrived in the post. Philippa has written that she wishes you to visit for Christmas." She turned to her husband. "George, there will be plenty of time to talk of marriage arrangements after the festive season."

George grunted. "I only wanted to know Katherine's view on the matter so that I might write to Sir Herbert and inform him." He shook his head. "In my opinion, he's not good enough for her anyway."

It was only after she was alone with her grandmother that Katherine admitted her true feelings. "For all I dream of marrying I know I cannot." She held her grandmother's blue-veined hand against her cheek, forcing away stinging tears. "But why did Sir Herbert ask for me?"

"For offspring, my dear child. He wishes to sire a son and he had no luck with his previous wives. A much younger wife will make that possible."

Katherine turned her head away to hide her troubled expression.

CHAPTER TWO

The coach pulled up at the main entrance to the Court and the waiting groom came forward to open the door. Katherine stepped down and surveyed the expansive, gloomy edifice spread around her. She looked up at the grey stonework remembering what Sebastian had said about 'his lordship's gloomy ancestral pile'. Her gaze roamed over every nook and cranny and she smiled since the earl's ancestors had certainly employed the Gothic style when building their home. But there again, the Goths came from Germany, she remembered, so perhaps his lordship's German ancestry went back many centuries. She stared up at the battlements and turrets, where the occasional gargoyle stared back down at her from their position below the parapets that edged the balcony running along the roof. The windows were made up of small panes of glass and each one glinted in the sun.

Suddenly, she was almost knocked over by the force of Philippa's greeting, as she threw herself at her with such force that she staggered back, laughing. Philippa had been watching the driveway for the last thirty minutes and when the coach finally appeared, her desperate flight through the house had caused havoc in her haste to run down the steps and fling her arms round her cousin's neck.

"Kate! Oh, Kate, you're here at last. I've been waiting all day for you. I feared the wheel had come off or the driver had lost his way. I'm so pleased you've arrived."

Katherine laughed and hugged her. "You silly goose, we've been parted barely six weeks and you talk as if it had been six years."

"Sixty years more like."

Arms linked, they made their way into the Court and were immediately greeted by a large mastiff that bounded about barking loudly at all the excitement.

Katherine knelt to stroke his soft, black ears. "And what's your name?" she asked and he whined in appreciation of the gentle touch.

"His name is Socrates and he seems to have taken a liking to you," said the earl, suddenly appearing from one of the many doorways that led into the vast entrance hall. He smiled and walked across the marble floor to greet their guest, taking her hand and lightly kissing her fingers. "Thank goodness you've arrived, Cousin. Philippa has done nothing but talk about your visit for the entire week." A tall, lanky man appeared in the doorway of one of the interior rooms and the earl beckoned to him. "Allow me to introduce you to Frobisher, my secretary."

The young man pushed his spectacles further up his nose and greeted the new arrival in an awkward, clumsy manner.

"W…w…welcome to the C…Court," he stuttered, his face becoming bright red with embarrassment.

Katherine's heart softened at his obvious discomfort. "I'm pleased to meet you," she answered with a smile. She offered her hand but pulled it back when he started coughing and spluttering. Pulling out a large, white handkerchief, he blew his nose. "Oh dear, Mr Frobisher. You seem to have a bad head cold," she added in amusement.

"P…please ma'am, p…people just call me Frobisher and I do have a c…cold, indeed. I still haven't recovered from my chest trouble and what with my b…bad back and…"

The earl turned his eyes to the ceiling in exasperation. "Our guest doesn't want to stand around here, listening to you complaining about all your aches and pains. Philippa take your cousin to her room and help her get settled in. And then I'm sure she'd like a tour of the Court." He hurried his secretary away before another word could be said.

After settling in, Katherine followed Philippa around on the Grand Tour. If the outside had been gloomy, then the inside was in sharp contrast. The cousins wandered from room to room and down each corridor with Socrates padding softly behind them. Philippa overflowed with the splendours of the Court, pointing out every feature in turn. All the main rooms were sumptuous with ornate woodcarvings and dramatic chimneypieces. Katherine nodded at the lavish tapestries still in place even though they were a remnant from times past.

As they climbed the impressive staircase Katherine saw evidence that Philippa was making her mark on her new home. In certain rooms, ladders were still erected and pots of paint stood beside them. Workmen's tools lay in tidy piles.

"Conrad told me that I must do as I wished with the Court and I've been redecorating ever since I arrived," she giggled. "The place has been a hive of activity what with workmen sawing and hammering and painting. It's been so noisy and dear Conrad has had to escape from room to room in danger of having his head lopped off by swinging objects." She bent to stroke the dog's ears. "And Socrates has been very confused, haven't you, you old thing?"

"You've done remarkably well." Katherine placed her arm round her cousin's waist. "I was so worried about you, but it seems I had nothing to worry about at all."

Philippa pulled a face. "But I've missed you. And Grandmama and Papa and Mama and dear, dear Sebastian."

"We've missed you." Katherine glanced around and sighed. "Well, now that the tour is over, I think some tea would be lovely."

"Would you mind if I didn't use my best Wedgwood?" asked Philippa, biting her lip.

Katherine tried to suppress a smile. "Of course not. I'm only family, after all."

That afternoon while they dined, Katherine watched the staff with interest. The Court seemed filled with servants, many more than at the Hall and the maids and footmen who carried the various dishes of meats, pies, fish and the nuts and sweetmeats to the table did so with all the pomp and ceremony that was inherent in the below stairs hierarchy. Their respect for the earl was evident and it was obvious that this was spilling over to include his new wife. Katherine nodded in approval; for all she was just seventeen years old, Philippa was managing this large household exceptionally well.

The evening was spent in the drawing room and it was on her first evening at the Court that Katherine met Anne Fletcher, Philippa's companion. Anne had been employed by the countess only a week after her marriage and it was the earl's idea to allow her to join them on an evening, in order to alleviate any loneliness his wife might experience with being constantly in the presence of men. It was then that Katherine realised that the earl was struggling somewhat with married life, since he seemed to find it difficult to communicate with his wife.

Katherine had brought her tapestry and she spent the first hour engrossed in her work while listening to her cousin chatting with her companion, but keeping an eye on the door waiting for the earl and Frobisher to appear and join the ladies. Eventually, they arrived and the secretary settled down with a book, while his lordship set out the chess pieces and started playing against himself. His wife watched him for a couple of seconds and then resumed her conversation with Anne, but Katherine noticed the sadness in her face and dismay flooded through her. No wonder Philippa had written of her loneliness; her husband was being quite neglectful of her. Katherine caught the companion's eye and realised that she also was aware of the deep divide between the earl and his wife.

Anne was a small, pretty woman in her early twenties. She had a round, sweet face which was almost childlike in quality, framed with dark curly hair and the most beautiful brown eyes. It didn't take much guesswork to see why Philippa had employed her, since they both seemed like two schoolgirls sitting together on the couch with their embroidery.

It became obvious there was someone else in the room who also admired Miss Fletcher. From his vantage point behind his book, Frobisher would often peep over the binding to cast secret little glances towards the pretty girl sitting next to the countess. Sometimes Katherine would see her quickly return the look, go quite red and then feverishly concentrate on her work as if it was an urgent commission. Only the occasional polite conversation passed between them and Katherine surmised the two were equally attracted, but deathly shy.

Halfway through the evening, Katherine wandered over to the earl's chair.

"Would you like me to play against you, sir? It would make it more interesting."

He smiled. "You play chess?"

"I play excellent chess," she said, her chin in the air.

He extended his hand to the seat opposite. "Then if milady would care to sit, battle may commence."

Katherine made herself comfortable and after he had set out the men, moved the first piece. She felt confident. This game was one she had enjoyed since her grandmother had taught her as a child.

As the game settled down, she glanced at Conrad. "It seems your secretary and my cousin's companion are attracted to each other."

"You noticed that, eh?"

"It's not hard to miss. He keeps peering over his book like a love-sick calf."

He grinned. "Well, we shall have to wait and see the outcome of that." He studied her for a moment. He had thought her pretty when first they met, but now sitting opposite him, he noticed the glow of her blonde hair in the candlelight and the rosy hue of her skin. Candlelight became her and he smiled. "I'm glad you're here Cousin Kate."

"As am I, my lord."

"Tell me about your parents."

The request had come unexpectedly and she looked at him in alarm.

"Why do you want to know about *my* parents?"

"Because I know all there is to know about Philippa's and your parents intrigue me."

"Do they?"

"It sounds like a love story."

Katherine nodded as she moved one of her chessmen. "It was. At least that's what Aunt Beatrice told me. She said that my father fell in love with my mother at their first meeting."

Conrad was just about to say that if she was as beautiful as her daughter then it was little wonder, but held his tongue.

"But it must have been difficult for her with your father away at sea?"

"I suppose it must have been." She drew in a deep breath. "My mother was a lady's companion." She glanced across at Philippa and her companion. "Just like Anne."

"A lady's companion, indeed."

Detecting a tone of disapproval she bristled with indignation. "I suppose you think that my mother had no right to *set her cap* at someone so high as the son of a baronet. But I would just like to say my mother was a gentlewoman fallen on hard…"

He opened his eyes wide in surprise and interrupted. "My dear Kate. I'm not thinking anything of the kind. I'm simply listening to your story."

Duly rebuked, she gulped furiously. "I beg your pardon, my lord."

There was a moment of uncomfortable silence.

"Do you know if your father travelled far? Sea voyages can take years sometimes."

Katherine smiled again. "I was told he went to Portugal to pick up oranges and Madeira for casks of wine." A look of sadness crossed her face. "It was when he was sailing to Madeira that my mother decided to accompany him. I was only six months old and I suppose she thought her parting from me would not be for long." She lifted the locket over her head and passed it to him. He opened it to reveal miniature versions of the portraits she kept on her dressing table. "But it would be the first and last voyage she would take with him. My father's ship never returned to Bristol."

Conrad looked at the portraits. Yes, he thought, the mother is as beautiful as the daughter. He gave it back to her.

"I'm so sorry for your loss, Kate, but why didn't your mother's family take you in?"

"My Aunt Sybil is a spinster lady on a meagre income. She couldn't afford to bring me up so Uncle George and Aunt Beatrice fetched me away to live at the Hall with them." Her thoughts wandered to her aunt and she sighed as she moved the queen. "I never knew my parents so I suppose I can't feel loss for something I never had. It's just that," she licked her lips, "when I was ten, my uncle told me that my father had left debts and there was no money for a wedding settlement for me. I didn't really understand the implication until I was fourteen." She added dryly, "My uncle has arranged a small settlement for me."

He nodded, understanding. "I know it's considered important in the marriage stakes for a substantial dowry and I must admit I know many a young dandy who would not consider marrying for less than ten thousand a year. But for me, I think that compatibility is more important than wealth. A man and his wife might live together a great number of years and if there is no contentment in the marriage, then I believe that life would be intolerable." He glanced uneasily at his wife and picked up a chessman, examining its detail.

She caught his glance and a shock wave pulsated through her. Was he having regrets about his marriage? It didn't seem possible after only six weeks.

"Philippa has done extremely well with the household, don't you think?" she said, wanting to change the subject.

"Indeed," he nodded.

"Despite her youth, she has taken on a great deal of responsibility."

"Yes, I'm pleased with my wife's efficiency."

Efficiency! She stared at him hardly believing she had heard correctly. He was talking about his wife as though she was a new parlour maid. Her heart sank into her stomach.

"She talked of new curtains and…making new seats for the chairs," she said without enthusiasm.

Conrad glanced up, detecting her change in manner. "My wife has *carte blanche* to do as she pleases. I'll not object to anything she decides."

"She also mentioned a party." Katherine moved her bishop to put him in check. "A small Christmas party. And only if the weather stays clement, of course." She watched him move his king out of the way, before sliding her castle across the board.

He sat back in his seat, studying his wife, his head inclined thoughtfully. Without warning he called across the room, "Philippa, dearest, would you come and sit with us for a moment." She came obediently, seating herself in the chair that Conrad had pulled back from the table. "Your cousin has just told me that you wish to have a party for Christmas."

She let out a delighted cry. "Oh yes, Conrad. Only the families in the neighbourhood. No more than thirty guests."

Her husband nodded. "Very well, then we shall."

Philippa clapped her hands like a child. "Then I will tell the workmen to hurry with the improvements and we must start on the curtains and upholstery immediately. I want to throw the doors of the Court open and proclaim to the entire world that I'm the Countess of Croston."

Conrad smiled at the two of them. "Then we will settle on a date and send out the invitations."

Katherine smiled, her despondency evaporating with Philippa's delight.

"It will be wonderful," said Katherine and then pointing at the game, she added, "By the way, I believe that's checkmate."

Plans for the party started the following day and Philippa compiled a list of the prominent families that she would invite. Katherine sat at the table in the parlour and wrote down the names as her cousin called them out. Mrs Craddock, the housekeeper, had already been informed what was to take place and she went to her sitting room to draw up a suitable menu. The best dishes, Philippa had told her sternly; the table had to groan with food. It didn't matter that his lordship had never been one for hosting parties whilst a bachelor. He was a married man now and things were different.

At the end of two weeks the Court was ready. With the work completed the servants started decorating the rooms with mistletoe, holly and scented candles since it was only six days before Christmas. Replies to the invitations had started arriving and Philippa's excitement heightened.

The evening before the party was spent in the drawing room as usual. Philippa whiled away her time playing on the harpsichord and Katherine was again sitting opposite Conrad, engaged in yet another battle of chess. She was winning by eight games to seven and he was determined to equal the score that evening.

"I'm sure to beat you tonight," he said.

"May the best man win, then," she answered, tossing her head.

He gave a slight smile. "How about a wager?"

"What kind of wager?"

"The loser has to pay a forfeit."

"What kind of forfeit, sir?"

He thought for a moment. "The loser must confess to the worst thing that has ever happened to them, or they have done to someone else, no matter how dreadful."

Katherine felt the colour drain from her face. "I don't think…"

Seeing her expression like that of a china doll, he laughed, "And what would a young girl like you have to confess to? No, dear Kate, perhaps a wager like that would be pointless."

"And what about you, Conrad? Would you have much to confess to?"

He chuckled. "I could tell you many stories that would make your hair stand up on end. But I won't, since I would hate to corrupt you." He became serious. "When we talked of marriage settlements the first evening you were here, you said that your uncle had arranged something?"

She nodded. "Three hundred pounds and I doubt that will attract any gentleman." She added, "Not that I want to get married."

He thought this over. "You don't?"

"Never."

He sat back in his chair, the game of chess now forgotten. "Not many young ladies decide such a bleak and lonely future for themselves. Usually they're more than eager to make a good match. For security if for nothing else."

"And what good match will I make with three hundred pounds?"

"That depends on the wealth of the gentleman in question. Someone short of funds might be glad of it."

He closed his eyes at his crass remark. "I apologise, Kate. That didn't come out as I meant it. What I mean is that…"

She raised her hand to stop him. "You don't need to explain." Suddenly, the devil was at her elbow and she felt an overwhelming urge to tease him. "Of course, there is one who is quite happy with my three hundred pounds."

"Oh, who might that be?"

"Sir Herbert Fox."

Conrad sat upright in alarm. "Dear Lord, not that buffoon."

"He was very charming when I met him in Cheltenham last spring."

"Never! I'll not allow it. Seems I'm going to have to pay a visit to your uncle and have words with him."

Katherine was taken aback by the vehement tone in his voice. "Please don't do that, it would be too embarrassing."

He shook his head in dismay. "I can't believe that a beautiful woman such as yourself, cannot find a much younger and better placed husband. Heavens above, Fox is nearly fifty and he's already buried two wives."

Katherine gave a wry smile. "But you seem to forget that I don't intend marrying."

He hesitated for a few moments before asking, "Will you tell me why you don't wish to marry? It seems so unusual."

She looked down at the chessboard. "Because I'm not suited to marriage."

Conrad took in a sharp breath. What she was saying was illogical. She was more than suited to marriage, but not to the likes of Sir Herbert Fox. Watching her make her move, anger boiled up inside him causing his heart to pound in his throat. It was an abomination to even suggest the man, surely Sir George was aware of his reputation?

But then he smiled. "If you are going to move your queen there, then I will take her with my bishop," he warned.

Startled she moved the queen out of danger and then watched him with amusement as he studied his next move. Why was this handsome man sitting opposite her, feeling so hostile about her offer from Sir Herbert? And yet hostility suited him just as much as amiability. In the latter mood his violet eyes would sparkle and his smile could charm the coldest of hearts. But in the former, his eyes would turn darker, the muscles of his chin tensing and emphasising his high cheekbones. And it was this part of his character that worried her. Did she sense unkindness in him? He could certainly be curt with anyone who crossed him.

As he bent over the board, planning his next move, her gaze drifted from his face and down his body, to his cream-coloured cravat, the high collar of his shirt and his embroidered waistcoat. Small ruffles peeped out from the cuffs of his coat and she felt mesmerised as she watched his long, elegant fingers move the knight. She pursed her lips. He was an earl and as such had been indulged as a child; his every desire granted. He was used to the world revolving round him and her only wish was that he would be kind to her cousin.

Philippa had abandoned her tinkering on the harpsichord and had resumed her embroidery on the couch with Anne.

Suddenly, the countess gave a scornful laugh. "And Lady Belverton helped this servant and her child?"

"Yes, my lady. She was such a kind lady. So understanding," nodded Anne, her eyes glistening with memories of her former mistress. "The maid's sweetheart had been killed in Flanders at the start of the war so there could be no marriage for the poor girl."

Philippa sniffed in contempt. "Well, I wouldn't care about the circumstances. If one of my maids found herself in trouble, she would be dismissed forthwith without a character. That would teach her a lesson."

Conrad suspended his movement over the chessboard. "What good would that do, pray?" he snapped. "Throwing a young girl out in the cold because she has made a mistake, is hardly going to help her or the situation."

Katherine started at his tone of voice. She had never heard him speak so harshly to his wife.

Philippa jerked her head in his direction. "Conrad, I'm sorry...I didn't mean...Oh!" Her face turned white.

He ignored her distress. "For God's sake, Philippa, don't be such a moralist. You haven't seen enough of life to make such judgements. There is no such thing as complete right or wrong. The world is not black or white."

Tears spilled onto his wife's cheeks, her eyes searched the room in panic. Finally, the humiliation became too much and not being able to bear it any longer, she stood up, her embroidery frame thudding to the rug. In a moment she had scurried to the door and was gone. Anne followed her like a frightened spaniel.

Conrad turned to look at Katherine's blanched face. "I suppose you thought that very cruel of me?"

"Yes, I did." She saw no advantage in lying.

"And I suppose you'll tell me that you thought the world black or white when you were seventeen?"

Katherine paused before replying, "No, my lord. At seventeen I did not think the world black and white. But...then again...my experience of life was very different from Philippa's."

43

He raised his eyebrows in surprise. "In what way was your experience different?"

Katherine declined to answer, her throat tight at the altercation that had just taken place. She couldn't understand why his temper had flared over a simple observation from her cousin. An observation that would surely alter with the passing years.

"Please go after her…and bring her back," she said softly. She was risking his disapproval, but she had to take the chance.

The anger left his face and was followed by amusement. "You think I should go and ask forgiveness?" he asked, watching her. She nodded. He sat back in his chair and sighed. "I think not, Kate. It would teach her a valuable lesson to let her sleep on it for tonight."

Courage swept through her. "Please, my lord. Philippa will be so distraught and she will already be remorseful for speaking so."

His expression softened, but his tone was still harsh, even though he couldn't ignore the eagerness in her eyes.

"I will do this just once. But never ask me again." Rising to his feet, he left the room. She turned to look at Frobisher who seemed to be absorbed by the pattern in the rug. Five minutes later Conrad returned with a very subdued Anne, but an exhilarated Philippa. He led his wife back to her seat and dropped a hurried peck on her forehead, before resuming his place at the chessboard. "Satisfied now?" he said.

"Thank you," Katherine whispered

They continued their game in silence.

The evening of the party was cold, the chilly air turning the guests' breath into white mist as they alighted from their coaches. But the bitter cold couldn't prevent the merriment as everyone hurried indoors through the hallway and into the drawing room where a huge fire roared in the fireplace.

The supper table was laden with poached carp, turkey pies, and a large tureen of soup. Philippa insisted that everyone must down a bowl to drive away the cold and no one needed a second invitation since the chicken soup was flavoured with pieces of bacon, basil, bay leaves and coriander and just a few cloves to add a tang. It was thickened with rice, coloured with saffron and Philippa was delighted when she had to call for more within a very short time.

Amongst this feast were the customary sweetmeats, nuts and choux pastry swans filled with cream that were the cook's speciality. Glasses of champagne flowed freely and entertainment was provided in plenty, many of the guests bringing violins and flutes, eager to demonstrate their expertise. Two lady guests sang a duet from Mozart's *The Marriage of Figaro* and Philippa enchanted the guests with a piece by Haydn on the harpsichord. And when it was time to leave, everyone collected their capes and cloaks and spilled out into the forecourt to their waiting coaches.

"Wonderful party. Top notch," said Lord Newburgh, shaking Conrad's hand.

Conrad nodded in delight. "Yes, it was very pleasant."

Lord Newburgh winked. "Pretty girl that Miss Widcombe. Lucky the man that weds that one. Well, good night and I will see you at my card party on Christmas Eve."

Katherine felt restless after the guests had left. Watching Philippa playing hostess had filled her with pride and she had received a great deal of attention herself and enjoyed the flattery from the younger male guests and some from the older, married ones too. But she needed fresh air, so flinging her cloak round her shoulders and pulling the hood over the silk flowers pinned in her hair, she took a walk outside. She wouldn't go far, she decided, just along the drive a little. She paused halfway down and looked back at the Court. The light shining from it seemed to give a magical effect, somehow diminishing and softening the grim exterior of the building. She imagined it not in the Cotswolds of England, but in far distant lands where dragons roamed and brave knights rode on white horses.

She was halted from her fantasy by the sound of footsteps coming along the drive towards her. They crunched on the loose gravel for a few seconds and then suddenly stopped. Alarm swept through her. Clouds obscured the moon and the light from the Court faded into dark, forbidding shadows. Who had come down the drive?

In a ridiculous attempt to conceal herself, she hid behind the bare branches of the large hawthorn bush that bordered the drive. She listened intently but then realised that whoever it was had disappeared into the gloom and been swallowed by the night. Her next thought was to escape inside, back to the warmth and security of the drawing room. But before she could leave her hiding place, a hand came from behind her covering her eyes. Plunged into darkness she let out a cry of panic and then twisting herself round she did something she had never done before. Raising her right fist she swung it in the direction of her assailant catching him a vicious blow on the jaw.

The sound of fist on jaw was followed by a yell of pain and someone falling heavily into the shrubbery.

"How dare you," she screamed. "Who are you?"

Conrad rubbed his sore face and tried focusing on the figure standing over him. "Well, that's a sure way of making a man sober up."

Horror swept through her and as she saw him trying to rise to his feet, she fled the scene. Her heart pounding in her ears, she ran up the drive and back to the safety of the Court, oblivious to the cries behind her.

"Kate! Kate, don't run away. I meant you no harm."

CHAPTER THREE

The next morning had brought the terrible memories flooding back for Katherine. As she descended the stairs to breakfast, her courage failed her for a moment and she had to pause momentarily. The night before, she had flung herself face down on the bed and pulled the pillow under her, mortified at her actions. Yes, his lordship had surprised and terrified her, but to strike out like that was not the behaviour of a lady. She would apologise and hope that Conrad didn't send her back to Widcombe Hall.

But when she walked into the breakfast room, she was pleased to see only Philippa sitting at the table. Helping herself from a tray of poached eggs set out with many other dishes on the sideboard, she then took a seat while the footman served her with coffee.

Katherine tried to eat, but the food seemed to stick in her throat.

"Are you feeling unwell today, Kate? You've hardly touched your breakfast."

Katherine shrugged. "I don't feel very hungry."

"Perhaps we should take a walk outside. That's always the best tonic for renewing your appetite."

Katherine didn't answer but waited patiently for her cousin to inform her that she must pack and leave immediately. However, Philippa continued to chatter about the mundane topics concerning the Court.

Eventually, she could bear the suspense no longer. "Philippa, if you have something to tell me, then please get on with it before I burst with apprehension."

Her eyes opened wide in surprise. "Something to tell you? What might that be?"

"That I must leave, perhaps?"

"Why would I want you to leave, Kate? Your company these last weeks has meant so much to me."

"But not to his lordship, I wager," Katherine murmured.

"I don't understand. What do you mean?"

"Did Conrad say anything about last night?"

"What about last night?"

"I insulted your husband and disgraced myself."

Philippa placed her hand over her mouth, trying to stifle a giggle. "What on earth did you do?"

"I struck him. I didn't mean to, well, I wouldn't have done it if I'd known it was him."

Philippa squealed with delight. "You struck him?"

"Yes, I knocked him to the ground."

Philippa tried to control herself. "Why did you do that?"

"It was nothing. Something so silly, I feel embarrassed to say." Katherine stared down at her uneaten food feeling despondent. "He didn't say anything this morning before he left for Cheltenham?"

Philippa shook her head, her hand still over her mouth. "I'm sure he doesn't want you to leave. I shall speak to him when he returns."

Katherine bit her lip. "No, please, Philippa, don't mention it. Let's wait and see what develops. But if he asks me to leave then I will go."

"No you shan't. I'll tell him that you must stay."

Katherine squeezed her hand tenderly. "You seem to have forgotten that you promised to *obey*."

It started raining mid-morning and the residents of the Court were forced to stay indoors. But by the afternoon, the dark clouds cleared and a weak sun tried to warm the sodden earth. Philippa was busy with the preparations for Christmas so Katherine decided she would go for a walk. A maid went to fetch her cloak from her room and she set off. In minutes she was hurrying along the path that skirted the front of the house and heading towards the meadow.

The air smelt of wet grass and damp soil and she wrapped her cloak more closely round her, shivering in the bitter cold. When she reached the end of the building, she stopped and looked back. The battlements stood out against a pale blue sky and she smiled. She wondered if there was a way up to them. It must be a wonderful view across the estate if a person could stand so high up.

There was a small walled garden to the left of her and she decided to wander through it, following the paths. Here she halted in delight for the hazy sun made the spiders' webs that were caught in the shrubbery and the thorny rose plants glisten like tiny diamonds. So engrossed was she, that she didn't see Conrad standing at the end of the path, leaning on the wall, his arms folded, watching with mounting pleasure, her steady progress towards him.

"Hello. I've caught you at last," he said softly, his voice from out of the shadows startling her.

"How did you get here?"

"I know every short cut." He cocked his head. "I thought you might try and avoid me."

"No, I wouldn't do that," she lied.

"I don't believe you." She blushed and he gave a low chuckle. "I feel in need of a walk too. Shall we walk together?" He offered his arm.

Katherine sighed. "If you can bear my company. I really must apologise…"

He clicked his tongue. "It's I who must apologise. Forgive me, Kate. Now, let's not mention the incident, shall we? It's all forgotten."

Smiling, she took his arm. "Very well, sir. Then I would be pleased to walk with you."

They walked in silence at first until Conrad looked about him.

"My father loved this garden. Oh, it wasn't fashionable to have a walled garden, but he insisted on keeping it, nonetheless. When I was a small boy I helped him plant many of the shrubs and trees at the Court."

"Your father died about five years ago, didn't he?"

"Yes. I'm afraid he was ill for quite a while." He pointed to the front of the house that could be seen just beyond the wall. "In my grandfather's day, there were ponds there and a very large garden in a geometric pattern. But Capability Brown came along and swept that all away. From then on it was lawns and pastures as far as the eye could see. And trees. Thousands of trees."

"Grandmama says that trees mean life."

"I'm sure she's right. Have you been to the folly?"

Katherine nodded. "Yes, but I would like to go again."

They crossed over the rustic stone bridge that straddled a small manmade stream and finally reached a half-ruined tower. Inside was a wooden seat and they sat down.

"You can see why it's called a folly," said Conrad, looking around. "There's no point to it except to add a bit of interest." He smiled. "Mind you, I found it wonderful as a child. I would come here with my toy sword and hobby horse and pretend I was a knight saving a damsel in distress."

Katherine's heart softened at the expression on his face. "And would you save a lady in peril, sir? Are you the kind of man who would fight for a lady's honour?"

His lips twitched. "How fanciful. Do you mean pistols at dawn and such?"

"Not exactly. I suppose I'm asking if you adhere to the chivalric code of honour. To be willing to fight for a noble cause at risk to your life."

He rubbed his chin lightly. "Well, I certainly didn't adhere to the chivalric code last night," he sighed. She made to speak but was silenced by a finger over her lips. "You've already apologised and so have I. We said we wouldn't speak of it."

But Katherine realised she couldn't be silenced. "It was a stupid thing for me to do, to strike out at you simply for putting your hand over my eyes. I should have realised it was a game."

He stayed quiet for a moment, thinking.

"Why were you so afraid?"

She swallowed with difficulty before saying, "I'm afraid of the dark."

He bent towards her and Katherine, for one breathtaking moment, thought he was about to take her hand. But then he leaned back in his seat, frowning. They sat together in silence. Katherine bit her lip. She knew he was suspicious; that her reason didn't convince him. But he was the last person she could confide in. He must never know what had happened to her to make her fear the dark.

The following morning, Philippa was absent from the breakfast table.

"Is she unwell?" asked Katherine, as the footman poured out her coffee.

Conrad folded his newspaper and lay it down on the table. "Anne tells me she is suffering from a cold so is staying in her room for a while."

"I will go up and see her," said Katherine, standing, but was restrained by a firm hand.

"It's only a cold. It can wait until you've had your breakfast." He looked at her sternly. "What do you plan to do today?"

"Oh, nothing in particular."

"The gamekeeper has told me that gypsies have set up camp near the woods. If you go out riding, then I would prefer it if you stayed away from them."

Katherine climbed the oak staircase and made her way along the corridor smiling at the pretty rugs that covered the uneven but highly polished floorboards, the rich fabric that adorned the casement windows of leaded light. The Court was a wonderful place to live and as much as she loved Widcombe Hall, she was contented in Philippa and Conrad's home. The house seemed to smile at her, the whispering shadows in the alcoves and long passages urging her to stay and never leave.

She finally reached the east wing and knocked on the door of Philippa's peach and cream bedchamber.

"How are you, dearest?" she said, coming to the bedside.

Philippa was sitting up, propped aloft with many pillows. She held a handkerchief to her streaming nose that was already looking very red.

Turning her face, she grimaced. "I feel terrible," she said thickly. "My head aches, my nose won't stop running and I have a horrid sore throat."

"Perhaps we should call the physician?"

Philippa shook her head and then winced at the pain. "Mrs Craddock has the remedies and I'll recover soon."

Anne looked down at her mistress. "Yes, Mrs Craddock is making up some hot lemon and honey and an excellent embrocation."

Philippa pulled a face. "Of all the things, to catch a cold three days before Christmas."

Katherine and Anne exchanged amused glances.

"I'll stay with you," said Katherine. "I know, I'll read to you until you fall asleep."

"That would be most agreeable," Philippa sniffed and then went into a fit of sneezing.

Katherine went back downstairs to choose a book. There was no one in the library and she looked about her at the quantity of books that adorned the shelves. She had brought her own reading material from the Hall so had had no need to examine these books, in fact, this was the first time she had been in the library since Philippa had shown her round the Court. Now, she trailed her fingers along the spines, reading the titles. There were volumes of Milton's poetry, plays and sonnets by Shakespeare, the philosophical works of Francis Bacon and novels by the French writer Voltaire. Quite a few books by modern poets graced the shelves, Robert Burns, William Blake and Thomas Gray.

Katherine thought to read some poetry to Philippa, but near the top were some smaller, thinner books and pulling the ladder towards her she climbed up. Here she saw *Gulliver's Travels* by Swift and Defoe's *Robinson Crusoe* and two other books entitled *Fanny Hill* written by John Cleland and *Tom Jones* by Henry Fielding. My goodness, she thought in surprise, the Earls of Croston certainly enjoyed the more lurid taste in literature. She had a mind to snatch *Tom Jones* from the shelf and take that up to Philippa, but instead she chose *Gulliver's Travels*. Philippa had always enjoyed that particular story and it would cheer her up. The door opened and Conrad entered the room.

At first he didn't seem to see her until she gave a polite cough. He glanced up and smiled.

"Philippa said you were going to read to her. What have you chosen?"

Katherine grinned. "I can't decide between *Tom Jones* or *Fanny Hill*." His expression made her burst into laughter. "No, I've chosen *Gulliver's Travels*." She narrowed her eyes, trying to be serious, "But one day I might purloin the others and read them in the privacy of my room."

Chuckling, he stepped forward and reached out to help her descend the ladder. "Come, take my hand. There are two steps down."

The words, so familiar and yet so terrible, made her gasp with shock and she shrank back from him, pressing herself against the steps. "I can…manage perfectly well on my own, thank you."

Conrad had not realised he had said anything untoward, but the fear in her eyes startled him. She eased herself past him and with a brief glance over her shoulder, hurried from the room. The earl stayed in the library for some time, deep in thought.

Katherine had resolved to spend the entire day with Philippa, but after only three chapters of *Gulliver's Travels*, the patient had fallen into a deep sleep and leaving her in the capable hands of her maid, Katherine decided to go out riding.

She trotted along the lane and then turned the horse's head towards the woods. Looking up into a very grey sky, she realised that the long awaited snow might finally arrive therefore she must not stay out too long. And then she saw the gypsy camp.

It was an encampment of about twenty adults and a dozen children, but their living conditions were poor. The wagons and packhorses that carried all their possessions stood amongst the shabby tents. Katherine could see that the tents were no more than hazel rods driven into the ground and then course blankets thrown over the rough frame. She did notice one particular wagon with a makeshift covering of sailcloth, which must have afforded better shelter through the harsh winter. But otherwise she shuddered at the appalling circumstances of the Romany people.

Both adults and children were dressed in a motley assortment of clothes and they all looked as though they needed a good meal. On the edges of the camp, washing was flung over the bushes and dogs rooted in the rubbish thrown at the side. The residents huddled round a fire and playing in the dirt in front of a tent were the very small children, watched over by an old woman with a wrinkled face and broken teeth. Katherine drew back in alarm. Conrad had told her not to go near them, but it was too late, they had seen her.

A man came forward. Despite his rough appearance he didn't seem threatening, but Katherine gripped the reins ready to escape should he mean her harm.

"What do you want, miss?"

Katherine took in a breath. "Do you have permission to camp here?"

The man narrowed his eyes. "Aye, miss. His lordship has given us leave. We'll be moving along in a few days. Spending the Yuletide in Cheltenham, we are, plying our trade."

She looked up at the clouds filled with snow and thought of their life, always travelling, always being moved on. And in the towns and villages they passed through they would mend cooking utensils, tell fortunes, dance and entertain and perform any task that they could to earn the odd shilling.

Katherine nodded. "Very well." The old woman sitting with the children had risen from the stool and come forward, frowning at the young girl sitting on the horse. "Is there anything you need?"

"His lordship has been kind. He sent us food and some blankets," said the man.

Katherine smiled. Usually gypsies were not tolerated at any cost and she was relieved to discover that Conrad had a kind heart in that direction.

"You've got a secret," said the old woman, eyeing Katherine. "You've got a dark secret that follows you through your days and nights."

Katherine tossed her head in disdain. "You're wrong. I have no secret." All eyes were turned to her and some of the women had also stood and joined the old woman.

"You have, miss, I know," she insisted, pointing a claw-like hand at her. "And your heart is too tender, too young to bear it. If you don't unburden yourself of it, it'll become too heavy and it'll drag you down. It'll mark the end of you."

"Don't talk nonsense."

"I see it in your face, your eyes." She blinked hard. "Beware a devil pretending to be an angel."

Katherine had heard enough and urging the mare forward, cantered away from the camp. She galloped faster knowing the danger of speeding through woodland, but she didn't care. She must escape the words of the old gypsy woman.

Perhaps the horse sensed her fear or perhaps she simply took offence at being ridden so hard. Whatever it was, three miles from the Court, as Katherine galloped through a muddy stream, Lady decided to throw her. Hurtling through the air, she landed in a sea of black clinging slime. The mare didn't wait, but tossing her head with contempt, turned and galloped in the direction of the Court.

Katherine lay there dazed. She had banged her head against a boulder and blood trickled down her temple and into her eye. Somehow she pulled herself up and staggered to the mossy bank at the side of the stream where she sank to her knees. She felt dizzy and decided to lie down until the world stopped spinning.

The earl and Frobisher cantered their horses into the stable yard, where the young groom held the bridles while they dismounted. Conrad was relieved to be home early, having completed his business on the estate in plenty of time for dinner that was usually served about three o'clock. The weather was turning bitterly cold and he was looking forward to warming himself by a roaring fire.

They were just about to make their way to the main entrance of the Court when they were forced to jump to one side as a dapple grey mare careered into the yard and pranced backwards and forwards in an agitated state. She raised herself up on her hind legs and whinnied, her front hooves flailing in the air. Socrates jumped at her, barking furiously. Seconds later, the mastiff was racing out of the yard and heading along the drive to the main gate.

All the grooms rushed out and after several minutes managed to catch the horse and calm her down, leading her to her stall at the end of the low buildings.

"Who was riding Lady?" cried Conrad to one of the men.

"It was Miss Katherine, my lord. She took her out about an hour ago. She must have thrown her, although I don't know why. She's fairly quiet and very good with the ladies."

"You let her go out without a groom!"

The man turned scarlet. "I'm sorry, my lord. She said that you had given leave to do so."

Cursing under his breath, Conrad didn't care to wait for any more excuses, but called for his horse to be saddled once again.

"It's already getting dark, my lord," said Frobisher, looking towards the ominous gloom that was spreading across the hills. "I shall come with you."

"Indeed you must. But we will separate at the edge of the woodland and take different directions. In that way, we'll cover more ground." He called to the stable hands. "Light torches and two of you search the road to the village. The rest of you be prepared to spread out in a more thorough search if we should come back without her." He swung his leg over the saddle and turned to look at his secretary who was also ready to go. "Chances are Miss Widcombe is already on the road and making her own way home. There is little point in worrying until we've investigated all possibilities."

Minutes later they were galloping out of the yard and heading towards the gate, taking the direction the grooms thought Katherine had taken. Once near the hill, they stopped and scanned the fields, desperately searching for a moving figure amongst the sombre tones of a winter landscape.

Katherine pulled herself up into a sitting position, not knowing how long she had been lying there, but relieved that the dizziness had lessened. Wincing at the pain, she spent a few minutes rubbing her shoulder, before taking a handkerchief from her sleeve and dabbing at the cut on her temple, thankful that the injury had stopped bleeding. She looked around her, panic rising in her throat as she realised the light was going. Then she heard a noise.

It was a snuffling, grunting noise coming from her right and Katherine instinctively moved towards a bush in order to find some cover. She thought of the dogs from the camp and fear made her heart beat rapidly. Suddenly a black shape came out of nowhere and lunged at her with a force that knocked her to one side. She let out a scream and put up her hands to protect herself from the teeth that she was sure would go for her throat. A sloppy, wet tongue caught her cheek and a paw rested on her shoulder.

"Oh, Socrates." Katherine sat up and put her arms round the big head. "You frightened me half to death, you silly dog."

Leaning on his broad back, she dragged herself to her feet and steadied herself for a moment. Then she looked up the bank of the stream and towards the woods. She had ridden through those woods so there was nothing else to be done but start walking back the same way and hope she didn't happen on the gypsies again. At least Socrates would be her guide and guardian now. Groaning with the pain in her ribs and back she set off.

Conrad's heart raced with fear, as he tried to keep his mind free of sinister thoughts. He and Frobisher had separated at the edge of the woods and while Frobisher had gone to alert the gamekeeper to help in the search, Conrad had skirted round to pick up the lane that led from his estates to the small hamlet of Hazleton. The daylight was fading much faster than usual and he had barely ten minutes of light left. If he didn't find Katherine soon, then he knew he would have to return to the Court for men and torches.

Making his way round the wood, he prayed that at any moment he would meet her walking along the road. As the time and light disappeared, panic surged up from his stomach. If she was badly hurt or knocked senseless behind a hedge, she wouldn't be seen. As the freezing night closed in around her, she would die from exposure.

He had to give up his search, the light was so bad it was impossible to see any colour amongst the undergrowth. His heart in his mouth he made for the main highway that led back to the Court, galloping hard to fetch help. It was then that he saw the slim figure of a woman, her hair down her back, walking wearily by the side of the road. A black shape loped alongside her and he recognised it as that of Socrates. Conrad smiled that his faithful dog had done what he could not.

As he came alongside her and she turned her head to look at him, he gave out a cry. He sprang from the height of the saddle and gripped her shoulders, his face close to hers.

"Dear Lord, you're hurt."

"I've hurt my shoulder and cut my head. No mortal injuries, I assure you."

"I thought you were dead, Kate." Relief turned to anger. "And what do you mean by telling the grooms that I gave you permission to ride out alone?"

She was glad the gloom hid her blushes. "That was rude of me, Conrad. I do apologise but I'm quite capable of looking after myself."

"Oh, really! And that's why the horse galloped into the stable yard without a rider, eh? You sent her home so you could prove your independence?"

"Lady threw me in a muddy stream. I'm sure she did it on purpose."

Her bedraggled state made him smile. "Well, do you want to ride home with me, or would milady prefer to *look after herself* and continue with her walk?"

Annoyed at his sarcasm, she retaliated. "Socrates can see me safely home, but thank you for the offer." She turned as if to carry on with her interrupted journey, but was halted by his hand on her arm.

"Don't be so stubborn." His voice softened. "Dear Kate, I really thought you were dead. Frobisher and I have been chasing around the countryside for the last twenty minutes searching for you."

"Have you? Why didn't you send your men to look for me?"

"I did, but there wasn't enough time to stop and collect a large search party."

She studied his earnest expression and relented. "Very well. I'll ride home with you."

He climbed into the saddle and pulled her up behind him. She was forced to put her arms round his body to keep her balance, pressing her dirty face on the back of his thick, woollen coat. As they trotted along, neither spoke for a while.

"Hold on tightly. I don't want you falling off," he said, finally breaking the silence.

"I'm afraid your coat is getting terribly muddy."

"Worse things have happened."

A further minute of silence passed until she said, "I came across the gypsy camp. They scared me a little."

Conrad frowned. "They didn't harm you?"

"No, they were quite amiable really. They said you had given them permission to be there."

"Yes, I did. But I'd rather you kept away from them."

"It's the first time I've seen a gypsy camp so close. They live in the most appalling conditions."

"I know and I often pity them. But they try to find employment. I see the older children earning money in the village and the adults have various talents."

Katherine considered this. "Conrad, do you ever fear that the revolution that took hold of France, might happen here? I've often thought it could."

Conrad squeezed her hand, smiling that he could always rely on Kate's mind and conversation rising above the mundane. Not for her, the everyday talk of gowns and bonnets, of balls and social events. And so, for the rest of the journey they discussed the merits of the Revolution in France and the plight of the starving poor that had instigated it.

Katherine kept a tight hold on Conrad, her arms wrapped round his waist. Only the dull clomp of Shah's hooves on the dirt road and the snuffling of Socrates as he tormented a hedgehog, impinged on their quiet conversation. Katherine turned her head to look up at the threatening snow clouds and wished it would start to snow, the gentle flakes falling on them, white and pure. But then Socrates started barking and looking ahead she saw that the Court was straight in front of them.

Once inside, she ran up to her room. Sliding open the drawer in her dressing table, she took out a red silk handkerchief. In one corner was embroidered the initial 'R'.

Philippa looked down at her clenched hands and struggled with her conscience. "Papa told me that I must never speak of it."

Her husband was sprawled in the armchair opposite her and gave a sigh. "Then so be it, I wouldn't want you in trouble with your father."

She glanced at him and licked her lips nervously. She still felt in awe of her new husband and wistful at leaving her family. They were sitting in her room two days after Katherine's eventful ride and Conrad had slept badly ever since. Philippa had hardly risen from her bed before her husband had come in, half-dressed and asked the maid to leave them alone. He had to speak with his wife.

"But you're my husband," said Philippa. "And I have vowed to obey."

Conrad shook his head, laughing. "I'm not ordering you to say anything, my dear. I simply wanted to know what ails your cousin. Why is she so afraid? And obviously there is a secret there that I must not be privy to."

Philippa leaned forward in her seat. "It wasn't exactly a secret. In fact, I'm sure all the servants knew about it. It's so difficult to keep anything from the servants."

"Indeed."

She narrowed her eyes at him. "If I tell you, will you promise not to say a word?"

"On my honour."

"Not to Kate, or anyone?"

"Promise."

She gathered her thoughts before speaking. Her husband waited. "I was only a child, of course." She tapped her chin, thinking. "Yes, Kate and I had just celebrated our birthdays. I was eleven and she was fifteen. We were inseparable, like sisters. So, when she visited her Aunt Sybil in Bristol, I missed her so much. She was due home and I was waiting at the window for the coach, but instead a messenger came galloping up the drive and hurried into the Hall."

"What message did he bring?"

"The message was from her aunt saying that Kate was missing."

"What do you mean? Missing?"

"Just that. Her aunt had found her gone in the morning. Her bed had been slept in, but she was nowhere to be seen. The adults tried to keep this from me, but I overheard their conversation."

"How long was she gone?"

Philippa shook her head. "I'm not sure. A few days, perhaps. All I know is that I was so relieved when she turned up at the Hall. I really thought she was gone for good."

"I wonder what happened?"

"When I was older, I did have a thought that she had eloped, but something went wrong and she had to come home."

"She doesn't seem the character to elope."

Philippa gave him a knowing smile. "But she's against marrying. To my mind, that smacks of someone crossed in love, someone that has a broken heart. I think she was supposed to meet someone and he jilted her." She tilted her head. "Or she could have changed her mind and decided to jilt him."

Conrad grinned. "I wish you wouldn't read the novels serialised in the paper, my dear. It's filling your head with such romantic absurdity."

Philippa pulled a face as he rose from his chair. "Well, that's my opinion and remember you promised not to say a word."

He gave a slight smile and nodded. But as he went to his own room to find Robert, his valet and get properly dressed for breakfast, he knew that his wife's conjectures were false. Even if Katherine had eloped and then changed her mind, that didn't explain the glimpses of fear he had detected in her eyes. No, thought Conrad, there was something else amiss with Miss Widcombe. But what it was, he had no idea.

Katherine had awoken that morning still aching from head to toe. She lifted herself from the mattress and tried to stand, but then sank back down. There was a huge bruise on her arm, cuts and scrapes everywhere and her forehead was dressed with a gauze bandage applied with liniment. Mrs Craddock and Anne had fussed over her when she had arrived back with Conrad, but the following day, it was Philippa who had ordered her cousin to stay in bed and rest. It was Christmas Eve and Katherine felt as though she had been a participant in a tavern brawl.

She was brought out of these melancholy thoughts by the appearance of the maid at the door.

"Come in Molly. I must get up today and start moving about. I'm aching more than yesterday."

Molly squinted at the young woman slumped on the bed. "Miss Katherine! I think you need a little care and attention. I will call for the bath immediately, and then you will let me do your hair and make you presentable. My lady has sent me away and will call when she needs me, so there's time."

The tin hip-bath was brought in and placed by the blazing hearth. The maid instructed the servants to bring in the hot water and when all was ready, Katherine sank into the sweet scented balm with a sigh and Molly washed her hair. As jugs of warm water flowed over her head, her spirits lifted and after she had stepped from the bath, the maid seated her by the fire, spreading out Katherine's golden locks so that the heat would reach every strand.

In the breakfast room, the gentlemen stood as she took her place next to Philippa.

"No more riding, I think, until the weather improves," smiled Conrad, watching her.

Philippa looked towards the window. "I didn't notice it was snowing, but see, Kate, it's coming down in large flurries."

Katherine also looked and smiled. "Snow at Christmas, how wonderful. We won't be going far today but it would be fun to take a little walk, just as far as the walled garden." She suddenly remembered her stroll with Conrad and her thoughts about the battlements. "Can we get up on the roof, my lord?"

"Oh, yes. There are some steps in the attic that lead to a door to the outside. I haven't been up there for years."

Philippa was delighted. "We must all go after breakfast. It's my Christmas wish, that we walk along the battlements."

Her husband agreed that it would be interesting, so after they had eaten they dressed warmly and he collected the key from Mrs Craddock, who guarded all the keys with the tenacity of a gaoler. They climbed to the top of the house, walked along a cramped passageway in the attic and then up a narrow flight of stairs. At the low wooden door, Conrad turned the key in the rusty lock and pushed with all his strength until it flew open. The cold air and a flurry of snow blew over them. And then they were outside and walking along the battlements just above the gargoyles.

"It's wonderful!" cried Philippa. "Why, we can see for miles."

Katherine nodded in agreement. "You can see Hazleton. I wager you can see Widcombe Hall on a clear day."

Conrad smiled with amusement. "Not quite."

Frobisher wasn't impressed. Taking off his spectacles and wiping the snowflakes from the lens, he replaced them before looking over the ledge.

"It's a long way down. I wouldn't like to have to jump from this height."

They were having too much fun to take any heed of him, until Philippa remembered their social engagement that evening.

"The snow is delightful, but oh, Conrad, what shall we do about Lord Newburgh's card party tonight? The coach can't travel in all this snow."

"We will have to send a message that we are unable to attend."

"You could still go. You can take Shah and cut across country. You'll be there in ten minutes."

"And leave you on our first Christmas together? No, my dear, we will send a message and have our own little card party tonight. What say you to that?"

Philippa couldn't hide her delight and Katherine smiled. His lordship's initial irritation with his wife seemed to have evaporated.

The excitement of Christmas affected Katherine when she went to bed that night. She almost felt like a child again, waiting for the gifts and treats that she would receive when the morning came. And just like a child she found sleep difficult. She lay there trying to force her body to rest, until in frustration, she jumped out of bed and crossed to the window. The sight that greeted her made her smile. It had stopped snowing, but a white blanket covered the ground, the bare trees bent and swaying with their icy burden. The moon came from behind a cloud and the landscape glowed with a supernatural light that seemed to turn night into day. Turning from the window she headed for her bed, but realising that she was still not sleepy, she suddenly remembered the improper books tucked away in the library. Everyone was in bed and if she sneaked down she could borrow one and bring it to her room.

Katherine opened the top drawer of the dresser and pulled out the woollen shawl that her grandmother had crocheted and given her for her eighteenth birthday. Spreading it over her shoulders, she held the soft fibres to her cheek, breathing in the smell of jasmine, which had never left the garment since her grandmother had given it to her.

She took a candle and tiptoed barefoot down the corridor and stairs and into the hall. The library was at the far end of the hallway and as she opened the door, she saw that the fire was still glowing in the hearth. She lit the candelabra and put another log on the fire, deciding to stay in the warmth of the library until she felt sleepy. The large grandfather clock in the hallway began to strike midnight.

It was easy to climb the ladder and select *Tom Jones* from the shelf and curling up in the chair, she began to read.

"What are you doing?" The voice from the doorway made her jump out of her seat.

She held the book against her breast, realising that Conrad must have been in the drawing room all this time and heard her come into the library since he was in his shirtsleeves, his cravat unloosened.

"Just reading."

"Let me see," said Conrad, stepping forward and holding out his hand.

She handed him the book. "I was just taking a quick…I didn't mean to read it…"

To her astonishment, he passed it back to her. "You're old enough to read it, so do so."

"I couldn't sleep," she said, placing the book down on a small table. "For some strange reason I'm excited about tomorrow, just like a child."

"It's already tomorrow. Merry Christmas, Kate." He took her hand and kissed it.

"Merry Christmas to you, sir, but I'd better retire. It's so late."

She was startled when he held her hand tighter and said, "Please stay with me. Keep me company for a short while."

"I must not. This is not appropriate, Conrad. If you want company then go to your wife."

He moved away from her, running his fingers through his hair.

"I've been such a fool, Kate. Such a damned fool."

"Why? What have you done?" Fear made her catch her breath.

He took a step towards her, his eyes pleading. "I've married in haste. I should have waited."

She tried to swallow the lump in her throat. "What are you talking about?"

Straightening himself to his full height, he stared down at her, his expression grim. "When I was in Germany, I was surrounded by family, by children playing. And when I travelled home I decided that I wanted to see the Court filled with children. I was gone thirty years old and it was time I took a wife. I met your cousin in Worcester and was enchanted with her smile and her capricious ways. So, I proposed. Dear Lord, how I wish she had turned me down." He stepped closer. "Why weren't you in Worcester last summer, when I visited my Aunt Sarah? If you had, then I would have called on you and got to know you better." He reached out pulling her into his arms. "And I know for certain I would have asked for your hand."

"Please Conrad, don't say these things. I'm sure you don't mean them."

"Oh, but I do mean it."

Katherine couldn't believe her ears. "Let me retire. In the morning you'll feel different."

He shook his head. "I have to tell you the truth. I have to tell you how much I admire you and how that admiration has turned into love." His voice became hushed. "And that's the way it's supposed to be, that's the way I've always wanted it to be."

Katherine started to panic. "You do not love me. For Philippa's sake, let's not speak of this or you'll regret everything in the morning."

Seeing her anxious expression, he loosened his hold and stepped back. "I've disgusted you, haven't I? I've lost your respect?"

She took in a breath and spoke firmly. "Yes, my lord, you have."

A look of pain flittered across his face, but then this was replaced by disappointment. "I thought you would…"

"Thought what, sir? That I would be flattered by your attentions?" She stared at him. "You are married to my dear cousin and you stand there and profess love to me. Your behaviour is despicable."

"I apologise…this was unforgivable of me."

But his contrition went unheard. "Perhaps I should return home?"

He placed a tender hand on her arm and was alarmed when she shook it away. "Please don't go home. Stay for Christmas as Philippa has planned. She would be so disappointed if you left us now."

Katherine shook her head slowly, the anger inside her starting to subside. Yes, she must think of Philippa who had worked so hard to make Christmas a delight. Her eyes lifted to his and she sighed. His wife was his trump card and when he showed it then he had won. But

Conrad Fitzwilliam, the fifth Earl of Croston had lost her respect.

As she turned to go, he caught her hand. "Kate, just tell me one thing. If I had asked for you, would you have accepted me?"

She shook her head. "No, my lord. Without doubt, I would have refused you."

Conrad swung his legs over the side of the mattress and sat up. He looked down at the woman lying on the bed, who smiled seductively as she stroked his back.

"I didn't think to see you in my bed again. After your marriage you said…"

"I know what I said," he bit back. "But I was passing your door and I didn't think you would mind. For old times' sake."

Geraldine shrugged complacently, wanting to pacify him. "Well, we spoke of always being friends."

He took her hand and kissed her fingers. "I'm sorry. I'm a bit out of sorts. You are a good friend and always will be."

She studied him for a moment." "You have a fine bruise on your chin. Not from your wife, I suspect."

He rubbed his chin and grinned. "No, not my wife. Miss Widcombe decided to strike me to the ground."

"Now why would she do that?"

"I don't know," he said slowly. "There is much about Miss Widcombe I don't understand."

"She intrigues you?"

Conrad didn't answer at first and instead rose from the bed and gathered up his clothes. Pulling on his underwear and breeches, he thought about his wife's cousin. He had noticed the sadness in her eyes when first they were introduced and it had alarmed him.

"Yes, she intrigues me. But something else. I feel a desire to protect her from something but what it is I have no idea."

"She must have a secret," said Geraldine dryly.

Conrad turned to look at her. "You think so?"

"I had many secrets at that age," smiled Geraldine, snuggling down under the covers.

He continued dressing, returning her smile. "I dare say you did."

Conrad was well aware of her past. Geraldine Rondelet had been married to a wine merchant and living in Paris when revolution took it by storm. The Terror had plunged the country in a bloodbath and yet the Rondelets had felt untouched by it, even though every day, the tumbrel rumbled its way along the cobblestones, taking its victims to Madam Guillotine. After all, they were not aristocrats, so why should they be concerned by a mob of unruly, unwashed peasants?

But the wheels of the revolution turned quickly and after it had sated itself on the blood of the nobles, it turned its attention to those who had served them. Servants, dressmakers and tailors found themselves facing judgement in court, where their pleas for mercy went unheard.

Geraldine's husband had finally been arrested for 'crimes against the republic of France' and incarcerated in the Temple awaiting trial. His wife had then slept and bribed her way through every official she met, trying to find clemency for him. But it was to no avail and he was brought before the judges with many other unfortunate souls. He had put forward a sound defence that he was simply an honest wine merchant who had done business with all who wished to buy his product. He was a good citizen of France, he told them, and often contributed money to the poor, but the stony faces and cold words of the judges told him what they thought of him. Wasn't it mostly the aristocracy that bought his expensive wines? Therefore, hadn't he helped them perpetuate their decadent lifestyle? He was guilty by implication and sentenced to death.

Geraldine had watched him take his final journey, keeping to the back of the mob that jeered at him and the other two men and four women who would join him on the scaffold. Dressed in the poorest of clothing, she had pulled her shawl over her head, knowing that she could be recognised at any moment. But she was determined to be with him until the end and his end came swiftly, for the executioner was efficient at his job. Hardly daring to show any emotion, Geraldine had blown him a kiss as he climbed the steps, his head held high and when he was gone, she fled Paris, her jewellery sewn in her skirts. There was only one place to go and only one person who would help her now.

She watched Conrad complete his dressing. "Would you like me to do some investigating? I could find out if Miss Widcombe has a past that she needs to keep hidden?"

Conrad stopped tying his cravat and swung round, horrified. "Certainly not! Whatever it is, I'm sure she wouldn't want anyone prying. Leave her be." He paused for a moment. "Your uncle has asked for her hand."

"Uncle Herbert? Goodness me, he's a great deal older than she is. No wonder you feel she needs protecting. It's from my uncle."

"She won't marry him. In truth, she says she'll never marry."

Geraldine made herself comfortable against the pillows and ran her fingers through dark hair that flowed over her shoulders.

"A young girl doesn't usually decide that for herself. Often it's fate and circumstances that brings a girl to the altar or not." She narrowed her eyes at him. "But I think your interest in Miss Widcombe goes far beyond that of a kindly relative's. I think you care for her a great deal."

"Poppycock! She's family and nothing more."

Smiling smugly, Geraldine turned her head towards the window. Her smile turned into a grimace. "Ugh! It's raining. English weather! So different from Italy."

CHAPTER FOUR

Two weeks after Christmas, it was time for Katherine to return to Widcombe Hall. The cousins sat together on the chaise longue holding hands, watching the maid pack the trunk.

"Must you go, Kate?" Philippa sighed. "The time has gone so fast. Could you not stay another month?"

Katherine shook her head. "I must go, the family will be expecting me."

"But you will come back and visit again?"

Katherine put her arms round the forlorn figure. "Of course I will and you'll come to Widcombe Hall to visit us. We will write often."

"Conrad says we'll probably travel to Germany in May. Promise you'll think about coming with us. I'll need your companionship. I'll be so lonely without you."

She sounded so sad that Katherine couldn't find the words to reassure her and was glad when the maid shut the trunk and snapped the locks. Picking up the cloak that lay over the chair, she held it open and Katherine stood while she slipped it over her shoulders.

"You've packed everything, Molly?"

"Indeed, miss."

"Then you'd better call the footmen to take the trunk downstairs. The coach must be waiting at the door by now."

Molly nodded and disappeared. Seconds later, two men came into the room and lifted the leather trunk and carried it down to the coach. The two cousins followed them walking arm in arm. Conrad was waiting in the hallway and escorted her out to the coach.

To her amazement, most of the staff was waiting to see her off and the cook gave her a basket of food and wine to keep her going on the journey. Kissing Philippa on the cheek, she turned to Conrad who took her hand and kissed her fingers. She tried to avert her eyes. Their relationship had been strained since their encounter in the library and their battles over the chessboard had stopped, conversation between them becoming stilted and uneasy.

As soon as she was seated, the horses pulled forward causing the coach to sway for a few seconds before righting itself. Katherine waved from the window until Philippa and Conrad became a small speck in the distance. She closed her eyes, her hands tucked in the sable muff that had been a Christmas present from the earl and countess and pondered on the fact that her world had been turned upside down.

She thought of her future, something she had avoided for many years, but now she had come to a decision. A decision she needed to discuss with her grandmother.

When the horses trotted up the drive, she leaned out of the window catching glimpses of the large sash windows shining in the winter sun and then she smiled when the white portico and huge pair of Corinthian columns came into view. Katherine arrived at the main door and took the groom's hand as she alighted, enquiring the whereabouts of her family. She was told that her aunt and uncle were visiting friends but her grandmother was in the parlour.

Katherine hurried through the hall, only stopping briefly to give her cloak and bonnet to the maid, before being shown into the room by a footman. Her grandmother was seated by the fire as usual, her cane leaning up against the chair and Katherine's sudden entrance pulled her out of sleep. Katherine flung herself at her knee and put her arms round the frail body.

Her grandmother returned her hug. "Child, you're home at last. I have missed you."

"I've enjoyed your letters, but it's wonderful to be back."

The old lady nodded. "Your uncle has received another letter from Sir Herbert, but he wanted to speak further with you before he replied."

Katherine found swallowing difficult. "And I need to discuss something with you," she whispered. "But it can wait until tomorrow."

The following day was the anniversary of her grandfather's death and her grandmother wished to visit his grave and pay her respects. Katherine decided to accompany her. A short drive in the coach and then a rambling walk down a dirt track brought them to the family vault. It was a cold day, but the sun tried to shine as grandmother and granddaughter made their way to the large, round building with a domed roof, just to the rear of the village church. Inside, the place was full of light, since the windows set in the dome caught the sunshine and sent it dancing along the stone walls. It was easy to see where her grandfather had been laid to rest, since the coat-of-arms embellished his tomb and a basalt urn was placed on the stone slab with small sprigs of holly sticking out at awkward angles. Katherine and her grandmother didn't speak, each lost in their own deep thoughts. Katherine couldn't remember her grandfather and remained silent as her grandmother leaned heavily on her arm, her head nodding gently as she tried to focus on the inscription with watery eyes.

"Seems such a long time ago now. I remember what he looks like since I have his portrait to remind me, but it's his voice I cannot recall and I find that very painful."

Katherine didn't answer as she fought back tears for her grandmother's grief. "I wish I'd known him."

Her grandmother squeezed her hand. "You didn't know your parents, child. And that's more a pity."

Katherine gathered her courage. "Lord Croston and I had a terrible disagreement."

It was so matter-of-fact that the grandmother thought she had misheard, but then realised she hadn't.

"Ah, so that's the measure of it? I thought you seemed different when you returned home."

"Oh, Grandmama, I was so angry with him."

"And what was this disagreement over?"

"He said...he had made a mistake in marrying Philippa and that he wished he had chosen me as his bride."

"A natural mistake." She glanced at her granddaughter. "It is the way of young, wealthy men of rank. To marry in haste and regret at leisure."

"Was it in haste?" Katherine couldn't hide her horror.

"I believe he didn't take enough thought over it. I advised him that Philippa was too young and perhaps a year or two of waiting would not go amiss." She eyed her granddaughter curiously. "How did you feel when he said he wished you'd been his bride? Tell the truth, child, were you not flattered?"

"Of course not," said Katherine, feeling aghast that her grandmother should ask such a question. "Even feelings of flattery would have been a terrible betrayal of Philippa."

The old lady chuckled. "I've lived a long life and seen much. And people...men never surprise me now.

A man of his status with all the trappings that goes with a comfortable life, often have no thought for anyone but themselves. They take life for granted expecting other people to conform to their wishes."

Katherine rounded on her grandmother in alarm. "Oh, but that doesn't bode well for Philippa."

Her grandmother patted her hand. "And for your cousin's sake I beseech you to heal your rift with his lordship. At least try to be cordial with him if you can't bring yourself to be friends with him. If Philippa has already seen there is a coolness between you and her husband it will distress her and add to any unhappiness she might already feel."

Katherine looked down at the tiny woman leaning on a stick. "I will do everything in my power to achieve that, but..." she took a large breath, "I've decided to marry too."

Her grandmother couldn't hide her astonishment. "You want to marry? But you've always said that you would never marry."

"I've changed my mind. Now I believe it's imperative that I do marry."

"To remove yourself from Lord Croston? You think that by being wed your feelings will alter towards Conrad?"

"Oh no, his lordship has nothing to do with my decision." She thought of the gypsy's warning. "It's because of...well, I believe it's time."

Her grandmother stared at the tomb of her long dead husband and sighed. "You do realise that certain...arrangements will have to be made when you marry?" Katherine nodded again. "But we can discuss that nearer the time."

Her grandmother gave a reassuring toothless grin and arm in arm they made their way back to the waiting coach.

During the next seven days, Katherine resumed her riding, galloping around the estate and over the hills, rejoicing in the fact that she was partially free from the feelings that had tormented her, since not having Conrad's relentless presence gave her the opportunity to put her thoughts in order. Yes, he had declared his love for her and she was glad she had given him a piece of her mind. But her grandmother was right, she must put their confrontation into the past. Besides, her future was taking shape.

Her uncle had been astonished when Katherine had requested that he write to Sir Herbert and invite him for a visit, with the view to a formal marriage proposal.

"Are you sure, my dear?" her uncle asked one evening when they were gathered round the fire after supper.

Katherine lifted her eyes from her tapestry. "Yes, Uncle. I think Sir Herbert will be most acceptable."

She saw her aunt and uncle exchange worried glances. Her grandmother stared into the fire.

Her aunt frowned. "But you've always spoken of staying unmarried. What has changed your mind?"

Katherine gave a forced laugh. "I'm twenty-one and it's about time I settled down. It was folly of me to say that I wished to remain a spinster. Now I feel different."

Aunt Beatrice took in a breath and let it out gently. "Being in Philippa's company must have influenced you. Well, at twenty-one I was expecting my first child, although God saw fit to take him from me." Her husband placed a tender arm round her shoulders. "It just seems so sudden, my dear."

Katherine snipped the silk thread with her scissors and smiled. "Perhaps I've finally seen sense."

Philippa walked into her husband's study and was pleased to find him alone.

"Have you a minute, Conrad? I've something to show you," she said, her eyes sparkling with delight.

He pulled out a chair and smiled. "By your expression, it's something very interesting."

She settled herself against the cushions and gave him a smug look.

"Do you remember when we talked of Katherine's disappearance and I thought she had eloped but events had gone awry?" Conrad nodded. "I think I was quite correct since now I have evidence."

Conrad's lips twitched. "What evidence?"

"The maid was dusting Katherine's room and decided to look in the drawers. She found something and gave it to Anne who then gave it to me."

"And what is this *something*?"

Philippa opened her hand revealing a red, silk handkerchief.

"Look, Conrad. It has a gold initial embroidered in the corner. The letter 'R'. Now I wonder who that could be?"

Her husband took the handkerchief and examined it. It was of fine silk and had obviously cost a great deal of money.

"No idea. But I think we should send it back to her."

"It's six years since she went missing and she's kept it all this time. That means she was jilted." Suddenly the implication of the handkerchief washed over her. "Oh, Conrad, she must have been heartbroken to keep a memento of her love. Poor, poor Katherine."

Three weeks after Katherine arrived home, Sir Herbert Fox came to visit, resplendent in his best clothes in order to woo a young lady nearly thirty years his junior. He was quite tall with stout proportions, dressed in his long tailed coat with a square-cut front and just a couple of inches of waistcoat showing beneath it. Katherine thought he looked every inch the wealthy landowner and knight of the realm although rather old-fashioned in his dress sense. His collar was high and he sported a becoming peach cravat. On his head he still wore the short wig, favoured by older men. Fifty years old last Christmas, he told her sombrely, and honoured that she had accepted his offer.

The dressmaker had been busy on Katherine's gown of pale blue brocade, gathered slightly under her bosom with a wide band, the skirt flowing round her slender figure. The low neckline showed off her feminine curves to advantage and her hair was curled into ringlets at the sides and fashioned into a coil at the back. It was obvious to her family that Sir Herbert was very taken with her.

They walked slowly up and down the long gallery as the weather wasn't suitable for a stroll outdoors.

Sir Herbert cleared his throat. "I was delighted to receive your uncle's letter inviting me here today. And you must come and visit Westcroft, my love, before we are wed. It's a large estate and I'm sure you'll be happy there. Plenty of opportunity for riding and the house is a pretty manor set in a beautiful area of the Cotswolds." He gave a smile that she thought very pleasant.

"I look forward to seeing it, sir," said Katherine, smiling.

He took her hand. "I have a splendid house in Cheltenham and I'm not adverse to the social calendar. Despite my age, I enjoy the balls and parties as much as any gentleman. You'll not be buried away in the country. Mind you, I have been told that my dancing leaves a lot to be desired. Two left feet, my late wife used to tell me. But my enthusiasm always seems to win the day."

Katherine couldn't help laughing. "Then, sir, we must dance together and I will tutor you."

"That would be delightful." He kissed her hand. "I will be the envy of every man in the county."

Katherine found him very kind and although she remembered Conrad describe him as a 'buffoon' and not worthy of her, she thought otherwise. She could be happy with this man and settled at Westcroft, she would be safe. And so on that wet Sunday afternoon in February, Miss Katherine Widcombe and Sir Herbert Fox announced their betrothal and preparations were made for their wedding in early May.

A strange feeling of trepidation mixed with relief crept over Katherine during the next few weeks. As the Hall bustled with the organisation of her wedding, she knew for certain that she had made the right decision. One way or another she would put an end to the guilt that had plagued her since Conrad's confession, the terrible feeling of having done something wrong when she had not.

Standing in front of the mirror and obeying the instructions to stand and turn as she was measured and fitted for her wedding dress, she knew that Sir Herbert was the perfect husband for her. Being older and more experienced, he would no doubt be more understanding than a younger man. She would care for him and he would protect her from the troubles of the world.

Philippa's letters came regularly, expressing surprise that her cousin should have accepted Sir Herbert's marriage proposal, but Katherine replied that she was happy and looking forward to the ceremony and her life at Westcroft with her new husband. Sir Herbert had come to the Hall to dine with the family many times, she told Philippa, and he was pleasant, kind and had a witty sense of humour. He talked of spending only a month in the country after their wedding and then they would travel to Cheltenham for the summer season. When Philippa wrote to say that Conrad had agreed to open up his house in Cheltenham, Katherine smiled with delight. She and Philippa would be able to spend every day together and as for his lordship? Well, she would be a married woman by then, belonging to another man.

On a sparkling morning in April, Katherine along with her aunt and uncle set off for Westcroft to visit Sir Herbert and inspect the bride's new home some twelve miles from Widcombe Hall. As they travelled through the beautiful Cotswolds, Katherine's spirits soared at the prospect of springtime and she breathed in the sweet air.

The approach to Westcroft was delightful and as the carriage rumbled along the drive, Katherine's gaze took in the Tudor manor set in a semicircle of elm trees. The house was three- storeys high with small windows and many chimneys and to Katherine's mind, it seemed unchanged since the days of Queen Elizabeth. Lush gardens surrounded it on the west side and the east side looked out onto a rolling meadow and an orchard. Sir Herbert had already told her that a bowling green was just beyond the orchard and a place to play shuttlecocks.

He met them at the door with great self-confidence and ushered them indoors to take tea. And then he guided them round his property, showing off his wealth and directing his guests' attention to anything particular that he felt they must be made aware of. Katherine was impressed, as Westcroft was very pleasing and seemed to have been run efficiently, the staff well organised.

"It's eighteen months since my wife died," said Sir Herbert. "My home lacks the female presence. I'm sure you'll enjoy making it your own." The tour of the house also included her apartments that were in a state of upheaval due to redecoration. "They'll be complete by the time we are wed, my love. The housekeeper has ordered new curtains." Katherine nodded with approval at the small chambers with low ceilings that seemed filled with light from two windows.

The rooms upstairs were numerous but small in size. Downstairs, the main rooms were just that bit bigger, although nowhere near the size of those at the Hall or the sumptuous apartments at Croston Court, and as they continued their tour, Sir Herbert explained that he liked it that way, since modest rooms were more intimate and homely.

But it was the grounds that enchanted her the most and it was at this point in the visit, that her aunt and uncle decided to leave the couple alone together to enable them to talk privately. Sir Herbert took Katherine's hand and they walked through the gardens and past the orchard. It was then that she saw the folly on the far side of the meadow, nestled amongst the trees on the edge of the woodland.

"May we go and see? I adore follies," she said, pointing in the direction of what looked like a ruined church.

Sir Herbert pulled out his pocket watch and grimaced. "It's almost time to dine, my love. It's nothing more than a representation of a church. There's very little inside."

"Do you ever use it?" She squinted against the glare of the sun. "It seems to have a sound roof. I thought perhaps you used it as a summer house."

"I dare say we could have picnics there when the weather is fine."

His reluctance to cross the meadow seemed strange and the very mention of the folly had suddenly subdued his bright nature. Glancing at him, Katherine wondered if he had fearful memories of the place. Perhaps something had happened there that made him want to avoid the church and if that was the case, then in time he was sure to confide in her.

Their visit lasted most of the day and Sir Herbert had organised an elaborate meal, having fetched his best wines from the cellar. He had ordered his cook to use all her skill in the preparation of the dinner with the added incentive of a small pay increase if she 'did him proud'. And she did just that since the stuffed perch and roast capon looked appetising as the guests sat down to eat. A side dish of mushrooms cooked in butter were placed next to slices of ham and beef and at the end of the table were small cakes with pistachio nuts and apple meringues.

When they left Sir Herbert kissed Katherine's hand and then her cheek. She smiled and bowed her head as the carriage pulled away. The next time she would meet him would be at the altar.

Philippa and Conrad arrived three days before the wedding. Katherine stayed in her room and watched from the window as they alighted from the coach. In minutes, Philippa had run upstairs to fling her arms round her cousin's waist.

"Oh, Kate. I've missed you so much."

"Well, it's been nearly four months since we last said goodbye. But how well you look." She stroked Philippa's hair and kissed her cheek.

"I'm in the best of health," she said, but then reached up and touched Katherine's face. "But what of you? You look pale."

Katherine shrugged indifferently. "I'm in good health too."

"You might be in good health but are you in sound mind?"

Katherine threw back her head and laughed. "I'm happy, Philippa. You must understand that I want to marry Sir Herbert."

"But you said you would never marry. And he's so old," she protested. "Fifty is not an age to marry. Why, he'll be in his Bath chair in no time and..." She was silenced with a finger over her lips.

"Shush now." Katherine gave a bright smile. "Remember what we spoke of? Of visiting each other as married ladies? Well, soon that will be so. Aren't you happy about that?"

"Yes," said Philippa reluctantly.

"Then speak of it no more and be content with my decision."

They went downstairs and joined the others in the parlour. All the family seemed to have collected together, the room filled with people. Her grandmother sat in her usual armchair with Aunt Beatrice sitting opposite her on the couch with her sister Charlotte, next to her. Conrad and Uncle George stood together by the fire on the far side of the room. Sebastian seemed occupied at a small card table tossing dice and writing down the score.

Conrad came across to Katherine and kissed her hand, smiling. "Dearest Kate," he murmured. "Your presence at the Court has been sorely missed."

"I was sorry to leave my cousin, my lord," she said politely, removing her hand and then herself, noticing his eyes darken at her aloofness.

She went to sit next to Philippa.

"I've some good news of my own," said Philippa, slipping her arm through Katherine's.

Katherine bent her head towards her. "Then do tell me. I'm desperate to speak of anything other than my blessed wedding and the common opinion that no doubt my husband-to-be will not live long enough to reach the altar."

Philippa giggled. "Well, firstly we've decided to postpone our trip to Germany." Seeing Katherine's quizzical glance she said, her eyes shining, "And secondly, I'm expecting a child."

Katherine gave a gasp. "Oh, Philippa, that's wonderful."

"Conrad is so delighted. Of course, he would like a son and I've told him I'll do my best," she said with a chuckle.

"I'm sure you will. When are you due?"

"About November. And I do hope you will come to the Court when I'm confined. I can't have this child without you."

Katherine gave a low sigh. "I'll see what I can do. I'm certain my new husband will not keep me from you."

They spent the rest of the morning in Katherine's room examining her trousseau and especially the diamond necklace Sir Herbert had sent her as a wedding gift. They were left in peace and Katherine was more than relieved that Conrad made no attempt to search her out or speak with her.

They ate their dinner at two and then everyone dispersed to separate areas of the house and garden. The weather had become very warm and Katherine decided to go upstairs and sit on the couch in the bay window. She pulled open the sash to let in the gentle breeze and for a moment breathed in the scent of the spring flowers that wafted in from the garden. She looked about her and remembered she had sat there when Conrad had visited to make arrangements for his wedding to Philippa. And now she was waiting for her own wedding day.

Suddenly, she saw Conrad walking along the passage and when he reached her he stopped. She heard him take in a breath and let it out slowly.

"Hello, Kate. Are you enjoying a moment of contemplation?"

She inclined her head. "Indeed, sir. A quiet moment of reflection is always good for the soul."

"Sounds like something your grandmother would say."

"Yes, it is."

He hesitated a few seconds. "May I take a seat?"

She coughed nervously. "You wish to discuss something with me, sir?"

He sat next to her. "Did my wife tell you our wonderful news?"

Katherine's face brightened. "Yes, indeed. I'm very happy for you both."

He glanced away for a moment and when he looked back his eyes were troubled. "Kate, please tell me that your marriage is not any of my doing?"

"What do you mean?"

"You wished never to marry and then suddenly we receive a wedding invitation. If it has anything to do with what I spoke of in the library that night, then please tell me."

"No, sir. It has nothing to do with that," she lied.

He nodded in compliance. "Then so be it. However I must say that it was wrong and ungallant of me to say such things. I let the situation get out of hand and I must ask your forgiveness."

"I'm not sure if I can forgive you," she said, averting her gaze.

He took her hand and kissed it. "Dearest Kate. I've not had a moment of peace since you left, believing that I had upset and embarrassed you so greatly."

She turned her face away to hide her discomfort. His very proximity made her heart race and she wished he would leave her alone.

Katherine shook her head. "Let's put it in the past and speak of it no more." She turned her head to gaze out of the window. "It's so lovely here. I now know why Philippa didn't want to leave when she married."

He smiled. "It must be heartbreaking for a young girl to leave her home. But where is the rest of your family? Your aunt that lives in Bristol doesn't seem to be here."

"Aunt Sybil is in very poor health and cannot make the journey."

"That's a pity, since she seems to be your only relative on your mother's side."

She nodded. "She has sent me a small gift and a very kind letter. I will visit her as soon as I can."

He paused before asking, "Are you sure about this marriage? It's not too late if you have a change of heart."

Katherine opened her eyes wide in surprise. "Are you asking me to jilt Sir Herbert? I would never do that, it would be too cruel."

Conrad remembered why he had come upstairs after dinner. "I have something that belongs to you. It was found in a drawer in your room at the Court."

He pulled the red, silk handkerchief from his pocket and was not at all surprised to see the colour drain from her cheeks, her lips part in a gasp.

"Oh, that. You didn't need to return it," she said, regaining her composure.

"It's of no importance to you?"

She gave a strained laugh. "No, sir. It's of no importance whatsoever."

"Do you want it back?" he asked.

She tentatively reached out to take it. "Since you've brought it then I might as well have it." She took it from him and crushed it in a tight ball in her fist.

He watched her nervous actions with concern. Miss Widcombe's secret was obviously buried deep inside her and she was determined to take it into her marriage. From his experience that spelt heartache, since secrets taken into a marriage were apt to reveal themselves at the most unfortunate times.

The night before her wedding, Katherine was called into her grandmother's bedchamber. Making her way to the end of the passage she entered the large vaulted room, where her grandmother sat up in bed, her shawl round her shoulders and a cotton nightcap perched on wispy grey hair. Her maid fussed about her.

"Go, now," she ordered. "My granddaughter is here and I do not wish to be disturbed until she leaves." Mathilda grunted in compliance and picking up the chamberpot, left the room. The grandmother patted the mattress. "Come, child. We must speak."

Katherine made herself comfortable. "I've always enjoyed our conversations," she said, biting her lip. "But I've dreaded this one."

Her grandmother nodded. "I want you to be contented and happy with Sir Herbert and that can only come about if certain arrangements are made." She sucked in a breath. "I want you to take Mathilda with you as your personal maid."

"Oh, no, surely not, Mathilda has been with you since before I was born."

"I can spare her."

"But she's so old. And she has trouble with her legs. She'll not be able to cope with the demands made on her."

Her grandmother raised her hand to silence her. "No, Katherine, you need someone who understands and knows what to do."

"You've told her?" Katherine couldn't hide her horror.

"Not yet. But I will once I have your agreement."

"I'm not sure. Mathilda?"

Lady Widcombe squeezed her hand. "Take her for two weeks and then send her back to me. By then everything should be settled. You can tell Sir Herbert that you made a mistake in her appointment and that will allow you to employ a much younger maid. One to your liking."

"Sir Herbert mentioned his late wife's maid. What was her name? Oh, yes, Betsy. I could ask for her."

"Good! Then it is all arranged. Now, go to your bed, child. You have a long day ahead of you."

Katherine stood and leaned over to kiss the thin cheek. As she walked to her own room she felt angry.

Damn everything, she thought, I shall burn the silk handkerchief and remove it forever from my life. I'll not look backwards but forwards and I will be happy.

"Try a little rouge?" suggested Anne, looking Katherine up and down.

"Am I that pale?"

"Yes, you are. Pinch your cheeks," said Philippa and then reached up to do it herself.

Katherine had already bathed and had her hair dressed. Standing in her bridal gown, she looked stunning and Philippa nodded in satisfaction. If only there was more bloom in her cheeks, she thought, then she would look perfect.

Katherine scrutinised her image in the glass. Her dress was elegant and yet simple in design. Made from fine muslin, it was white in colour, the material, embroidered in satin stitching, tumbled in folds from under her bosom and all the way to the hem. She ran her hand over the tight bodice and adjusted the low neckline and puffed sleeves that fell from her shoulders. Underneath she wore a white chemise and underskirt. Philippa placed the wreath of pink, silk rosebuds on the golden hair that was piled up on her head and then handed her the small posy of the same pink, silk rosebuds.

Finally satisfied, the bride made her way downstairs to where her uncle waited to accompany her to their private chapel where Philippa and Conrad had taken their vows. Conrad took her hand and kissed her fingers, murmuring words of admiration. The rest of the family kissed her and wished her well and she watched as they all disappeared through the door to go ahead of her.

The walk through the house on her uncle's arm didn't take long and the servants lined up to give their best wishes and throw petals and blossom at her feet. And then she was walking up the aisle past the smiling faces of her friends and family, towards the groom waiting for her at the altar.

Katherine enjoyed the ceremony and repeated her vows in a quiet but clear voice. The hymns were sung, the prayers said and the ring placed on her finger. Only as they turned to walk back down the aisle did Katherine catch Conrad's gaze and she quickly looked away.

Sir Herbert patted her hand. "Well, my love, you look an absolute vision. I told you I would be the envy of every man and I was right."

At the wedding breakfast, Katherine sat next to her new husband, chatting to the guests, but keeping her face turned from Conrad. As they rose from the table she saw Conrad coming towards her.

"I wish you every happiness, Kate. I hope your new husband proves worthy of you," he said softly.

Katherine smiled, but didn't answer. Perhaps I'm not worthy of him she thought and tried to fight the growing feelings of apprehension.

It was time to go upstairs and get changed for the journey to Westcroft. Katherine wanted the farewells to be as brief as possible, the pain starting to grow in her chest was becoming unbearable and she kept swallowing to hold back her tears. Dressed in a cherry red day dress with matching cape and bonnet, Katherine climbed into the coach with Sir Herbert. As the coach lurched forward, tears filled her eyes and the watery images standing in the drive of Widcombe Hall waved like ghostly apparitions.

Katherine turned to her new husband. "Will Mathilda reach Westcroft before us?"

He took the gold watch from his waistcoat pocket. "They set out an hour ago with the luggage, so everything will be prepared when we arrive." He took her hand and kissed it. "I was surprised that you chose such an elderly maid. I would have thought a much younger one would have suited you. Remember I spoke of Betsy?"

She grimaced. "Grandmama suggested her, but let's see how she manages. I can send her back to the Hall if she proves unequal to the task."

The rest of the journey was spent in idle gossip, mostly from Sir Herbert, who appeared to be full of energy, despite his age. Katherine, however, felt utterly exhausted and listened to her husband's chatter with her mind elsewhere. She watched her husband, knowing that she belonged to him now and yet she was already starting to believe that her married state would not protect her, save her, from the old shame of her past. Could her grandmama prove to be wrong? The ruse was in place but even so, Sir Herbert might still discover the truth.

They arrived at Westcroft just as the sun was setting. Mathilda was there to meet her and had unpacked her possessions, hanging up garments in the cupboard and placing underwear in the large chest of drawers. Katherine's toiletries were neatly arranged on the dressing table and a fire burnt brightly in the grate, as the evenings were still quite chilly. Katherine looked round her new apartments. There was still a smell of paint and new wood, but the curtains were pretty and the Persian rug was soft under her feet.

The maid removed Katherine's travelling clothes and helped her on with a cream evening dress, fastening a single rope of pearls round her neck. She was to have a private supper with her husband before it was time to retire. Katherine picked up her fan and was about to leave her room when she had an afterthought.

"My grandmama spoke to you?" she said quietly.

The maid lowered her eyes. "Yes, my lady. I know exactly what to do."

Katherine nodded and left the room.

The meal was simple and Katherine again, spent most of the time listening to her husband speaking of his plans for the estate, of their trip to Cheltenham and other things that interested him.

The clock struck ten o'clock and Sir Herbert yawned. "It's been a long day, my love," he murmured. Katherine's heart began to speed up. "If you'd like to retire now, then I'll be along shortly."

Katherine left the table and climbed the stairs to her rooms. Mathilda was waiting for her and helped her into the linen nightgown that had been warmed by the fire and then she gently brushed her lady's hair. The new Lady Fox stayed quiet, deep in thought.

Mathilda finally stopped brushing and lay the brush down. "Let's put you in bed so you'll be more comfortable, my lady," she said and ambled across the floor to the large four-poster and drew back the covers. Katherine slipped between the linen sheets and pulled the blankets round her. Mathilda had sprinkled lavender water over the pillows and the new wife breathed in the calming scent with pleasure. The maid went across to the dresser and lifted a metal plate from its top. On it was a small parcel wrapped in layers of cotton material that was already stained red with blood. Katherine gave a cry of fright. "There, there, my lady, there's nothing to worry yourself about. This will only take a moment."

Five minutes later there was a sharp rap at the door and Sir Herbert appeared. Mathilda quickly dropped an awkward curtsey and left the room.

Katherine studied her new husband's physique. He had removed his wig and his bald head seemed small against his stout figure. His nightgown could have been a tent for a regiment of soldiers and as he stood in the centre of the room, he seemed hesitant.

He pointed round the room. "You're happy with your apartments, my love?" Katherine nodded and pulled the covers more closely round her. "If you want any other improvements, you only have to say." He climbed into bed next to her, dipping the mattress alarmingly. "It's a rare night for a young girl, is it not? Her first time." He smiled and she suddenly detected a look of amusement on his face instead of the concern she had expected.

She shrank back against the pillows, trying to control her breathing. "I'm your wife, sir. And I've been told what to expect."

"I'm sure you have." He turned to face her and ran a large hand over her breasts, resting it on her stomach. Katherine gasped with shock at the roughness of his touch and closed her eyes as he lifted her nightdress and parted her knees, his fingers probing inside her, his moist mouth pressing down on hers.

"You're quite lovely," he murmured. Raising himself up, he pushed between her thighs and penetrated her. Her hands gripped the covers as her body shook and she couldn't control the trembling in her legs that encompassed him. He buried his face in her neck and she thought his thrusts would go on forever. She gritted her teeth until she heard him gasp and groan with satisfaction. And then he withdrew from her and fell to one side.

"Thank you, my love. I hope you'll not be offended if I leave you. I'm an old man and need the comfort of my own bed." He kissed her forehead and left the room.

Mathilda appeared with a jug of hot water and Katherine climbed out of bed, pulling the soiled nightwear over her head. As she bathed, Mathilda changed the sheets and then helped her on with a clean nightgown.

"It's all over now, ma'am," she said, her voice smooth as honey. "I believe everything will be all right. I saw Sir Herbert leaving your room and his countenance told me that he suspected nothing."

"Do you really think so?"

"A few weeks should do it, my lady and then with your permission I would like to return to the Hall."

CHAPTER FIVE

Her first sight of Mrs Geraldine Rondelet was certainly memorable. Katherine was riding along the riverbank and Sir Herbert had ordered that a groom must always accompany her. Her horse was named Valentine and her husband couldn't have found her a more gentle or quieter mount to ride.

Katherine had tried to explain that she liked to ride a spirited horse and ride it hard, but he wouldn't listen. It wasn't seemly for the new Lady Fox to be seen galloping furiously around the countryside, he had told her. But if there was one thing she had learnt in the two weeks since her wedding, it was that her husband had a kind nature. He tried to be the firm husband but she knew he was quite malleable when it came to the persuasions from the female sex. And Katherine was growing fond of him.

The grey mare was hitched to a phaeton that seemed to be without an owner. The horse had obviously freed herself from being tethered to a bush and was wandering about nibbling at the grass. On the seat lay a very becoming jockey-style satin bonnet and next to it a pair of leather button boots.

Katherine looked around, expecting to see the owner any minute. Then she saw something that made her smile. A young woman was standing in the river up to her thighs, her skirts floating round her like a balloon.

"Do you need help?" called Katherine, scrambling down from her horse.

The young woman gave an embarrassed laugh. "My gown is caught on something and I seem to be stuck."

The groom had also jumped down. "If you wait here, my lady, I'll see what I can do." Katherine held the reins of both horses and watched as the groom waded out to the young woman quietly standing in the lapping water. He struggled for a few minutes with the snagged material before shouting, "I'm sorry ma'am, her gown is caught fast. On some old farming equipment by my reckoning."

"Can you tear the cloth?"

The groom shook his head. "It's too thick and I haven't a knife to cut it with."

"And neither have I," said the young woman. "I'll have to take the damn thing off!"

The groom came back to Katherine, trying to suppress his amusement.

"The lady says she must take her gown off."

Katherine passed the reins to him. "Is that so, Harry? Then, I think that's woman's work."

"Yes, my lady," he said and then grinning, he unfastened his cloak and gave it to his mistress. "If I may, I'll leave this to cover her modesty while I go and catch her horse and phaeton." He stepped towards the grey mare.

Katherine waded out into the river. "Would you like me to help you out of your dress? My groom has offered his cloak."

"You're very kind."

Unable to hide their laughter, they fumbled with the buttons and ribbons and finally managed to get the dress over her head. And then they both pulled at the garment trying to release it from the snag.

"It's no good," said Katherine. "It's not going to give."

"Well, we'd better leave it there."

Katherine pulled a face. "I hope no one thinks it's a body in the water."

"That should stir up this dull neighbourhood."

They waded to the bank and the young woman picked up the cloak and flung it round her shoulders, covering fine linen petticoats trimmed with lace.

"My name is Mrs Geraldine Rondelet," she said, bobbing a curtsey. "And a good guess is that you're Sir Herbert's new wife."

Katherine was a little taken aback. "Yes, I am. But how did you know?"

"Oh, you're the talk of society. An old man like that, taking a third wife and such a young and lovely one at that." She laughed mischievously and Katherine saw a beautiful woman with black hair and eyes that seemed to reflect deep pools of brilliant light. She had an infectious laugh as she said, "Obviously Uncle Herbert didn't tell you about me."

"No, not at all," said Katherine in surprise. "He never mentioned a thing about having a niece. If I had known, I would have invited you to our home long before this."

Geraldine sighed. "Uncle Herbert and I haven't always got along." She leaned closer and whispered, "He thinks I'm a bad influence."

"Goodness me, I can't imagine my husband thinking that of anyone."

"Well, he does of me. My mother was his younger sister. She's been dead many years now and I've been abroad for a good ten years. Living in France and then Italy. Now I live in Cheltenham."

"Is Mr Rondelet with you?"

Geraldine's expression softened. "My darling Roderique was guillotined at the height of The Terror."

Katherine felt shocked. "I'm so sorry."

Geraldine shrugged. "It was a long time ago." She gave a charming smile. "Thank you my lady, for saving my dignity."

"Why were you in the river?"

Geraldine shook her head and grinned. "A duck was caught in the weeds so I went in to release her. Then I found I was trapped. I knew someone would ride along eventually. My only problem was *who* would ride along. There are some folk I'd not appreciate seeing me in that predicament. I'm glad it was you."

They studied each other for a moment.

"I'm sorry you were not invited to our wedding. It was a terrible oversight on the part of my husband."

Geraldine seemed nonchalant about the whole affair. "As I said, my uncle and I are not on speaking terms. So, your wedding is the last place he would invite me. And that is why I'm here. To introduce myself to you and also give you both an invitation to my birthday celebrations in June. Perhaps you could help heal the rift between us?"

"I would certainly like to do that," said Katherine. She looked about her and shivered. "We must get indoors or we'll catch our death in these wet clothes."

The groom appeared guiding three horses and the phaeton. "Is everything all right, ma'am?"

"Yes, Harry. But we must see Mrs Rondelet safely to Westcroft."

"Thank you," said Geraldine. She grimaced. "I hope Uncle doesn't throw me out before my clothes have dried."

They climbed up on the phaeton and Katherine decided to drive while the groom rode behind, guiding Valentine.

"I'm looking forward to going to Cheltenham," said Katherine. "It must be wonderful living there all the year round."

Geraldine nodded. "It's a very pleasant town and taking the waters does attract some interesting people."

"Last year my entire family went to Cheltenham, even my grandmother. They've decided to stay at the Hall this year," laughed Katherine. "But my cousin Philippa will be there."

Geraldine thought for a moment. "Do you mean the Countess of Croston? Conrad's new wife?"

Katherine turned to her in surprise. "You know her?"

"Well, not his wife. But I know...Conrad."

Suddenly Westcroft came into sight and they trotted up the drive to the main entrance. They alighted from the phaeton and left it in the capable hands of Harry and the stable boy.

Sir Herbert was just making his way to his study when they entered the hallway.

"Geraldine! Where did you come from?"

"I had a little misadventure, Uncle. That's all. But your lovely wife came to my rescue."

He narrowed his eyes. "Did she, indeed." He noticed that his niece was wearing a rough cloak of course wool. "To whom does that cloak belong?"

"To Harry." Katherine grinned at her husband's expression. "Now, perhaps we should get dried off. We'll go to my room and you can borrow one of my gowns. It can be returned when we attend your birthday party."

"What birthday party?" asked her husband, as they ran upstairs, laughing.

Four days later, Sir Herbert's stepson came to supper and then spent the night. The only son of the previous Lady Fox, Richard Melford, Viscount Haighton, had inherited the title from his late father, her first husband. He had been invited in order to meet his stepfather's new wife and the meeting between them proved to be a delight. He was an attractive young man with dark hair and deep brown eyes and Katherine took to him instantly.

When she entered the room, Richard immediately sprang to his feet and kissed her hand in an elegant flourish. Throughout the meal he and Katherine talked amicably, while Sir Herbert left them to it, more concerned with his supper.

"I know you're not strictly my stepmother, but may I call you such, just for the fun of it?"

"Of course you may," she laughed with glee.

"You're related to the Countess of Croston?" he asked, as he took a sip of his wine.

"She's my cousin. Marriage has forced us apart somewhat, but when we travel to Cheltenham I'll be spending a wonderful three months in her company."

"I know Croston. We were at Oxford together."

Katherine couldn't help feeling surprised. "You're the second person I've met this week, who knows Conrad."

Richard shook his head. "I've not seen him for a while. But it will be pleasant to meet him again."

"My cousin is very young. Only seventeen," said Katherine wistfully. "I'm glad that I'll be in Cheltenham too, then I can keep an eye on her."

"So, who was the first person you met, that knew Lord Croston?"

"Mrs Geraldine Rondelet."

"Ah, yes, the captivating Mrs Rondelet." He smiled at her over his wineglass. "How did you meet Geraldine?" Katherine grinned and told him how she had found her in the river. Richard laughed with her. "How very like Geraldine to risk her life saving a blessed duck. It's a good thing you weren't galloping by at speed or you might have missed her."

"Gallop," said Katherine dryly. "I'm not allowed to go faster than a brisk trot."

"You're not confident on a horse, eh!"

Katherine glanced towards her husband who had not joined in with the conversation although he seemed to be listening.

"Herbert thinks it unseemly for me to ride any faster."

Sir Herbert cleared his throat. "You might fall off, my love."

"I've ridden since I was a small child. I'm quite capable."

Richard narrowed his eyes. "So, you're quite capable, are you? How about a race tomorrow?"

"No," said Sir Herbert. "I don't want my wife tearing round the countryside."

"It won't hurt her. Not if she's used to it."

"I used to race Philippa, before she married," Katherine mused. "I only lost when she cheated."

"Just for my visit," said Richard, eyeing his stepfather. "And then she can go back to trotting after I leave." He raised his eyebrows and Katherine got the impression that he was goading his stepfather.

Sir Herbert's complexion reddened. "No, sir." He shook his head. "You know that I lost my first wife in a riding accident. I don't want it to happen again."

Katherine's heart went into her mouth. "Oh, Herbert. You should have told me."

He glanced away. "It was a long time ago. Her horse threw her right outside the folly. She fractured her skull and never regained consciousness."

Katherine reached out to take his hand. "Then I will definitely stay with Valentine. I wouldn't want to cause you any worry."

He gave a half-smile and raised her hand to his lips. "No, my love. My stepson is quite right. I must not mollycoddle you. Go out riding tomorrow and take any horse you wish." He looked sternly at the young man sitting opposite him. "But you had better look after her, or you'll answer to me."

After breakfast they walked round to the stables and Richard insisted that Katherine be given a more spirited mount. And so the groom led out a black stallion called Midnight and from then on their ride was exciting as well as enjoyable. For the first time in weeks, Katherine was able to urge her horse on and with the wind in her face, she gave a cry of exhilaration when she took the lead. When Midnight jumped a high stone wall, while Richard's horse stopped short and refused, Katherine watched gleefully as he tried to find a way round the obstacle, shaking his head in annoyance.

"Shall I wait for you?" she smiled. "Or shall I go home and tell them that you will be leaving a little later than expected?"

"I'll have to guide him through the gate," he said, grinning. Jumping down, he led the horse to the wooden gate and out into the lane.

"Have I won, then?" she asked tongue in cheek.

He joined her and jumped back up into the saddle. "Yes, sweet stepmother of mine. We can take it you've won. But next time I visit I'll expect a return match."

As they crossed the meadow, Katherine spied the folly and she brought Midnight to a halt.

"It's so sad about Herbert's first wife. She must have been very young. I've been thrown many times, but never received any major injuries."

"They hadn't been married long. Just twelve months, I believe."

Sliding down from the saddle, she took the bridle. "I've never visited the folly. Shall we go now? It's on our way home."

She was surprised that Richard seemed reluctant. "I must be leaving shortly." She caught his wary glance and puzzled over the fact that the death of her husband's first wife must have been before his time. So why was he so hesitant in visiting the folly? He licked his lips nervously. "Very well, we shall go. But we must not stay for long."

They led the horses across the small stretch of meadow towards the woodland and soon they were standing in front of the ruined church. At least, it was supposed to be a church. It was built in stone with a tower and three arched windows, painted to represent leaded lights. A double door made of wood marked its entrance and Katherine went to open it. A hand on her arm stopped her.

"I only want to see inside," she said quietly.

Richard removed his hand and she pushed open the door. Inside there were no pews, only an area of stone-flagged floor covered with rugs. And in the middle of this area was a stone altar, cushions scattered over its top. Luxurious, velvet couches lined the walls, these walls painted in vivid colours depicting men and women dancing about naked. At one end was a grate where a fire could be lit, although she had not noticed a chimney. Perhaps the tower acted as a chimney, she thought. There was a strange odour and there were candles everywhere, some burnt out. The words *Lucifer's Lair* was inscribed on one wall and on the other *Gabriel's Garden*.

Suddenly, fear gripped her and she turned to Richard, who had followed close behind. "I don't like this place. Please take me home."

He nodded and held the door open for her.

When Katherine reached her bedchamber, Mathilda was busy sorting out some fresh linen. She was still shaking from her visit to the folly and sank down on her dressing table stool.

The maid closed the drawer. "I wondered if you had considered my returning to the Hall, my lady?"

Katherine looked up. "Oh yes. You mentioned it yesterday, didn't you? You must go back to Grandmama. She needs you. I'll talk to my husband about a new maid."

Mathilda smiled with delight. She wanted to leave Westcroft as soon as possible. It was an ungodly place despite its beauty. She wondered if she should tell her ladyship about it when she arrived back at the Hall. She would pray, she decided and God would tell her what to do.

After she had freshened up, Katherine made her way downstairs to say farewell to Lord Haighton. At the parlour door she halted, as it seemed her husband and his stepson were having an argument.

"Why the blazes did you marry her?" Richard's tone sounded desperate.

"She's a beautiful woman, so why shouldn't I?"

"But of all the women in the world."

"I found it interesting."

"Interesting? What happens if she finds out?"

"How could she. Unless you tell her."

"I wouldn't do that. But she's been in the church. I couldn't stop her."

There was a moment of silence before she heard her husband say, "So, she's seen the church. It's a summer house and nothing more."

"A summer house," scoffed Richard. "Lord, I wish I was back in Italy."

Katherine bit her lip anxiously. The church had alarmed her, but this altercation between her husband and his stepson made the hair stand up on the back of her neck. She was in no doubt that she was the subject of the conversation and the words *of all the women in the world*, sounded ominous. What did Richard mean? And her husband found it interesting to marry her! Was it because of their age difference? Yes, that must be it; a young wife to show off to society.

Strangely, the only sentence that seemed to pacify her was the fact she mustn't find out something. It must have something to do with her husband's business, she reasoned; perhaps some deal that had gone wrong and he was too embarrassed to admit it to her.

She took in a deep breath and forced herself to smile as she entered the room.

Two days later, Katherine plucked up the courage to ask her husband about the ruined church and she was told that it was 'a bit of nonsense' when he had hosted a costume party for his birthday. The guests had dressed up as either angels or devils and the decoration simply reflected that. He had not had time to put it to rights, since shortly after he reminded her, he had received the letter from her uncle inviting him to Widcombe Hall.

"As you can imagine, my love," he told her apologetically, "from that moment on, my time was taken up with preparing a life for us. But if it upsets you, I will get the folly repainted."

She agreed that that would probably be the right thing to do and until it was completed, she would stay away from it. And then she remembered Mathilda's request to return to the Hall.

"I must find a new maid if Mathilda wishes to leave me. I wondered about the person you spoke of. Betsy?"

Her husband nodded. "A good girl. My late wife was very pleased with her. I will find her address and you can write and ask her to attend an interview."

Three days before their journey to Cheltenham, Betsy came to Westcroft. She stood in front of Lady Fox, who looked her up and down.

"I was born in Durham, my lady," explained Betsy Hardcastle. "I come from a poor mining family, but I taught myself to read and write."

Lady Fox glanced down at the neatly penned character in her hand. Betsy had originally come to Westcroft to work as a scullery maid, but had worked her way up to parlour maid and then lady's maid. She could style hair, wash and starch linen, embroider and mend. She had spent eight years in the household of Sir Herbert and Lady Fox becoming almost indispensable. But the death of her lady had sent her back to Durham to become a parlour maid once more.

"It's my accent that seems to let me down," said Betsy, frowning slightly. "No matter how much I practise I can't seem to get rid of the Durham lilt."

Katherine nodded. Some prospective employers would believe her accent too strong and therefore think her unsuitable as a lady's maid, no matter her skill. Now, standing in her boudoir, Katherine could see by the young girl's eager expression that Betsy desperately wanted the new Lady Fox to like her.

And the new Lady Fox did like her. Katherine thought her accent pleasing to the ear and as she asked her questions about her abilities and her life in Durham, she knew that Betsy would be perfectly acceptable. Although rather tall for a woman, her arms and legs too long, she reminded Katherine of the fallow deer that roamed the woodland on the estate. Yes, Betsy Hardcastle would be an asset to the Westcroft household and in a short time she moved her possessions into the room next door to her lady's.

Her appointment came just in time. Mathilda had already started packing for their visit to Cheltenham and immediately handed the task to the new maid. And then with very little fuss, Mathilda left Westcroft and travelled back to Widcombe Hall and back to the life she loved.

The journey to Cheltenham was taken in an open carriage that day in early June since the weather couldn't have been better for the start of their holiday. When Katherine saw the spire of Saint Mary's church and they trotted into the outskirts of the town, she couldn't contain her smiles. The elegant whitewashed houses with colonnades each side of the door, the intricate ironwork fencing, the civic buildings, the parks, all added to the beauty of a town where the wealthy residents promenaded daily for the enjoyment of all.

And yet in the early years of the century, Cheltenham was no more than a small hamlet. That was until the mineral springs were discovered when it was noticed that the pigeons took pleasure in pecking the small white specks of crystal that had dried by the water's edge. But it was King George III that brought the town into the public domain, by visiting to take the waters. And whatever the king did, his subjects were bound to follow.

When they arrived at Sir Herbert's townhouse, Katherine couldn't hold back her rapture. Forty-seven the High Street was a cream and white-fronted dwelling, three storeys high, with iron railings and framed with imposing columns either side of the door. It was near the gardens and although every house along the terrace was identical, this didn't seem to detract from its beauty. Katherine ran from room to room, crying with pleasure and even Sir Herbert smiled at her utter delight.

"I'm glad you approve, my love." He picked up the invitations already lying on the small hall table. "It looks like we'll be very busy with all our social engagements."

They had hardly arrived when Philippa came to visit. The two cousins hugged each other as though they had been apart for years and to Katherine's delight, she discovered that the earl and countess would be living just round the corner in Saint George's Place.

"We're going to the Pump Room tomorrow," said Philippa, her eyes shining. "I've heard it helps the baby to grow stronger if the mother takes the waters."

Katherine glanced at her waistline. "You don't seem very big. I hope you're not wearing a corset."

Philippa patted her stomach. "I'm only four months gone and I'm certainly not wearing a corset. Conrad would be furious if I did."

Katherine smiled and put her arm round her cousin. "Well, we must enjoy ourselves for the next three months before you return to the Court to have your baby."

Katherine and Philippa watched as Betsy unpacked her clothes. The bed was covered with silk, satin and muslin dresses. Some were plain, with delicate lace frills round the bodice, the sleeves short. Others were embroidered with coloured gold or silver thread. Katherine sighed as she told Philippa that her husband had insisted that the most beautiful gowns be made for her.

"You're going to look wonderful for Mrs Rondelet's birthday party. You'll turn the heads of all the young men, I'm sure," teased Philippa.

Katherine decided to ignore her remark. "What did you think of Mrs Rondelet?"

"So beautiful and charming. She's lived in France and Italy. Did you know that?" Katherine nodded. "But did you know her husband was guillotined?" Katherine nodded again. Philippa pulled a face. "Seems you know everything."

A visit to the Pump Room was always interesting. It was a large spacious hall with huge windows and decorated with palm trees and plush seating. The mineral water was distributed in small lead crystal glasses and Katherine grimaced at the bitter taste. She had tried it on many occasions in the past and could never get used to it.

It was while she was waiting for Sir Herbert to fetch a second glass for himself, that Conrad and Philippa arrived followed closely by Lord Haighton and then Mrs Rondelet. They made their way straight to Katherine and after she had kissed her cousin on the cheek she turned to Conrad.

She tried not to look at him as he kissed her hand and was relieved when he moved away to talk to Richard. Her heart had suddenly speeded up the moment he had walked into the Pump Room and she felt annoyed with herself for having such uncomfortable feelings. She turned her attention to Philippa, delighting in the bloom on her cheeks and the happiness that sparkled in her eyes. It was foolish and very ungracious of her to carry a grudge for Conrad. He had made a terrible error of judgement when he had confessed his feelings to her in the library last Christmas. But he had apologised and she decided that she must forgive and forget. It was apparent that he was making Philippa happy now and she would be thankful for that.

So, when Conrad came to her side once more, she smiled at him.

"I haven't had the chance to ask how you are," he said. "It seems a long time since your wedding."

"It's only been four weeks and thank you, I'm quite well."

"And settled down to married life?"

"Westcroft is a beautiful place and I'm very happy."

He raised his eyebrows. "Good."

"I look forward to seeing you at Mrs Rondelet's party."

"And I hope you'll honour me with a dance," he said, his lips twitching slightly.

"Of course, sir."

He smiled. "Then that's settled. You'll want the first dance with your husband, of course, so I'll have the second." Conrad tried not to laugh but found it impossible. "Unless you've already promised that one to someone else?"

"No, my lord. I haven't."

They had been talking together a little apart from their friends and Sir Herbert had noticed. Katherine removed herself from Conrad and went to her husband's side.

"Is everything all right, my love?" he asked, squeezing her hand.

"Oh, yes. But I think I'd like to take a walk in the gardens. It seems the summer has finally arrived and I want to take full advantage of it."

They all agreed that that would be a splendid idea.

The evening of Geraldine's birthday ball arrived and Betsy dressed her lady with care. Katherine had chosen a very special gown for the occasion, wanting to look her best for her first engagement since her wedding. The dress was made of muslin embroidered in silver, the low bodice edged with delicate lace frills.

The maid dressed her hair in a simple fashion, pulling it back from her forehead and then piling it up on top of Katherine's head. She left tiny curls to frame her mistress's face and then teased out a flowing ringlet of golden hair to hang over one shoulder. On the left side, she pinned a small cluster of silk orange blossom. A beautiful blue silk fan with a design of exotic oriental birds complemented her dress.

When she had finished, Betsy stood back to survey her mistress. "You look wonderful, my lady."

Katherine responded with a satisfied smile. "You certainly have a remarkable skill, Betsy." She turned to look at the young girl with green eyes and red hair. "I think you will do well."

Betsy's face flushed with pleasure. This was the first time she had dressed her lady for a social occasion and she had wanted to impress.

"I'm willing to serve my lady in any way I can."

Katherine smiled and nodded.

Sir Herbert grinned as she made her way down the staircase and across the hallway towards him. He had to admit to swelling with self-satisfaction with such a young and beautiful wife on his arm. Many people took them for father and daughter and it amused him seeing the young bucks gawk at them when discovering their true relationship.

It was a pleasantly warm evening as they travelled in the carriage to the far end of the High Street and the home of Geraldine Rondelet. At the door of the large reception room that was doubling as a ballroom for that evening, Katherine spotted Lord Haighton standing by the fireplace.

Sir Herbert had also seen him. "Ah, I see my stepson is here," he smiled. "Shall we join him?"

Richard was delighted to see them and took Katherine's hand, murmuring a polite greeting that she could barely hear.

Richard bowed to his stepfather and after hesitating for the briefest of seconds said, "Have you tried the punch? It's absolute poison." He gestured towards the punch bowl. "I don't know what's in it but it's enough to blow your brains out. Shall I get you some?"

Sir Herbert nodded. "Yes, fetch us a drop. I'm sure my dear wife will be able to manage it."

Katherine watched his retreating back. "He's such a charming young man. I'm surprised he's not married."

Her husband chuckled. "Are you going to do some matchmaking while in Cheltenham, my love?"

"If I meet a suitable lady, then why not?" She smiled as Philippa and Conrad entered the room and made their way towards her.

"I believe the lady you seek might be closer than you think," said Sir Herbert, grinning from ear to ear.

She puzzled on this, but then Geraldine appeared and everyone clapped as she entered the room.

The small orchestra started to play and Geraldine and Richard opened up the dancing. At first, Katherine felt startled. Yes, they were related by marriage, but the way they were talking so intimately together it was obvious that they were much more than friends. As Katherine danced with her husband she knew that Mrs Rondelet and Lord Haighton were romantically involved and that was what her husband had been hinting at. Yes, she thought, Geraldine would make a suitable match for Richard.

But when the music ended, the matchmaking between Geraldine and Richard was forgotten with the gentle hand on her arm. She turned to see Conrad, his violet eyes looking directly into hers. He had come to claim her for the promised dance.

CHAPTER SIX

It was three days later that a distressing letter arrived for Katherine. It had been forwarded from Westcroft and came from Mrs Owen, her Aunt Sybil's neighbour and friend who sounded distraught that her aunt had taken ill. It seemed she had developed a severe cold that had settled on her lungs.

"I must visit her, Herbert," said Katherine, after reading the letter a second time.

"Yes, you must. I'll accompany you, of course. We'll set off after breakfast tomorrow. I know an excellent hotel where we can stay. The King George."

"It's not necessary for you to accompany me. I've often travelled to Bristol on my own. There's no reason why I shouldn't do that again."

He shuffled in his seat. "But, my love, I can't let you travel alone. I wouldn't be fulfilling my responsibilities as a husband…" He paused, his mouth twisting in an inexplicable smile. "Very well, if you don't wish my company, then I'll find other things to do with my time."

"Please don't feel hurt, sir. You wouldn't wish to visit a sick woman you've never met." Hoping that a little humour would ease the situation she said, "I shall travel by public coach."

Her husband nearly choked on his tea. "You'll do no such thing! Travel on a public coach indeed, when I have coaches and carriages in plenty. What are you thinking of." He saw the mischievous glint in her eyes and burst out laughing. "Oh, I see, you jest. Good! Humour becomes you. But I'll still expect you to travel with your own personal maid as well as a coachman and two grooms."

Katherine sighed. "My aunt lives in a small cottage," she explained. "It will be far simpler if I travel alone. It's not necessary to take an entourage. They'll only get in the way." She fiddled with her wedding ring to hide her discomfort. "I don't intend staying long, only three or four days." Her husband's overprotectiveness could be stifling at times.

Sir Herbert thought this over, pursing his lips. "I insist Betsy accompany you. Harry will drive and just one groom then...yes, Thomas, I think. Both are good men and quite dependable. They can sleep above the stables while they tend to the coach and horses. Surely your aunt could accommodate the maid?"

"I suppose an extra bed could be found for her," said Katherine reluctantly.

The following day, Katherine started her journey. She would return to Cheltenham when she was reassured about her aunt's health, hopefully only a week or so since she couldn't bear to be away from Philippa. However, a nagging suspicion had developed that it was both Philippa *and* Conrad that she truly couldn't be parted from. Were her feelings slowly changing towards her cousin's husband? At Geraldine's ball they had danced twice together and their conversation had been animated. She had thoroughly enjoyed the evening and returned home dancing on air. Yes, there had been a change in their relationship and it felt wonderful. And if she enjoyed Conrad's company she saw no harm in that.

As the coach wheels bumped over the ruts in the road, she fixed her eyes on the scenery and contemplated her life since her marriage. It had turned out happier than she had expected. She was content with Sir Herbert, but she knew she did not love him. He was the gentlest of souls and generous to a fault when it came to money. He liked to live well and didn't stint himself when it came to the trappings of a good life. His home was finely furnished with the tasteful décor associated with a country gentleman and his cellar and larder were brimming with all the sustenance a body could need. In his stables there was a good stock of fine horses and two richly upholstered coaches and gleaming carriages stood in the coach house. Katherine had jewellery and gowns that were the envy of the neighbourhood. Smiling to herself, she knew she would be a good wife to Sir Herbert and they would be happy together.

They had completed over half their journey when the coach suddenly lurched violently and there came a sickening crack from somewhere under the floor. Then the vehicle jerked to one side and Katherine hurtled forward on top of her maid. In a flurry of arms, legs and muslin gowns, they were flung onto the floor. Seconds later, Thomas yanked open the door.

"I'm afraid there's been a bit of an accident, my lady," he murmured, helping the shaking mistress and maid onto the road.

"You've hurt your arm," said Katherine, noticing he was holding his left arm as if to protect it.

"Aye, my lady. But I'm not as bad as poor Harry there."

It was then that Katherine saw Harry sprawled in the road, his head bleeding above his left eye, his cheek and chin grazed.

They hurried over to him and with Thomas using his good arm, they managed to move Harry so that he was propped up against the coach that was tipped at an angle of forty-five degrees, the back left wheel almost cracked in two. Katherine quickly assessed the situation. Both men had sustained serious injuries when they had been thrown from the seat. The horses were still hitched and were agitated, their hooves thudding the ground.

"Are you hurt?" asked Katherine, watching the maid rub her back.

"No, my lady. Just a bruise here and there."

Katherine knew she had to take charge. "Thomas, sit down next to Harry and try not to move that arm. Betsy, you clean up Harry's head. I must deal with the horses before they harm themselves."

She approached them with a soft tread, speaking gently and making them calm down. Once they were more composed, she was able to unhitch them and lead them to an area of grass, where they started to chomp voraciously. Patting their necks, she returned to the distressed Betsy.

"He's almost insensible," the maid said, dabbing Harry's head with her handkerchief. "And Thomas is in a lot of pain. What are we going to do now?"

Katherine studied the two men. Thomas sat with his head bowed, hugging his arm, biting his lip against the pain. Harry's eyes were glazed and he was breathing rapidly.

Katherine scanned her eyes over the countryside. "I'm going to walk to Dursley."

"But that's nearly four miles, my lady."

"I should be able to do it in under an hour." She looked down at the injured men. "They need a physician and the coach needs a wheelwright."

"And you'll need an escort," said Betsy. "It's not right for you to be alone on the road."

"Don't talk such nonsense. At the Hall I went out walking and riding many times on my own." Katherine smiled and then her face brightened even more. "I could ride to Dursley."

"What! Bareback?"

"Did you pack a saddle?"

"No, I didn't."

Katherine clicked her tongue. "How very forgetful of you." She headed towards the horses.

"You'll have to ride astride, my lady. It's not decent," answered the maid, chasing after her.

"You know what they say about 'needs must when the devil drives'. And I'm riding to Dursley. Bareback and astride."

"What will people say if they see you?"

"Probably that my husband should take a whip to me." Katherine chose a horse. It still wore its bridle and it was a simple matter to shorten the traces to make reins. She led him to a stile set in a stone wall and climbed up and then clambered astride the horse. He pranced backwards and forwards, threatening to throw her off, but she held on. "I'll be as quick as I can. Take care of Harry and Thomas." She turned the horse's head and galloped away.

Thomas lifted his head. "You'd better bring me the pistol, miss. It's under the driver's seat. If you put it in my good hand, I should be able to use it if necessary."

Betsy's face blanched with fright, but then she raised her chin. "If anyone is going to use a pistol, it's going to be me."

Katherine reached the crossroads and took the left turn towards the market town, confident that she would be there in no time. She was heartened when she spotted a stone slab and clearly engraved DURSLEY 1 MILE.

She was nearly there but she was starting to feel cold. Despite it being June, the warm weather had deserted her and it was quite chilly. And then the heavens opened and a deluge soaked her thoroughly. Staying on a horse bareback was difficult at the best of times, but holding on when his hair was slippery was almost impossible. Shivering, she gritted her teeth and spurred him on, bending her body low against his warm flesh.

The storm was short lived and soon passed over, the sun suddenly breaking through the clouds, making the puddles in the rutted road sparkle. Despite its comforting heat, Katherine was glad when she reached her destination.

She was even more surprised to find a carnival in progress. The inhabitants had run for cover during the downpour, but were out in the street again, dressed in fancy costume and dancing around with enjoyment. Katherine passed amongst them, conscious that she must look a frightful sight, soaked to the skin with her bonnet flattened against her head.

A young man grabbed the horse by its mane and pulled him up. "You're supposed to take your clothes off, darling, if you're playing Lady Godiva," he leered at her.

She kicked him away and his three companions laughed and cheered as he fell backwards into a pile of horse manure. She pushed past them and looked around for some form of help. Suddenly, she saw a tall man standing near an inn door. His face was hidden under the brim of his hat, but he looked well dressed and respectable.

"You, sir," she called. "I need the physician and a wheelwright urgently. Can you assist me?" He lifted his face and she gasped, "Lord Haighton?"

Richard seemed just as surprised as she. "Lady Fox, for goodness sake. What are you doing here, riding bareback and wet through?" He helped her down.

"It's a long story," she laughed, relieved that she had met someone that she could trust.

In seconds, she had told him the story of the unfortunate accident on the road and he immediately took charge. "Let's get you inside the inn and then I'll collect together some men and bring back your maid and grooms." He guided her through the door. "Landlord, show Lady Fox to a decent chamber and see she has a hot drink and a change of clothes." The rather weedy man behind the bar shuffled over. "And she'll need someone to act as maid. The young serving girl will have to do for the time being." Richard turned to Katherine. "I won't be long. Don't worry, everything will be all right." He was gone before she could say thank you.

She looked around the inn. She had been in one before when travelling with her aunt and uncle, but then they were always shown to a private sitting room. Now, she was alone and when thirty pairs of male eyes strayed in her direction, she wondered if she should leave. But Richard had already issued his orders and she was under his protection.

"I'm sorry, my lady," drawled the landlord, "but every chamber is taken with the carnival and coach travellers. There's only small attic room available. I'd have told his lordship, if he'd stopped a moment longer."

"Then I'll take that. I need to get out of these wet clothes."

"Fire's not lit. I'll get Meg to do it, but be a while before room's warm enough."

Katherine saw the fire blazing in the main saloon. "I'll go in there until it is."

"Best not, ma'am. Not a place for a lady."

"What do you suggest?" A shiver ran through her.

The landlord shook his head and rubbed his chin. "There be only Lord Haighton's room that'd suit lady such as yourself."

Katherine gathered her patience and smiled. "You should have said his lordship was staying here. Take me to his room immediately. I can dry off in there."

She followed the bent, hunched figure of the landlord up the stairs and to the large front-facing bedchamber. Although the best room in the house, it was still meagre in appearance. A spacious bed stood in the corner and the rest of the furniture consisted of a broken down washstand, dresser and wardrobe. But the blazing fire was a joy and Katherine ran straight to it.

"Meg will fetch some towels and she might have some clothes for you to change into." He closed the door and she could hear him shuffling down the stairs.

Katherine discovered that Meg was the pleasant little serving girl who bobbed and curtsied when she brought the towels along with a cotton underskirt and faded yellow dress. When she went to fetch her lady a drink, Katherine knelt before the fire and eased off her wet clothing. After drying herself with the rather coarse towel, she slipped the underskirt over her head and tied the ribbons at the front. Then she started on her hair, rubbing it vigorously and holding out the strands in front of the dancing flames. The young girl returned with the required hot chocolate and a few candles as not much light was coming through the single window. They had stopped in Stroud for breakfast, but now it was gone midday and Katherine was starting to feel hungry. Pulling the dress over her head, she managed to fasten the buttons and after straightening the skirt, she sank down in the armchair and sipped her drink. She glanced around the room.

Richard's possessions were scattered about. A clean shirt hung over a chair; his shaving kit lay on the washstand. By the side of the bed was a saddlebag. Thank goodness Richard had been there to help, thought Katherine, as her eyes started to feel heavy. Tiredness washed over her and in minutes the warm drink and blazing fire had lulled her to sleep.

Katherine was awakened from her sleep by a gentle voice calling her name. She opened her eyes to find Richard bending over her.

"I shouldn't have come in, I know," he smiled. "But I did knock and there was no answer."

She rubbed her eyes. "I must have dozed off with the warmth from the fire."

"I thought you'd want to know how everything went." Richard grinned, noticing the faded yellow gown. "Looks much better on you than on the serving girl."

"It will do for now," she grimaced. "Now tell me of the others."

"They're all well," he laughed. "Harry had regained his senses by the time we arrived although Thomas was still in a lot of pain. Your maid waved a pistol at us until she recognised me. They're at the physician's home now, although he says that the injury to the groom's head isn't as bad as first appeared. He's set Thomas's arm and given him laudanum for the pain. Betsy is staying with them to make sure they're cared for, but she's bringing some things over to you shortly. So, at least you'll look more yourself when you dine with me."

"Dinner sounds wonderful."

He looked at his pocket watch. "I thought we'd dine early. Then we can set off for Bristol immediately after."

"You're coming with me?" she said, trying to smile.

"Well, Bristol was my destination also, so I see no reason why we shouldn't enjoy each other's company. The wheelwright is working as I speak and I've organised another driver and groom. And Harry and Thomas will be accompanied back to Cheltenham when they're well enough."

Katherine found speech difficult. "That's kind of you, sir. I'm very grateful that their welfare is taken care of." She thought for a moment. "Why are you going to Bristol?"

He gave a mischievous grin. "I have many business interests there, as well as family. I thought I would take the opportunity of dealing with the former and visiting the latter." There was a knock on the door. "Ah, that will be your maid so I will leave you in private."

Katherine was delighted to see Betsy, who brought her toilet accessories, a lime-green gown and clean underwear.

"I came just at the right moment," the maid sniffed, seeing her lady in the faded yellow gown. "You do look a sight."

"Don't you like it?" Katherine asked, twirling round the room.

"A scullery maid wears better." She shook out her ladyship's damp clothing. "Now, let me dress you in something more suitable."

Katherine smiled and nodded.

A short time later, Lord Haighton came to escort Katherine to the private parlour where a table was set and covered with various dishes of food. He pulled back a chair for her, his eyes sparkling with elation.

"If anyone had told me this morning that I'd be dining with you, I would never have believed them." He poured out two glasses of wine from a decanter.

"Is it such a wonderful thing?"

He took her hand and kissed it. "It is for me," he murmured, peering at her over his glass of wine. "You're certainly the most beautiful woman I've ever met." Katherine smiled in response. He added quickly, "I thought that when I first met you. My stepfather is a very fortunate man."

"Why were you not at our wedding?" she asked.

"I'm afraid I was in Italy and couldn't get back in time. More's the pity. I would have liked to have been there."

She smiled coyly and looked around the parlour. "My husband will be very pleased that you came to my rescue."

He nodded. "We will have a pleasant journey together, I'm sure. I came on horseback, but travelling with you will be an absolute pleasure."

She sipped her wine.

Richard was right, their journey turned out to be very pleasant and they rode through the outskirts of Bristol in the late afternoon. Katherine looked out of the window. The difference between Cheltenham and Bristol was immense since the houses of the rich merchants on the edges of the city were soon replaced by the rundown cottages, business premises, alleyways and shops that dominated the centre. The stink of the river drifted over the buildings and as they travelled closer the stench from the slave ships made them put hands to their noses. It was rank and after a while it would seep into clothes and hair, seeming impossible to eradicate.

"William Wilberforce has his work cut out, I think," said Katherine, trying not to retch. She knew the smell, but it often took a day or two to get used to it.

Richard nodded. "Those in the slave trade will be reluctant to relinquish such vast profits. But it's a terrible business and should be stamped out. I hope Wilberforce succeeds in passing a bill though Parliament."

"My husband says he's an advocate of Wilberforce and always supports him."

He smiled as the coach came to a halt. "The driver will want to know the directions to your aunt's cottage," he reminded her. She gave them and he passed them on. The coach lurched forward once more.

They travelled down roads that seemed to get narrower and then the coach turned a tight corner into a dirt lane. Along this lane was five cottages and the coach drew up in front of the end one.

"Well, we're here," Katherine sighed.

Richard opened the door and helped her alight, looking about him.

"Yes, this is your aunt's dwelling," he said, biting his lip. He cleared his throat. "Is it not?"

Katherine frowned at the strange statement that had suddenly turned into a question. "For more years than the neighbours can remember." She put up her hand to stop him following her. "You don't need to come in. Betsy and I will do very well now. If you could see the coach safely to the stables, I would be very grateful."

Richard studied the row of dilapidated cottages while helping Betsy from the coach. They seemed like neglected dolls' houses, made of rough brick with grey slate roofs and small windows and doors. Her aunt's home was in better condition than the rest, with pretty lace curtains hanging in the window and a flower box full of marigolds, giving an overall appearance of gentility.

"No, I'll come in with you, if you don't mind. I would like to meet your aunt."

He didn't wait for her answer but knocked on the door. A woman answered, as round as a barrel and wearing black. A white cloth cap covered her head.

"Miss Kate. You're here at last."

Katherine took her hand. "Yes, Mrs Owen. I came as soon as I received your letter."

"Then come in. Your aunt is in her chair by the fire. Refuses to go to bed, she does."

Katherine followed her into the cottage with Betsy and Richard close behind. The front door led directly into a room that was a tight squeeze to fit everyone into such a small space. Once the door was closed, Katherine introduced Lord Haighton.

"Such illustrious company," said Mrs Owen, giving an awkward curtsey.

Katherine went into her reticule dangling from her wrist and pulled out a small packet. "I've brought some tea, Mrs Owen. Would you be so kind as to make us a pot?"

Mrs Owen curtsied again. "Yes, of course. Do sit down and I'll do it now."

Aunt Sybil was staring into the fire of the range, unaware that visitors had arrived. She was so small that the armchair seemed to be devouring her, the plain grey dress and white cap too big for her, so shrunken was her frame.

Richard looked about him. The room was as small as his dressing room and in fact, he had had to bend his head as he passed through the door. The ceiling was low and had he been an inch taller he would have had to stoop. The furniture was sparse with only two armchairs, two rickety chairs, a table and a dresser against the wall, containing the crockery. A clock ticked on the mantelpiece, with a polished candlestick holding a burnt down candle on one side and a vase of bright red poppies on the other. Copper pots and pans shone down on them from a shelf above a cupboard. And to the right of the cupboard was the kitchen range, a kettle of water just coming to the boil over the flames.

Katherine took off her cloak, handed it to Betsy and then kneeled beside the chair of her aunt.

"Aunt Sybil. I've come to visit you."

The frail figure turned her head and looked at her through dull, lifeless eyes. "Do I know you, my dear?"

Katherine glanced away briefly but then took her hand, holding it against her cheek.

"It's Kate, Aunt. Don't you recognise me?"

Mrs Owen had finished her task. "Now, I'll leave your tea here," she said, gesturing towards the pot and dishes on the table. "Must pop next door and see what mischief Mr Owen has got up to. Can't leave him too long."

They watched her disappear through the door.

"Who are you?" asked her aunt once more, squinting at Katherine.

"I'll...I'll pour the tea," whispered her niece, trying to rise to her feet. But then seeing her aunt's careworn expression she sank down once more fighting to control herself. "I'm Kate. Your sister Juliet's daughter." She gave a weak smile.

Her aunt's face completely transformed. "Oh, yes. I know you. My dear Juliet's little baby. Kate, my precious Kate. You're safe and back home with me."

Katherine put her arms round her and held her close, tears streaming down her face.

They drank their tea in silence and then Betsy went outside to organise the trunk from the coach. Aunt Sybil had fallen asleep, her chin on her chest.

"I must get her into bed," said Katherine, placing her dish of tea down on the table.

"Allow me," said Richard. He rose from the chair and lifted her aunt into his arms as though she was a small child. "Dear Lord, she weighs nothing. Up here?" He nodded towards the narrow flight of stairs.

"Yes, her room is on the right of the landing." She gestured to the only other door leading from the sitting room. "That leads to a small courtyard where the washing tub is kept." She lowered her voice. "And the privy."

She led the way up the stairs to the small landing and opened the door on the right. He carried her aunt into the room and placed her on the bed. Katherine slipped off her house shoes and covered her with a blanket. They stared down at her.

"How long has she been like this," said Richard quietly.

Katherine hesitated before replying. "She's been growing increasingly deaf since I was a child, but her mind has grown...sick these last seven years. Ever since..."

"Ever since?" he asked.

"Ever since she received a terrible shock. She never really recovered from it." She glanced up to see Richard pass a shaking hand over his face. "Does her condition repel you?"

He forced a crooked smile. "No, indeed not. Why should it?"

"She's quite harmless even though she forgets nearly everything now."

Richard looked around the small bedchamber that had room for a bed and dresser and nothing more.

"Where do you sleep?" He gestured towards the door across the landing. "In that bedroom?"

She frowned wondering how he knew that was a bedroom; after all it could have been a cupboard. "No, I haven't slept in that room for a long time. I always sleep in here with my aunt now. Betsy can sleep in my old room."

"There's very little space."

"We manage."

Back in the sitting room, they found themselves alone. Glancing through the window, Katherine saw Betsy standing by the coach in conversation with Mrs Owen, while the coachman unloaded the trunk and bags.

Richard sat down and Katherine peeped into the teapot.

"There's some tea left. Would you like another dish?"

He nodded and watched her pour it out.

"Why don't I take you and Betsy to the hotel. The King George is a wonderful establishment and you'll be far more comfortable there."

Katherine felt anger rise up inside her. "Are you trying to say that this cottage is not good enough for me?"

He sipped his tea. "You deserve better."

She grunted in annoyance. This was why she wanted to travel alone. Independence brought a certain amount of privacy.

"Richard, I'm not ashamed of my humble beginnings." Her gaze swept round the room. "It was here my mother lived and she probably sat at that window waiting for my father to return from sea. I was born in this cottage and spent my first six months here."

Colour flooded his cheeks but she didn't notice. "In this cottage I'm Miss Kate and sometimes just plain Kate."

"You'll never be plain."

She chuckled, her annoyance evaporating. "What I'm saying is that I accept that I live in two worlds. Before her marriage, my mother worked as a lady's companion and that places her on the same footing as a servant."

"But you're also the niece of a baronet."

"True, but my papa was only the third son. The title passed to Uncle George because Uncle Edward died suddenly. And my uncle has been very kind to Aunt Sybil settling a small allowance on her. He didn't have to. After all, she was only the sister of his sister-in-law." She shook her head. "No, from what I've been told, my papa was a sailor first and an aristocrat second. Until he met my mother, of course. Aunt Beatrice said she became his world and called her his 'cherished Juliet'."

"And then they had you."

"For a short time, yes."

He smiled. "Juliet? That's a beautiful name."

"My mama was a beautiful woman."

The death of her aunt came as a shock to Katherine even though she had expected it for some time. Aunt Sybil had not been able to rise from her bed the following morning, so Katherine and Betsy bathed her and changed her into a fresh nightgown. The maid had then accompanied Mrs Owen to the market, while Katherine set about making some bread, something she loved doing and a household chore that she never got the chance to do either at the Hall or at Westcroft. She was surprised when Richard arrived and making himself comfortable on the rickety kitchen chair, they chatted as she kneaded the dough.

He grinned with delight. "You're getting flour everywhere. It's on your face and in your hair."

She gave a girlish giggle. "I don't get much practice doing this, but it's wonderful work. I can thump away pretending the dough is someone I dislike." She looked at the clock. "I'll just put this to prove and then I will see if Aunt Sybil is awake. She'll be wanting some tea soon."

Richard sat forward in his seat. "You seem happy here."

She smiled as she pressed the dough into a tin and placed it by the small kitchen range that stood on a low plinth of stone.

"Yes, I am. I believe I would be quite content to live in a small cottage like this, without the trappings of wealth and status."

"But you will never have to. Whatever you say, you have aristocratic blood and that puts you above living in a dwelling such as this."

"So Uncle George keeps telling me. But I think after what happened in France every aristocrat should look into his own heart. Don't you agree?" He didn't answer and she shrugged. "Goodness it's getting hot in here," she said, mopping her forehead with her apron.

"I have a villa in Italy. It's situated on the banks of Lake Garda, at a place called Riva. It's some fifty miles from Verona and a hundred from Venice."

"Verona? Isn't that the home of Romeo and Juliet?"

He nodded. "Yes, and I would think it an honour if you and Sir Herbert would visit me there one day."

"Then thank you, my lord. I will mention your invitation to my husband when I return home. Now, I must go and see to my aunt. She should be awake by now."

A few minutes later she returned; the pain on her face telling him what had happened.

Katherine sat by the window, looking out at the rain. It was only the beginning of July and yet again, the good weather had deserted them. She had come back to Cheltenham with her husband only the week before and the rain had persisted for the last two days, mirroring her sorrow. Richard had been wonderful throughout her grief, sending couriers from Bristol to inform everyone of the sad news. Sir Herbert, Uncle George and Aunt Beatrice had arrived within a day and she had left the arrangements to them. The funeral had been simple but dignified and many friends and neighbours had attended. But how sad the cottage seemed when she finally locked the door and gave the key to the landlord.

Katherine sighed as she watched people hurrying by and drivers trying to manoeuvre coaches and wagons over rain-logged cobbles. She turned to look at the room in which she sat. It was so different from the cottage. Chippendale furniture and the plain marble fireplace enhanced the green and red rug covering the floor. Chairs and couches were placed against the walls and a three-legged table stood to one side. The walls were covered with paintings and two small mirrors holding candle brackets were fixed above the mantelpiece. It was a pleasant room and one that she and Sir Herbert spent a great deal of time in.

Her husband appeared. "It's a pity about the weather, my love. I hoped we could take a walk in the gardens."

She gave a half-smile. "I suppose we must leave Cheltenham now?"

He thought this over. "I know you're in mourning, but I don't see any reason why we shouldn't stay here. Providing we don't attend any balls or lavish entertainment then I'm sure it would be quite acceptable. We could walk and go riding in the park."

She breathed a sigh of relief. "I'm so pleased. I want to stay here and be with Philippa."

"I thought you would. When you feel well enough we will plan our itinerary for the next two months."

"I'm not sick, Herbert. Just sad."

The maid showed in Lord and Lady Croston. Philippa ran to kiss her. Conrad smiled that even in mourning Katherine looked lovely, her gown of a black velvet skirt and white bodice set off her rather pale complexion.

"How are you, Kate?" said Philippa.

"I'm well, dearest."

She took a seat.

"Would you care for a glass of brandy, good sir?" said Sir Herbert.

"Yes, indeed," said Conrad.

"And for the ladies, I think some hot water would be in order for your tea." Her husband gestured to the footman who left the room.

Katherine let the conversation go over her head until the footman returned carrying a silver kettle and placed it on the table next to the milk jug, teapot and dishes.

"Poor Aunt Sybil," Philippa sighed. "Such a sad little woman. And living in such a tiny cottage."

Katherine nodded. "I loved that cottage, but the landlord told me that a young couple might be taking the lease and so it should be. Life must go on." She paused in her task of making the tea, holding the spoon heaped with leaves over the teapot. "I wonder if I'll ever go to Bristol again? I have no one there now to visit."

The maid announcing another visitor interrupted her melancholy thoughts. Lord Haighton came in, striding across the room to kiss her hand.

"I had to call on you and ask how you are."

"I'm well, sir."

"Mrs Rondelet has invited you and Lady Croston to take tea tomorrow." He took a seat and his stepfather ordered a brandy for him.

"We were just talking about Aunt Sybil's cottage," said Philippa.

Richard grinned. "I've never been in a place so small. I felt like Lemuel Gulliver. And I shall always remember Lady Fox baking bread."

"You baked bread, Kate?" said Philippa in disgust. "That's servants' work."

"I did many things in the cottage that were servants' work."

Philippa's face brightened. "Did you tell Sir Herbert about meeting Prince Rasheid?"

"Prince Rasheid?" queried Sir Herbert.

Katherine was amused that anyone should be interested. "It was a long time ago. Aunt Sybil and I heard that a royal yacht was docking in Bristol. At first we thought it was King George, but it turned out to be the Turkish sultan visiting His Majesty. Selim, I think his name was. But his son was Prince Rasheid, I remember that most distinctly. They were on their way to take the waters in Bath. So, Aunt Sybil and I went down to the quayside to watch them disembark. Oh, what a spectacle it was. The yacht was beautiful, like a palace with sails and covered with colourful flags. And the sultan and his son wore the most marvellous clothes and jewels. It was all so exotic."

"And you met them?" said Conrad in amazement.

"The prince saw me in the crowd and spoke to one of his advisors. Before I knew it, I was being ushered along to meet him. He spoke very good English and was so charming. It was a wonderful moment."

"How old were you?" asked Conrad.

"Fifteen."

Katherine glanced round the room and although her cousin seemed deep in thought, she couldn't help noticing that Sir Herbert had the strangest expression, while Lord Haighton had suddenly become interested in examining the toes of his boots.

"Conrad, you're not listening to me," complained Philippa.

Lord Croston carefully lay his newspaper to one side and smiled. "I heard every word you said, my dear. You believe that it was this Prince Rasheid that your cousin eloped with, but circumstances forced them apart."

"Don't patronise me, I'm not a schoolgirl," came back her petulant answer. Conrad laughed, raised himself from his seat and bent to kiss her. He resumed his paper and she watched him with a yearning that almost bordered on pain. "But it all makes sense. She was fifteen when she went missing and that was when Prince Rasheid came to Bristol."

Conrad considered this morsel of information. "True. But if your cousin did make an attachment to a royal prince then it would have been frowned upon. She would not have been a suitable consort for a Turkish prince."

"And that's why they had to part. And he gave her the red silk handkerchief as a token of his love."

"Rather a paltry gift to give, considering his wealth," said Conrad, pursing his mouth.

"His father and the royal court would have torn them apart. And he would have gone back to Turkey with a broken heart."

"And she would have stayed in England with her heart duly broken." She threw her napkin at him. "I'm sorry, my dear. But I think you're letting your imagination run away with itself."

"Well, the initial on the handkerchief is 'R' and that could stand for Rasheid."

Conrad grinned. "It could also be Lord Haighton, since his name is Richard. Or my valet, Robert. What about…"

Philippa's withering look silenced him and chuckling he resumed his paper.

Katherine looked down at her husband in utter dismay. Sir Herbert had not appeared for breakfast and when the parlour maid had told her that he was still sleeping, a fact very strange indeed, she had decided to go to his rooms and see if he was unwell. What she found was his large, slumbering body stretched across the bed from corner to corner, his mouth open and loud snores reverberating round the room. She placed a gentle hand on the prone arm and shook it, expecting no response and receiving none. Grimacing, she decided to continue with her plans and leave Sir Herbert in the capable hands of his valet, Albert.

"I'm going to visit my cousin, Lady Croston," she told the hunched and elderly servant. "When my husband wakes up, please tell him that I'm going shopping and then taking tea with Mrs Rondelet. I should be home in time for dinner."

Albert nodded and lifted the overfull chamberpot to carry it down to the kitchen for disposal. Katherine picked up a shirt from the floor, folded it and placed it tidily on the dresser. It was obvious that Sir Herbert had vomited and Albert would have his work cut out to clean up the mess.

She decided to walk to Philippa's home in Saint George's Place since the weather was glorious, now that the rain had gone. Raising her parasol, she smiled and greeted the people she passed and as she walked she thought over the discussion the day before when she had told her story of the sultan's visit and her meeting with the prince. She couldn't understand why recounting the story had unsettled her husband and Lord Haighton.

They had spent the evening together cloistered in the study and although they were trying to keep their voices low, they were having a terrible disagreement. They had also drunk a lot of brandy and port and that is why her husband couldn't rise from his bed that morning. It had surprised her to see him in such a state; since their marriage he had never imbibed large quantities of alcohol. This disturbing change in his character worried her.

That afternoon Katherine went out riding, with a groom trotting discreetly behind her. Sir Herbert had planned to accompany her, but his condition was no better and she had left him groaning in his armchair, with a cold, damp cloth across his forehead.

She kept the horse to the wide promenade, as the grass was still wet, but the sky was a glorious blue, the sun now drying the sodden ground.

"Good afternoon, dear stepmother," said a cheerful voice to Katherine's left.

She turned to find Richard trotting towards her. Katherine smiled with pleasure.

"Why, good afternoon, Lord Haighton." He was riding a powerful black stallion and she noticed he handled it with great expertise. "That's a wonderful horse you have there."

Lord Haighton came alongside, grinning. "Borrowed him from my generous stepfather."

"Have you now. Are you sure you can handle him?"

"I will do my best," Richard chuckled. "I look forward to racing with you again, Lady Fox."

She sighed and bent to stroke the smooth, silky mane. "Unfortunately that will not be for some time. Not until my mourning is over."

"Of course. But when it is, I will call on you at the first opportunity."

And then Katherine noticed two riders a short way ahead. Their horses were standing nose to tail, enabling their owners to talk comfortably together.

Conrad had met Geraldine in the park by accident, but he was pleased to speak with her.

"I wanted to have a word. We have seen very little of each other since I came to Cheltenham."

Geraldine lowered seductive eyelashes. "I think that's for the best. The place for a former mistress is in the background."

Conrad clicked his tongue. "You might be my former mistress, but I'll always consider you a friend."

Suddenly, Geraldine shielded her eyes. "Ah, the delightful Lady Fox is over there talking with Lord Haighton. How sad that she's lost her bloom since her aunt died."

"It will return as soon as she's recovered."

She eyed him curiously. "You think a lot about her, don't you?" He didn't answer. "In fact, I'll go so far in saying that your heart is lost to her."

"What utter nonsense. You're worse than my wife and her theory about her cousin's unsuitable love affair."

Geraldine was intrigued. "Oh, yes. I had forgotten. You thought Katherine had a secret."

"No, you thought Kate had a secret."

She pursed her lips. "Well, did you discover what it was?" Again he didn't answer. "Then tell me your wife's theory."

Conrad sighed. "We found a handkerchief after Kate had left the Court."

"How interesting."

"It was red silk with an embroidered 'R' in the corner. Philippa believes that it belonged to Kate's lost love. Of course it's all poppycock and I think..." He turned to see Geraldine's blanched face. "What is it?"

"It's nothing."

"That's not so. Something has unsettled you."

"No, Conrad, leave it be." She tried to smile as Katherine and Lord Haighton joined them and as they spoke pleasantries, she studied Lady Fox through hostile eyes.

CHAPTER SEVEN

In the middle of August, Katherine and Philippa celebrated their birthdays. Since they were only four days apart, Sir Herbert suggested a private birthday supper at their home for family only, since Katherine was in mourning. She would be twenty-two and her cousin would be eighteen and somehow that year, the first year of their marriages, it seemed an appropriate time to mark the occasion. It was also only two weeks before Conrad and Philippa would be returning to Croston Court to await the arrival of their child.

Philippa and Conrad were the first to arrive, followed by Geraldine and Richard and as was always the case, Geraldine became the centre of attention, manipulating the conversation and regaling the party with stories of her years in France and Italy. Katherine had been the last person to believe that Geraldine would become her friend, but since their first meeting, they had established a bond. And it was not only the binds of being aunt and niece, a fact that Geraldine found very amusing since she was eight years older, but also the binds of friendship. Katherine had grown to respect this worldlier woman and was secretly delighted at the way she relished in shaking up the establishment in any way she could. Her audacious comments would cause many a lady to flutter their fan in embarrassment or a gentleman to raise his eyebrows in surprise. Geraldine simply did not care what people thought of her.

But at the birthday supper, Katherine noticed that Geraldine couldn't look her in the eye. And then she realised that her conversation was never directed towards her. Yes, Geraldine spoke to everyone round the table, but when it came to her hostess, she seemed to be avoiding any discussion with her. Katherine then remembered that Geraldine had been strangely distant towards her for quite a while. She had remained pleasant when they had met, but the innate friendliness, so obvious at their previous meetings, had somehow disappeared.

When Katherine received a note the morning following the supper, asking her to call on Geraldine at her home any time before one o'clock, she was more than relieved. Geraldine's manner had unsettled her and leaving the house soon after breakfast, she hoped the reason behind Geraldine's aloofness would soon be made clear.

Geraldine's home was very much like her own, constructed of warm brick with tall, sash windows, a small portico and a fanlight over the main door. The maid showed her into the parlour where her mistress was sitting on the chaise longue in front of the window. Glancing round the room with pretty cushions, curtains and elegant spun glass figurines adorning the fireplace, so very much a female domain, it was obvious why Geraldine was the envy of every female in society. She was an independent woman of means and admired by every gentleman she met.

Geraldine gave a half-smile and after asking her to take a seat, ordered the maid to bring in some hot water for the tea.

"You're probably wondering why I asked you to visit?" she said, glancing away briefly.

Katherine detected her discomfort. "Your note was intriguing," she said, sitting on the couch.

The maid brought in the hot water and then disappeared back to the nether regions of the house. Katherine watched as Geraldine carefully spooned the tea into a silver pot and poured hot water over the leaves. On a small table, exquisite bone china dishes, and a milk jug and sugar bowl were laid out, all beautifully hand-painted in a blue and silver pattern that seemed French in design.

"As well as being related by marriage, my lady, I've always considered us friends too."

"As have I."

"Indeed. And as friends I hope I can speak plainly to you." She poured out two dishes of tea and offered one to Katherine.

"Of course. If there is something troubling you then please don't be afraid to say."

Geraldine sipped her tea and then took in a shuddering breath. "I must ask you if you've ever met Monsieur Roderique Rondelet?"

"Your husband I assume?" Geraldine nodded. "I don't think so."

"Are you absolutely sure?" She leaned forward. "You have never met him?"

Katherine couldn't help laughing at her serious expression. "How could I have? I've never left England."

"That is of no account. As a wine merchant, my husband frequently travelled around the country and came to England often. Many of his best customers were English including the king, the Prince of Wales and William Pitt, the prime minister."

Katherine was impressed, but shook her head. "No, I can truthfully say that the name of Monsieur Roderique Rondclct doesn't come to mind. And I'm sure I would have remembered him had I met him."

"Yes, you would have. He was a handsome man and he could charm the birds off the trees."

Katherine studied her for a moment before saying, "May I ask why you want to know?"

Geraldine shrugged. "It's of no importance now. If you say that you never met my husband then I am content."

Katherine placed her dish down on the table and laughed. "Geraldine, if anything is worrying you and it concerns me, then I would rather know. I value your friendship and I don't wish any animosity between us."

For the first time in weeks, Geraldine laughed with her. "If I did tell you then you would think it a lot of nonsense." Seeing Katherine's blue eyes sparkle in amusement she added, "It would be breaking a confidence if I told you." She gave an exasperated sigh. "But there again, you are a beautiful woman and must have had your own fair share of admirers, so I'm sure you would understand."

"I'm certain I would."

Geraldine smiled and nodded. "When Roderique and I were betrothed, I ordered a dozen red, silk handkerchiefs for him. And I spent many weeks embroidering the initial 'R' in gold thread...Goodness, what is it?" Katherine had become deathly pale and her hands started to shake. "My lady, are you suddenly feeling unwell?" Katherine tried to rise from her seat, but her legs gave way under her and she sank back down. "Let me call the physician," said Geraldine in alarm.

Katherine brushed it off. "No, I'm quite well. I suddenly felt dizzy."

"Then sit quietly until it passes." Geraldine came to sit next to her and held her hand.

"You did what?" Conrad couldn't hold back his anger.

"I asked her about the handkerchief, that is all."

"That is all? How could you Geraldine? Not only did you distress her, but also she'll know from where you received your information."

Geraldine stood and walked about the parlour, her body rigid with tension.

"It was foolish of me, I know that now. But it had been a torment to me for weeks and I had to know."

"So, what did you accomplish? Except to upset her."

"Only that she never knew my husband, but that she does have a secret of her own."

"In other words you accomplished nothing."

She sank down beside him on the chaise longue and sighed. "I loved my husband and he loved me, but we were not faithful to each other. He had his dalliances and I had mine. We accepted it."

"And you thought that Lady Fox was one of his *dalliances*?"

"Yes, I did."

He gave a snort of contempt. "Do you really think your husband would be interested in a girl of fifteen?"

"Fifteen?"

"That was the age that my wife thinks she came in possession of the handkerchief."

Geraldine made a quick calculation. "Lady Fox has just celebrated her twenty-second birthday. Seven years ago she would have been fifteen. What year would that be? '92? My husband came to England in the October of that year. I remember it clearly since he was arrested just before Christmas and was executed only six weeks after King Louis."

"Why did he come to England?"

"The king was entertaining various foreign royalties and he wanted the best wines for his guests. My husband was the obvious choice."

Conrad remained silent. So, Roderique and Prince Rasheid were in England at the same time. Katherine's secret was becoming perplexing and his fears became more acute. Since if she could fall ill at the very mention of something as ordinary as a handkerchief, then her secret must be terrible indeed.

Philippa entered the room with a silver-edged card in her hand.

"See what's just been delivered, Kate. From Lord Newburgh."

She took it from her cousin and saw that Lord Newburgh was hosting a special race meeting to celebrate the birth of his firstborn son. There was to be a buffet and all guests were invited to bring along their favourite mounts and race them against each other.

"Yes, we received one also. I don't think Lord and Lady Newburgh remembered that my aunt died in June."

Philippa sat down next to her. "Well, they've been too taken up with their new baby. But you could still go, surely?"

"It sounds delightful, but society forbids it."

Philippa tapped her finger against her chin in thought. "What if you stayed in the carriage? You could just watch. Oh Kate, do say yes. It'll be such fun."

Sir Herbert thought it quite acceptable to attend if Katherine sat in the carriage and took no actual part in the racing. And when he suggested that he enter Midnight in a race, Katherine was delighted and asked that Richard should be the rider. He agreed that that would be a splendid idea.

And when the day arrived, the weather could not have been kinder, the sun glorious in a sparkling blue sky.

"Not good weather for racing, though," said Sir Herbert, as he climbed aboard the carriage and mopped his face with a large handkerchief.

Katherine had decided to wear a white lace dress with a broad black ribbon under her bosom. Her bonnet was white and trimmed with the same black ribbon. She carried her black and white parasol and sitting serenely in the carriage, she was content to watch the proceedings from a distance.

The racecourse was filled with the guests all in their best gowns and suits and all intent in having a good time. Laughter floated in the air and the constant neighing of horses and stamping hooves echoed above the merriment.

Richard appeared guiding Midnight, with Geraldine at his side.

"Do you think I can win?" he said, as they reached the carriage.

Katherine leaned over to stroke the horse's nose. "I'm sure of it."

"Would be better if you rode him. Then we would be sure of a win."

Sir Herbert lumbered down from the carriage. "My wife is a good rider, but I'm glad that women are forbidden to ride in races." He blew out a breath. "Lord, it's hot today."

Conrad and Philippa arrived. Conrad was entering Shah, his favourite chestnut stallion.

"Wonderful horse, sir," said Sir Herbert.

Conrad nodded. "Yes, he's a horse I've always been proud of."

"Will you be able to see the race, Kate?" asked Philippa, looking around.

Katherine nodded. "Oh, yes. This is a very good position."

Glasses of champagne were being handed out and then there was a call for the first race to begin. Lord Newburgh had organised the race meeting with flair, deciding that there would be six races in all, three before the buffet and three after. Katherine looked about her and saw that a huge marquee had been erected where guests would eat their meal, but all the time, maids and footmen hurried hither and thither with trays of champagne.

And then she noticed the fair. "Where did that come from?"

Conrad smiled. "Lord Newburgh has allowed them to set up their tents so that the common folk of Cheltenham can enjoy themselves too."

The scene before her was one of total mayhem and confusion. People moved back and forth shouting and laughing. The sellers had set up brightly coloured tents and stalls and a multitude of flags fluttered in the hot breeze. Their calls to buy their wares were vociferous and carried easily across to the wealthy residents of the town. The second call came for the riders to take their places at the start line and in eager anticipation Katherine was left alone while everyone went to the fence to see what was happening. There were twelve horses in the first race and there was a lot of to and fro before the race began accompanied by a loud cheer. She watched keenly and although the horses disappeared from sight, she eventually discovered the winner was Lord Newburgh's horse, Comet.

Katherine turned her head to look at the fair.

"Buy some lucky heather, my lady?"

She hadn't heard the gypsy woman come up to the carriage, the same gypsy who had known so much about her on her visit to the Court. But this time she was dressed in a brightly patterned skirt and white blouse, her head wrapped in a scarf and gold rings dangling from her ears and wrists.

Katherine went into her reticule. "Yes, yes indeed. I will need all the luck I can get."

She offered the woman some money and took the small sprig of heather, tied with a blue ribbon.

"My lady is in mourning?"

"My aunt died."

"I too, have lost someone I love recently and I understand your pain."

"Thank you. You're very kind."

Suddenly, the gypsy's expression contorted into one of desperation and she grabbed Katherine's hand in a vice-like grip. "Beware of a devil pretending to be an angel. Your health and happiness and yes, your very life is in peril."

Katherine pulled away in fright. "You said that before, when we met on Lord Croston's estate. What do you mean? Of what danger do you speak?"

The gypsy shook her head, her dark eyes suddenly wary.

Katherine breathed a sigh of relief when she saw her husband making his way towards her. When she turned her head to look for the gypsy woman, she had gone, lost amongst the crowds of the fair.

"What are you doing here? I thought you would want to watch the race and see how Midnight fared."

He gave a wry smile. "I wondered what you were up to. Have you been lonely, my love? I've been neglecting you disgracefully."

She paused for a moment. "Lord Croston has been to speak with me and Philippa and Geraldine keep coming by. I can't expect people to dance attendance on me."

He shook his head. "Drat this mourning period. Why the deuce must we closet ourselves away from society simply because of a death? Life must be lived to the full, don't you agree, my love?"

Katherine looked across to where Philippa and Geraldine were excitedly waiting for the second race to begin. "Yes, but society expects otherwise."

Sir Herbert grunted. "The pox on society. Life is for pleasure and pleasure makes life worth living."

Katherine felt puzzled. "What are you talking about, sir?"

"I've someone I want you to meet."

"Who?"

"An old friend of mine." Katherine looked about her expecting to see his friend. "She lives just a few streets away. Come on, she's waiting to be introduced to my young and beautiful new wife."

He gave an order to Harry. As the carriage started to turn and ease its way through the throng, Katherine became alarmed.

"You want to go now? May we not write to her first and invite her to tea?"

"No, she's a busy lady and has precious little time for socialising."

Katherine tried to ease herself away from him, apprehension making her mouth dry. "We had better inform the others that we're leaving. They'll be worried if we just disappear."

Her husband shook his head. "They'll know you're with me and there'll be no cause for concern."

She saw Harry turn his head and noticed his grim expression.

"Where are we going?" asked Katherine, as Harry manoeuvred the carriage into the road and set off at a steady trot.

"I've told you. To meet an old friend of mine."

She decided to stay quiet but her misgivings were growing by the minute. Also, she felt uneasy that Sir Herbert had whisked her away without warning the others. What would they think when they found her missing?

They left the noise of the racecourse and went past the fair. Soon they were travelling along silent, forbidding streets, since it seemed everyone had joined in with the day's entertainment. Suddenly, Katherine realised they were driving through an area of Cheltenham that was not deemed respectable and her breath quickened with alarm. Harry reined in the horses and they stopped outside a three-storey dwelling that must have been an impressive house in its time. Even now, it still kept its aura of grandeur despite needing a lick of paint. But the columns either side of the door were imposing and the large sash windows were covered with brocade curtains.

Sir Herbert climbed down from the carriage and helped Katherine to alight. She stood in the road feeling lost and frightened.

"Your friend lives here?" she murmured.

Her husband didn't answer but snapped an order to the groom. "Go back to the racecourse, Harry. We'll find our own way home."

Harry glanced at Katherine, biting his lip. "Shall I stay, sir? You might need…"

Sir Herbert stepped across to him and spent a few seconds in muffled conversation before coming back to his wife and gripping her arm.

Without turning his head he sent his final order to the groom. "I said go, you're not needed."

Katherine watched her husband in dismay, her heart turning cold. His usually pleasant face had changed, not smiling, only determination shone from his blue-grey eyes. I don't want to be here, thought Katherine, but for some strange reason she dare not voice her thoughts.

He knocked on the door and it was answered by a heavily painted, young girl. She must have been barely twelve, perhaps younger, but her clothes and makeup made her look much older.

She gave a smile that showed a mouth full of decaying teeth. "Come to visit Madam, have you?" Sir Herbert nodded and she opened the door wider.

Katherine stepped over the threshold and looked about her. They were in a hallway that could have been in any house in the wealthy part of Cheltenham. Richly decorated and furnished in Hepplewhite, it had a grand staircase leading to the upper rooms. And upstairs she could hear doors banging and the sound of girlish laughter. Intermingled were the lower tones of men's laughter.

Katherine finally found the courage to speak. "I want to leave, sir."

"For once in your life, do as you're bid," he snapped, pushing her in front of him.

They walked across the hallway to a door on the left and after the young maid knocked they were shown into what was obviously the parlour of the lady of the house. It was a large room and its decoration and furnishings reflected the style and taste of the woman who rose from her seat to greet them. She must have been a great beauty once, but now her shape was rotund, her face absurd, with an angry streak of rouge across each cheek and her mouth no more than a bright red slash. Matted black hair poked out from under her turban and her throat and fingers were covered with jewellery.

"Oh, Sir Herbert. You've arrived at last. And your good lady too. Please sit down and I'll order some tea. It's a special and very expensive blend from China and I keep it in reserve for only my honoured guests." She caressed Katherine's cheek. "My goodness, you were not exaggerating, Lady Fox is absolutely breathtaking."

Katherine glanced at her husband in confusion. He had a look of pleasure as though he enjoyed being in this house, being in company with this woman.

"Yes, Mrs Percy. We will enjoy taking tea with you. Wouldn't we, my love?" He turned to Katherine and then chuckled at her horrified expression.

He pressed her down on a couch of faded velvet and took a seat next to her. She perched herself on the edge of the cushion, feeling uncomfortable, desperation making her mouth dry. Escape from this dreadful place seemed impossible; it was obvious that both her husband and this Mrs Percy would prevent it. Katherine tried to swallow but instead gave a nervous cough. There was something about this house that filled her with dread. The smell, the sounds, all had a familiar ring to them. Please, please, let me go home, she prayed. And that frightened her too, for deep in her memory she knew she had said the same words before, long, long ago, when she was just a girl of fifteen.

CHAPTER EIGHT

Katherine sipped the tea. She didn't like the sweet taste and the chipped china dish was none too clean. She glanced around the room and noticed the heavy brocade curtains at the window and the furniture with just the few porcelain ornaments. She left the conversation to her husband and Mrs Percy, only nodding when an occasional remark was directed towards her. She began to think that everything would be all right. They would have their tea and then they would leave. After that they would go back to the racecourse and their friends. Yes, everything would be all right.

Katherine couldn't remember when she started feeling sleepy. First came calmness, then lethargy, before she realised she couldn't keep her eyes open. She blinked hard, but the room seemed to be swimming in front of her, the murmured conversation between Sir Herbert and Mrs Percy drifted in and out of her consciousness. Eventually her head became so heavy she found it difficult to raise it and all she could do was stare down at the dish resting on her lap.

A hand appeared from nowhere and took the crockery from her and she heard a gentle laugh as her bonnet was untied and removed from her head. Someone was lifting her to her feet and guiding her through the door and into another room. And then she was lying on a bed and someone was unfastening the bodice on her gown.

Conrad looked about him.

"Where did she go?" he said.

"We don't know. We were busy watching the race and when we returned the carriage had gone," said Philippa.

Richard nodded. "She must have gone with my stepfather, since he's missing too."

Geraldine came to his side. "Yes, that's what it is. He's probably taken her for a drive to stop her getting bored."

"He could have said something first," said Conrad. He placed a tender arm round his wife, sensing her anxiety. "There's nothing to do except wait until they come back."

Richard looked across the field. "The food will be served soon, so perhaps by then they'll have returned. Shame though. I can't believe my stepfather missed seeing Midnight run."

Conrad grinned. "And win, damn you."

Richard grinned with him. "You came second and that's not bad for an old nag like Shah."

"How dare you," laughed Conrad.

Geraldine took Philippa's arm. "Shall we go and speak with Lady Newburgh?"

Philippa agreed it was a good idea and taking their leave of the gentlemen, they walked across the grass to where Lady Newburgh sat in a large high-backed armchair like a queen on her throne and surrounded by her court.

Conrad groaned with relief. "Well, there's the carriage at least. Perhaps Harry knows where they've gone." The groom reined in the horses and then sprang down from the seat. "Have you seen Sir Herbert and Lady Fox?"

"May I have a private word with you, sir?"

He took Conrad to one side and although they were talking in hushed tones, Richard overheard the words 'Mrs Percy'.

"I know that woman," he said angrily, taking a step towards them. "Dear Lord, if Katherine is in that house of ill repute then we must get her out immediately."

Conrad stepped towards him. "The House of Venus?"

Richard nodded.

All three men sprang into the carriage and Harry cracked the whip, urging the horses forward.

Philippa saw them leave. "Now where are they going?" she said.

"Probably to the cider tent," said Geraldine, smiling.

They made their way through deserted streets.

Lord Croston looked round at Harry. "Go as fast as possible." The groom nodded. Conrad gave a wry smile. "Harry has put his situation in jeopardy by telling us where she is. Sir Herbert told him to say nothing, only that he was taking his wife to visit an old friend."

"An old friend," scoffed Richard. "Mrs Percy used to be his parlour maid some twenty years ago. From what I was told she had more beauty than brains and thought that her looks would win her a good match. She ended up as a plaything for rich men, then she worked the streets before managing the House of Venus."

Conrad shook his head in dismay. They didn't speak for the rest of the journey and five minutes later they arrived in front of the house where Conrad jumped down and banged on the door.

Richard stood next to him and grimaced. "We should have come armed."

"Let's hope it doesn't come to that," said Conrad through clenched teeth.

The same young girl who welcomed all visitors opened the door. Only this time her crooked smile vanished as Conrad pushed her to one side and stepped over the threshold.

"Where is Sir Herbert and Lady Fox?" The girl refused to answer and shook her head, a sly expression creasing her face. He reached into his pocket and gave her sixpence. "Tell me where they are and you'll get another sixpence when we leave."

She held the silver coin in her fingers before putting it between her teeth and biting down on it. Then grinning she closed her hand round her treasure.

"They're in Madam's private boudoir," she said, pointing to a door on the far side of the hallway.

Conrad ran across the tiled floor with Richard close behind him. At the door, he knocked loudly. At first there was no answer. And then the key grated in the lock and the door opened a little. Mrs Percy peeped through the crack.

"What do you want?" she said.

"We've come for Lady Fox," said Conrad. He was surprised how polite he sounded although his heart was pounding in his head.

"Her husband is here with her," she said, glancing over her shoulder. "He'll see his lady safely home."

She went to slam the door, but Conrad stuck out his boot preventing her. He pushed against the wood and stepped into the room.

Katherine was lying on the bed, her hair unpinned and cascading over the pillow in a golden shower of curls. She was wearing only her underskirt, the straps hanging loosely over her shoulders and the skirt pulled up above her knees. Lying next to her was a young woman in a state of undress, who was kissing and caressing her face and neck, her hand resting on

Katherine's inner thigh. It was obvious that Katherine was totally unaware of this, since her eyelashes flickered occasionally, revealing pupils that were unfocused.

Conrad gave a cry of anger and rushing forward, lifted her from the bed and carried her out of the room. From the corner of his eye he saw Sir Herbert rising from a chair positioned to one side, his breeches undone and another young girl scrambling to her feet from a kneeling position. Sir Herbert looked at the intruders in horror.

Richard turned on his stepfather. "I hope my mother didn't know this about you." He followed on Conrad's heels and on the way out gave the girl another sixpence. The girl curtsied with pleasure. "Poor child," he murmured.

Harry set off as soon as they were aboard and his lady had been covered with a blanket.

"Where should we take her?" asked Richard. "We can't take her home to await Sir Herbert's anger."

Conrad thought for a moment. "I would like to take her to my home. She would be safe there." He grimaced. "But my wife would want to know what had happened. Could you go back to the racecourse and find Geraldine? Tell her we need her help and if she would allow Lady Fox to spend some time at her home."

"And your wife?"

"Try and allay her fears, if you can. As soon as Katherine is safe with Geraldine, I'll return and hopefully the day can continue as normally as possible. I can't let my wife become upset in her present condition."

Richard leaned forward to study Katherine, her cheek resting on Conrad's shoulder, her eyes closed in peaceful sleep.

"She's been drugged. Opium no doubt."

"Then hopefully she'll not remember anything."

"What about my stepfather?"

Conrad clenched his fist. "I swear he'll be dealt with."

Richard turned his head to watch the houses passing. "Let me speak with him. He can make life very awkward for you if you cross him." When he turned back, Conrad noticed that his deep brown eyes had turned almost black. But he couldn't decide if that was through anger or anxiety. "I'll have more sway over him being a relative. I can make the kind of threats he'll understand and he'll be forced to treat Lady Fox with more respect in future."

Conrad shook his head. "I don't understand. For years I heard rumours about Sir Herbert and I was very alarmed when I discovered he was to marry Katherine, but then my opinion changed after his marriage. I found him such a pleasant man. I was beginning to believe that his reputation was ill-deserved."

Richard didn't answer and turned his face away, his expression grim.

Katherine opened her eyes slowly, blinking at the light shining through the curtains. But then she realised she was in a strange room. Easing her legs over the edge of the mattress she stepped onto the rug surprised that she was wearing her underskirt. There was a gentle knock on the door and Betsy came in carrying a large pitcher of hot water.

"How are you this evening, my lady?"

"Evening! Where am I?"

Betsy gave a giggle. "You're in the home of Mrs Rondelet."

Katherine felt more confused. "Why am I here?"

"I'm sure the mistress herself, will explain everything. She says that tea will be served in thirty minutes so that gives me time to get you ready."

She allowed Betsy to fuss over her, not having the strength or willpower to resist. The maid removed her underskirt and allowed her to bathe before putting on fresh underwear. And then she lifted the day dress over her head and fastened the buttons and ribbons. Seating her at the dressing table, she carefully brushed her lady's hair, sweeping it up onto her head and pinning it into place.

Katherine peered at herself in the mirror. Who was this woman staring back at her? Was that face really hers? It looked so white and sickly, hardly recognisable. She tried to remember what had happened. She recalled the races. And then Sir Herbert had suddenly taken her to visit that strange woman. What was her name? Oh, yes, Mrs Percy. In horror, she remembered the house and then the overwhelming desire to put her head on a pillow and sleep.

Betsy's work complete, Katherine made her way downstairs where Geraldine waited for her in the parlour.

"Just in time," she said brightly, patting the seat next to her on the couch. "I've just prepared a fresh pot of tea and if you are hungry, you can order what you like to eat. How about some toast?"

Katherine sat down. "Just tea for now. I don't know why but I feel very queasy."

"Then sweet, weak tea for you, I think," Geraldine said, frowning. "But please try and take just a little food, you've not eaten since breakfast and it will give you strength."

Katherine shook her head. "Thank you, but I'll try some later." She quickly glanced around. "What am I doing in your home? What happened? Is it still the same day as the races?"

Geraldine gave a strained laugh. She had been shocked to see how ill Katherine looked when she came in, so heavy-eyed as though she had not slept for weeks, her complexion pale.

"Yes, it's the same day."

There was a moment of silence before Katherine said, "I remember Sir Herbert took me to visit a friend of his. But why am I here?"

"Do you feel strong enough to talk?" Katherine nodded. Geraldine turned her head away for moment. "You took ill and my uncle sent for the carriage. I helped him bring you home."

Katherine couldn't help thinking that her explanation sounded rather stilted. "But why am I in your house?" she repeated.

"I insisted that you stay with me and immediately sent for Betsy."

Katherine shook her head in disbelief. "What about the others? Were they worried when I suddenly went missing?"

Geraldine grimaced. "They were very worried, of course. Especially your cousin."

"Oh, poor Philippa. I didn't want to leave, but Sir Herbert insisted." A footman announced the arrival of Lord Croston before Geraldine could answer.

He kissed Katherine's hand, studying her pallid complexion. As he had carried her upstairs and placed her on the bed, he had wondered how much opium she had been given and had wanted to call a physician. But Geraldine had convinced him that all she needed was sleep and he had been forced to accept her advice.

"I think a stroll in the fresh air will bring the roses back to your cheeks," he smiled, taking a seat in the armchair.

"Then I shall walk along the High Street with Betsy, if you would accompany us, sir."

Conrad glanced uneasily at Geraldine.

"Why don't you stay here for a few days?" she said, smiling.

"My husband will be missing me. Where is he?"

Geraldine poured out a dish of tea for Conrad. "He'll be here soon. So, you might as well have your tea until he arrives."

Katherine sipped her tea and her gaze drifted from Conrad to Geraldine and then back to Conrad.

"That house I went to. Mrs Percy's? I know what kind of house it is."

"You can't possibly know," said Geraldine, her smile fading.

Katherine looked towards the window. "It's a bordello isn't it? And the smell and sounds…they reminded me…reminded me…as if I had been there before."

Conrad shook his head. "No, that's impossible. I assure you that you will never have been in that house before."

"How can you be so sure?" Katherine blinked away frustrating tears before gathering her courage and saying more adamantly, "I've been in a place like that before. I know I have."

Geraldine felt fear gush up from her stomach as she wondered what her uncle had been up to and she moved closer to Katherine, taking her hand. Conrad bent forward in his seat, his elbows resting on his knees.

"What are you saying?" Geraldine whispered.

166

Katherine opened her eyes and large tears finally trickled down her cheeks. "You asked about the red, silk handkerchief and I never gave you a proper answer."

"That doesn't matter now. Especially since you're not well."

"Oh, yes it does. That house was so familiar. I need to tell you. I've prayed to God for help to bring me through this, but sometimes he doesn't hear me." Her face twisted in pain.

Geraldine and Conrad exchanged anxious glances. Geraldine licked her lips and then pulling out a lace handkerchief, offered it to Katherine. "Then tell us."

"It's about the red, silk handkerchief," she said, wiping her cheeks. She took in a steadying breath. "When I was fifteen..." she started and then swallowed before continuing, "I was visiting my aunt in Bristol and was taken from my bed in the middle of the night."

"What do you mean 'taken'?" said Conrad, his pulse throbbing painfully in his throat.

"I was asleep and...two men came into my room and took me away. I don't know how they broke in, but it happened."

"Where did they take you?"

"I don't know that. They carried me out of the cottage and put me in a coach."

"Didn't your aunt hear anything?" said Geraldine.

"She was already going deaf by then. No, the poor dear wouldn't have heard a sound. One man put his hand over my mouth until we were in the coach and then a cloth bag was placed over my head. We drove for quite a while." Katherine thought for a moment. "When we reached our destination, I was given something to drink that made me sleepy."

Conrad found it difficult to speak. "What else do you remember?"

"Only that I had it in my mind that I must have been kidnapped for ransom. I assumed that Uncle George would receive a demand for money. But all the time, when I could, I kept begging them to let me go, that I wanted to go home. And I'm sure that I heard the same sounds in the house in which I was imprisoned, as I did at Mrs Percy's." Conrad muttered something under his breath that neither Katherine nor Geraldine could hear. "They let me go. I was given some old clothes to wear."

"Because you were in your nightgown?" asked Geraldine, horrified.

Katherine nodded. "They took me to the crossroads six miles from Lenchwick and from there I walked back to the Hall."

"Your uncle had paid the ransom?" asked Conrad, his voice husky.

Katherine shook her head. "No ransom was asked for. I had been gone a day and a night."

"Did they find the kidnappers?" said Geraldine.

"No, I'm afraid the constables were not very efficient. A ransom wasn't paid and I was safely home. As far as they were concerned, nothing more could be done."

"The parish constables can be very lackadaisical at times," cursed Conrad.

The three fell silent until Geraldine remembered. "But what has this to do with the handkerchief?"

Katherine winced. "They tied it over my eyes. When they released me, they also left the handkerchief behind." She looked at Conrad. "It was the one found at the Court and you gave back to me before my wedding."

"Do you still have it?" he asked.

Katherine stared at him for a full ten seconds. "No, my lord. I threw it on the fire the night before I married."

The maid came in to say that Sir Herbert had arrived to take his wife home. Before they left, Geraldine took him to one side and urged her uncle to give Katherine an explanation for his actions that day.

"She deserves more respect, Uncle."

Sir Herbert looked like a schoolboy who had been caught in a misdemeanour. "I know and I'll explain. I only hope my dear wife understands," he said.

After they had left, Geraldine ran upstairs to her bedchamber and then came back down to the parlour to say farewell to Conrad.

"I must be leaving," he said, coming away from the window where he had been watching Katherine and Sir Herbert climb into their carriage.

"I need to ask you something," she said and then she opened her hand. "Was the handkerchief like this one?"

He took it from her and examined it closely. "I think it was. At least it was very similar."

She caught her breath. "This is one of the twelve I ordered for my husband when we became betrothed. I embroidered the initial."

He stared at her aghast. "Surely your husband wasn't involved in this sordid affair?"

She turned from him in an attempt to conceal her anxiety. "My husband was in England when Lady Fox went missing. I can't deny the fact that the handkerchief might have been his. There is something else. My husband was in debt. The Revolution had denied his customers the opportunity of paying their bills by sending them to the guillotine. In return, he was finding it difficult to pay his suppliers. He needed money." Her dark eyes became wide with horror. "Oh, dear God, surely he wouldn't contemplate kidnapping a young girl for ransom?"

Katherine had never seen her husband so distressed. When they arrived home, he took her into the study and on his knees asked for her forgiveness. And then he threw his arms round her waist, burying his face in her gown. It was a moment of weakness, he told her. It had been such a hot day and the heat had addled his senses. It would never, never happen again. Her heart softened and she found she could do nothing else but forgive him. He was her husband and forgiveness was all part of being married. But she would always remember his change in character at the home of Mrs Percy and from that moment on, she wondered if she would ever trust him again.

It was a few days later that Katherine realised that Harry was missing. When she asked Betsy about him she was surprised by her answer.

"He's been dismissed, ma'am," said the maid.

"But why? What did he do?"

"He won't tell me although I keep asking."

"I'll have a word with Sir Herbert. It must be a misunderstanding that needs clearing up."

Betsy shook her head. "He's told me he's all right and I mustn't worry. He's got a position as groom with Mrs Rondelet."

"Has he?"

"Yes, my lady. It seems she's been in need of a groom since the last one left. A footman has been doing an excellent job, but she said she'd much prefer a man who knows about horses."

"Well, she's got a good man in Harry," murmured Katherine.

She asked her husband why he had dismissed Harry and was told that he had become dissatisfied with his work. She decided not to pursue the matter further.

In the hallway, the earl and countess's bags and trunks were being loaded into the coach, but Philippa couldn't leave without saying goodbye to her cousin. Katherine had promised to be there but had not arrived yet.

"She'll be visiting the Court at the end of next month. You'll see her again very soon," said Conrad. Philippa wouldn't be pacified and then he gave a cry of relief. "Oh, there she is, just getting out of the carriage." Conrad smiled and dropped a kiss on her forehead. "I told you not to worry yourself."

Katherine was shown into the parlour where Philippa hugged her cousin, chastising her for being late.

"I'm so sorry, dearest. I was waiting for the physician and he was detained because of a child with mumps."

Philippa narrowed her eyes at her. "Why was the physician calling on you? Are you sick?"

Katherine threw back her head and laughed. "Only something that will be cured in six months' time."

Philippa glanced down at Katherine's stomach. "You're with child?" she asked softly.

Katherine nodded. "I had suspected it for the last month, but it's finally been confirmed."

Conrad came forward and kissed her cheek. "Many congratulation, my dear cousin-in-law."

Philippa took both her hands. "Oh, Kate. Do you remember how we spoke of visiting each other as married ladies? Soon we'll be able to do the same as mothers. How wonderful."

Conrad smiled with them. "Unfortunately, ladies, we must be on our way."

Katherine walked outside with them and after another brief farewell, the coach pulled away from the house in which they had lived for the last three months. Conrad's spirits sank to their lowest level, a deep despair that had never left him since Katherine had told him about her kidnapping.

Suddenly, he wished that his wife had had the correct theory, that Katherine had eloped and then been brought back. Somehow it seemed a more manageable pill to swallow. But to be kidnapped and held prisoner in darkness for a day and a night was monstrous. And then there were the suspicions that Geraldine's husband might be implicated. Poor Geraldine, she had not known what to make of it all. He sighed and thought of Katherine, now with child. Perhaps motherhood would ease her pain, calm her memories? But he had very little hope on that account. Although Haighton had told him that he had had strong words with his stepfather and Sir Herbert was a reformed man after his misdemeanour, Conrad knew he would never trust him again.

Katherine returned to her home relieved that the sickness had left her, the physician confirming that she was in good health. Added to this was the fact that Sir Herbert had been kindness itself since the events at Mrs Percy's and her every wish had been granted.

Their final evening in Cheltenham was spent in the lively company of Lord Haighton and Geraldine who had been invited to supper, even though the house was filled with the furore of maids and footmen packing for their departure.

"You look very well, Katherine," said Geraldine, kissing her on the cheek.

"Yes, we are both quite well, thank you," said Sir Herbert, rising unsteadily to his feet, to greet their guests. "But I'll be happy to get back to Westcroft."

"I can't understand why you like to spend the winter in the country," said Geraldine. "You always get snowed in and company is very limited."

"And that's the way I like it," grinned Sir Herbert. He took Katherine's hand. "Shall we tell them the good news, my love?"

Katherine nodded. "I'm with child."

Geraldine gave a cry of delight. "Oh, what wonderful news."

"I do hope you'll come and visit us once we are back at Westcroft?"

"Of course we will."

"I'll be travelling to Croston Court next month to be with Philippa. I'll write to you and tell you how everything goes with her baby."

"Yes, do. Oh, Conrad will be so delighted if he has a son," said Geraldine.

"You'll only travel if you're well enough," said Sir Herbert, watching his wife. The footman had poured her a sherry, but Sir Herbert took it from her. "No, Katherine. No spirits for you, my dear and certainly no more riding once we get back to Westcroft."

"But Herbert…"

He shook his head. "I too, will be delighted to have a son and I want nothing to jeopardise your pregnancy."

Katherine knew that her husband was right and that her health was important now she was carrying a child. But during the following week, the weather became very warm and there was no cool breeze to be had either in the garden or in the meadow. Not that she walked in the meadow often since the folly still filled her with dread.

However, she missed her rides on Valentine and when the horses were allowed in the pasture to stretch their legs, she would often go with an apple or two. There never seemed to be enough for her to do since Mrs Chambers was more than capable and the problems she had to deal with, such as the under parlour maid leaving without giving notice and the scullery maid coming down with chickenpox, didn't exactly challenge her.

And then came the morning when Katherine opened her eyes and lifted gently out of sleep. Rolling over onto her back, she stretched, yawned and looked about her. It was early and behind the curtains she could see a bright, inviting glow. Stepping barefoot across the carpet, she went to the window and peeped out. The heat was already oppressive and she opened the casement to allow some cooler air to waft in her face.

The cloudless sky was a clear azure blue cradling the swifts and larks that soared and glided as though they were full of the joys of life. The sun was already heating the landscape, causing the colours to shimmer. But in the distance, the dark storm clouds were starting to gather.

She could hear the dogs barking and the sound of the grooms tending the horses in the stable and suddenly, she decided she would have an early morning ride and visit old Mrs Peacock, the elderly mother of the gamekeeper. Yes, her husband had forbidden her to ride, but Mrs Peacock lived in a small cottage on the edge of the estate, a distance of only three miles and had not been too well of late. It would mean a pleasant trot along the country lanes and across the meadow and would make a perfect ride for an hour or two as well as discovering that the old lady was comfortable. Surely, Sir Herbert couldn't object to her doing that? Of course, she should take the carriage, but Valentine would be quicker and easier.

It was far too early to summon Betsy and besides, she craved her freedom and independence. She was delighted when she discovered the pitcher of water left over from her previous evening's bath and started her toilet. The water was refreshingly cold and felt luxurious on her warm skin. She dressed in a frilled, linen shirt, black skirt and jacket, brushed her hair and tied it up with a black ribbon. And then she pulled on her riding boots.

She crept downstairs, just as the clock started striking seven. She moved furtively through the hallway, avoiding the drawing room from where the sound of activity echoed, as two maids dusted and polished. Instead, she hurried into the dining room, snatched an apple from the fruit bowl and fled outside like a thief.

Katherine lifted her face to the September sun for a couple of seconds, before heading for the stables. She wondered whether she would have the opportunity to saddle Valentine herself and be away before anyone realised. But standing right in front of the stable block was Thomas, busily moving the night's manure with a very large pitchfork.

Katherine smiled as she approached the hardworking groom. "Good morning, Thomas."

He spun round in surprise. "You're up early this morning, my lady."

"It's a beautiful morning. How's your arm?"

Thomas grinned and flexed his hand. "Mending nicely, thank you, my lady. Feels a bit weak but physician says I must use it and strengthen the muscles." He looked towards the horizon. "Are you considering going out riding, my lady? Storm's coming. Not good to get caught in it."

"I want to visit Mrs Peacock. I'll be gone only a few hours," said Katherine.

The groom nodded and rubbing the dirt from his hands, disappeared into the stable, where he appeared moments later leading Valentine. She was quickly saddled and Katherine trotted away from the house and down the drive.

Once out of sight, she let the horse canter a little through the park, before bringing Valentine to a trot. Katherine relaxed in the saddle and let the reins fall loosely between her fingers. Valentine meandered along the road at will while her mistress sat deep in thought as she travelled through the fields and woods to the boundary of the estate. The miles fell behind her and finally Mrs Peacock's small cottage came into sight.

But even after her visit was over, Katherine continued her ride towards the village and onwards, not caring which path was taken or road followed, as the weather became sultrier. While sitting under a tree munching an apple, her thoughts were very much on Conrad and especially her confession to him and Geraldine. She was glad she had shared her burden, somehow it had lifted a weight from her shoulders even though she hadn't told them the whole story. But there again, the total truth of her ordeal was only known by her grandmother.

When she had finished eating the apple, she took the core over to Valentine who was splashing in a stream. It was only when she heard the clap of thunder in the distance that her attention was alerted. In alarm, she realised that she was near Chipping Campden and had travelled more than fifteen miles.

She turned the horse's head for home. Keeping to a trot, she was constantly aware of the darkening clouds behind her and the continual drop in temperature.

Everything was still and waiting, the very air holding its breath for the deluge that was sure to arrive very soon.

When the storm finally caught up with her, she had travelled barely a mile, the thunder and lightning warring over her head. She knew that Valentine was jittery and slipped down from the saddle to lead her along the road, speaking words of comfort. Suddenly a crack of lightning made the mare rear up, pulling on the reins and jerking Katherine off her feet. She landed on her side, but not before hitting the surface of the road with an impact that winded her for a moment. She gave out a muted cry as a sharp pain shot through her back and stomach and alarm swept through her that she had caused damage to her child. Katherine waited for the pain to pass and was relieved that it seemed to abate very quickly.

Valentine pranced about and then a crash of thunder sent her hurtling amongst the trees by the side of the road to stumble over what appeared to be a hidden tree root. Seeing the mare's plight, Katherine's reaction was instinctive and springing to her feet, she approached the horse and pacified her. Calm was restored and then the fear that had gripped her for the wellbeing of her child also subsided. She breathed deeply, feeling her injuries and sighed with relief. She was young and healthy and her baby was snug and safe, tucked away in her womb, oblivious that its mother had suddenly had a mishap.

But then Katherine realised that Valentine was injured. The mare limped along the road, whinnying and holding her right foreleg in the air. A quick examination filled Katherine with dismay, since a stone had embedded itself against the side of her shoe. She tried pulling it out, cursing that she had no other tool but her fingers. And her fingers were just not strong enough to grip onto the stone.

She quickly looked around trying to assess her situation. Toddington was about a mile away and if she could reach it then she could find a blacksmith. She led Valentine forward, stroking and encouraging her with words of comfort, knowing their only hope was to press on the best they could and somehow reach the village. Valentine obediently followed her mistress's entreaties, holding her foreleg up away from the hard surface that caused her so much pain.

The rain came slowly at first but with each passing minute became a shower and then a torrent. She and Valentine were soon soaked to the skin and it was a very bedraggled Lady Fox who guided a limping Valentine through the village and into the blacksmith's.

Her return to Westcroft was greeted with relief although Katherine brushed off the incident as unimportant. With an indifferent shrug of her shoulders, she gave the reason for her delay as the bad weather. Betsy surveyed her with a mixture of gratitude that she was safe and disgust at her appearance. Thinking that her mistress would be discovered lying face down dead in a ditch, she couldn't stop scolding her for the worry she had caused. But when she instructed the servants to bring up hot water to fill the bath, Katherine sank into the water with pleasure, breathing in the scent of rose oil that wafted round her like a garden.

"You obviously stirred up the entire household with your shenanigans," said Sir Herbert at dinner. "Why didn't you take the carriage?"

Katherine unfolded her napkin and placed it across her knee. "I wanted to visit Mrs Peacock and I didn't think the storm was so close."

He waved a fork at her. "You went out riding when I expressly forbade it."

Katherine nodded guiltily. "I know I did wrong, Herbert. I promise never to do it again. I've learnt my lesson I assure you." She lowered her eyes submissively.

He grunted. "But, did you not think of your child? Our child."

"I have to keep reminding myself that I am with child."

Sir Herbert shook his head in exasperation. "I've seen a piebald mare in the stable and Valentine seems to be missing." She told him of the accident and winced when his expression became scornful. "You endangered your life and that of my son. I expected more sense from you."

"I'm sorry, Herbert. I was very thoughtless."

"From now on you will stay close to the house and you will not ride."

Katherine stared at her husband. Yes, she had been foolish but his harsh manner dismayed her.

"May I still visit Philippa?"

"I'll decide that at the time."

The following morning he gave his orders to the head groom. Lady Fox, must not, on any account, go out riding. And when Valentine was collected from Toddington, she was to be shot immediately.

Over the next four days, Katherine felt like a prisoner. She walked through the gardens with Betsy as her constant companion and if the weather proved inclement she would sit by the window and work on her tapestry. The day she was picking wild flowers in the meadow and heard the sound of a gunshot, she thought nothing of it, since the gamekeeper was always shooting rabbits. But then she went to the stables to see if Valentine had been collected and being surprised at the stall still being empty, she asked Thomas about her whereabouts. His hesitancy alarmed her and she had to confront her husband.

"No horse will endanger the life of my son," he said with bitter coldness.

Katherine was too horrified to argue with him.

It was the nagging pain that brought Katherine out of sleep in the early hours of the morning. She had had a restless night thinking of poor Valentine and had finally fallen asleep long after the clock had struck midnight. But now the pain was too severe to ignore.

Waking up in discomfort was terrible and at first she thought it was a dream. But then she lit the candle by the side of her bed and tried to sit up. The pain got worse. She tried to get off the bed and after a few attempts, she stood unsteadily. The blood gushed down her legs and the pain intensified. She sank to her knees, trying to call for help as she bent over, her hand clutching her stomach. And then Betsy came running in, wearing her nightgown and a shawl, her long, red hair tucked under a nightcap.

Katherine barely heard the terrifying scream, as her maid went for help.

"Mrs Chambers! Please come quickly. It's my lady."

It seemed as though countless hands were lifting her from the floor and putting her back on the bed.

Sir Herbert appeared. "Should we call the physician?" Mrs Chambers agreed and a groom was sent to fetch him. "What is it, woman? What's wrong with my wife?"

"We fear that Lady Fox might be miscarrying, sir."

"But she's already three months gone."

"The most dangerous time, I'm afraid."

Sir Herbert let out a curse. "She had no call to go out riding last week. I told her she was foolish."

Mrs Chambers didn't answer and concentrated on making her mistress comfortable.

Katherine was dressed in a fresh nightgown and an old sheet was put under her. Rags were placed between her thighs to catch the blood that seeped continuously. And just after the physician arrived, the pain intensified and clutching onto Betsy's hand, the baby came away from her with very little difficulty. She was relieved that the bleeding and pain started to lessen, but this was immediately followed by grief.

Betsy washed her gently, soothing her with comforting words. "It was hardly a baby, ma'am. Just a tiny thing, really. And you'll be able to have more."

Mrs Chambers nodded. "She's quite right. I lost two babes in the same way, but went on to have three healthy daughters."

Sir Herbert came to visit and stared down at her. "So, you've lost the child?" he said. "But I've been told you'll recover quickly and at least I know you're not barren. There's no reason why you shouldn't conceive again."

Katherine closed her eyes, sadness sweeping over her. She had not realised how much she wanted this child. It would have put right all the wrong done to her. Made her feel whole again.

The weeks passed slowly and Katherine was pleased that Mrs Rondelet and Lord Haighton called on her to offer their sympathies, for she seemed to get very little from Sir Herbert. His absences were getting more frequent and Katherine began to feel that her husband would never forgive her for losing their child. But at least she was improving in health day by day and was looking forward to travelling to Croston Court to be with Philippa for the birth of her baby.

Letters from the Court and Widcombe Hall arrived regularly. Philippa sounded happy to the point of ecstatic, full of health as she entered her ninth month. She informed her cousin that she was all prepared, the cradle ready, the layette put away in drawers and a nurse already arranged although not set for employment until the baby was born. Anne was still crocheting a shawl and Frobisher was ready to fetch the physician as soon as he was needed. Philippa was saddened by the loss of Katherine's baby. She had only just got used to the idea when the child was no more.

Letters from her grandmother were a joy, giving encouragement as well as wisdom. Lady Widcombe was suffering from too much Aunt Charlotte, Aunt Beatrice's sister, who had come to visit and was constantly bickering with the family and servants. *'I will be heartily glad when she goes home'*, her grandmama had written and Katherine smiled as she read.

It was the last week of October and only three days before Katherine's departure to Croston Court. Her husband had given his permission reluctantly, finding no reason why he shouldn't. In fact, he expressed the opinion that the visit would be beneficial for his wife and Katherine had breathed a sigh of relief.

And then the last day dawned. Autumn was now merging into winter and the trees were slowly losing their leaves, but the weather was mild and perfect for a journey. Twenty-four hours, thought Katherine, as she descended the stairs for breakfast. Only twenty-four hours and I'll be on my way.

She had recovered quickly in the last six weeks and Sir Herbert had started coming to her room again. At first, she had found his podgy fingers painful as he poked and prodded her. It seemed that making her pregnant and her losing the child had unleashed an inexplicable urgency in him and when he penetrated her, he would often stop and look down on her with a strange expression that caused her to blush.

Betsy made her way down the path to the garden. Her lady's best underskirt still hung on the line and she had to bring it in for ironing. There seemed so much to do before she and Lady Fox departed the following morning and she had left her lady's room littered with clothes and possessions, lying on the bed, over the chest of drawers and across chairs.

As she rounded the stables, two arms reached out and grabbed her, pulling her close and smothering her face with soft, warm kisses.

"Harry!" she shrieked, trying to catch her breath. "What are you doing here?"

He grinned mischievously. "Mrs Rondelet gave me a few hours free so I could say farewell."

She returned his kisses. "That was very kind of her."

"She knows we'll be parted a good two months." He blew out a breath. "And I shall miss you."
He pulled her into the stable and they went into the end stall that was temporarily empty.

"Eeh, you can't delay me for long, pet. I've still quite a bit of packing to do," giggled Betsy.

Harry glanced to the far end where Thomas was busy grooming Midnight.

"If I hadn't been dismissed then I would have been driving you to Croston Court."

"But you were, so nothing can be done about it." She pulled his head down and pressed his lips on hers. After the kiss had come to a lingering conclusion she studied her intended through narrowed eyes. "Are you ever going to tell me why the master let you go?"

He pulled her closer. "Perhaps one day. When we're old and grey and the young ones have flown the nest."

Betsy opened her mouth to speak but was halted by the appearance of Sir Herbert entering the stable by the far door.

Thomas stopped his grooming and came towards him. "Afternoon, sir. Is everything to your liking?"

Sir Herbert ran his plump fingers over Midnight's silky back. "It is, Thomas." He studied the horse for a few moments before his gaze was directed down the row of stalls where the horses were feeding. The couple hiding at the end shrank back against the wall amongst the shadows. "I want you to take one of the coaches into Cheltenham this evening and pick up my supper guests."

Thomas touched his forelock and smiled. "Of course, sir. And what be the address?"

"Mrs Percy's residence." He turned his ample back on the groom and left the stable.

Thomas stood motionless, his smile just a ghost of what it had been. So engrossed was he in his own thoughts that he didn't see Harry, holding Betsy's hand, come to his side.

He turned and noticed his old friend. "Harry. It's good to see you," he said, clapping him on the shoulder.

"So, he's still up to his old tricks," murmured Harry, nodding in the direction of Sir Herbert's retreating figure.

Thomas nodded. "You heard, did you?" He blew out a breath. "Mrs Chambers has the worst job preparing the folly."

"What old tricks?" asked Betsy. "And what's that about the folly?" They didn't answer. She persisted with her questioning. "Sir Herbert and Lady Fox have often hosted a supper. There's nothing unusual about that."

"It's not that kind of supper. This is a private party," said Harry.

"I don't understand," said Betsy, starting to feel irritated.

The two grooms exchanged worried glances.

"Perhaps you ought to tell her," said Thomas. "Then she can warn Lady Fox."

Harry placed an arm round her waist. "Walk with me to the gate. I've left my horse tethered to the trough there and as we go I'll tell you." Suddenly he turned back to Thomas. "Oh, by the way. Mrs Rondelet is looking for a second groom if you're interested."

Thomas shrugged. He would certainly think it over. But at the moment he had to wash the coach ready for his passengers. He just hoped they were in a fit state for the journey and didn't vomit all over the leather upholstery.

Betsy stumbled into the house and up the stairs, hardly aware of each step she was taking. Her mind felt numb both with shock and horror. Harry had told her about Sir Herbert's 'private parties' in the folly, something she wasn't aware of since they had never taken place in the late Lady Fox's time. She had to warn her ladyship, had to tell her. It was going to take place tonight, her last night at Westcroft. She reached her lady's room and knocked on the door before entering. Katherine was sitting at her desk, writing yet another letter to her grandmother.

She turned and smiled. "We must get everything packed this afternoon, Betsy." The maid nodded and then without warning, tears began to flood down her cheeks. Katherine jumped to her feet, alarmed at her distress. "What is it? Is it Harry?"

"It's Sir Herbert, ma'am. I've just been told he's hosting a special supper tonight."

Katherine frowned. "He told me nothing of this. Are there many guests invited?"

"I'm not sure. Only you mustn't go...you must keep away...you..."

Guiding the trembling Betsy over to the chaise longue, Katherine made her sit down.

"Now tell me what this is all about. Why must I keep away from a perfectly harmless supper? Sir Herbert has probably organised it as a farewell meal for me and invited all our friends."

The maid's red-rimmed eyes stared into the intense blue ones of her mistress. "Aye, it might be a farewell supper for you, but the guests are not your friends."

"Mrs Percy," murmured Katherine. The very mention of the name made her shudder.

She had tried to forget the day of the races and Sir Herbert's insistence that she meet his 'good friend', although she couldn't actually recall what happened while she was there. It was like viewing a scene through the bottom of a wineglass.

"What shall we do, my lady?" whispered Betsy.

Katherine rose from her seat. "You're right, I mustn't go down to supper tonight. Not if that woman is coming here." She glanced around the room. "Get these things in the trunks immediately."

Betsy rushed over to the bed and scooped up the gown lying across the quilt.

"I still need to do some ironing."

Katherine shook her head. "Never mind that. We must leave as soon as possible." The maid began to run backwards and forwards, from chest of drawers to the trunks and then to the clothes on the chairs. "Where's my husband?"

"I saw him riding out with the estate manager about ten minutes ago. I think they're going to visit some of the tenants."

"Good," said Katherine.

She sat down at her desk and began to write rapidly, stabbing her quill into the inkpot in her haste. Betsy continued darting to different parts of the room, collecting together the underwear, nightgowns and accessories. She finished the packing and slammed the lids shut, wincing at the way she had thrown in her lady's best gowns, even though she had done her best to fold them.

"All done, my lady," said Betsy.

Katherine glanced round. "Splendid." She tapped her finger on her lips. "I take it that Thomas will be going for the supper guests?"

"Yes, ma'am. But Reuben will be free to drive us."

Katherine came to a decision. "Go to your room and put on your bonnet and cloak and bring your bags in here. Then run to the stables and find Reuben. Tell him that if he can hitch up the horses and bring the coach to the main entrance in ten minutes, I'll give him two shillings. And if he can drive us to Croston Court in the fastest time possible, I'll give him two more."

Betsy ran from the room and was soon in her own small bedchamber. In minutes she was dressed in her outdoor clothing and carrying her bag and valise to her mistress's room, grateful that she had packed her possessions straight after breakfast. And then she was away, hurrying to the stables as fast as her long legs would carry her.

Katherine looked down at the letter and continued writing. She knew her husband would recognise her handwriting and since she was right-handed, she used her left hand and tried to slant the words to mask the writer's identity. She then blotted the wet ink. The letter was written as though it had come from the Earl of Croston and he was urgently requesting her immediate presence at the Court owing to the fact his wife was not too well.

The paper was good quality, but without any embossment that would reveal its true origin. She gave a sigh. But the seal would give the game away. Conrad's seal was his coat-of-arms, while Sir Herbert's was a sheaf of corn, since he was descended from a wealthy farming family. There was only one thing to do. Katherine folded the paper and dripped the sealing wax onto the edge before pressing a diamond brooch into it. Blowing on it to cool it down, she then examined it and was surprised that it did look like a coat-of-arms. She broke the seal and re-read the letter. It sounded plausible, but would Sir Herbert fall for her little trick?

Betsy burst into the room. "He's on his way, my lady. Reuben is bringing the coach round directly. His eyes lit up when I told him about the four shillings."

Despite the grim circumstances, Katherine couldn't help laughing. "Ring for the footmen, Betsy and we'll get the trunks downstairs. And you'd better summon Mrs Chambers."

The footmen arrived within minutes and were soon carrying the luggage down to the waiting coach and pair. Thomas had not been surprised when Betsy had come running into the stables and he had immediately helped Reuben in getting the coach ready. Offers of a share in the four shillings had been brushed aside.

"You just get her ladyship safely to her cousin," he had said.

It would take Reuben an hour to get to Croston Court and then he would have to bring the coach back. This meant he wouldn't get back to Westcroft until later that evening and there would be hell to pay when the master found out. But they were only servants and their duty was to obey, not pass judgement.

Mrs Chambers was of a different mind. "You're going, my lady? But I thought it wasn't until tomorrow."

Katherine sported the saddest expression she could. "I received this," she said, waving the letter in front of her face. "It seems my dear cousin needs me today not tomorrow."

The housekeeper tried to read what was on the paper, but failed.

"But what will Sir Herbert say? He's only gone to see the tenants. He'll be back in an hour."

Lady Fox shrugged as Betsy placed the cloak over her shoulders. "There is no time to wait. You will have to explain it to him," she said, tying on her bonnet.

Katherine didn't wait for any further protest but glided out of the room with Betsy in her wake and Mrs Chambers following them like a black, bouncing ball. They made their way downstairs and into the hall and then out into the bright sunshine. The trunks and bags had been stored aboard and a footman helped Lady Fox and then her maid into the coach. As Reuben cracked the whip and urged the horses forward, Katherine watched as the housekeeper's perplexed face faded out of sight. And she continued watching as the ancient manor of Westcroft began to diminish in size until all she could see was the chimney pots.

"I think we did it, my lady," said Betsy.

Katherine shook her head. "We'll not be safe until we reach the Court." Thomas had advised Reuben to take the back road to the main highway, thereby avoiding the cottages where the master might be. The last thing they wanted was to meet him on the journey. "Well, I hope Sir Herbert enjoys his supper," said Katherine softly, a terrible despondency sweeping through her.

Sir Herbert stood in his wife's empty bedchamber and looked around. There were obvious signs of hurried packing and on the dressing table was the letter. He picked it up.

"When did this arrive?"

Mrs Chambers looked uncomfortable. "I can't tell you, sir. I didn't see the courier."

"So, she's gone."

He pursed his lips and examined the seal, tracing his finger over the wax. The impression was indistinct and he couldn't quite make out the emblem. Even so, there was something very peculiar about it all.

"There was nothing I could do, sir," said the housekeeper. "Your wife was adamant that she had to leave to be with her cousin."

Sir Herbert shrugged. "My little supper party will go ahead as planned, so prepare the church." He gave a low chuckle. "Lady Fox will have ample opportunity to enjoy one of my special parties when she returns."

Mrs Chambers remained silent and looked away, her round face devoid of any emotion. On occasions like these she would much prefer to turn a blind eye. Of the servants, only she was permitted to enter the ruined church. Church! She wrinkled her nose in contempt. There was nothing holy about that place; it was a place of sin. But it was her duty to clean the folly, make the fire and put new candles into the holders. And this she did with trepidation, clutching her rosary and muttering Hail Mary over and over again. She would spend the rest of the night on her knees in her room, praying furiously until that dreadful woman and her entourage had left. She was grateful that her lady had escaped and if she had her way, Lady Fox would never return to Westcroft.

CHAPTER NINE

It was Socrates who saw the coach first. Rising from his place in the sun, he stood and sniffed the air before giving half a dozen sharp barks, his body rigid with expectation.

"Hush, noisy dog," said Frobisher. "You'll disturb the countess and she needs her rest." The secretary had been making notes on the building work that needed doing before the winter set in. There wasn't much to do since the Court was of sound construction. Should get rid of those gargoyles, thought Frobisher with a grimace, enough to frighten the poor little babe to death. But there again, the earl had grown up with them and they hadn't done him any harm. Socrates kept on barking. "Are you going to hush? Or shall I lock you up in the stables?"

Socrates bounded forward heading along the drive. It was then the coach came into sight and swept round the courtyard, stopping in front of the main entrance.

"Good afternoon, Frobisher," said Katherine, as the footman helped her to alight.

He stepped forward, pushing his spectacles further up his nose. "L...Lady F...Fox. There s...seems to have been an error for we were t...told you were arriving t...tomorrow."

Katherine grinned that Frobisher's speech impediment had returned. "You must be surprised at seeing me if you've started stammering again."

His face broke into a beaming smile and he took her hand. "My dear lady, I'm so delighted to see you. Although when I last saw you, you were Miss Katherine Widcombe."

She grimaced. "That was a hundred years ago."

"Well, everything is prepared for you, so what does twenty-four hours matter? The countess will be overjoyed to see you. She's taking some rest in her room."

Katherine turned to see Reuben unloading the coach along with the footman.

"Go straight back to Westcroft. You'll not be blamed. My husband will understand that you must follow my orders." She went into her reticule. "And here's your four shillings. Don't gamble it all away tonight with the other grooms."

Reuben grinned as he guided the horses round to the stables so that they could be fed and watered before their journey home.

Frobisher offered his arm and he and Katherine strolled through the main door into the hallway of the Court.

"It's wonderful to be back." She cast him a shy smile. "I can't believe it's nine months since I left." She felt more than just happiness to be back at the Court. Relief mixed with peace engulfed her. It was as if she had stepped into a cathedral and asked for sanctuary. Here she was safe.

"You've been missed, ma'am. Mrs Craddock suggested a special meal and Cook has made all your favourite dishes."

"How kind," said Katherine, smiling.

Mrs Craddock was waiting for them in the hall, having been told of the unexpected arrival of their guest. She had hurried from her parlour, her body quivering with excitement, her thin face all aglow with anticipation.

"Lady Fox, I'm so delighted you're visiting the Court again," she said, making a dignified curtsey. "Your rooms are ready and your maid will be sharing with Molly, if that's agreeable with you."

Katherine nodded. "Yes, that will suit perfectly." She looked around. Nothing had changed. "I'd like to go up and see my cousin straight away."

"Of course, ma'am. She'll be so surprised and delighted to see you."

Katherine followed the ramrod back of the housekeeper up the stairs to Philippa's rooms where Mrs Craddock knocked on the door and then turned the handle. Katherine passed through into her cousin's peach and cream bedchamber.

Philippa was lying on the bed, propped up on many pillows. More pillows supported her swollen body and Katherine was amazed how she had expanded in just seven weeks. Perhaps her dates are wrong, thought Katherine, perhaps the baby will come earlier than expected.

"Kate, you're here," Philippa squealed, holding out her arms. Katherine ran into them, caressing the waves of brown hair that billowed over her shoulders and down her back.

"You look so well," said Katherine, kissing her cheek. "You're absolutely blooming with health."

"The physician is very pleased with my progress. But he thinks I might deliver a few weeks earlier as he says the baby has grown quite a lot." She frowned. "Oh, Kate, I'm so sad about your baby. You must be heartbroken."

Katherine shrugged. "Some things are not meant to be. Where's Anne?" She knew the devoted companion had never left her cousin's side.

"She's just gone to fetch me a drink."

"And…Conrad?"

Philippa shuffled herself into a more comfortable position.

"He's gone to see Zachary. The gamekeeper came across the gypsies again." Katherine's smile faded, but Philippa didn't notice. "Do you realise that Conrad and I have just celebrated our first wedding anniversary?"

"Yes, I remembered."

Anne came into the room, all smiles and carrying two steaming cups of chocolate.

"I've just heard of your arrival, ma'am, so I took the liberty of bringing you a drink also. Please let me take your cloak." She put the cups on the side table and took the garment, laying it over a chair. "Betsy is already unpacking your trunks." Anne offered the drink to her mistress, while Katherine sipped hers perched on the edge of the mattress. "Mrs Craddock has asked me to inform you that dinner will be served in an hour."

Katherine nodded. "Excellent. I'm quite hungry."

She looked towards the window thinking of her husband only eight miles away. What would he do now that she had gone so suddenly? Would he come after her? She prayed not. He had a side to his nature that frightened her and she needed to be apart from him. She needed to decide her future and whether she could consider leaving her husband. It would mean social suicide; no one in society would want anything to do with her if she took that road.

Conrad arrived back in time for dinner. Striding across the hall, the first person he met was Katherine who was just coming down the stairs. She stopped and turned in surprise.

He smiled and came towards her. "I heard that you had already arrived." He came closer and took her hand raising it to his lips. She felt something leap between them, a tingling sensation that she knew he experienced also. "Welcome back to the Court, Cousin Kate."

Conrad watched Katherine across the chessboard as she made her move. Her head was tilted slightly so that her eyelashes cast long shadows on her cheeks and in the flickering glow of the candles, her skin had a rosy hue that he found irresistible.

He cleared his throat. "Has Philippa shown you the nursery?"

She lifted her head and smiled. "The nursery. The layette. The cradle. Absolutely everything, many times over."

He leaned back in his chair and chuckled. "I feel she's been preparing forever. Sometimes I believe this child will never arrive."

"You won't think so when he's seventeen and you're chastising him for his unacceptable behaviour or his choice in sweetheart," she laughed.

Conrad grimaced. "Yes, we've all that to come." His hand reached out and covered hers, knocking over the bishop. His voice was so low it seemed part of his breathing. "Kate, I'm so sorry about your child."

"Thank you, my lord," she whispered, easing her hand away. "But I'm coming to terms with my loss."

He righted the bishop and made his move. "I think you've had too much loss for one so young."

"The physician believes that I can have another child."

"I'm sure you can. You're young and healthy and that's a good sign." He saw her glance across the room to where Philippa was sitting with Anne and Frobisher. The secretary was entertaining them with card tricks and the sound of Philippa's giggles echoed round the room. Conrad followed her glance and smiled. "My wife is content with our life." He turned to gaze at Katherine. "And I'm pleased that we've patched up our differences."

"I'm pleased too," she said softly, moving her knight.

He nodded. "I wish the same happiness for you, Cousin Kate."

She looked up catching his eye and feeling uncomfortable. Yes, his lordship knew more about her than she would have liked. He was well aware now of Sir Herbert's inclinations for the seedier side of life; perhaps he had been told about the folly. The thought horrified her. She picked up her fan and spread it in front of her face to hide her blushes.

But then he smiled and moved his queen. "Checkmate."

Philippa hadn't meant to climb up onto a chair in order to lift down the basket of baby clothes that had been sent from the Hall. They had arrived the week before, lovingly packed in a brown box tied with a bow and she had been delighted with the tiny garments that she and Katherine had worn as infants. Anne had put them in the cupboard, but on a high shelf that Philippa couldn't reach and although Philippa had called Anne and the maid, neither had answered. And so, she had dragged a chair across the floor and stood on it. Her foot slipped on the seat and she came crashing down, hitting the rug with a thud that jarred her body. Everyone heard her scream of pain.

In seconds, the room was filled with people who lifted her onto the bed. Katherine and Anne removed her clothing and it was then that they noticed the blood seeping through her underwear. Frobisher was despatched for the physician.

Mrs Craddock tried to stay calm. "She's only two weeks before her time, ma'am," she told Katherine. "And that means nothing since a baby can arrive a few weeks either way."

"But the bleeding?" Katherine's heart turned cold remembering the loss of her own baby.

The housekeeper pressed her lips together drawing on her expertise.

"She's probably ruptured a blood vessel in the fall. Let's wait and see what the physician says. But until he arrives, her ladyship should remain in bed and rest as much as possible."

The physician was in complete agreement. Except for the bleeding, Philippa wasn't experiencing any pain and staying off her feet should solve the problem.

"How is she?" asked Conrad, when passing Katherine in the hall.

She smiled. "She's doing quite well, really. She just needs to keep still. The physician says he can hear the baby's heart and it's strong and regular."

"Thank goodness. What possessed her to climb up on a chair?"

"Mrs Craddock says that expectant mothers can do the strangest of things when they're about to give birth."

He touched her hand for a brief moment. "Take care of her, Kate. I'm glad you're here."

"You know I'll do everything possible. But I think Aunt Beatrice should be sent for."

He nodded and left the hall to organise a messenger.

The following morning, events took a turn for the worse. Philippa's pains started and this time it was obvious that the baby was on its way. At first, everything seemed to progress well, as Katherine sat by her bedside, trying to soothe her with a flannel dipped in lemon water. But her shrieks of pain could be heard all round the house.

Aunt Beatrice arrived and hurried upstairs to her daughter's room.

"Should it be this painful?" asked Katherine, after greeting her aunt with a kiss on both cheeks.

Beatrice took over the task of bathing the patient's head. "I'm afraid so, my dear. And it's going to get worse before it gets better. But we will see her through it."

The physician arrived once more and examined the patient. He was surprised at the frequency and severity of her contractions but decided that this baby was in a hurry to come into the world and that was nothing unusual. He gave her some laudanum to alleviate the pain and help her sleep for a few hours. But when she awoke the contractions ripped her apart, causing her to scream and grip the blankets in an effort to control herself.

After twelve hours the baby started coming and although the countess tried to push as hard as she could, the baby refused to move. With her mother on one side of her and Katherine on the other, she leaned on them and bore down with all the intensity she could muster. Mrs Craddock assisted the physician but Katherine knew from their concerned glances that events were not going well.

The physician placed the funnel on the mother's abdomen and listened. "The child is in some distress," he said, wiping the sweat from his forehead. "And he seems to have got himself jammed. I will need you two ladies to hold onto her while I use the forceps."

Philippa's mother put her arms round her, speaking words of comfort, but her face white as chalk. The physician took the instrument from the table, where his equipment had been laid out and tried to grip the baby's head. Philippa's screams became louder, as the cruel metal tore her tender tissues and caused more bleeding. It seemed an eternity before the baby started to move and finally the small, wet body emerged into the world. At first there was relief but then Katherine was aware of the terrible silence. A silence that seemed to cut through the air and bring with it the depressing truth.

Her aunt's face became wet with tears. "Oh, no," she murmured. "This can't be. Philippa, my beautiful daughter, you have a son. But he didn't take his first breath."

Conrad came into the room and studied his wife lying so still on the bed. It must have been a terrible ordeal, he thought, an absolute nightmare and it wasn't over yet. The next few days would determine if Philippa would survive or not. The physician wouldn't commit himself to a prognosis saying only that he had done his best and now it was in God's hands.

Conrad glanced across at Katherine, sitting as close to her cousin as possible and saw her tuck the covers under the pale, oval face. And then she reached beneath the quilt and drew out the tiny hand, holding it to her cheek. Conrad knew she was forcing back painful tears.

He took a seat next to her. "Kate, why don't you go to your room and get some rest. I'll stay with her."

Katherine nodded, but didn't move from her seat. She couldn't move, even though she ached to lie down and close her eyes. There was a gentle knock on the door and Mrs Craddock entered the room, followed by the Reverend Penny. The vicar came to the side of the bed and after letting out a long sigh, opened his Bible and mumbled a prayer.

He started to make the sign of the cross on Philippa's ash-grey forehead, her dark brown hair tucked into a white cap. She didn't stir but murmured in her sleep. Katherine stared at him, narrowing her eyes, her expression showing total bewilderment. But then awareness seeped into her brain as her gaze rested on the book in his hands. Conrad would have called him, probably with advice from Aunt Beatrice, since Philippa's condition was critical. Katherine's nerves became a jangled mess. It had to be done, she knew that, but it was only customary. Philippa wouldn't die. God couldn't take her now. She leaned forward and caressed her cousin's pale cheek.

Philippa half-opened her eyes, the light from the candles filtering through to her numbed brain in waves of dazzling colour. She was in bed, but she was so disorientated that she hardly recognised the room. She smiled when she saw Conrad slumped in the chair his head bowed in sleep. Suddenly, she was aware of a bright aura on the covers and her searching hand found the mass of golden hair.

Katherine's exhaustion had got the better of her and she had rested her head on folded arms. Philippa stroked her face causing her to stir. Raising herself, she blinked away the tiredness and glanced around the room, not quite realising where she was. Suddenly she remembered and jerked upright. In a moment she was holding Philippa close, whispering words that were neither intelligible nor important, her thoughts and feelings only that her dear cousin was still with her.

"Have you been here all the time?" Philippa asked, struggling to speak through a desperately parched throat.

Katherine supported her head and helped her drink some water.

"Yes," she smiled and then whispered, "How do you feel?"

"As though I've sat on a bayonet," she grimaced. "What time is it?"

She looked over at the clock. "Just after five."

"At night?"

"No, it's morning now."

"How long have I been here?"

"It was yesterday morning when your pains began. And you had the baby last night."

"Not twenty-four hours yet?" she said in surprise.

Katherine nodded. "Yes. Your mama will be here soon." She waited for the next question and was relieved when it didn't come.

Their whispered words permeated through Conrad's sleep and he stirred, sat up and drew his chair closer to the bed.

"The baby died, didn't he?" said Philippa, as her husband took her hand.

They both started with shock, not expecting such plain speaking from one so ill.

Conrad nodded. "Yes, he died. The doctor did his best but…"

"I knew. I don't know how, but I knew everything." A reply failed to come from either of them. She sank back on the pillows, a shadow crossing her face. "Where is he?"

"In your dressing room," said Conrad in a hushed voice.

"I want to see him."

"No, Philippa," Katherine began, but then thought better of it. "Are you sure?"

She gave a half-smile in answer.

Conrad stood and left the room as though in a daze. He returned a few seconds later with a small bundle wrapped in a white shawl and placed it in his wife's arms. Aunt Beatrice appeared and stopped in shock that her daughter was holding her dead child. Her lips parted in a vain attempt to protest, but then thought better of it. She took a seat next to her niece.

Philippa held the child she had carried for nine months, staring into the tiny features, caressing the perfect little fingers. The transparent lids were closed as if in dreamless sleep.

"They bury still-born babies in other people's graves," she whispered.

"Not this child," Conrad answered. Philippa glanced at her husband, puzzled at the vehemence in his tone. But then he explained, his voice husky with silent grief, "I'm going to arrange a proper funeral for him, with a service and flowers. He'll have his own little piece of earth."

"You're so kind," she murmured. She began to shake with the sheer effort of trying to stay awake.

Her trembling lasted only a few seconds before she became still. And then when her mother saw that she had fallen into peaceful sleep, tears trickling from behind her closed eyelids, she pulled out her handkerchief and wiped them away. Conrad removed the child from his wife's arms.

The next two days seemed endless as they waited for some kind of recovery; some sign that Philippa was improving. But then fever set in and her temperature soared. Katherine and her aunt stayed with her, bathing her burning skin and changing her nightdress. They didn't leave her side, not even to snatch some hours of rest themselves.

At the end of two days, her aunt persuaded Katherine to leave the bedside and Betsy undressed her, and helped her into the hip-bath of warm water. But afterwards, when she was in clean clothes and her hair had been dressed, nothing would stop her from returning to her cousin's bedchamber to resume her vigil.

The fever continued and didn't break. And then came the morning of the fourth day and Katherine stirred from her chair to hear the rasping, laboured breathing that she knew heralded the end of her cousin's struggle.

"Find Lord Croston and Lady Widcombe," she cried and Anne ran from the room in fright.

They arrived and came to Katherine's side. Conrad took his wife's hand, while her aunt leaned over her daughter, caressing her face. Katherine clenched her fingers together in a painful grip, her eyes never leaving the gasping figure lying beneath the covers.

The rasping became quieter and it seemed as though she would stop breathing and then start again. Until she took her final breath. Letting it out slowly, Philippa remained still and quiet.

Katherine let out a small sob of pain and she felt Conrad's hand squeeze her shoulder, but she couldn't take her eyes from the slight figure on the bed, the face still glistening with perspiration. There was no sound from the rest of the house; not one murmur from the servants as the news filtered through that their beloved countess was dead. Katherine remained by the bedside, motionless like an alabaster statue until her aunt put her arms round her. And then they were hugging each other lost in mutual grief.

"My lady, I think Kate should go to her room," said Conrad, his voice sounding gritty to his ears.

"Please let me stay a little longer," she said. "I'm not ready to leave her just yet."

Her aunt shook her head. "She's gone, my dear. There's nothing more to do."

"I know that, but please let me remain here with her."

Conrad and her aunt left the room, she to her own bedchamber, he downstairs, where he saw Frobisher holding Anne in a tight embrace. She had buried her face against his chest and was clutching his jacket as she sobbed.

"We need to write some letters and make arrangements," said Conrad to his secretary.

Frobisher acknowledged and kissed Anne's hair. "Come on, my love. There's matters to be dealt with."

"Go and help Betsy," said Conrad to Anne. "Try and get Lady Fox to take some rest, before she becomes ill too."

It was an hour before Katherine could be persuaded to let go of Philippa's hand and go to her own room. Once there, she lay on the bed with a shawl across her legs. But Katherine's eyes wouldn't close. Her tears were locked away in a grief so deep that it was unreachable.

Four footmen carried the casket to the drawing room and placed it on mahogany stands. Mrs Craddock lit a candle at each end and the maids arranged the flowers that were arriving by the hour.

Katherine stayed in her room, restlessly walking up and down and only nibbling at the food brought to her on a tray. Conrad sent constant messages entreating her to join them for meals, but Katherine knew she was in no fit state to bear company. She just couldn't stop crying.

The letters had been written and despatched. One went to Widcombe Hall and others went to Geraldine Rondelet and Lord Haighton. The letter to Sir Herbert was difficult to write. Conrad had never thought to have to invite him to the Court and the knowledge that he would be sleeping under his roof, filled him with repugnance.

The grandfather clock struck one in the morning. The Court was as silent as the grave, it was a grave as far as Conrad was concerned. He had been in the library most of the evening and it was only as he was crossing the hallway to climb the stairs to retire for the night that he decided to go into the drawing room.

He walked to the side of the casket and gathered his strength before looking down at the figure that seemed only sleeping. "Oh, Philippa. What have I done to you?" he whispered. He contemplated his brief married life and the wife and child he had lost. The funeral was to be held in two days and the following afternoon, everyone would be arriving at the Court. He placed a tender hand on the body of his tiny son. "What have I done to both of you?" He followed the outline of his wife's cheek very lightly with his forefinger. "I'm so sorry." He raised himself to his full height and covered Philippa's small hand with his. "Please forgive me for falling in love with your cousin. I believe you were in ignorance and for that I am glad." He grimaced. "I've lost you now, but I cannot lose Kate. I must convince her to stay at the Court with me, safe from that wretched husband of hers. I know you would have understood. You loved her too."

CHAPTER TEN

She could hear Socrates barking and the sound of a footman and maid talking in hushed tones just outside the door. But she didn't open her eyes. She didn't wish to open her eyes, not just yet. Katherine knew that once she could see the world, she would have to face its troubles and she wasn't ready for that at the moment. She felt peaceful, like being in a boat gently drifting down a river.

The door opened and somebody entered the room.

"My lady, it's time to wake up," said Betsy. Katherine opened her eyes, but lay still. The sun shone brightly behind the curtains and it was going to be a beautiful day. How many days had passed? She couldn't remember. "His lordship wants me to dress you immediately and then you must join him for breakfast."

She pulled herself up on the pillows and then swung her legs over the edge of the mattress, shaking her head at the fact she had lost all sense of reality, not knowing what was real or dreamt. Betsy took her in hand and helped her bathe and dress in her black gown trimmed with white lace. Another period of mourning thought Katherine sadly. Her maid brushed her hair and tied it up, interlacing a black ribbon among the soft curls.

Katherine made her way downstairs but stopped at the bottom unable to go further, her eyes fixed on the closed door leading to the drawing room. A parlour maid curtsied and then murmured something that Katherine couldn't quite understand. And then the maid ran into the dining room to fetch Lord Croston. Moments later, Conrad appeared.

He walked towards Katherine, relieved that she looked much more rested.

"Kate, are you ready for breakfast?" She didn't answer. He took her hand and tucked it through his arm. "Would you like to see her?" he said softly.

Katherine nodded. "Is she in there? I thought she might be."

Conrad guided her over to the large oak door and turned the handle. They stepped into the room and the scent of flowers took their breath away. They were everywhere, large floral displays exploded from elaborate metal stands, wreaths were propped up on chairs, bouquets, baskets and vases, covered every possible surface. And in the centre of this garden was the casket, the lid still raised.

Katherine stepped forward and viewed the figure lying amongst the cream satin lining, her head resting on a silk pillow trimmed with blue lace.

"She looks so peaceful," she said. "But she was only eighteen. She should have had her whole life ahead of her."

"The physician said she would have recovered from the birth if it hadn't been for the fever."

"Physicians! It was those damned forceps that brought on the fever. I know for certain that the midwife in Lenchwick lost only a handful of mothers in twenty years. And she doesn't use such instruments of torture."

"I'm pleased to see you've regained your fighting spirit."

"Where did all the flowers come from?" she said, trying to change the subject.

"From everywhere and everyone. I don't think there's a bloom left in England."

"She was much thought of," she sighed.

They turned to go and minutes later, Katherine was sitting next to her aunt, nibbling her breakfast.

Aunt Beatrice watched her, frowning. "You must eat more than that, Katherine."

"I'm not very hungry, Aunt."

She let out a sigh. "The family will be arriving this afternoon and we all must be brave...and keep up our strength." She pulled out a handkerchief.

Katherine jumped out of her chair and wrapped her arms round her aunt's shaking body. "Oh, Aunt Beatrice. I think I want to remain childless. How can a person bear to lose a grown child? I thought losing my own baby was grief enough."

Her aunt patted her hand. "We bear it because we must. Now, eat my dear. Give me some comfort that you are well." Katherine picked up her fork and forced a piece of sausage into her mouth. Her aunt gave her a watery smile. "Only don't choke on your food."

"I thought we might go out riding this morning, Kate," said Conrad, watching her.

"Is it seemly with...?"

Conrad raised his eyebrows in surprise. "I don't mean to race you over the hills. Just a gentle trot in the fresh air. It might give you an appetite for dinner."

"Indeed, it will do you the world of good," said her aunt.

Katherine had to admit that there was some sense in what they were saying and agreed.

In fact, she enjoyed her ride and they stayed on the paths of the estate and woodlands, meandering along at a steady pace. Katherine looked up at the rays of the sun filtering through the canopy that was slowly losing its abundance of shade. In a short while all the leaves would be gone and the branches would be stark and bare.

Conrad smiled. "I knew this would do you good. You've not been outside for nearly a week with nursing Philippa and..." Words suddenly failed him.

"Has it been that long?"

"Well, I must admit I lost count of the days too."

She thought for a moment. "She died only two days ago and yet I feel as though it were weeks."

They emerged from the trees and a cottage came into view. Katherine realised that it was the gamekeeper's. Zachary was chopping wood, a large pile already growing at his side, his wife was pegging clothes on the line. The children were running about squealing with enjoyment as they played their game in the warm morning sun. The scene was one of complete harmony as the family laughed and called to one another.

"Family is important," whispered Katherine.

"Well, there's plenty of them arriving shortly."

"What about Geraldine and Lord Haighton?"

"They hope to join us later this afternoon in time for dinner."

"Sir Herbert?" she murmured.

Conrad studied her anxiously, noticing her complexion turning pale.

"I believe he'll be the last to arrive." She turned her head away. "Are you all right?"

She turned to face him. "Yes, I'm all right," she nodded, but knew she wasn't fooling him.

Conrad led the way down the narrow track. Minutes passed before he asked, "I always wondered why you arrived a day earlier than expected. Perhaps now would be a good time to tell me."

"I had to leave Sir Herbert." She sucked in a breath. "He used to be so kind and considerate. And then he seemed to change after I lost the baby. He hates me for it. And little wonder, it was all my fault."

Conrad gave her a sidelong glance. "Don't blame yourself, Kate."

"But I am to blame. I went out riding when I shouldn't have. I was very foolish."

Conrad shook his head. "But it wasn't your fault. Riding accidents happen all the time."

"I was with child and I should have known better." They rode in silence until they reached the gates and Katherine saw two coaches parked in the forecourt, their passengers just alighting. "It's Grandmama! They've arrived at last."

Conrad grinned and reached for the reins of her horse. "You go and welcome them and I'll see to the horses. Tell them I'll be along shortly."

Katherine jumped from the saddle and ran down the drive. Conrad watched her and smiled.

Her family turned to see her.

"For goodness sake, girl," snapped Aunt Charlotte. "Have you no sense of decency. Running about with your cousin not yet in her grave."

"Oh, do stop complaining and leave the child alone," said her grandmother, holding out her arms.

Katherine hugged the thin frame of her grandmother, kissed Aunt Charlotte and gave Sebastian a bright smile.

"I'm sure you've grown another six inches," she said, ruffling his hair.

He came to his grandmother's side and took her arm.

"He's my right arm, dear Kate," she smiled. "And I would be lost without him. Reminds me of you when you were his age."

Katherine noticed Uncle George standing a little to one side, his arms round his wife's shoulders. They were lost in their own grief and as she watched, she felt tears welling up inside her. She was relieved when they all went into the Court where Mrs Craddock hovered, waiting to be of service.

"Tea will be served in the parlour, my lady."

"Thank you. His lordship is on his way."

"I think we should pay our respects to Philippa first," said her grandmother.

Katherine left them to go into the drawing room alone and made her way to the parlour. She didn't want to be party to another viewing.

Conrad appeared moments later and decided to join them in their vigil. And after ten minutes he accompanied them in to have their tea. As Katherine poured and passed round the dishes, her grandmother watched her through worried eyes. Her granddaughter had had to endure much these last months, but she was strong. But something else was going on here. Yes, by the glances that his lordship sent in her granddaughter's direction, it was clear he was in love with her. How very interesting, thought the old lady.

Taking tea was pleasant, although Aunt Charlotte's outspoken comments on the grandeur of the Court became quite embarrassing. Afterwards they all went their separate ways, the two aunts and uncle to walk round the grounds, the grandmother to her room to take some rest after their journey.

A footman announcing the arrival of more guests made Katherine jump to her feet as Geraldine and Lord Haighton came into the room. And when her aunts, uncle and grandmother appeared once more there was the mayhem of introductions and more tea, before the new arrivals went into the drawing room to see Philippa.

Geraldine emerged a few minutes later, tearful and with Lord Haighton's steadying arm round her.

"Oh, she's too young," she wept. "And she left Cheltenham so very excited and happy."

When everyone had collected in the parlour, Katherine noticed Conrad standing near the window talking to Lord Haighton. Suddenly they both turned their heads and looked out of the window. Katherine's heart lurched in her chest. Only one more person was expected and she dreaded his appearance. In minutes he was shown in. Dressed in his best red coat and wearing a smart wig, he clutched a gold-tipped cane, striking it on the floor as he walked. He bowed to Lord Croston who responded politely and then proceeded to greet every person present, the men with a flamboyant bow, the ladies with a kiss on the hand.

"Never liked the man," said Katherine's grandmother under her breath.

He left Katherine until last. She stared at him as though he was a stranger, hardly believing he was standing in the parlour of Croston Court.

"Well, Katherine, my love, aren't you going to give your husband a kiss," he smiled, holding out his hand.

She went towards him, took his hand and kissed his cheek. Sir Herbert was still her husband and despite her feelings of repugnance, she had to obey the rules of society. But she felt as though she had kissed her executioner.

That evening, they gathered in the parlour. Katherine watched her husband from across the room. She had been apart from him for nearly three weeks and yet the indignation she felt at his obscene intentions towards her, still rankled. After the funeral she would confront him and ask him to explain himself. It was the only way she would find peace.

Geraldine was sitting next to her and took her hand. "Mrs Craddock has put me in the Chinese Room," she said with a mischievous grin.

"It's a beautiful room. Conrad told me that his father had it decorated after his trip to Shanghai."

"Hmm. Too many dragons for my liking."

"Really! Shall I ask Mrs Craddock to move you to another room?"

Geraldine smiled and shook her head.

Katherine yearned to play chess with Conrad as she had done so many times before, but when Sir Herbert took his place next to her, she was forced to listen to his conversation, shivering every time he touched her arm or showed her the slightest bit of affection. Sometimes her gaze would fall on Conrad who was being the perfect host, sharing his time and conversation with each guest. But when he felt Katherine's eyes on him, he would turn his head and smile reassuringly at her.

Finally, Katherine decided to go upstairs.

"Yes, you retire, my love," said Sir Herbert. "I will remain a little longer, but I will be along shortly."

She left the room in a hurry and in the wake of Aunt Charlotte's insufferable critique on the beautiful carriage clock and the delicate china figurines.

Geraldine jumped into bed, blew out the candle and snuggled under the covers. She smiled to herself musing over the fact that it was so obvious to her that some spark had been ignited between Conrad and Katherine. But it seemed she was the only one. Even Richard had been surprised when she had mentioned it to him.

The door opened and she pulled the blanket over her head. Heavy footsteps crossed the floor and then a hand pulled back the quilt, revealing her in her nightgown.

"Uncle! What the blazes do you think you're doing?"

Sir Herbert stared at her and then looked around in bewilderment.

"I thought this was my wife's bedchamber. I do beg your pardon."

"Katherine and I exchanged rooms. She's somewhere along the corridor. You'll have to wake Mrs Craddock and ask her."

Perplexed, he stumbled back through the door and Geraldine pulled herself up on the pillows, putting her hand over her mouth to stop her giggles. She re-lit the candle and waited a few minutes as she heard the door close across the corridor and knew her uncle had returned to his own room.

Moments later, Richard peered round the door. "Did it work?" he smiled. He came into the room and jumped into bed beside her.

Geraldine grinned. "Of course it worked. He got the shock of his life, the silly old fool. He'll never find the Chinese Room tonight."

Richard wrapped his arms round her and kissed her lips.

"I hope not." Suddenly he raised himself up on his elbow. "This Mrs Percy business is getting out of hand. Perhaps we could invite Katherine to the Continent. The change would certainly do her good."

"It's a wonderful notion," she whispered. "But unfortunately, Sir Herbert will never let Katherine go without him. And the last thing I need is my uncle's company in Italy."

In the Chinese Room, Katherine snuggled against the pillows. Suddenly she felt happier, but only because Geraldine had given her a night of peace. Exchanging rooms had been a wonderful idea and she didn't mind the dragons at all. They will frighten away the monster, she thought, as her eyelids became heavy. And tomorrow she would say goodbye to darling Philippa. God grant me the strength to bear my grief, she prayed. And God grant me the courage to face my fears.

The rest of the mourners had left the vault and were wandering about outside, talking and admiring the horses and coaches. Lord Croston decided to linger a while, mainly because Lady Fox seemed unable to leave her cousin, even though her earthly remains had already been placed in the marble sarcophagus. Katherine's veil was now raised, after hiding her features for most of the morning and Conrad was surprised that she now seemed serene and dignified in her grief. He stood quietly in the resting-place of his ancestors and watched the lovely woman standing so tall and straight and to his mind, looking every inch a countess.

The private chapel had been overflowing with those wanting to attend and the service had been quite beautiful. Lord Haighton had surprised them all by giving a short eulogy on behalf of Lady Croston's friends in Cheltenham and Conrad had been quite touched by that. In fact, everything had gone very well, although it had started to drizzle with rain for a short while.

Katherine turned her head and seeing Conrad, gave a watery smile. "It's difficult to say goodbye."

He stepped over to her and put his hand on her elbow. "You can stay if you wish, but it is rather chilly in here."

"I suppose it is," she said, looking around. "I hadn't noticed." She turned sad eyes towards him. "Oh, Conrad, I'm going to miss her so much. I hope she's not lonely."

"She's got plenty of company." He gestured to the many slabs around the floor and inscriptions on the walls. "And one day I'll be joining her."

Katherine felt aghast at such bluntness and took his arm. "Not for many, many years I hope."

"Well, I hope so too," he grinned. "But this is the family vault of the Earls of Croston, so I must accept that I will lie here eventually."

Katherine looked around her once more. "Is that your father and grandfather?" She pointed to the two slabs at one side of the vault, with the coat-of-arms emblazoned on the side.

He smiled. "Yes, and many others too, all in one long line." His eyes darkened. "And that little babe lying there with his mother, would have come after me." Shaking his head, he added, "What drives a man to want a son, an heir, at the cost of a woman's life?"

"Not all women die. My grandmama had three sons."

He squeezed her hand. "But how can I ask the woman I love to risk her life in such a way?"

"The woman who loves you will know the risks and accept them gladly." She held his arm even tighter. "Let's go outside and join the others."

Once in the fresh air, Katherine went straight to her husband and slipped her hand through his arm. He patted her hand in a fatherly way and smiled down at her. She studied him, trying desperately to see the man she was once so fond of.

"Have you said your farewell?" asked Sir Herbert, giving Lord Croston a bow as he passed.

Katherine nodded. "It was difficult but it's all done now."

Sir Herbert looked at her, his small, grey eyes glistening with concealed frustration. "I went to your room last night."

"Did you, sir?" She turned her head away so that he couldn't see her smiling.

"And made an utter fool of myself. Why did you not tell me that you exchanged rooms with my niece?"

She turned back, her expression impassive. "I thought you would be tired after your journey. And I know I was exhausted. I'm sorry that you're upset."

They were making their way to the carriages.

"I've missed you, Katherine and when you left Westcroft so unexpectedly, I wondered why."

The words came out before she could stop herself. "After Mrs Percy, you begged forgiveness from me. And I forgave you. So, why, sir, did you then invite that woman to our home?"

He grinned. "Not to our home, my love. To the folly, the ruined church. Just for a bit of fun."

"Fun you call it. To want to take me there is dishonourable, you must realise that, Herbert."

He seemed unrepentant. "You're my wife and must accept whatever I do. Anyway, I saw no harm in it."

She pressed her lips together to keep back her anger.

Katherine spent the rest of the day agitated. Her husband's glib comments had shocked and annoyed her. Did she not deserve some respect from him? How could she return to Westcroft knowing that it could happen again? If she had her way she would burn the folly down to the ground.

That evening they all went into the drawing room that had now been cleared of flowers and cleaned and swept. But when they entered, the fragrance still lingered.

Katherine looked around the room with sadness. Here she had fought his lordship over the chessboard. Here she had watched Philippa with her sewing as she gossiped with Anne. Here she had seen love grow between the secretary and the companion. It was a sad room and yet a happy room, filled with memories.

Her grandmother came in leaning heavily on Sebastian's arm. "Dear Lord, but I ache with my rheumatism tonight. I think I might have to retire early."

Her grandson lowered her into the armchair next to his aunt.

"We needn't go home tomorrow if you feel disinclined," said Aunt Charlotte dryly. "I'm sure Lord Croston can grant us a further night."

Conrad nodded. "Yes. Yes, of course. If Lady Widcombe is unable to travel then she must stay another night." He bowed to the dowager sitting in his best armchair. "Please feel free to use my home as your home."

She gave a toothless grin. "You're very kind, my lord. But when a person gets to my age they like to be in their own bed and have their own possessions round them. I shall travel home tomorrow and suffer the consequences."

Katherine felt very concerned for her grandmother and came to sit at her knee on a footstool. "Are you sure, Grandmama? If Lord Croston has invited you to stay a third night, then perhaps you should accept it? I wouldn't like you to get overtired and become ill. These last few days have been quite arduous."

She patted her hand. "No, my dear child. I want to be back at the Hall."

Charlotte pursed her mouth. "Such a pity. It's been very pleasant at the Court. So much more refined than at Widcombe Hall. It's a beautiful place and full of the finest furniture and paintings. Not to mention the exquisite china and…"

Aunt Beatrice was losing her patience. "Sister! We don't need to hear a blessed inventory."

"No, of course not. I'm just saying that this is the best seat in the county."

Sir Herbert gave a polite cough. "Well, Katherine organises Westcroft very efficiently and her presence is needed. So, we will be returning home tomorrow straight after dinner."

Katherine glanced at her husband in dismay. "Tomorrow? We are returning so soon? I thought you might want to stay a little longer."

"Yes, Uncle," said Geraldine. "Katherine has just buried her dear cousin. She needs time to grieve and her household duties will be too much for her at the moment."

Sir Herbert glared at her. "Not that it has anything to do with you, but I believe it is exactly what she needs. Immersing herself in her responsibilities will help her get over her cousin's death."

Katherine knew that she ought to obey her husband but fear gripped her, making her feel faint.

She looked at Geraldine and steadied her breathing. "I know you're trying to be kind but if my husband says I must go home tomorrow then that's what I must do."

Sir Herbert smiled, his face twisted in arrogant victory. "Good. I'm glad you agree."

Katherine clasped her hands together on her knee. She mustn't make a scene in front of Conrad's guests and certainly not at such a sad time.

Her grandmother's weary voice broke through the hum of conversation. "Sebastian, call for that wretched chair. I must be away to my bed." The young boy went to do as he was bid and two footmen arrived carrying a chair with poles either side. She was helped unsteadily to her feet and into the contrivance where she sniffed in contempt. "To think I was once a young girl running about the place with little effort or thought. And now I've come to this, to be carried about like an invalid."

Katherine laughed. "Oh no, Grandmama. Like a queen."

Her grandmother chuckled but then groaned with pain. "Sir Herbert, I think I must deprive you of your wife tonight."

He stopped his discussion with Lord Haighton. "What do you mean, Lady Widcombe?"

"I'm speaking about my granddaughter, sir. My knees pain me enough to make me weep and I need Katherine to rub liniment into my joints. I'd like her to spend the night in my room in case I should need her."

Sir Herbert frowned. "Surely your attendants and personal maid have the required skills to treat your ailments?"

Laughter gurgled up from her throat. "They're nearly as ancient as I and besides Katherine's hands are young and supple. She has the ability to massage in a manner that I find very soothing." She looked at him through eyes that were determined. "It's only for one night, sir. You can do without her for one night. Come Katherine, follow my chair."

Mystified, Sir Herbert watched them go, anger consuming him. His voice was gritty as he turned to the rest of the company. "I surmise my wife will make an excellent nurse when I'm in need of one." He tried to force a smile.

Katherine reached her grandmother's room and helped her onto the bed. Mathilda took over the task of getting her ready.

"Child, I need something to read. What has Lord Croston got on his shelves?"

"Many books, Grandmama. Milton, Shakespeare, *Fanny Hill*."

"What was that, Katherine? Did you say *Fanny Hill*?"

Katherine blushed. "Yes, Grandmama."

The old lady grunted. "Read that one years ago. Fetch me some Milton."

Smiling, Katherine made her way down to the library, passing through the quietness of the grand hall like an apparition and only briefly pausing outside the drawing room where the sound of conversation hummed behind the solid oak door.

She stepped into the magnificent library and searched along the shelves.

"Kate." The words were almost a murmur but she heard and spun round.

"Oh, Conrad. I'm just looking for a book for Grandmama."

"What are you looking for?"

"Milton."

He slipped the book from the shelf and handed it to her.

"You're determined to go home tomorrow? I don't think I can bear it. Can you not persuade your husband to stay a little longer?"

"I could try, but he sees no purpose in staying." Conrad nodded in defeat. Katherine smiled. "I've not spent the night with Grandmama since I was a child and used to suffer with nightmares."

"You suffered with nightmares?"

"Only occasionally. I used to dream that I was in the sea with my parents, trying to swim to a ship that was moving away from us."

"Dear Lord. Perhaps you shouldn't have been told what happened to your parents?"

"Unfortunately, I was the kind of child who asked far too many questions and my grandmama thought it better to tell me the truth."

He took her hand and kissed it. "Then, I hope you sleep well tonight, despite the grievous circumstances."

"I will try. And I know my grandmama, once asleep, she'll not stir until dawn."

He let out a slow breath and held her hand tighter. "You're looking much healthier."

"The physician advised me to drink red wine to build up my blood. And I've been well looked after at the Court. I have you to thank for that." He gave a misty smile, but she noticed the sadness in his eyes. He turned to go but she didn't want him to leave and placed a tender hand on his arm. "Conrad, my heart goes out to you. If there's anything I can do…"

He looked at her, his pain so obvious. "Stay with me, Kate. Stay here at the Court."

"It's not my place to fill your loneliness." Suddenly, she wished it were.

"I'm not talking of my loneliness. I will get by. No, it's you that I worry about."

"Why?"

He shook his head. "I can't explain. But please stay with me."

"I can't do that. Society wouldn't understand. Your wife has just died and I have a husband."

"And I do understand. You want to be a good wife and I respect you for that." Before she could answer he said hurriedly, "When I spoke of my feelings last Christmas, I was speaking from the heart. I want you to know that my feelings will never change. You must believe that before you go back to Westcroft and take up your life there."

There was a sharp knock and Frobisher came in. "I'm sorry, my lord. I was going to complete the funeral accounts."

Katherine climbed the stairs. She felt exhausted, as though she could sleep for a hundred years and yet, she felt stronger and more determined. Conrad's confirmation of his love for her had given her strength. Tonight she would sleep next to her grandmother and the following day she would go back to Westcroft and take up her household duties. But if her husband invited Mrs Percy to her home, she would walk out. Yes, she would walk all the way back to Croston Court if she had to.

She halted halfway up the staircase gasping with shock. How had it happened? When had it happened? Her feelings had grown over the months without her realising it and now he was a part of her. Conrad had somehow won her heart and she loved him. She swallowed with difficulty thinking of Philippa. I'm so sorry, my dearest cousin, she thought. I didn't mean it to happen but it has. Oh, what am I to do?

Conrad raised his hand to stop the maid speaking.

"You don't have to explain further, Betsy. I understand."

She hesitated briefly. She knew that the man standing opposite her cared for her mistress and would do anything to protect her.

"My lord, her ladyship mustn't return to Westcroft. She's not safe there. Not with *him*."

"You may go, Betsy. Make sure your mistress is comfortable."

Betsy curtsied and left the room. Conrad turned and looked out of the window his thoughts in turmoil.

It was just before breakfast the day after the funeral and Katherine's family was leaving for Widcombe Hall as soon as they had finished their meal. Geraldine and Lord Haighton were leaving after dinner and Sir Herbert and Lady Fox some time later. The Court would be very quiet.

Frobisher had brought Betsy into the study to explain about the letter that her ladyship had written before leaving Westcroft. The maid had heard Sir Herbert speaking about it to Frobisher and seeing the puzzled look on the secretary's face, she had decided to take matters into her own hands and tell Frobisher why her mistress had had to write such a letter. In turn, the secretary had insisted that she tell his lordship.

Frobisher watched his master anxiously. The death of the countess was taking its toll on him and he could see that his lordship was deeply grieved. Frobisher had worked for him for many years and the thought of having to leave him when he married Anne, made him very despondent. But that morning, his lordship had given them a wonderful wedding gift in the form of a cottage on the edge of the estate and only two miles from the village. Marlborough Cottage was an ideal home for the young couple and Frobisher's delight had been overwhelming. He would be able to keep his position at the Court, but at the same time enjoy married bliss with his lovely Anne. At that moment, there was nothing he would do for his lordship.

Conrad turned back to face his secretary. "I'm sure I don't have to remind you to be discreet about what you've heard this morning?"

"Of course not, sir." He sighed. "Although it does seem common knowledge amongst the servants at Westcroft."

"It's a dreadful business and Lady Fox's situation is far worse than I suspected."

Conrad frowned as his secretary left the room. He sat down and leaned back in his chair. Now it seemed imperative that Katherine leave her husband. If only she would stay safely at the Court where he could protect her. But persuading her would be impossible. He thought over what the maid had told him and his blood ran cold. It was not just the House of Venus that was a threat, but a damned folly in the grounds of Westcroft. A ruin, put there to add a bit of interest to the landscape was now a place of debauchery and shame. It was not a place for his Kate.

Two coaches pulling up at the door interrupted his grim thoughts. Katherine's family was ready to leave and he needed to play the perfect host and see them on their way.

It didn't take long to get ready for dinner. And when Betsy had finished dressing her hair, sweeping it up into coils and placing a dainty lace cap on top of the curls, Katherine went down to the dining room just as the others were taking their places. There was a scraping of chairs as the gentlemen rose to their feet.

Katherine smiled and allowed Conrad to guide her to a seat. Sir Herbert came to kiss her hand. "You look very well, my love."

Katherine smiled at him and then turned to her friends. "You're leaving straight after dinner?"

Geraldine nodded. "Yes, our bags and trunks are being loaded as I speak."

"And we will be leaving soon after. Oh, I'll miss you so much."

Sir Herbert cleared his throat. "I've decided that we must celebrate Christmas, my love, even though you are in mourning again." He looked around the table. "I would like to invite you all to Christmas dinner. Perhaps a quiet game of cards would not go amiss afterwards, but definitely no parlour games."

"And a little riding if the weather is clement," smiled Richard, ignoring the hostile looks from his stepfather. "Although I think Valentine ought to be retired and a more spirited animal put her ladyship's way."

Katherine tried to swallow the lump in her throat. "Valentine is no longer with us."

"Oh, what happened to her?"

"She had to be destroyed," said Sir Herbert curtly.

"Then Midnight would be a good alternative. A very apt Christmas present for an excellent horsewoman and a courageous lady who has endured so much."

Katherine smiled at him. "Thank you, my lord."

The meal continued with the idle chatter associated with a meal before a long journey. They talked about the weather and the condition of the roads. The news that a notorious highwayman named Edward Quinn had been hanged for robbing the Bristol Mail, brought a grin from Sir Herbert.

"I'd have liked to have seen that," he said. "There's nothing better in life than a good hanging."

By the time Richard and Geraldine's coach rolled down the drive, the footmen were bringing the trunks out to be loaded into Sir Herbert's coach. Katherine ran upstairs to put on her cloak and bonnet.

As she was coming downstairs, Conrad came out of the study and beckoned her inside. He shut the door behind her. Puzzled she waited for him to speak.

"So, tell me about the letter."

"What letter?"

"The one you wrote to yourself requesting your presence at the Court."

She blushed in embarrassment. "I…I couldn't think of what to do. I had to get away immediately. How did you know about the letter?"

He squeezed her hand. "Betsy told me about Sir Herbert's supper…guests."

"I wish she hadn't told you. What must you think."

"Your maid did the right thing in telling me. Your husband was questioning Frobisher about the letter and she didn't want to see you in trouble. As to what I think? Well, I think that you should not return to Westcroft." He stepped towards her. "You must stay here now, where you will be safe."

Katherine closed her eyes for moment and when she opened them again, tears made them shine.

"I can't leave him. I'm his wife."

Lord Croston stared at her, hardly believing what he was hearing. "You're staying with him out of loyalty and duty?"

"Yes, I am."

"When he has no respect, no loyalty for you."

"I have to do what I think is right."

Conrad paced the floor. He couldn't look at her. "I've spoken with Lord Haighton and Mrs Rondelet. They're planning a trip to Italy in the summer. We could go, you and I." He put his hands on her shoulders and then she saw again the pain, the hopelessness in his eyes. "Or we could travel to Germany to visit my family. We could stay in my cousin's schloss. You would be made so welcome there. I would keep you safe."

She struggled with her feelings. "I know I would be safe with you, but it would also be wrong. You know it would be wrong."

He drew her closer to him. "Do you think Philippa would want you to go back to your husband if she knew? No, indeed. Had she lived she would have begged me to help you. Kate, please do not go with that man."

She gave a half-smile and after a moment's pause, lifted her chin. "I will make you a promise. I promise that I'll not let Sir Herbert treat me with such scorn again. If he does then I will come to you and be with you." Tears stung her eyes and she held his hand to her cheek. "And I promise you that no matter where I am, I will always love you. There will be no other man for me, not if I'm married to Sir Herbert for the next thirty years and I'm an old lady with grandchildren at my knee. You have my heart, Conrad, so take good care of it."

He gave a low moan of relief at her confession and pulled her towards him, his mouth finding hers with intense passion that swallowed her up, body, mind and soul. Their kiss only broke when voices were heard outside the door. Conrad let her go and stepped back a few paces, his eyes glistening, the muscles tense in his jaw. Katherine had never seen him look so handsome as he did at that moment as he battled with his emotions.

Sir Herbert's voice rang out from the hallway supervising the loading of their luggage and Lord Croston and Lady Fox left the study separately.

Everyone had been given stone flasks containing boiling water and these had been placed under blankets to keep them warm. Even the coachman had one secreted away under his covers. And when everyone was ready, the coach set off. Katherine's hands had only touched Conrad's briefly as they said goodbye. But their eyes had said everything. As she watched his figure recede into the distance, she felt subdued and suddenly very lost.

She turned to her husband and saw that he was more interested in watching the parklands of Croston Court than talking to her. She looked down at her wedding ring. She was Lady Fox and she couldn't change that. The future seemed more uncertain than ever.

For Sir Herbert, the future was far from uncertain and he smiled to himself thinking about it. He had been too premature in his dealings with his new wife, believing her youth would make her more amenable. He would need to rein in his desires if he wished to win her round. And win her round he would, for he enjoyed nothing more than corrupting the innocent. Yes, he would go back to playing the loving and devoted husband and in time Katherine would become as pliable as soft clay, fashioned into any shape he desired. So struck was he by this notion, he was forced to hide his mouth with his hand, so that his wife couldn't see his lips twitching.

CHAPTER ELEVEN

Katherine threw herself into the domestic routine of Westcroft, taking up the reins of managing the household as she had done before. If the weather were tolerable, she would walk with Sir Herbert round the garden and she was amazed that his manner had reverted to the early days of their marriage. Perhaps he had learnt his lesson, she thought. Her heart filled with hope that her life would be peaceful since thoughts of Conrad had not left her since they had arrived back.

As the festive season approached, the weather turned colder and snow powdered the hills and fields. Katherine sat at the window and watched the delicate flakes fluttering to the ground and remembered the Christmas before when she had tried to come to terms with Conrad's avowal of love. And this Christmas she was grieving for not only her aunt, but also her cousin.

And yet, Conrad's idea of leaving England and journeying to Italy or Germany intrigued her and deep down she wished it could be made a reality. If only she could persuade her husband to join Richard and Geraldine in Italy. He would be away from that woman, Mrs Percy, removed from the folly. A scheme began to drift through her mind. Life could be different or made to be different. Yes, but sometimes destiny needed a helping hand. She jumped from the window seat and paced the room. If only she had the courage.

It was the night before Christmas Eve and Sir Herbert had gone to Cheltenham on business. He would return the following evening in time to greet their guests on Christmas Day. Katherine lay in bed, sleep escaping her; the idea that had started as just an acorn had grown into a veritable oak tree. She jumped out of bed and stood in the centre of the room trying to come to some sort of decision. And then she decided, flung a cloak over her shoulders, pulled on a pair of shoes and ran into the maid's room, shaking her by the shoulder.

"Get up, Betsy. I need your help."

The maid rubbed her eyes. "But, my lady, it's a quarter to midnight. What do you need to do at this hour of the night?"

Katherine didn't answer, but took her hands and helped her to her feet. Soon they were making their way through the house, Betsy's entreaties waking up Mrs Chambers who opened her door.

"What's going on?" she asked the maid, but Betsy could only answer with a gesture of alarm.

The housekeeper pulled on her robe and followed them down the stairs.

Outside it was bitterly cold. There were no clouds and the stars were brilliant in a purple sky, the moon shining with a halo round it. Katherine picked up one of the flaming torches that studded the drive.

"Do you think she's gone mad?" whispered Mrs Chambers to Betsy. "Just like our poor king?"

Betsy frowned. "Eeh, don't ask me." She ran forward and caught up with her mistress. "What are you doing, my lady?"

Katherine threw back her head and laughed. "Marching to salvation, my dear. Marching to salvation."

By now the entire household were awake as maids and footmen appeared in a motley assortment of night attire including the grooms and stable boys that had been roused by a footman and were running to join the procession. And Lady Fox, like the leader in some spontaneous rebellion, marched down the path, past the gardens and towards the meadow.

They crossed the meadow and finally came to a halt in front of the ruined church. "Break the door down, if you please," said Katherine to Thomas.

He kicked at the flimsy wood and it cracked in two. She stepped through. The building was bathed in moonlight, the furniture just black shadows. She paused for a few seconds, the torch held high, before thrusting it deep into the fabric of a couch. The fire took hold and then she looked about her. It was just as she remembered it; the walls adorned with naked figures, the flickering flames causing them to dance maniacally; the rugs and velvet couches; the words inscribed on the wall.

Thomas came to her side his eyes agog at finally seeing inside a forbidden place that had been the gossip of servants for years. After glancing about, the groom guided her outside and they stood with the others. The spectators remained silent as the furniture inside caught alight with a sizzle, then a crack and finally a roar, smoke billowing in black clouds out of the door and up the tower.

Suddenly, there was a loud cheer from the household and some started to dance about in front of the flames.

"Hallelujah," cried Mrs Chambers, crossing herself.

The chimes of a clock made them silent once more.

"What's the hour?" asked Lady Fox.

"Midnight, my lady," said Mrs Chambers. "Christmas Eve."

"Christmas Eve," Katherine smiled. "And a new beginning."

Thomas grimaced. "There'll be hell to pay for when Master gets wind of this."

"Aye, but it's a grand sight nonetheless," whispered Betsy.

It was Christmas morning and Katherine jumped out of bed with excitement. Their guests were arriving today for dinner and then staying until after the New Year.

Katherine hurried Betsy with her dressing and then went down to breakfast. Her husband was already sitting and rose to his feet as she took the seat next to him.

"Merry Christmas, my love."

She nodded. "Merry Christmas. I believe this is going to be a happy Christmas for us, despite everything."

He chuckled in delight. "We have certainly lived quietly this last month and I think a little company will be very welcome." He smiled benignly. "Your gift is in my study. I picked it specially for you whilst in Cheltenham."

After breakfast, he brought the gift to her and to her amazement it was a diamond headband.

"It's beautiful," she breathed.

"For when we can attend balls again. And I can take up my dancing lessons with you."

She looked at him in wonder. In an impetuous gesture she reached to kiss his cheek.

"Thank you," she whispered and slipped her arm through his.

The rest of the morning was spent in making sure the house was ready for her guests. The main rooms had been decorated with garlands of mistletoe and holly, the red and white berries bright against the luscious leaves. Bay and rosemary were put in bowls giving a pleasing fragrance while candles were renewed ready for the evening. Fires were built up to capacity in the dining room and drawing room and the entire house was filled with the smell of baking pies and puddings and roasting meats. And these delicious smells mingled with the intoxicating tang of mulled wine.

It was time to get ready and Katherine ran to her rooms where Betsy waited for her. The gown she had chosen to wear was hanging up on the ornamental screen that gave her privacy when she bathed. It was royal blue and its sleeves and bodice were trimmed with white lace intertwined with silver thread. On her head, Betsy pinned a matching lace cap with a satin bow at the back, the same colour as her gown. Since Philippa's death she had been wearing black and white and still ought to for some time yet. But it was Christmas Day and she needed to bring a little colour into her life and had decided that royal blue wouldn't show any disrespect to her cousin whatsoever.

And when she was told that a coach was approaching the house, she couldn't help going outside to meet it. She knew she was breaking the rules by waiting for her guests outside since decorum dictated that they should be shown into the drawing room where she would welcome them into her home. But her excitement had got the better of her and she had to be at the door as the coach pulled up.

Cries of 'Merry Christmas' filled the air as Lord Haighton jumped out and helped Mrs Rondelet to alight. Footmen carried the gifts in to be placed on the table with the others.

"Mrs Chambers has organised a wonderful dinner in the servants' parlour," said Lady Fox to Harry. "And I won't be needing Betsy until this evening."

The groom inclined his head in thanks. Soon he was urging the horses forward towards the stables where Thomas and Reuben waited to unhitch them. The guests trooped into the hall where footmen and maids were ready to take hats and cloaks. And then another coach came up the drive and Katherine waited.

Conrad stepped down followed by Frobisher.

"Merry Christmas," he whispered, taking her hand and kissing her fingers. "You look absolutely wonderful."

She smiled and gave a slight curtsey. "Thank you, my lord. It's so good to see you again." She turned to Frobisher, hovering just behind his lordship. "Welcome to Westcroft."

"Thank you, my lady. I hope I won't be intruding on your celebrations."

Conrad gave a low chuckle. "Anne begged him to accompany me. She wants to get on with plans for their wedding and it seems he is nothing but a nuisance." He turned to his secretary. "Take the gifts in and I will be with you shortly." Frobisher left without comment.

Katherine stared after him. "I think that was a very obvious ruse, my lord."

He threw back his head and laughed. "Frobisher is discretion itself. And why shouldn't I grab a few private moments with you?" He held her hand against the front of his coat. "I've enjoyed receiving your letters."

"And I yours. Although it wasn't the same as seeing you in person."

"You won't believe how much I've missed you," he whispered.

Katherine realised they were forgetting themselves as well as her guests and laughing, steered him through the door and into the hallway.

They went into the drawing room where Sir Herbert was organising the footman with a tray of drinks.

Geraldine was full of news. "Richard and I are betrothed. We're marrying on the first day of June at

Saint Mary's and I'll be sending out invitations in March."

There was a cry of delight from Katherine. "When did you decide this?"

"Richard plucked up the courage to ask me only last week." She turned to Sir Herbert. "And you will give me away, Uncle?"

"Glad to get shot of you," he grinned.

"Croston is to be best man," said Richard, winking at him.

Geraldine wanted to tell them more of their plans. "And after the wedding we'll be going to Italy on an extended honeymoon," she said, taking Lord Haighton's hand. "I long to see Richard's villa again."

"Again?" said Katherine.

Geraldine nodded. "It was where I escaped to after my husband died. It was the only place I knew I would be safe, so I stayed there for nearly five years until I decided to return to England."

Dinner was announced.

Katherine's spirits soared as she acted as hostess to her lively guests. Conrad watched her, happy that she looked in good health and Sir Herbert too seemed to have improved in character, the banter between Katherine and her husband often quite amusing. They seem genuinely fond of each other, he thought, could Sir Herbert really be reformed and was now the good husband? He frowned and glanced at Haighton. Despite beaming with happiness at his impending marriage, Richard too was watching his stepfather.

Conrad, Richard and Geraldine had made a solemn pact. Katherine must be protected from her husband by regular visits from both Geraldine and Richard, with the added help of Mrs Chambers who had also been recruited. It was the job of the housekeeper to send a message to Cheltenham if her master called for Mrs Percy. Although everyone had been on their guard, nothing had occurred to cause concern and the last month had passed without incident. Even so, Conrad had decided to open up his house in Cheltenham after the festivities so that he too would be on hand should Katherine need help. He glanced across at Sir Herbert, chuckling over a clever quip from his stepson. He looked the genial host, the country gentleman and the perfect husband. But Conrad had a feeling of dread that made the hairs stand up on the back of his neck.

After dinner they went into the drawing room to open up their gifts that were displayed on the table. Another log was thrown on the fire and they started opening the brightly coloured parcels and appreciative sounds echoed round the room. Conrad's gift to Katherine had already arrived a few days before in the shape of a beautiful mahogany writing desk. His card had simply said: 'So we never lose touch'.

Outside it was getting dark and the servants were lighting the torches along the drive. They had also lit all the candles in the drawing room and with the blazing fire, the room was warm and inviting. Sir Herbert, Geraldine, Richard and Frobisher settled down to play cards for the rest of the evening, while Katherine and Conrad played chess.

"This appears to be our game," she said in amusement.

"Yes, and we are perfectly matched." He glanced at her. "You seem to be happy with Sir Herbert?"

"I believe I've tamed him."

"Like a horse?"

Katherine couldn't help laughing. "Perhaps."

"I still want to take you to the Continent," he whispered. "I will never feel easy until you are away from him."

She leaned forward eagerly. "You don't understand. I've cut out the canker that was destroying our marriage. My husband is a reformed man." She smiled in her innocence.

Conrad viewed the scene with distaste. He and Katherine had gone for a walk and across the meadow he could see the blackened shell of the church standing at the edge of the woodland. To Katherine's mind it looked more ominous than it had as a ruin.

"It wasn't like the folly at the Court," she murmured. "The one where you played as a child."

He couldn't have agreed more. "No, indeed." He gave her a quizzical glance. "Does your husband know what you have done?"

She shook her head. "Well, he's not mentioned it. But he only arrived home Christmas Eve night and I don't think he's had time to think about the folly. And it's plain the servants haven't said anything to him, or he would have said something."

"Perhaps you ought to tell him soon while Richard and I are still here. Just in case..." He didn't dare finish the sentence.

Katherine tilted her head as she viewed the scene. "I've been in it once. I was riding with Lord Haighton and insisted that he take me in. I wish I hadn't. It frightened me."

He turned to stare at her. "Lord Haighton took you into the folly? That was rather insensitive of him."

"But as I said, I insisted. He was being agreeable. I could see that he didn't want to go in either but I ignored him. That was my folly." She smiled at her quip and was relieved when he chuckled.

They continued their walk arm in arm and he told her more of the news from the Court. Not that much had happened since Philippa's funeral. Katherine got the impression that Conrad was living a solitary, bachelor life and as he spoke, she watched him, marvelling at how his violet eyes sparkled in the handsome face she loved.

Katherine had found it difficult these last three days, having him near but not being able to hold him close. They had walked and talked and played chess and when they had walked, it had been arm in arm. Frequently, they would meet in the hallway or in a corridor and would always stop and speak, their hands brushing against each other, as though accidentally.

On a particularly windy day, Conrad, Richard and Frobisher decided to go out riding before the daylight vanished. Since Geraldine was taking a bath in her room, Katherine went into the parlour where a roaring fire burnt in the grate and the room had been made bright with winter pansies. She warmed her hands over the welcoming flames and her eyes alighted on her tapestry lying on the side table. It was a depiction of Widcombe Hall and Katherine smiled. She had nearly finished it and then it would be framed and hung on the wall. She carried it over to the large armchair by the fire and after making herself comfortable, began to weave the needle in and out of the canvas, pulling along the emerald green thread as she completed the oak tree. The very one she had climbed as a young girl. She would finish the tapestry in time for the New Year, she decided.

"Now, ain't you the picture of domestic harmony," laughed Sir Herbert, coming into the room and taking a seat in the armchair opposite her. "For all the world, you look like a contented wife."

She smiled. "I am a contented wife."

"Good! Good, that's what I like to hear." He appeared agitated, restless.

"Didn't you want to ride this afternoon, sir?"

He pursed his mouth. "Too windy for me. Might get blown off me horse." He squinted at her, studying her closely. "You've not ridden since arriving back from Croston Court. Why's that?"

She hesitated before replying, "I don't wish to ride at present."

"Is it because of that damned nag, Valentine?"

"I think it might be," she said, keeping her eyes on her work.

He sniffed in disdain. "My horses, just like my wife and servants, should be obedient."

Katherine put down her sewing, feeling angry. "It was my fault. Valentine was only a dumb animal...she shouldn't have been blamed. It was a terrible act of cruelty, sir."

Sir Herbert shrugged. "I thought it necessary." And then smiling he said, "Let's not speak further on it. What's done is done." His smile widened. "Did you remember it was my birthday tomorrow?"

"Yes, I did. I have your gift ready."

"What gift would you like?"

She looked at him in amazement. "Me, sir? What do you mean? It's not my birthday."

"If you could have your heart's desire. Anything at all. What would it be?"

For a moment Katherine felt stunned, but then an idea slowly formed. "If I could have anything...anything at

241

all…then, with it being New Year, I would like to see changes made. A new understanding, so to speak."

"And what would this 'new understanding' entail?"

She bit her lip. During the last few days she had expected him to mention the folly. Surely, he had seen it? Perhaps he had, she surmised, and had decided its burning was for the best.

The idea gave her hope, but she had better test the ground first. "I would like to see the folly destroyed. I would like to see it burnt to the ground and then the stones taken away one by one and thrown down the hillside."

At first, her husband seemed surprised, but then his manner turned cold. "No, I don't think that would be very agreeable."

Bile rose in her throat. He didn't know! "Why not, Herbert? Get rid of it, please. It's not a pleasure to see, it's a monstrosity."

"I say again, no," he said quietly.

Desperation took her over and she slipped from her chair and dropped on the floor at his knee, sitting just as she did when talking to her grandmother.

She stroked his hand. "You asked me what I wanted and that would please me greatly." She looked up at him with sapphire blue eyes.

Herbert watched her. His wife was certainly a beautiful woman. His gaze wandered down to her cleavage showing above the low neckline of her gown, the soft breasts moving rhythmically with her breathing. He leaned forward and placed his hands on her shoulders and then his left hand slipped down to cup one of her breasts.

"The folly will stay. I know I'll have need of it," he said.

She hated the look in his eyes and twisted away from him. "Don't Herbert, please, don't." She gasped with dread at her confession. "I've burnt it down. The folly is gone."

He stared at her, hardly understanding, but then gave a snort of derision. "Is this one of your jests?"

She shook her head. "No, Herbert. Take a look for yourself if you don't believe me."

He threw back his head and let out a raucous laugh, but the smile faded when he saw her expression. Grabbing her chin, he held it up so that his face was inches from hers.

"You had better be jesting, Madam!" He frowned. "You burnt down...the folly! How dare you!" He gritted his teeth and swore under his breath.

"I had to do it," she pleaded. The fury in his eyes terrified her, but she still felt she could persuade him. "It was a terrible place, Herbert. It corrupted you, as did Mrs Percy. I know you can be a better man."

"You had no right!"

"I'm your wife..."

"My wife!" His tone was scornful and full of hate. "The blue-blooded girl who would give me many healthy sons, but couldn't hold onto one."

"I apologised for that. When will you forgive me? I thought you were happy with me. Perhaps you should never have married me."

"If I hadn't married you, then who would have? Who would have had a girl already spoilt?"

She gasped, her mouth drying up. "Already spoilt?"

"The virgin from an aristocratic family," he grinned, seeing her face pale. "But you weren't a virgin were you, my love? Where did you learn the trick with the slice of liver? That made our wedding night very interesting. The idea must have come from your grandmother. Yes, I wager the old bird knows a few tricks."

"You knew?"

He pushed her away and she fell backwards, falling onto the floor.

"Of course I did." He stood and glared down at her. "Did you really think I would be so ignorant?"

"Then why didn't you say something when you discovered it? And if you were so disgusted with me, then why didn't you send me back to my aunt and uncle?"

"I didn't say I was disgusted with you. It was your utter carelessness in losing the child that offended me." He gave a half-smile. "Being married to you amused me. A little game. But like all games, it's becoming tedious." He almost spat out the next words. "And now you have the audacity to burn down the folly!"

Katherine stared at her husband in disbelief. "A game? What are you talking about?"

He stroked his chin, smiling smugly. "I wanted you to tell me that you had lost your virtue. I was eager for you to tell me. How disappointed I was when you cared not to."

She rose to her feet, shock making her stagger. He gripped her arm.

"Herbert, you don't understand. It was not my fault."

"Whose fault was it, then?"

"I was kidnapped. When I was just a girl. Taken from my bed. I don't know why…except that…that."

He threw back his head and laughed. "Except that someone decided to send you home…defiled. Now I wonder who that was?"

She shook her head. "I don't know. They covered my eyes and gave me a drug that made me sleepy. I don't know what happened only that I knew I had been…violated. Only my grandmama knew. She took me to Oxford and I was examined by a physician who confirmed it."

He studied her. "When I first lay with you on our wedding night, I really thought you would remember."

She tried to stay calm. "Remember what?"

He put his mouth close to her ear. "But the dose of opium was too much for a fifteen-year-old girl. You were insensible, if I recall. And that was a shame."

She looked at him aghast. "You…?"

He nodded, his eyes full of malice. "Mmm…And how I savoured having you. So young and fresh with an arse as round and firm as an apple." He grinned relishing the memory. "It was difficult to give you up." He sighed. "But I was persuaded to send you home." He chuckled at her horrified expression. "Not that it was supposed to be me claiming your innocence. I had you hand-picked for the Turkish prince. Wanted him to take you in exchange for…well, it doesn't matter now. But I had a mind for him to take you back to Constantinople to the beautiful Topkapi Palace. I've heard the harem is full of beauties that could take a man's breath away. You would have been at home there."

She turned from him but he caught her by the wrist. She struggled to escape. "Let me go."

"That's what you kept saying. Screaming and carrying on like you did. And when the prince saw you he baulked at the idea. Seems he was a man of principle and couldn't bring himself to take a woman against her will. Unlike me, who has no qualms whatsoever."

Katherine wrenched her hand away from him. "You! You ruined me."

He frowned. "I was angry that you had destroyed my plans, making all that fuss when I was offering you a better life. I was angry with myself. I've owned the House of Venus for many years and procured girls to work there. I know the business, or thought I did, but I was certainly wrong when it came to you. I believed you a commoner, a young girl living with her aunt in a small cottage in Bristol. But when you told me your name and that your uncle was Sir George Widcombe, a baronet, I realised what a colossal mistake I had made."

"The House of Venus?" she whispered.

He gave a low chortle that set her nerves on edge. "Commonly known as a house of disrepute. But a high-class establishment, nonetheless."

"Oh, God," she murmured. "Mrs Percy…is in your employ?" She struggled away from him, but he grabbed her by the hair.

"Yes, indeed. So, my love, now that you know, I'll not expect you to object when she and her delicious girls attend my parties, since you're no better than they. I'll soon rebuild the folly and I'm sure it will become as dear to your heart as it is to mine. What fun we shall have."

Katherine thrashed out, trying to release her hair from his grip. Stumbling over the footstool, she stretched out her arms to steady her balance and her fingers curled round the handle of the metal poker that was hooked on a stand. It scraped against the fender. Then raising it above her head, she struck him across the temple with a sickening crack. The blow registered in his expression and he stayed still, staring at her, his eyes wide with surprise. Blood trickled from the wound above his eyebrow and then he blinked twice, before dropping at her feet.

She gaped at the fire iron in her hand and then at her husband. What she saw filled her with horror. Sir Herbert was lying on his side, his face against the side of the fender that surrounded the fire. And round his head, a pool of blood was forming that was soaking into the rug.

CHAPTER TWELVE

They left the horses at the stables and walked round to the main entrance of the house. The daylight was fading fast and the windows of the manor glowed invitingly, welcoming them inside for their dinner. Just as they were nearing the entrance, Conrad noticed a figure wrapped in a cloak, hurrying up the drive, her skirts flowing out behind her in the strong breeze.

They all stopped and stared.

"Was that Lady Fox?" asked Frobisher, peering into the gloom.

Richard shook his head. "I hardly think so. Most probably a maid, eager to see her beau."

In the hall, the footman took their hats and coats.

"Where is everyone?" said Lord Haighton and was told that Mrs Rondelet was still in her room, but Sir Herbert and Lady Fox were in the parlour. Richard grinned. "Good, I could do with a brandy before dinner."

They stepped into the parlour and looked about them. For a moment they thought the room empty until Frobisher gave a gasp and pointed.

"Dear Lord! Sir Herbert?"

Horrified, they looked to where he was pointing. They crossed the room swiftly and Conrad crouched by the side of the large shape on the rug in front of the fireplace.

"He's dead. Struck on the head." He picked up the poker and grimaced at its bloodied end. "The weapon, no doubt." He turned to Frobisher. "Go upstairs and find Mrs Rondelet and Lady Fox. Bring them down here, but don't say anything to them just yet." He stood and turned to Richard. "Close the door, we don't want any servants coming in."

Frobisher returned with Geraldine and informed his master that Lady Fox was nowhere in the house. Geraldine knelt by her uncle's body and took his hand. She didn't speak as her gaze swept over the blood and the large gash across his temple.

The three men stood together.

"Do you think it was Katherine?" said Richard, biting his lip. "Perhaps it was she we saw running up the drive."

Conrad shook his head. "What makes you think she did this? Why would she murder her husband?"

"We should call for the parish constable," said Richard.

"No! Let's find Katherine first. In God's name, let's discover the truth."

Frobisher took off his spectacles and wiped them on his handkerchief. "My lords, we cannot do anything other than call the constable."

Geraldine had risen to her feet. She looked down at the crumpled body. "He was an evil man, and if Katherine did this, then she must have had just cause."

"Katherine can't be responsible for this." Conrad knew he sounded desperate.

"Then let's find her and ask her," whispered Geraldine, trying to pacify him.

Conrad walked a few steps into the room, rubbing his hand through his hair and then he turned to face his companions. "Frobisher, send someone to fetch the constable. And when he arrives, I will tell him that I did this."

They exchanged stunned glances.

"How very noble, but may I ask why?" asked Richard.

Conrad gave a strained laugh. "Because I love Kate," he said softly. "And I will not see her stand on the scaffold. I would rather die in her place."

Frobisher left to find a groom and send him to Cheltenham.

Katherine ran and ran. Where the drive curved, she cut across the field and clambered over the stone wall. It was dark and the wind tore at her cloak as if trying to pull it from her. The moon was bright and the landscape seemed ghostly and unreal. She had been horrified to see her husband lying dead at her feet and her first instinct was to run, run away and hide. But she knew she was not running from the mere fact she had killed him, but from the revelations before she had struck the fatal blow. He had been responsible for her kidnapping when she was just a girl. All for the sake of currying favour with a foreign prince. She had been a prize, a gift. And when the prince had rejected her, Sir Herbert had lost his temper and violated her. What unkindness that six years later, he should ask for her hand in marriage. A cruel jest at her expense.

She wrapped the cloak more closely round her and realised that it was Sir Herbert's, thrown over a chair in the hallway when he had come in from walking in the garden. She had not remembered picking it up in the first place but had snatched it up in her haste. And now she was running, running. But where to? Where could she go on a windy December night when the stars twinkled behind rolling grey clouds? She stumbled along getting weary and then she saw more glittering lights in the distance. Was it the village? Surely she hadn't run so far? Her foot slipped and she felt herself falling down a steep incline.

Tumbling over and over, she finally landed in a hawthorn bush with a cry of fright and pain. She heard dogs barking and the sound of men's voices getting nearer and nearer, louder and louder. They were coming for her. Coming to arrest her and drag her to prison. A man was leaning over her although she couldn't see his features clearly because of the gloom. But she could see he was sturdy in build and the glimmer of the gold ring in his ear caught her eye. Then she realised he was the gypsy leader, the one she had spoken to when she was at Croston Court. The gypsies had found her. She didn't care. They could rob her of the little she had, slit her throat and throw her body in a ditch. She didn't care about that either. It was over and she accepted her fate.

"What are you saying?" Geraldine stared at Richard in disbelief.

They were still in the parlour. Frobisher had returned after sending a groom to fetch a constable, but Lord Haighton's words had made him turn the key in the lock. It was important that no one entered the room.

"I'm saying that I think I know why Katherine would do this and if I'm correct, then if anyone should be arrested, then it should be me."

"But you've done nothing wrong, my darling," said Geraldine. "Why should you be arrested for this?" She gestured towards the body of her uncle. "It's bad enough that Conrad insists on taking the blame."

Richard rubbed his hand over his mouth and stared at the three pairs of eyes that stared back at him.

"I'm not as innocent as you think." He took in a steadying breath. "I owed my stepfather a fortune and he agreed to wipe the slate clean if I performed a necessary task."

"What was this necessary task?" asked Conrad, his suspicions growing.

"Sir Herbert wanted me to discover the whereabouts of a certain…young girl and take her to…the House of Venus."

Conrad blinked hard. "Go on."

"I discovered her address and managed to lever a window and snatch her from her bed." His large brown eyes filled with tears. "And afterwards I returned her to within walking distance of her home."

Conrad stepped forward, his fists clenched. "It was Kate?" He turned to Geraldine. "Dear God, he's responsible for her kidnapping."

Richard backed away, holding up his hands to defend himself. "You know of it? Has Katherine told you? Believe me I loathed doing it. And afterwards I fled to Italy to escape my conscience."

Conrad took two steps towards him and grabbed him by the lapels. "Fleeing to the far side of the world should not have done that."

Geraldine came between them and pushed them apart. "Did you do it alone, Richard?"

Lord Haighton stared at her in bewilderment. "No, I had a companion."

"Who was your companion?" She shook his arm, as if trying to wake him from a daze. "I want to know if it was my husband?"

Richard seemed stunned. "Why should your husband be involved in this?"

"Because of the handkerchief. The red, silk handkerchief that she was blindfolded with. I believe that it belonged to Roderique."

Despite the dire situation, Richard smiled. "No, your husband was not involved."

"But the handkerchief?"

"Do you remember the duel when I was winged? Roderique was my second and he tied the handkerchief round the wound to stem the bleeding. I meant to return it, but never did. I suppose I must have used it to cover her eyes, although I don't remember using it."

Conrad still felt anger coursing through his veins. "And what happened when you met her after her marriage?" he asked sarcastically. "I wager that amused you."

Richard turned on him. "It did not. I was confounded when she walked into the room and my stepfather introduced her as his new wife. She was a lovely girl now grown into a beautiful woman and with no knowledge that we were responsible for her terrible secret." He looked down at the body of his stepfather. "As time passed, I grew to adore her." He took in a breath. "I can only assume that she discovered the truth. And that is why I should be arrested for the crime. I didn't wield the weapon, but I might as well, since I wished him dead a thousand times." His brown eyes became darker, as he grasped Conrad by the arm. "Go to the stables, have Midnight saddled and go and find Katherine. When the constable arrives I will surrender and then you can bring her home safely. It is the least I can do to make amends." Conrad stared at him. "In God's name, Croston, go!"

Conrad left the house and sprinted to the stables. Midnight was saddled and in a short time, he was galloping along the drive. He didn't know where to search and realised that his mission might be in vain. As he looked across the dark and forbidding landscape, he had a feeling of *deja vu*. He had done this before, only this time there was no Socrates to help him.

Katherine felt herself being lifted and then carried by the man who had found her. She kept her eyes closed and shivered. Bright lights danced in front of her eyelids and then she was being placed into a wagon.

"Put her on the bed, son. And then leave her to me." The voice sounded familiar. "Some cuts and bruises, I see, but no lasting damage." Someone was bathing her face and when she opened her eyes, she saw the crinkled smile of an old woman. She shrank back in horror. The old woman soothed her with gentle words. "Don't be afraid. You'll come to no harm here," she said, tucking a blanket round her.

Katherine looked about her and saw a covering overhead made of sailcloth. She was in a wagon, but inside was all manner of things; dried herbs hung from the sides and all around were strange objects in glass jars, bundles of feathers and bizarre metal instruments. Resting on a wooden trunk, a stub of a candle guttered in a brass holder giving only the barest of light.

"Where am I?"

"You're amongst the gypsies, my dear. Now, sit up and I'll give you something to drink." Katherine did as she was told and took a sip. "It's just a drop of rum with just a little something in to calm you down and help you sleep a little."

She looked at the old woman that had sold her the heather. "You told me to beware a devil pretending to be an angel?" she gasped. The woman nodded. "I killed that devil. I struck him a fatal blow and now he's dead."

"Is that why you were running?"

Katherine nodded. "And I don't know what to do."

The old woman laughed. "For now, you must rest. Later, we will talk."

She parted the flap in the sailcloth and then with a quick glance over her shoulder, she was gone and Katherine was alone. Pulling the blanket round her, she sank back against the cushions. Outside she could hear voices, men, women and children. They were obviously preparing a meal round the fire, as the smell of cooking meat wafted through the opening in the sailcloth. Her eyes began to close and she drifted off to sleep.

She didn't know the time when she finally stirred, but she had the feeling that she had not been asleep for long. Peering through the flap, she saw the moon shining brightly above skeletal trees and the sounds of the camp made her feel safe.

The old woman appeared carrying a plate of rabbit stew.

"Ah, I see you're awake. I want you to eat, dearie. You must build up your strength." Katherine pulled herself up on the cushions and the old woman placed the metal plate on her lap. She tasted the food and began to eat. The old woman nodded in satisfaction. "Good. You'll soon feel much better."

As she ate, Katherine looked around the small space. "This is your home?"

"Aye, it's all I need. I tell fortunes at fairs and do a little healing with my herbs," she said, sitting down on a small three-legged stool.

Katherine watched her. "It must be a difficult life?"

"A body gets used to it, my lady."

Katherine put down her spoon and the woman took the plate from her.

"What shall I do? I've killed a man." She tried to fight back tears. "The authorities will be looking for me by now."

"Yes, but I doubt they'll think you've joined a gypsy band."

"But I can't stay with you. Harbouring a criminal will get you into trouble."

"Do you care, my lady, if we should get into trouble or not?"

Katherine studied the wrinkled face, tanned from the sun; the grey hair tucked in a scarf.

"Yes, I do care. It would be wrong if I let your kindness to me be paid with imprisonment."

The old woman nodded. "You have a tender heart. Just like your parents."

Katherine felt stunned. "You knew my parents?" The gypsy grinned, showing uneven teeth and then slipped her hand under the mattress, pulling out a gilded picture frame. She handed it to Katherine who gave a cry of surprise when she saw a portrait of her father in naval uniform standing behind a chair on which sat her mother. "I don't understand."

The old woman took her hand. "My name is Orana and I had the privilege of meeting your ma and pa many years ago when you were just a tiny babe." She chuckled at Katherine's astonishment. "I keep their portraits close to me for I have much to thank them for."

"What did they do?" whispered Katherine.

"The man who carried you into the camp is my son, Patrick and the leader of this gypsy band. He too shares my gratitude." She sucked on her teeth as she mulled her thoughts over. "This is not the time to tell you our story. But the day will come when you'll know all."

"Time might be short when the constable comes for me."

Katherine fought back tears. She should be sitting in her parlour with her guests, not in a gypsy wagon hiding from the law. Thoughts of Conrad engulfed her and she let out a sob. Would he now know the terrible thing she had done? How he would hate her.

"Ah, yes, your husband. But didn't all this start the night you were taken from your bed?"

Katherine looked aghast at her. "You knew about that?" Even in the candlelight she could see the glint in the old woman's eyes.

"I knew all about Sir Herbert and his *House of Venus*. I was horrified when you married him and I persuaded my son to stay in the area while I watched and waited."

"That's how you knew about the devil pretending to be an angel?"

"Yes, that's how I knew. And I also knew that Lord Croston loved you." She grinned, her face crinkling. "Servants can be very useful for wheedling out information."

Katherine gave a sob. "I could never hurt Philippa. I pray she was never aware."

Orana smiled sadly. "It was already on the cards that your cousin would die." A cry of grief escaped Katherine's lips and the old gypsy woman clutched her hand. "Listen to me, girl, there are those whose futures are already destined and there's nothing that can be done about it. Your cousin was one of those. And there are others who can choose their destinies, like you."

"How can I choose my destiny?"

"You will have some important decisions to make and when the time comes, you will know what road to travel." She tucked the blanket more snugly round the slender figure. "Now sleep, dearie. I will be in the tent next door. The morning will bring fresh hope."

Katherine slipped further down the bed. "Goodnight, Orana."

After the gypsy had left, her mind buzzed with all she had heard. How could so much have happened in barely six hours? The morning will bring fresh hope, Orana had said. Was there really any hope? There was no getting away from the fact that she was a murderess and for good or ill, her husband's death would have to be reckoned with.

It was a short time later that a commotion outside the wagon pulled her out of restless slumber. The heavy beat of hooves and a man's voice calling out made her sit up in terror and she stared at the opening, waiting for the constables to burst in and arrest her. But when the flap was pushed aside, she saw Conrad climbing in. Giving a cry of surprise, she held out her arms to him and then his arms were round her and they were holding each other close.

Conrad could hardly believe that he had found her. Not knowing which way to go he had been alerted by the sounds and lights from the gypsy camp and thinking there was no harm in asking if they had seen her, he had ridden into the enclosure of tents and wagons, sending the women and children scurrying to safety. The men had immediately drawn their pistols and knives and held him at bay, but the leader recognised him and told his men to lower their weapons. A brief conversation confirmed that Katherine was with them and an old woman had shown him to the wagon. Now he sat on the side of the small bed and held her in his arms, kissing her hair and face.

"I thought I would never find you," he whispered.

"Have you come to take me back?"

He shook his head. "No, of course not."

Their arms tightened round each other.

"I killed him. I killed my husband. I should go back and admit it."

His mouth became dry. "Kate, I must tell you something. It will be difficult for you to believe but it's the truth." Conrad then told her about Richard's confession and she listened impassively as though there was nothing she could hear now that would surprise her. When he had finished, he held her chin in his hand. "And I can only assume that Sir Herbert told you his part in all this and that was why you did what you did."

She kissed his fingers. "I killed my husband because he violated me when I was his prisoner."

"He did what?" Conrad pulled her closer to him, his mind reeling with the knowledge of what Katherine had suffered at the hands of an evil man. And the suffering would continue for a young girl's innocence was valued and taken into her marriage along with her dowry. No man would look twice at a woman who was not a maid. "Oh, my poor darling."

"That is why I would have turned down your offer of marriage, should you have made me one," said Katherine. "You would have discovered that I wasn't pure."

Conrad smiled. "You're pure in heart and mind and I admire that more. No, my darling, if you had told me everything, I would have understood. I love you too much to let something like that spoil our happiness."

Large tears rolled down her cheeks. "What is to become of me?"

He gave a sigh. "Haighton wants to take the blame. He says it's the only way of making amends to you."

She pressed her face into his coat. "I can't let him do that. I did the deed so I must face the punishment." She lifted her face and stared into eyes that showed horror. "You do understand that, don't you?"

"No, Kate. I'll not see you hang. I can't let that happen."

"But I cannot see an innocent man go to the gallows."

Conrad let out a groan of despair. "Please, Kate. Don't ask me to take you back. The gypsies say that

259

they're on their way to Gloucester for the New Year fair. We could travel with them and then find someone to row us down river to Bristol. I will charter a yacht that would take us anywhere in the world, away from all this."

"I must do what I believe is right." Conrad sucked in a steadying breath, wrapping his arms more tightly round her. "Would you do one thing for me?" she asked.

"Anything."

"Will you stay with me tonight?"

His heart beat faster. "Of course."

"And in the morning, will you come with me to the nearest Justice of the Peace? And always be near to me, right to the end?"

"As you wish," he whispered.

He murmured words of comfort as he caressed her trembling body. Then he started kissing her neck and shoulders. Her breathing steadied and she lay still. He felt her softness and closed his eyes at the feelings that surged through him. He wanted to feel her close. He needed to be near her. He brushed his lips against hers.

Katherine didn't open her eyes, enjoying the warmth of his body next to hers and a yearning to feel him even closer made her tremble. She reached up and put her arms round his neck. His kisses became more ardent and she began to respond in a way she never could with her husband.

"I love you," she whispered.

She heard him gasp as if in pain, but then he pressed his lips on hers and her mouth parted. He pulled off his clothes and then helped her slip out of her gown and underskirt. Nothing seem to matter from that moment on as tears and sorrow were all swept away and forgotten, in the total and exhilarating joy of being loved. She nuzzled her face against his neck and stroked his back and shoulders. His lips moved over trembling skin, kissing areas of her naked body that had never been kissed before. He was so gentle that she moaned at the swollen sensations that made her ache with desire. It was like the misty unreal quality of a dream and she was melting like a piece of ice in hot water. Every touch was exquisite and as the camp became quiet and the wagon sheltered them, they became lost in each other. She matched her movements to his rhythm and lifted her body to meet his as she experienced the wonderful satisfaction of letting go until her feelings gushed to the surface in a cry of intense pleasure.

Even after the ecstasy had ebbed away they stayed coupled together. Conrad lifted himself so that he could gaze at her smiling face and then at their entwined bodies, her legs wrapped round his waist, enjoying the softness of her most intimate part pressed down by the hardness that was his.

"Kate. My Kate," he said, not wanting to let her go. And then she let her legs slide from their position and they rolled over onto their sides. He held her face in his hands and kissed her cheeks and nose and lips. "My darling girl. How I love you. I wish tonight would never end. I wish the sun would never rise again."

"But when it does, you'll always have tonight to remember me by," she smiled.

Conrad kissed her hair and held her tightly against his chest.

They didn't touch Sir Herbert's body, but left it lying by the fireside. The constable would take a while to ride from Cheltenham and until he arrived, the door to the parlour was kept locked. Mrs Chambers was told to keep all servants below stairs until further notice and Geraldine had spent some time pacifying Betsy.

"Is my lady unwell?" she wailed. "If she is then I should be with her."

"Lady Fox is downstairs with Sir Herbert," Geraldine lied. "Carry on with your duties and we will tell you when she needs you." Betsy went to the sewing room to do some mending, but she knew that something dire had happened and her lady was involved.

"You're still going through with it?" asked Geraldine. They were now in the drawing room and although the fire burnt brightly, the air seemed cold.

"Yes," Richard nodded. "I have no choice."

Geraldine turned away from him. "Dear Lord, I watched my husband climb the steps to the guillotine. Must I now watch you do the same to the gallows?"

He took her in his arms. "If it comes to that, then I would rather you stayed away."

She shook her head. "Can I assume that our wedding plans are cancelled?"

He smiled, despite himself. "Let's not pre-empt the judge. He might have me transported to the antipodes."

"That being the case, then I will go too."

"Would you?" he frowned. "To the far side of the world?"

She nodded. "I will be where you are." He made to protest. "And don't persuade me otherwise."

Frobisher entered the room. He had taken it upon himself to organise the household and allay the gossip that was already starting to circulate.

"I don't think we can keep this hidden for long," he said sombrely.

Richard and Geraldine turned to him.

"No, we don't think so, either," said Geraldine.

Frobisher had an idea. "When the constable arrives, would you like me to show him into the parlour? I have the key here." He patted his pocket.

"Yes, you do that. And until he does arrive, I think I will go into the study and write a few letters," said Richard.

He walked to the sideboard containing a tray of decanters and poured himself a large brandy, drinking it back in one gulp. They watched him stride to the door and out into the hall.

"I think I can do without days like these," said Geraldine.

"Indeed, ma'am.

She smiled at the bespectacled secretary who had been a tower of strength. "Thank you, Frobisher. I shall be in my room. Please call me when…" She licked her lips and shook her head.

When she had gone, Frobisher went out into the hallway and crossed the floor to the parlour. Smiling to himself, he took the key from his pocket and turning it in the lock, he entered the room and closed the door behind him.

Richard sat at the desk, his pen hovering over a sheet of paper. He wanted to write to Lady Fox and Croston and then there was his lawyer and bank manager to inform. His heart beat wildly at what he was doing. He knew it was the right course of action even though the prospect of swinging from a rope terrified him. His courage failed him and he let out a gasp of horror. Sitting back in his chair he thought of his luggage upstairs in his room. He had brought a pistol with him since every traveller carried some form of weapon, in the event of meeting trouble on the road. He could go upstairs now and take that pistol from its case. He could put the barrel in his mouth and pull the trigger. It would be messy but quick, unlike the hangman's noose.

But then Richard knew that his untimely death might raise questions on its own. No, he had to speak with the constable and admit his guilt. Only then would Lady Fox be safe from any suspicion. He looked around the study. The curtains had not been drawn, since the servants had been sent below stairs and the maid had not had time to complete her tasks. Outside the window, he could see the torches flaring in the wind, but beyond them was utter darkness. This was his stepfather's study where they had had many an argument over Lady Fox. He had wanted Sir Herbert to treat Katherine with utmost respect and never involve her in the activities of either the House of Venus or the folly. But his stepfather had just laughed at him. Now he was dead.

Richard blinked at the brightness of the candles in the candelabra standing on the cabinet. Portraits on the wall glared down at him. Round the fireplace, a similar fender to the one in the parlour and just as highly polished, reflected the dancing flames. For a split second, part of the intricate ironwork seemed to glow as red as blood, but then it vanished. He shuddered and started writing.

Some time later the jingle of the doorbell, brought Frobisher hurrying from the parlour and across the hall to the entrance. He let the two men in, the constable and the physician. The constable was in his middle years, with a stubbled chin and rough complexion, as though he had suffered from smallpox. The physician was Doctor Nichols who had attended Sir Herbert for many years and also treated Katherine when losing her child. Frobisher wasted no time in showing them into the parlour where he closed the door after them.

Richard had heard them come into the house and he smiled ruefully even though his breath had quickened. He tried to control himself as he blotted the ink and sealed the four letters lying on the desk. He was all finished and there was nothing more to do but meet his destiny. He left the study and walked with determined strides, towards the parlour door.

Frobisher was watching the physician examining the body, while the constable stood by waiting for his verdict. They turned when Richard entered the room.

Frobisher gave a half-smile. "This is Lord Haighton. Stepson to the deceased."

The constable raised a hand to the brim of his hat in acknowledgement.

"Sad business this, my lord," he said.

Richard nodded and waited. Geraldine came into the room.

"And this is Mrs Rondelet, Sir Herbert's niece," said Frobisher.

"My condolences ma'am."

The physician rose to his feet and sighed. "Oh, dear. I see this all the time especially at Christmas and the New Year. A gentleman imbibes too much alcohol, decides to revive the fire and stumbles into the blessed thing, often hitting his head on some sharp object. The fender usually, but sometimes the grate. I can't understand why people don't take more care."

"So what do you think, Doctor?" asked the constable.

"Accidental death. Very unfortunate. Very unfortunate, indeed." He snapped his bag shut.

The constable shrugged and turned to Richard. "Where is Lady Fox?"

Geraldine decided to answer for him. "She's upstairs in her room. As you'll understand, this has been very distressing for her."

265

Doctor Nichols seemed alarmed. "Then I must go up and see the dear lady. She might need something to help her sleep."

Geraldine shook her head. "Oh, no, she's sleeping now. The housekeeper gave her something to help her rest. She mustn't be disturbed."

The constable rubbed his chin. "May I ask who found Sir Herbert?"

Worried that he might be getting suspicious, when everything had been going so well, Frobisher said, "I did. I came in and discovered him like this. I could see he was dead immediately. And I summoned his lordship and Mrs Rondelet."

"You are the only guests of Sir Herbert and Lady Fox?" said the constable. They both affirmed it. He grunted. "Very well, we shall leave it as it is and may I again, offer my condolences. If I was you, I would get some footmen to carry the...Sir Herbert upstairs and make preparations. If you know what I mean?"

Doctor Nichols bowed his head in sympathy and stunned, Richard simply nodded. Geraldine looked blankly at them as she watched Frobisher show the two men out.

Alone together, Geraldine slipped closer to Richard who put his arm round her.

"Sweet Jesus, I thought we were done for when the physician asked to see Katherine," said Richard, blowing out a relieved breath.

Frowning, he took a step forward in order to examine the body more closely and realised it had been moved. Instead of being on its side, it was now on its stomach, the head turned so that the deep gash in the temple was against the bloodied fender. The right arm was stretched out, the hand clutching the ivory handle of the poker, its tip plunged deep into the fire. To the left of the body was a broken glass, its contents spilt over the carpet and mingling with the blood.

Frobisher came back in. "Well, I think they were satisfied."

Richard spun on his heel. "What the blazes did you do?"

He smiled. "Rearranged the scene to look more, what shall I call it? More reasonable."

"You made it look like an accident?"

Frobisher's smile broadened. "Nothing easier. Just a little adjustment here and there. Not to mention removing the evidence of the weapon. The flames would have scorched the blood on the tip of the poker."

Richard walked round the body of his stepfather. "You made it look as though he had been drinking?"

"Poured a little brandy into his mouth." He sighed. "Thankfully the pool of blood was big enough to hide the fact that his body had been moved."

Geraldine had been unable to speak, but gave a cry of delight. She clutched Richard's coat and hung onto him.

"I was preparing myself for losing you."

Richard nodded. "Lord knows what I was preparing myself for." He sighed with relief. "Frobisher, you are a man to be reckoned with."

Frobisher smiled. "May I suggest, my lord, that I organise two footmen to carry Sir Herbert up to his room? And then perhaps the parlour maid could be given the unenviable task of cleaning the fireplace and removing the rug?"

"Yes, indeed. Do it, Frobisher."

"And then we must hope that Lord Croston has found Lady Fox and is bringing her home."

Geraldine had remained silent, clinging onto Richard as though she was afraid to let him go. But Frobisher's last comments caught her attention.

"Do you think his lordship has found Katherine?" she asked.

Richard nodded. "If he had failed, I'm sure he would have returned by now. What of it? We will have some wonderful news for them when they do return."

Geraldine wasn't pacified and her face creased into a worried frown. "If he has found her then chances are he has told her about your intentions, to admit guilt in her place. And if she has been told that...!" Her eyes opened wide in horror. "Katherine won't accept it, not for one minute. She'll never allow an innocent man die for something she has done. She'll want to confess. She'll demand that his lordship take her to the nearest Justice of the Peace so that she can give herself up."

Frobisher became alarmed. "If that's the case, my lord, then our good fortune tonight will have been for nothing. For Lady Fox will tell them everything and they will not doubt her word. She'll be arrested and charged."

"We must find them immediately," said Richard.

"It will be difficult in the dark," said Frobisher.

"Even so, we must try. For if we are too late then it's the scaffold for Lady Fox and prison for us."

It didn't take long to don their outdoor clothing and have their horses saddled. Before he turned his horse's head, Richard stooped down and cupped Geraldine's face with his free hand, pressing his lips on hers.

"We shall be back before you know it."

And then they were galloping down the drive.

"Please find them," she cried. "And bring them safely home."

But she knew they hadn't heard. Her voice had been carried away by the wind that moaned through the branches of the birch trees that bordered the drive.

It was Conrad who first awoke. As he brushed the sleep from his eyes and looked about him, he was aware that it must be early in the morning. He guessed the time at being about seven o'clock as the inside of the wagon was cast in the indistinct shadows that occur just before the sun rises. He raised himself up on one elbow, amazed that not only had they fitted in such a small bed but also that they had slept well. He was also aware that the blanket and their cloaks that covered them were hiding the fact that they were naked. Conrad smiled as he remembered the previous night and the intense joy of their lovemaking. And then his smile faded as he also remembered that he had promised to accompany Katherine to Cheltenham, just three miles away.

He touched the sleeping woman next to him, if only to reassure himself that she was there and it hadn't been a dream. He looked about him and saw the trappings associated with life in a gypsy camp. Never would he have imagined sheltering amongst them and asking for their help.

Katherine sighed in her sleep and turned over away from him. He put his arms round her drawing her closer, moving her golden hair away from her neck and kissing the tender skin below her ear. The minutes ticked away and peace enveloped them. A peace so deep it seemed that there was no one else left in the world to trouble them. Gradually, the sun rose above the hills and the shimmering light filtered through the opening in the sailcloth.

He rolled off the bed and pulled on his clothes and then slipped through the flap to the ground. It was going to be a cold day, the stormy winds having moved away. The camp was already awake and women were cooking round a large fire. The comings and goings of the camp fascinated him, since everyone seemed to have work to do.

An old woman approached him. "You slept well, my lord?"

He smiled. "Yes, thank you. And thank you for giving up your home for us."

"I'm pleased it suited you," she nodded. She pointed over to one side. "There's a stream yonder, as cold as ice, but you'll be able to freshen up." She handed him a coarse towel and a small piece of soap. "My son can loan you a razor, if you wish to make yourself presentable." Conrad chuckled, knowing he must look like a vagabond with his unkempt look and stubbled chin. "And then a bite to eat won't go amiss, I'm sure."

"I'm certainly hungry." He looked over to the wagon. "My lady?"

"I will deal with her, my lord."

He found the stream and stripped before washing. As he struggled with trying to shave in cold water, he wondered if Katherine would agree to return to Westcroft. It was only a matter of a mile away and then the constable could be summoned to the house. The servants' tongues would wag, but he was sure that he could persuade the constable to be discreet and take Katherine into custody with all due correctness. He shivered with the cold and the fear that coursed through him.

In the wagon, Katherine rolled onto her back, trying to remember where she was.

"Come on, my lady. Time to rise."

She stared at the old woman standing over her. "Morning did come after all," she sighed.

"As it always does. I've brought you some water."

"Where's Con...Lord Croston?" she said, feeling alarmed.

"He's making himself presentable, as you must do. I've heated your water, unlike his lordship, who must wash in an icy stream."

Katherine couldn't help laughing and sat up, dragging her fingers through her hair. Swinging her legs over the edge of the mattress, she blushed realising she was naked. She glanced at Orana, but the gypsy seemed busy placing a comb and other toiletries by the bowl of water.

"Yes, I must make myself respectable."

"You intend to give yourself up?"

Katherine began to wash herself with a small scrap of rag and even tinier piece of soap. "I've made my decision."

The old woman sat down on the stool. "Did you tell his lordship everything?"

"Yes, everything. He knows that I killed my husband. My husband's stepson, Lord Haighton, intends to admit guilt. But I can't let him to do that. Today, I will do what I must."

"And face the consequences?"

Katherine nodded. "Yes and face the consequences."

Orana patted her arm, her expression sombre. "Now, I shall leave you to complete your washing and then come outside for something to eat."

Katherine finished washing and then pulled the comb through her tangled curls. Discovering a small tray containing buttons and ribbons, she selected a ribbon and tied her hair back. She dressed and then jumped down from the wagon.

Eyes momentarily turned towards her and her cheeks flushed scarlet. She felt relieved when Conrad came striding towards her.

He looked anxious as he took her in his arms and kissed the tip of her nose.

271

"Kate, my darling. We are invited to breakfast, but before we go, I must ask you to think on what I suggested last night. I've been talking to the leader of this band and he is very happy to take us to Gloucester. We could remain quite hidden and no one will suspect that we are here."

She returned his kiss. "No, Conrad. I'm resolved to help Richard."

Shame washed over him. "You're so determined. And, of course, you're right, Haighton shouldn't take the blame, despite his hand in all this." He pressed her close to him. "Then I must ask you one thing." He took in a calming breath. "Let me tell them that I did it. I can say I lost my temper with Sir Herbert. I'll say anything, only let me go in your place."

"I know you would do that," she said, staring up into intense violet eyes. "And I love you for it, but do you think I could live the rest of my life knowing that I hadn't faced the truth?"

He couldn't answer and was relieved when a voice called them to eat. They sat beside the huge fire and were given slices of bread with fried bacon. A large tin mug of coffee was also offered and for a short while, they forgot what they were about to do and enjoyed the simple pleasure of eating good food in excellent company.

They broke camp as soon as they had eaten and everything had been packed away. And then the line of wagons, carts and packhorses started on their journey towards Cheltenham. Katherine sat next to Orana while Conrad rode Midnight and kept pace with them. They travelled in silence, Conrad hoping that Katherine would change her mind and decide to stay with the gypsy band and go on to Gloucester as he wished. But then the spire of Saint Mary's came into sight and he knew that hope was fading fast.

The sound of shouts and thundering hooves made Patrick bring the train to a halt. Raising his hand, he pulled out the pistol tucked in his belt.

"Two men, riding fast," he said, shielding his eyes from the glaring sun. "Might be nothing, but better to be cautious."

Conrad too, looked in the direction of the riders and then he recognised them.

"Dear God, it's Haighton and Frobisher. How is this possible?" He jumped down from the horse and went to meet them.

Katherine watched in amazement that Lord Haighton was a free man and his peel of laughter at finding them told her that he could only be bringing good news. She saw them climb from the saddle and then become engrossed in earnest conversation with Conrad.

After only a few minutes, Conrad came to help her down. "Everything has turned out well," he grinned with delight. "The constable and physician accepted the entire situation as a tragic accident."

"How?" she said.

"I'll let Frobisher explain that. But for now, we must go home."

Patrick came to find out what had happened. "Is anything amiss, my lord?"

Conrad smiled. "Nothing whatsoever." He glanced about him. "For your kindness, you must feel free to camp on my estates whenever you are passing. I will inform my gamekeeper that you have the right to collect firewood and shoot game as you wish."

"Thank you, my lord."

Conrad kissed Katherine's hand. "It looks like our time with the gypsies is over."

She gave a half-smile and placed her hands on his chest and curled her fingers round the lapels of his coat.

"The authorities don't suspect me?" The sudden change in events left her breathless, every muscle in her body aching with tension.

"Not at all. But we must get you home."

He sprang up onto Midnight's back and then leaned down to lift Katherine up behind him. She wrapped her arms round his waist, holding him close. And then Conrad urged Midnight forward and Katherine held on tightly to the man she loved. And suddenly the world was beautiful and life was wonderful. And she didn't want to be anywhere else but there with him.

CHAPTER THIRTEEN

They arrived back at Westcroft within twenty minutes and Katherine was told what had happened. Lord Haighton and Frobisher had spent two hours searching for them the previous night, but had had to give up. As soon as dawn broke, they were in the saddle once more and by chance had decided to search along the Cheltenham road. There they saw the gypsy train and Midnight with Conrad sitting astride him.

When she arrived home, Katherine went upstairs to see her husband. She was shocked at his appearance, so cold and white with a dressing across his temple and then the horror of what she had done swept through her causing her to shudder.

"Oh, God," she whispered. "I did this." She went to his bedside and sat down on a chair feeling numb. The minutes ticked away until she leaned forward and took his hand. "I'm sorry, Herbert. I never meant to do this, but I was so afraid of you."

Sir Herbert's funeral took place three days later. Very few mourners attended the ceremony, just close family and friends. It seemed that Sir Herbert was widely disliked and Katherine wondered how many folk raised their glasses at his passing, not with sadness but with relief. And finally the coffin was carried to the cemetery where he was laid to rest in a solitary corner next to his previous wives.

Katherine wore a veil throughout the service, to hide the fact she couldn't shed one tear for her husband. She knew that the congregation might accept this as courage through grief, but Katherine feared that her lack of emotion for the death of her husband might give rise to suspicion. She sat quietly and listened to the vicar as he spoke highly of Sir Herbert and yet the words seemed hollow and echoed around the church like a lost soul in torment.

The day after the funeral, Mr Newton came to read the will. Everyone had gathered in the dining room so that the lawyer could lay his papers out in a correct and tidy manner. Mr Newton was a fastidious man and liked to be precise in his details. He spread the documents before him and after a few seconds of organising them, he took off his glasses and cleaned them on a cloth he kept for that purpose. He was a small, squat man with an impressive wig perched on a rather large head, but his eyes were a remarkable blue and twinkled as though he had just heard a good joke.

The conversation subsided as they saw he was ready to start. Katherine sat next to Conrad, who she had insisted attend also, along with Geraldine and Lord Haighton. Most of the main servants were present, the housekeeper, cook and valet, as well as a few members of the outdoor staff including Mr Knapp, the estate manager and Mr Peacock, the gamekeeper.

Mr Newton cleared his throat. "I, Sir Herbert Fox, being of sound mind…." The lawyer continued until he said, "Sir Herbert signed this will on the first day of April 1799." Katherine smiled realising this was a month before they married. "Sir Herbert has left a few bequests." The lawyer then went on to cite the minor ones before coming to the main ones. He then asked that the servants could be dismissed so that he could read the major part of the will. Katherine nodded and they all filed out and went straight to the servants' parlour to tell everyone what had happened. The lawyer continued. "The next part is very much straightforward. Your husband, Sir Herbert, leaves an annual income of one thousand pounds to his niece, Mrs Geraldine Rondelet and a legacy of five hundred pounds to his stepson, Lord Haighton. But the rest of his fortune, which I must say is quite substantial since not only does it include the proceeds from monies invested in stocks and shares and deposited in the bank, but also this house and its grounds, the stables, horses and all vehicles, everything appertaining to the estate including woodlands, farmlands and dairy, plus his townhouse in Cheltenham goes to, and here I must quote, 'to my dear wife, Katherine'. And if they are agreeable, my stepson and Lord Croston should act as trustees."

A stunned silence filled the room and Katherine stayed motionless. What she had heard seemed impossible. She expected Sir Herbert to leave her penniless. But then why should he?

Geraldine reached across and gripped her hand. "Oh, my dear, you are going to be one of the wealthiest women in the county. Your future can only be happy."

Katherine wondered if happiness was possible. What would her life be like now she had brought her husband's life to an end? That terrible knowledge would be with her always, no matter where she went or what she did.

After the reading of the will, Richard explained his part in her kidnapping, since now Katherine felt strong enough to hear the details. Sitting in the parlour, he told her everything, his large brown eyes full of sorrow. And he asked forgiveness. She could not believe that this quiet spoken man, had been the very one who had manhandled her and frightened her beyond belief.

There was a question Katherine had to ask. "Would you have really shot me in the head, if I had turned round?"

A gasp from Geraldine made him flinch.

"No, I would never have hurt you. How could I have hurt you?"

Conrad spoke up, his expression dark. "Good God, Haighton, I never thought you were capable of such things."

Richard closed his eyes for a moment. "Neither did I." His eyes shone with tears. "The money I owed my stepfather was vast, but I could have paid it off given time or I could have handed over my entire house and estates to him. I bitterly regret not turning my back on the whole terrible incident." He took Katherine's hand. "All I can say it that I'm truly sorry."

Katherine looked down at Richard's strong hand clutching hers. "It's not just I that suffered. My poor Aunt Sybil never recovered from the shock of finding me missing."

Richard nodded. "When I accompanied you to Bristol and met her, I was filled with overwhelming shame. I had a mind to help her if I could. But I was too late."

"I forgive you," smiled Katherine. "Please, let's put it all behind us now and live our lives happily."

Conrad was hosting a supper party at his townhouse with Katherine, Geraldine and Richard his only guests. It was February and the rain seemed continuous, causing grey days to blend into nights with very little sun to be seen.

It was at the end of the meal, that Richard decided to tell Katherine the news he had heard that day.

Frowning, he leaned forward in his seat. "I've talked this over with Geraldine and Croston and they're in agreement that you should know the circumstances of these last twenty-four hours."

Katherine turned startled eyes on him. "Goodness, this sounds serious. What has happened?"

"I've brought grievous news, although whether you'll think it grievous I have yet to find out. Last night Mrs Percy died."

"That women is dead?" she asked, not hiding her feelings.

Richard licked his lips. "And I'm to blame." His next words came almost apologetically. "You know of course, that my stepfather owned the business?" She nodded. "In his will, he bequeathed the House of Venus to me, only Mr Newton failed to mention Sir Herbert's *other interests* when reading the will. It was not for the ears of a lady."

Katherine gave a scornful laugh. "Little did Mr Newton know how I had suffered at the hands of my dear husband's *other interests.*"

"Indeed, he did not. However, I was in the process of selling the house and I had given Mrs Percy notice to leave and take her girls with her. I didn't want anything to do with them."

"So she left the house?"

"No, she did not! So, I gave her an ultimatum. Leave the premises willingly or be thrown out. She still refused so I sent my men to turf her into the street. I'm afraid Mrs Percy ran to fetch her money and jewels. In her haste she knocked over a candle and set fire to her gown. She went up in flames."

Katherine grimaced. "What a horrible way to die."

"Well deserved, I say," said Conrad and Geraldine nodded in agreement.

Richard ignored them. "Yes, it is a horrible way to die and I regret that incident, but now the girls are gone."

"And you and Geraldine can get on with your lives," said Katherine.

Richard smiled. "Indeed, and it's Italy for us."

Geraldine joined in. "Oh, yes, Italy. We intend travelling in May and when this period of mourning is over we will marry. I am so sick of England and its rain. I never want to see this country again." She reached out and squeezed Katherine's hand. "My only regret is leaving you."

Katherine's life became almost hedonistic after that. It seemed that all the evil in her life had been destroyed and only the good remained. She had taken on the full responsibility for the servants, workers and estate and there was plenty to keep her occupied. As she looked across the fertile fields that would harvest the rye and barley she swelled with pride. The milk yield was excellent and her dairy was producing good quality cheese, cream and butter. The estate was making more money than ever.

And then there was her time spent with Conrad. She found she couldn't express the joy she felt when in his company. But it was on the dark, cold evenings when they sat together by the fire, that she most enjoyed. Then they would toast crumpets with a long handled brass fork and spread it with butter from Katherine's own dairy. When they went to bed, their nights were filled with excitement as they tried to muffle their laughter while scrambling under the bedcovers, wrapping their limbs round each other and showering each other with warm tender kisses.

She had always found him a considerate lover, and except for their first time when caution had been thrown to the wind in the exhilarating passion of being together, he had agreed with her that a child would be out of the question under their present circumstances. Since she was innocent in these matters, he had introduced her to the method of withdrawing from her before the critical moment; a manner that amazed her and added to her deep respect and love for him.

However, this necessity plus the need to be discreet annoyed Conrad. He hated the hypocrisy and social conventions that restricted their happiness.

"I'm impatient, Kate," he told her one day. "I want you to be my countess and walk by my side in the sunlight, as my wife."

She reached up to kiss him. "I know, my darling. And one day I will. But until then we must obey the rules and stay in mourning for twelve months."

Spring arrived spreading its glory across the fields. Riding Midnight around the estate, she would often stop to pick wildflowers. Her hands brimming with primroses and bluebells that carpeted the woodlands, she would look across the meadow to where the folly had once stood. There was no evidence of it now; the stones used to mend a wall. And as she gazed about her, she took in big breaths of sweet air, overcome with a feeling of wonder and gratifying peace.

And on the first anniversary of her wedding, she visited Sir Herbert and placed a large bunch of bluebells on his grave. She kneeled beside the headstone and for the hundredth time asked his forgiveness. For now she was so extraordinarily happy, she suddenly had an overwhelming feeling that she did not deserve such happiness.

Even so, the next two months continued to be idyllic. Contrary to Geraldine's opinion, each day dawned a perfect summer's day, the meadow ablaze with foxgloves and poppies. Sometimes Katherine would spend them at the Court or Conrad would come to

Westcroft and they would picnic by the river. And after they had eaten, Katherine sat on a blanket under a tree, reading to Conrad with his head on her lap.

It was when she travelled to her townhouse in early July she decided to invite her family to spend the summer with her. The noise of their arrival and the hustle and bustle of trunks and bags being unloaded from the coach filled her with delight. Aunt Beatrice's sharp commands to the footmen to be careful with her hatboxes and Uncle George's firm instructions made her smile.

Her grandmother greeted her with open arms and her aunt and uncle kissed her warmly, commenting on her complexion.

"You're too brown, Katherine," said her uncle. "People will think you're a farm girl."

"Have you been putting plenty of lotion on your skin?" said her aunt.

"Yes, Aunt. But I've been riding around the estate a great deal and I often forget how long I'm outside."

"Have Lord Haighton and Mrs Rondelet set off for Italy?" said Sebastian. He was nearly seventeen and had grown as tall as his cousin. "That's where I intend to go on my Grand Tour. I want to be introduced to the Italian maidens."

"I've heard they're very beautiful in a dark and sensual way," she teased him. "You'll have to behave yourself. And you'll have to wait for the end of the war. You can't go gallivanting round Europe with armies still on the march."

Sebastian grimaced. "Bonaparte won't last much longer." His expression became distant as he imagined his future. "Yes, Italy will be my first port of call."

His mother clicked her tongue. "You have Oxford first, young man. And if you don't do well there, then I doubt your father will finance a jaunt on the Continent."

Uncle George chuckled, but then took Katherine's hand. "I'm expecting to take you up the aisle again soon. Have you and Lord Croston named the day yet?"

"Yes, where is he? I thought he would have been here to greet us," said her aunt.

Katherine smiled. "He'll be here shortly. He said he didn't want to get in your way while you settled in. And no, we haven't set a date yet, but we will soon and my family will be the first to know."

In fact, Conrad had been attempting to set a date for their wedding for some time, suggesting January or February, as soon as the twelve months of mourning was over. But for some strange reason, Katherine couldn't bring herself to settle on a date. Perhaps it was guilt or shame but the happiness she had felt that summer was turning on her. Conrad never spoke of her husband's death, or the manner of his death and Katherine knew the reasons behind this. He loved her so very much that he didn't want to hurt her by mentioning the subject. But for Katherine, it was becoming increasingly difficult to brush it under the carpet.

Katherine and Conrad stood in the garden at the rear of the house watching the sun setting. She had clung onto him and cried against his jacket, as he held her close. Why she had burst into tears she didn't know. His news that he had to visit Lady Sarah in Worcester since he had received word that she was seriously ill had unsettled her. Lady Sarah was Conrad's aunt and last surviving relative on his father's side and it was at Lady Sarah's ball that he and Philippa had first danced. Perhaps it was thoughts of Philippa that set her nerves on edge, or simply that Conrad had to leave her for a short time.

"You'll never be happy, my Kate, if you don't put the past into the past," he said, trying to soothe her.

"How can I? Oh, Conrad, I've been so happy this year. It's been a perfect year, but I feel a charlatan for being so happy."

"It's foolish to think like that. Let's set a date and then we can look to the future. You'll have a wedding to plan." He chucked her under the chin. "My new countess."

She sniffed with disdain. "Yes, the Countess of Lies, the Countess of Deception. That should be my true title."

"Don't be ridiculous. I'll not have you talk like this, Kate."

She turned away from him and watched two magpies squabbling over a tasty beetle.

"I'm a murderess," she said quietly. She glanced over her shoulder at him, her chin held defiantly. "There you are, I've said it. I'm a murderess and do you want that kind of woman as your wife? As the mother of your children?"

He put his arms round her. "You're the woman I love. You seem to forget that I know everything about you and I accept what I know about you. Can't you take that on trust? Can't you believe that I love you and nothing else matters?"

"Perhaps I have bad blood. Perhaps I was born with murderous tendencies."

"What utter nonsense are you saying now?"

She knew she was becoming hysterical, but she couldn't stop herself. "But I feel I should atone for my crime."

"Kate, you have cared for the servants and looked after the estate better than anyone. What more can be asked of you?" She shook her head in answer and he sighed in exasperation. "While I'm gone, wear sackcloth and ashes if you must, but please believe that you are a good person and always will be."

Katherine felt desolate when Conrad left for Worcester. He was worried about his aunt and now she had placed a further burden on him. Why couldn't she be happy? Why was she spoiling everything they had? And then anger consumed her. Sir Herbert had treated her abominably and although she shouldn't have ended his life, she knew that part of the attack had been in self-defence. She must put it all in the past if she was to have any hope of a life with Conrad.

She decided to pull herself together. When Conrad returned she would set a date for their wedding and she would be happy. To reinforce this idea she and her aunt went to the dressmaker and ordered her wedding gown. After a great deal of deliberation it was decided it would be of pale blue taffeta with silver thread round the bodice, sleeves and hem. Simple in design and loose fitting from the bosom, she decided that she would wear a bonnet of the same colour.

Even so, Katherine felt lonely over the next few weeks. She looked out for a letter from Conrad and when one arrived saying his aunt had recovered from her illness and he would be home shortly, her spirits lifted.

It was early September and the beautiful weather had disappeared. Katherine was sitting by the window watching the rain bounce off the cobbles and lash relentlessly down the windowpanes, when a coach pulled up. Her heart beat faster as she jumped to her feet. It must be Conrad. No other visitor was expected. She rushed to the door as the footman was showing the visitor in. Her heart plummeted when she saw it was Mr Newton, her lawyer.

She hadn't seen Mr Newton since the reading of her husband's will and his visit came as a surprise. He flung off his coat and hat and gave it to the footman and she noticed his ashen complexion, as he chewed his lip. Mr Newton, usually so calm and efficient, was in a high state of anxiety. He tucked a folder of papers under his arm.

"My dear lady. I had to come immediately."

"Is there a problem, Mr Newton?"

"There certainly is."

She pointed to the door of the parlour where her aunt, uncle and grandmother were spending a quiet afternoon round the fire.

"Is it confidential, Mr Newton?" she asked. "Would you mind if my family stayed to listen?"

"As you wish, my lady."

They entered the room and Katherine announced his arrival. She offered him a seat and he sat down heavily. Katherine smiled at him.

Mr Newton opened the folder. He glanced across at the beautiful woman in the black and white mourning gown and winced. She looked vivacious, but there again, the rumours that she was to marry Lord Croston, would make her so. How sad that he had to bring such terrible information.

"What on earth is the matter, Mr Newton?" she grinned, seeing his hands shaking.

"I think the good lawyer needs a brandy," said Uncle George, gesturing to the footman.

"That will do for me, although I don't usually take alcohol until the evening."

"Then, this must be grievous," Katherine murmured. "You had better get on with it and put your mind and ours at rest."

He shook his head. "Lady Fox, what I have to say is most distressing and I must apologise for the unutterable negligence of my establishment."

She glanced at her uncle, who had taken a seat next to her. "Then take courage, sir and tell it as it is."

Mr Newton wiped his perspiring forehead with his handkerchief.

"Your husband, Sir Herbert, left a will as you know and I read it to you after he was laid to rest." Katherine nodded, feeling puzzled. The lawyer coughed and again wiped his forehead. "Before I continue, Lady Fox, I must say something in my defence. When Sir Herbert called me to Westcroft to include a codicil in his will, I was not able to attend him. In fact, I was ill at the time, so my late brother dealt with it."

Katherine sucked in a breath. "A codicil?"

He nodded. "And if I had been present, I would have advised him against it, but it seems my dearly departed brother did no such thing." Mr Newton clicked his tongue. "To make matters worse, my clerk filed the codicil with the will for a certain Mrs Herbert, would you believe."

"The Mrs Herbert who died last week?"

"The very one. And when I went to find her will, what did I discover, but the codicil to Sir Herbert's will tucked amongst the papers. I was beside myself and I've dismissed the clerk forthwith."

"Read the codicil, if you please," said Katherine, wondering what was coming next.

Mr Newton cleared his throat. "The codicil is dated the thirty-first day of October 1799." Katherine thought this over. That was when she had travelled to Croston Court to be with Philippa. When she had escaped her husband's plans to 'entertain' in the folly. How ironic she thought, that the main will should be written on All Fool's Day and the codicil on All Hallows Eve, when witches and warlocks filled the night air on their broomsticks and good, Christian folk stayed behind closed doors. She brought her attention back to the lawyer. Mr Newton had paused as if he was in an enormous struggle with himself. "The codicil states that the will must stand as it is...providing Lady Fox does not marry..." the lawyer wiped his mouth with his handkerchief. "...for an interval of twenty years from the date of Sir Herbert's death. In other words, my lady, providing you stay unmarried until the year 1819, you will remain a very wealthy woman. But if you should enter into marriage during that time, you will forfeit everything and it will revert to Sir Herbert's niece, Mrs Geraldine Rondelet."

Her uncle frowned. "That is disgraceful," he cried. "Surely it can't be legal?"

"I'm afraid it is, my lord."

"Are you telling us that my niece must remain on her own at the risk of losing *everything*."

"For the next twenty years," he said, his face flushed with embarrassment. "Or more exactly, nineteen, since twelve months have almost elapsed."

"But Katherine is planning to marry Lord Croston," said her aunt.

"That's why I came as fast as I could," said Mr Newton.

"Oh, he's gone too far, that husband of yours," said her grandmother, who had remained silent up to that point. "Even from the grave he's ruining your life, stopping you from being happy. Did he really want you to spend your days alone, the vindictive old goat."

Katherine squeezed her hand.

Mr Newton gathered his papers together. "Lady Fox, I must give you my sincerest apologies. My firm has been very negligent and I really am quite distressed over it."

Katherine sighed. "It's done now, Mr Newton. I suppose it's an honest mistake."

"You know what it is," said her uncle, trying to calm his temper. "Sir Herbert knew that a young and beautiful widow, with a substantial fortune, would soon have admirers knocking on her door."

Aunt Beatrice nodded. "Yes, I agree. And by making her wait twenty years, he knew that by that time her youth and beauty will have faded."

Katherine's grandmother shook her head. "Not, my granddaughter. She might be twenty years older, but I wager she'll be just as beautiful. But what to do about it?" She turned to the lawyer. "Can anything be done? Could we not see a judge and have the codicil disputed?"

"I can but try," said Mr Newton. "But I really think it might be a lost cause."

Katherine remained quiet, letting the family debate over her head. What would Conrad say when he returned? He believed he was marrying a wealthy woman but she would forfeit everything if they married. As far as she was concerned, losing her fortune would not be so terrible, since she knew that the guilt at her husband's death was partially because he had left her such wealth. With her fortune gone, she would be free of Sir Herbert.

Mr Newton broke into her thoughts, coughing nervously. "I also have news about Lord Croston's secretary."

"Mr Frobisher?" said Katherine, feeling bewildered.

"It happened only a matter of hours ago, so the news is still relatively new. It's bad business, my lady. He's been arrested and charged with murder. It seems new evidence has come to light concerning Sir Herbert's death."

Katherine felt her mouth drying and licked her lips. "What new evidence?"

"You would have to speak to Mr Osborne about that." He sighed. "Yes, the poor man is languishing in gaol at this very moment. If he's found guilty, then it's the gallows for him."

CHAPTER FOURTEEN

Conrad had travelled to Worcester alone, leaving Frobisher and Anne to enjoy a short holiday together at Marlborough Cottage. Her husband's arrest spurred Anne into travelling to Cheltenham immediately to ask for help from the only person she knew could help. Lady Fox.

"Oh, my lady. What am I to do? Poor Edgar charged with murder? It's impossible, he couldn't have done it."

Katherine tried to pacify her and sat next to her in the parlour, holding her hand. The discussion of the details filled Anne with dread and Katherine with despair. It seemed that Doctor Nichols had suddenly had second thoughts about the accident suffered by Sir Herbert. It had occurred to him when he had been binding the hand of a valet who had inadvertently picked up his master's razor by the blade and sliced a deep gash in his thumb. The valet had made a joke that he would be hampered somewhat in playing cards and would have to use his left hand instead of his right.

Doctor Nichols had pondered on this for some time, until finally the awful truth had dawned on him. Sir Herbert had come by his accident after slipping and hitting his head on the fender whilst attempting to revive the fire. His hand on the poker handle signified that. But he was using his right hand and since Sir Herbert was left-handed, it should have been his left hand and not his right holding the poker.

At the end of the discussion, they all looked at Anne, who had turned a ghastly shade of grey.

"But Sir Herbert was also holding a glass of brandy," queried Katherine's uncle. "So, would that not have been in his left hand?"

Katherine's grandmother shook her head. "No, reviving the fire takes strength and a person always uses their strongest hand, that is, the one used naturally."

"But why has Mr Frobisher been arrested?" said Katherine thickly.

Her uncle grimaced. "I suppose because he said that he found the body and only he had the opportunity to rearrange Sir Herbert so that it looked like an accident."

"No. No, I will never believe that," wailed Anne. "Not my Edgar."

Katherine's heart beat wildly. "But he would have nothing to gain. Why would he want my husband dead?" Her family couldn't answer her. She nodded adamantly. "I will visit Mr Osborne as soon as possible. I've heard he's a good legal man." She turned to Anne. "I'll sort out this mess, don't you concern yourself. Your husband will be released from prison if I have any say in it."

She visited the lawyer the following morning. Tall and wiry, he seemed to tower over her as he bent to kiss her hand.

"Lady Fox. I'm not at all surprised to see you at my door. You will want to know what is happening, surely?"

Katherine glanced around his office, strewn with legal books, piles of documents, bits of paper, pens and inkwells. There were two small windows and the sun that came through, caught the dust motes in its rays. A fire burnt in the grate and sometimes the smoke would billow out as the wind howled down the chimney.

"Yes, Mr Osborne. Since this concerns my husband's death, then I feel I have the right to know why the law has brought charges against Mr Frobisher," she said.

The lawyer seemed taken aback by her sharp tone. "Because, my lady, the physician, in this case Doctor Nichols, has reason to believe that your husband did not die accidentally, but by malice aforethought."

"I've already been informed of the opinions of Doctor Nichols and it's all nonsense. What has Mr Frobisher to say?"

Mr Osborne shuffled the papers on his desk and looked uncomfortable.

"He says that he did not murder Sir Herbert and that it was an accident as Doctor Nichols first surmised."

"He's pleading not guilty?" said Katherine, relieved. For one dreadful moment she thought that Frobisher was admitting guilt. "What does that mean?"

"He will go to trial and let a jury decide his guilt or innocence."

After Katherine left the lawyer's office, she went to see Frobisher. Never in all her life had she been in a prison, not even a small lockup such as the one in Cheltenham where prisoners were detained until being transferred to the prison in Gloucester to await trial. The main door in the courtyard led into a small office and through another door made of solid oak with large iron hinges and locks, was a high vaulted room. As the constable pulled the door open, Katherine shrank back from the smell that made her want to retch. A shackled Frobisher was called forward and led to an old and very scratched table in the corner of the office. The constable found a second chair for Katherine. She sat down, horrified by Frobisher's appearance. His eyes were dark and sunken; his chin covered with stubble and his clothes crumpled and dirty.

He struggled to sit. "How k...kind of you to visit m...me, my lady. I fear I'm in n...no state to receive visitors."

His distress broke her heart. "I had to come, Frobisher. And you know why," she said, keeping her voice low.

"It's n...not so uncomfortable," he said, trying to calm himself. He pointed at the door through which he had just come. "There's seventeen of us in there, so it's a bit cramped at the moment. But they are taking me to Gloucester this afternoon. I have a letter for Anne. Would you take it to her, my lady?"

She nodded and then took in a breath. "The constable has told me that you're allowed a few little comforts. I will ask Anne to bring you fresh clothes and soap and a razor. At least you'll be able to stay clean."

"I want my wife to stay away, begging your pardon, my lady."

"This is no time to play the gallant husband...or the courageous servant." She stared down at her gloved hands. "Why didn't you tell them the truth?"

He smiled ruefully. "I wouldn't do that. That would be disloyal. Besides, I'm confident I will be found not guilty."

"Anne is not so sure."

"I know my Anne will understand what I'm doing. I owe his lordship a great deal and I have a debt of gratitude to pay him and therefore, you."

"You're doing this for his lordship?"

Frobisher nodded. "I could tell them that you did the deed. But, firstly, I don't think they would believe me. I'm only a servant while you are a lady. Secondly, if you were locked in that cell yonder instead of me, then his lordship might lose you and I would have to watch his pain for the rest of my life."

"What about your wife's pain?"

"I know that his lordship will take care of my Anne, as I've taken care of you."

Katherine came out into the street feeling sick with guilt. An innocent man will go to trial, for something I did, she thought. There was a time when she was ready to give herself up to the authorities, when she had had no hope and it didn't seem to matter what happened to her. But now that had changed. So much had happened, she had loved and been loved and now she felt so afraid.

"I don't want to die," she whispered.

Saint Mary's started striking midday. She looked up at the grey clouds racing across the sky and pushed her hands into the sable muff. It had grown cold for September. There seemed to be people everywhere. She walked slowly, passing gentlemen on their way to their clubs and tradesmen standing in shop doorways. She passed a wagon being unloaded with sacks of flour and then she turned the corner. A brisk wind blew up and dust swirled around her causing her to blink.

Suddenly, two soldiers very much the worse for drink, darted round the corner, prancing about and singing a vulgar song. Seeing the lovely lady in a black cloak and white sable muff, they caught hold of her arms and took turns in dancing with her. In a very short time she was spinning dizzily from one to the other. And then she lost her balance and was flung into the arms of someone walking behind them. The joviality stopped immediately.

"On your way, boys," said the gentleman. The young soldiers stared at him, looked at each other and then back at the lady, before shrugging indifferently and continuing on their drunken way. Katherine remained motionless and then opened her mouth to speak, but no words came out. Conrad took her hand and raised it to his lips kissing her fingers, smiling down at her. "So, my lady. Where are you going?"

It was then she realised she was on the corner of Saint George's Place and Conrad's home was in sight. He must have left the house just minutes before.

"I felt like a walk. When did you arrive back?"

"Late last night." He glanced around. "I was coming to invite you and your family to dine. Come, let's take a stroll in the park."

Katherine took his arm and a shiver ran through her that had nothing to do with the chilly weather.

"I'm so pleased you're home. I've missed you."

He took in a deep breath. "And I've missed you. I made sure that my aunt was well on the road to recovery and then came as soon as possible."

"You know about Frobisher?"

"Yes, I do. The housekeeper told me everything as soon as I returned."

"He intends to do the same as Richard. To take the blame in my place."

"Yes, I know. As soon as I heard the news, I went to see him. He believes he'll be found not guilty, but I doubt it." He added in a whisper, "I know I should help him, but I can't bear to lose you."

She gripped his arm. "I lived with a terrible secret for seven years and since Herbert died, I have had to live with a second even worse secret. Must I now spend the rest of my life weighed down by guilt?"

"What are you saying?" He frowned, as he guided her through the park gates.

"Do you remember when we stayed with the gypsies and you promised that you would always be with me?" He nodded. "In the morning will you come with me to see Mr Osborne?"

He almost stopped dead in his tracks. "I feared you would say that."

"I did such an awful thing and by the good grace of Frobisher, I escaped punishment. Now, I must do the same for him. It's what I should have done from the beginning and I must act now before it's too late."

He pulled her off the path into the shade of the trees where they were hidden from view. "Are you really going to be happier going to the law? Is your conscience going to be appeased if you are put aboard a convict ship bound for Australia and sentenced to years of hard labour? Or worse. Are you going to be happier being a gallows bird?"

She smiled, despite his harsh words. "Before you left for Worcester, I thought I was going mad. So, yes, I will be happier by doing the right thing."

"Then I will lose you."

She reached up to caress his cheek. He caught her hand and kissed it.

"We must put our trust in God," she sighed.

"Kate, please, please, forget this." He put his arms round her and pulled her close. His mouth was near her ear as he whispered, "Sir Herbert is dead and God forgive me, I am glad of it. He brought pain and suffering into the world and the world is a better place without him. And besides, you were protecting yourself. It was self-defence."

"Are you saying I should leave poor Frobisher to his fate?"

"Let's wait for the verdict and then decide. If he's found guilty then…"

"No, Conrad, by then, my courage might have failed me again. You say that no one would blame me for what I did, that it was in self-defence, but I still committed the act. Frobisher must not take the blame for it and you and I must not let him."

"You've made up your mind?"

Katherine's heart quickened. "Yes," she said. "All I ask is that you stay with me."

Conrad nodded and took in a shuddering breath.

They stood silently, holding each other close.

She was determined to keep to her decision. But that night, Conrad enclosed her in his arms and for a few brief hours, Katherine forgot what she was to do the following day. And after they had made love, they lay quietly in each other's arms, watching the flames of the fire and the flickering shadows dancing around the walls. The violent passion that had consumed them had now passed into peaceful satisfaction.

"Did I hurt you?" he asked tentatively.

"Not at all," she smiled.

"I should have been gentler."

"You're always gentle." She reached up for a kiss.

"How can I keep you safe?" He rolled over and raised himself up on his elbow to look down at her. The covers fell away revealing her breasts and he smiled that she made no attempt to cover herself. She wasn't shy with him. "If I had my way, I would spirit you away to a distant land where you can live in peace."

"I know you would and I love you for it."

He stroked her cheek with the edge of his forefinger. "On the way home the coach passed a gypsy selling lucky charms, so I bought one."

Katherine couldn't help feeling intrigued. "What did you buy?"

"An Irish symbol made into a pin. It's in my desk drawer, but I will give it to you tomorrow. Perhaps it really will bring you luck."

He pressed his lips on hers and then they were kissing and making love again, as though it was their last time together.

Mr Osborne set the wheels in motion to get Frobisher released immediately. And Katherine was taken into custody. Conrad stayed by her side the whole time and when the constable came to take her away, he and her uncle accompanied her to the prison in Gloucester. Her family realised that their stay at the house in Cheltenham was no longer a summer visit but for the duration as everyone awaited the decision of the judge who would consider her case and determine her fate.

There was much to consider. Katherine's testimony had been detailed and knowledge of Sir Herbert's crimes would go some way in mitigating her own. But the terrible news that Lady Fox had ended her husband's life became the main focus of social gossip and filled the newspapers daily, the pages often embellishing the slightest information.

Katherine was surprised when she first saw the prison. It had been built only ten years previously having been the central part of a castle site. It was three storeys high and ranged around three quadrangles with a gatehouse situated on the east side of the perimeter wall. The warden told her, quite proudly, that each prisoner had a separate cell and were allowed to exercise for one hour each day in the courtyard. Katherine felt like a visitor on a guided tour of a government building, but when the door was locked behind her, she too, was a prisoner within the walls.

Because of her status and rank, the warden had allocated two rooms for her at the top of the building and although the door was kept locked, Betsy was allowed to care for her. The maid would appear at the prison gate at eight each morning bringing clean clothes and the bits of finery that made Katherine's life more comfortable. At six o'clock, she would leave and the gate would be locked behind her.

But Katherine was filled with horror one morning when the warden told her to keep away from the window. Since her room was on the east side and she had sight of the gatehouse, this also meant she had a good view of any executions. And that morning they were executing a young woman for killing her newborn baby.

Only eight years before, executions took place in the nearby village of Over, the condemned person taken in a cart sitting on their own coffin. Now the 'new drop' method was employed on a raised gallows erected on the roof of the prison gatehouse. Katherine did as she was advised and stayed away from the window, but she couldn't ignore the roar of the crowd or the shouts of abuse as the unfortunate woman was led out, to climb the few steps to the scaffold.

Sitting at the table, her head held in her hands, Katherine concentrated on a large ink stain that resembled a tree, trying to sweep away the terrifying thought that she had heard the bolt withdrawn and the trapdoor swing open. She certainly heard the crowd cheer as it happened and couldn't prevent tears filling her eyes. Whether the tears were for the young girl who had just died or for herself she couldn't decide. But what she was certain about was that, should she be sentenced to death, she would ask her family to stay away. They must sit in Saint Mary's, she decided, and say prayers for her soul. She gave out a groan as she imagined her grandmama holding hands with Uncle George and Aunt Beatrice in the silence of the church, their thoughts in turmoil. She had already caused them so much pain and worry that she couldn't bear to think that more was to come.

She thought of Conrad, the only witness to her death, for his dear, handsome face was the last thing she wished to see before death claimed her. Her only prayer was that the hangman would be skilled enough to end her life quickly since it was a short drop through the trapdoor and the condemned didn't always die immediately.

After that terrible morning, Katherine was gratified to have the constant stream of visitors. Conrad, her aunt, uncle and grandmother came at regular intervals. But one day she had three very special visitors.

In the morning, Geraldine and Richard appeared with Conrad.

"We came back as soon as news reached us," said Geraldine, kissing her on the cheek and giving her a satin covered box of sweetmeats.

"Yes, and I've been to see the judge," said Richard. "I've told him my part in your kidnapping."

Katherine was horrified. "Oh, you shouldn't have done that. You might be arrested."

Richard smiled. "I thought it only right. If anything it verified your story." He paused for a few seconds. "Croston told us about Sir Herbert's codicil to the will." He glanced at Geraldine. "It's despicable, but so like my stepfather to ruin your happiness."

Katherine shrugged. "I think Westcroft is lost to me anyway. I've made out a power of attorney leaving you in complete control. I know you and Geraldine will look after the place and take care of the servants."

Geraldine looked about her. "You have these two rooms?"

"Yes," nodded Katherine. "I sleep through there and I'm able to have visitors in here. I'm very lucky. Frobisher had a small cell when he was here." She burst into strained laughter. "Now I know what Anne Boleyn felt like when she was in the Tower of London."

They didn't laugh with her, remembering the fate of that particular Queen of England.

In the afternoon, Conrad called again, much to Katherine's delight. "I didn't think to see you again today. I thought you said you were busy?"

He bent and kissed her lips. "I thought what I had to do would take until tomorrow." He took a seat next to her. "I sent men out to find the gypsies. They were camped outside Gloucester, so I was able to visit them without too much travelling."

"Why did you want to visit the gypsies?"

His expression softened. "I've brought someone to see you."

He strode to the door and knocked. The door was unlocked and on the threshold stood Orana.

Katherine opened her arms. "How wonderful that you should visit me."

Orana gave her a kiss and stroked her cheek. "You look well, dearie, considering your circumstances."

"It's the waiting that jangles my nerves. I wish they would make up their minds and put me out of my misery."

Orana and Conrad winced at her gallows humour.

And then Orana said quietly, "It's time to tell you the story that I mentioned. The story of your ma and pa." Katherine nodded. Orana took in a deep breath. "As I told you that night in the camp, you were a tiny babe when first I met your parents." Her voice faltered slightly and she gave a small cough. "It was after my dear little granddaughter, Patrick's child, went missing. She was gathering firewood and she couldn't be found."

"What had happened to her?" asked Katherine.

302

"We believed she'd been picked up by the rats that worked for Sir Herbert and taken to the House of Venus and into the coils of that wretched woman, Mrs Percy. Patrick went there and searched the place, but Tara had already been moved. He tracked her to Bristol and then London."

"Did he find her?" asked Katherine, glancing at Conrad, who was staring at the floorboards.

Orana shook her head. "No, he came back to Bristol a broken man and in poor health. He didn't make it back to the camp but collapsed on the dockside and that is where Captain Widcombe found him and brought him to your mother's small cottage. She nursed him back to full health."

"And that's why you're so grateful to my parents?"

"Ah, there's more. Patrick told your father everything and while Patrick recovered under the care of your ma, Captain Widcombe set off to search hither and thither and ask all manner of folk he was associated with. Other sea captains and port officials. And he found Tara on a ship ready to set sail for foreign parts. He brought her back to us." She smiled mistily. "And because of your pa she was with us until she died of consumption the same year you lost your Aunt Sybil."

"And my husband was responsible for her abduction?" asked Katherine, taking in a sobbing breath.

"Aye. Tara wasn't the only one to be taken. Many young girls disappeared…and boys too. All destined for wealthy clients, I'm led to believe, who request certain 'special' services."

"How old was Tara when she was taken?"

Orana sucked in another long breath. "Only ten."

"Dear Lord," gasped Katherine.

Conrad reached across and took her hand. "Don't you see, Kate. I suppose it has no bearing on your case,

303

but no one is going to regret Sir Herbert's death. In fact, there's jubilation now folk can breathe easily over their young ones. Something they've not been able to do for many a long year."

Katherine grimaced. "I still had no right to take my husband's life." She looked across at the failing light in the window.

Seeing the look of distress on her face, Orana said, "You have our thanks for the removal of that vile man. Lady Fox, you're a good person, a brave lass. I believe God must have guided your hand in this and He will protect you."

It was something to hold onto, something to ease her conscience. But the following morning she was told that the judge had made his decision and she would be brought before him the next day.

CHAPTER FIFTEEN

Betsy had brought her best clothes. Over her black gown, she wore a black pelisse with a royal blue paisley patterned panel round the bottom. She put on stout black boots and a black, silk bonnet with ribbon fastenings. And on her bodice was the pin that Conrad had bought from the gypsy woman. It was a Claddagh pin, the symbol of love, friendship and loyalty.

The maid looked her up and down. "You look every inch the lady and very feminine," she smiled. "You'll break the judge's heart."

Katherine pulled a face. "He's already made up his mind. What I look like is irrelevant. I want to look my best for myself and my family."

But Betsy would have none of it. "It doesn't hurt to soften his opinions, my lady," she said, following her out of the door. Katherine lifted her face to the warm October sun. Although she had been allowed to walk round the courtyard every day, it was pleasant to go through the gate and be outside the precincts of the prison. But then she noticed the throng of people standing outside, waiting. "Take no notice, my lady," said Betsy. "Flipping vultures!"

Katherine smiled and then she saw Conrad standing by his coach.

"I persuaded them to let me escort you to the courthouse, instead of going in the prison wagon. It's a bit more dignified."

He helped her in and then climbed in beside her. A constable sat with the driver and two more rode either side of the coach.

"Am I the most desperate criminal in England?" she said in amusement. "I seem to have a great many guards."

"They're worried that someone might help you escape. The papers are full of your ordeal at the hands of your husband and there's been an outcry about your incarceration. The populace have demanded your release."

"Shame the people weren't deciding my fate," she said softly.

Conrad took her hand and held it to his lips. His eyes closed and she could feel him trembling. How strange, she thought, I feel nothing, only resignation.

The courthouse stood at the centre of the town in the civic part of Gloucester next to the town hall. She was driven to the side of the building and into a courtyard where Conrad helped her alight and then watched, his heart in his mouth, as she was escorted through the entrance. She followed the constable along a maze of passages and finally she reached some narrow steps. Climbing them she was surprised to come out exactly in the dock that consisted of a square box enclosed by wood panelling. The musty smell of dust and sweat made her wrinkle her nose. She stepped forward, placed her hands on the bar and looked around.

The courtroom was large and full of people, spectators and officials as well as her family. She licked dry lips and suddenly her courage failed her. She wasn't on trial; she wouldn't stand for days listening to evidence. She had admitted her guilt and she was there to be sentenced. Conrad came through the door and took his seat next to Geraldine and Richard. And then the judge entered the room, in impressive wig and black gown, his expression stern. Katherine drew in a deep breath.

Conrad stood outside the courthouse with Richard and watched the people running past them, the babble of voices making them wince.

"Fourteen years!" said Conrad. "Fourteen years in New South Wales. That is unbelievably harsh."

Richard raised his eyebrows. "You must admit, transportation is better than execution." He studied the man standing next to him. "What do you intend doing?"

"I shall follow her."

"To the far side of the world?"

"To the moon if I must."

"You know that the voyage will be hard on her? I've heard that nearly a third of prisoners perish before getting to the colony."

Conrad grimaced. "I was considering a substantial bribe might smooth her passage, but I have another idea."

Richard didn't answer at first. He knew that the captain of a convict ship had nothing to lose by taking a bribe and then not fulfilling his side of the bargain.

"So, what are you considering?"

"I'm unable to say at the moment, but Bristol will serve my purposes."

"Geraldine and I will support you in whatever plans you make."

"Even if they are against the law?"

Richard nodded and looked across at the people hurrying by. "I've been told that my part in Katherine's kidnapping is a civil offence. In effect, Katherine's uncle must bring charges against me."

Conrad gave him a sidelong glance. "Is he?"

Richard shook his head. "I've spoken with him and he sees no purpose in it. But I can't help thinking that if

I had opposed my stepfather, Katherine would not be in this situation now."

Conrad tried to be practical. "Sir Herbert would have found others to do it for him."

Katherine went back to prison in a state of shock. Once in her room, she sank down on her small bed and stared at the wall. Details of her transportation would not be known until the spring, but for now she had to come to terms with the fact she was leaving England for a long time. If she didn't survive that meant she would never return, never see her family again. It was too hard to bear and yet she did have a chance at life and at least Conrad would not have to see her standing on the roof of the prison gatehouse.

She tried to be strong. Conrad had said he would follow her. He would live in the colony, always be by her and watch over her. It heartened her to think about him and yet, saddened her that he should be willing to give up his life in England to be with her.

Katherine stayed at the prison in Gloucester over the winter months, since she wouldn't set sail until April. And despite her incarceration, she was still treated with respect by the warders that locked and unlocked her door. But Christmas passed and 1801, a new century began.

In March she was escorted to the prison in Bristol where she realised that she was just one amongst many. The kindness and courtesy shown to her in Gloucester was not reflected at the prison in Bristol, where she was put into a cell of twelve women and their children and it was a case of fending for herself. There was no privilege due to her rank and when her family brought her gifts of fruit and sweetmeats, soap and cologne, they were stolen from her very quickly.

Only Mary Tunny and her grandson, Joshua, showed her any kindness.

Mary was in her late fifties and Joshua was only nine. It was Joshua who had committed the crime, having stolen clothing and a pistol, but his grandmother had made it worse by lying in court about the misdemeanour.

"Perjury, they called it," she told Katherine through toothless gums. "But I wanted to see Joshua set free."

"And they're sending you both to Port Jackson? I know there are other colonies."

"Aye, my lady, so at least we'll be together."

Katherine bent forward and whispered in her ear, "Please don't call me 'my lady'. If you must call me anything, then call me Kate. I'm a prisoner just like you."

Mary shook her head. "There was a lot of talk about you. Everyone knows what you did. But for me, well, you're gonna pay for your crime and that's that." Katherine looked across at the young boy asleep on a pallet of straw. His scrawny frame and tumbled fair hair made him look vulnerable. Mary followed her gaze. "I shall watch over him, though I dunno if I'll see old England again. But Joshua might make a life out there for himself, God willing."

News spread that they would sail on the fifteenth of April bound for Port Jackson in New South Wales. Katherine couldn't imagine what a convict ship was like. Often her thoughts would turn to the slave ships she had seen berthed in Bristol and a shudder would take her by surprise. She was to travel with one hundred and fifty other prisoners along with officials being sent out to govern the colony, members of the crew, marines and also the families and children who were accompanying their loved ones. The ship would be very crowded with little room for privacy.

HMS Guardian was an old frigate discarded by His Majesty's Navy, 879 tonnes and 140 feet long and ruled over by Captain Arthur Philips. It had been equipped with twenty cannon, ten on the portside and ten on the starboard, mostly to deter privateers. The voyage of almost eight months would take them 15,000 miles to the other side of the world and since a great number of the prisoners had not travelled more than thirty miles from their home, the journey terrified them.

Katherine felt their fear the morning she followed Mary and Joshua along the quayside and up the gangplank. Shackled together in chains, the prisoners stumbled along and some actually fell over, the other prisoners helping them up. Katherine stayed as close to Mary as possible, sometimes touching Joshua's shoulder in comfort. The marines stood either side of the line of ninety-two men and fifty-eight women, their muskets raised, as if they were afraid that anyone of their charges would break free.

As Katherine climbed the gangplank she looked about her and saw Conrad standing with Uncle George on the quayside. She had asked that her family stay away, but to see them made her want to call out. But she stayed quiet, fearing that any talking would bring a painful dig in the ribs from the butt of a musket.

They reached the deck and the gruff voice of the sergeant bellowed out,

"Take the prisoners below."

They were escorted down into the hold. Still shackled together, the prisoners were pushed and shoved and once inside, the hatch was slammed shut and secured. Katherine stared around her in horror. They had been given a blanket each and told to find a space to sleep, but there seemed precious little room since they were all crammed in together. Straw had been scattered about the floor and three lanterns gave them light, but in fact, it was a case of getting as comfortable as possible. She sank down against the bulkhead next to Mary and Joshua and pulled up her skirt revealing ankles that were red and bleeding from the iron chains. She tried to ease the cruel metal away from her tender skin.

"Are we to be like this for the entire journey?" she gasped, wrapping herself in her blanket.

"Yes, this is it," nodded Mary. "I heard tell that we go on deck for an hour each day for fresh air, but otherwise we stay here."

To live in such conditions seemed intolerable. At least she had been able to wash while in prison and Betsy had brought her a change of clothes and linen. But never to wash or change into fresh clothes seemed barbaric. She listened to the sound of the ship as it bumped against the quayside, the terrible creak and crack of timber. She had no idea when they were setting sail, since information had been scarce, so she closed her eyes and drifted off into another world, trying to fight the nausea that made her head swim.

Her eyes flew open to a cry from one of the men that the ship was moving. Katherine pulled herself up into a sitting position with no idea how long she had been on board, but it must have been quite a few hours. The ship rolled and the noise of creaking wood intensified, causing some of the women to start screaming with fright, others sobbed while holding their children close to them.

"We're being pulled down the river," said one woman. "Out into the estuary we'll be going and then we'll sail into the Bristol Channel before we reach the Atlantic."

"How do you know?" said another prisoner.

"My husband was a sailor," came back the sharp reply. "Until he was lost in the South Seas."

"Strikes me you could be joining him," said the first woman, laughing.

Her humour was not appreciated and a few minutes of bickering ensued until everyone fell silent again. Katherine felt the ship sway beneath her and she wished she could be out on deck. The air was already getting stale and the wooden buckets being used for bodily waste were full to overflowing and sending up a stink that made her gag. The ship heaved as the wind caught the sails and a young woman vomited down her gown. This is only the beginning, thought Katherine, how will we be after eight months?

The hatch opened and the sergeant appeared, scrutinising the prisoners.

"I want six of you men to carry out the buckets for emptying and sharp about it." The men volunteered quickly glad to have the opportunity of going out on deck. "You'll be fed shortly, but I've been instructed to release you from your chains." A sigh of relief filled the air. "It seems Captain Philips is a man with a soft heart."

He went round unlocking the irons with a bunch of keys. When he reached Katherine he knelt at her feet and seemed to take much longer over the job. As he undid the manacle, his hand slipped up her calf almost to her knee. She pushed him away and was horrified to see him leering at her. He was a big man, his head almost bald, with a nose that was pushed to one side and small, grey eyes. His grin turned into an arrogant smile as he passed to the next prisoner.

A short while later, a young soldier brought them all square pieces of very hard bread and Katherine bit into hers greedily. She grimaced at the taste.

"Sea biscuits," said the woman whose husband had been a sailor. "I'm afraid it's gonna be salt meat and sea biscuits from now on."

"Unless you can earn extra," said another woman.

"What do you mean?" asked Katherine.

The woman gave her a knowing smile. "Well, that sergeant certainly took a fancy to you. I'd give him what he wants, lovey, then you'll survive this voyage better than most." She glanced around at the other young women. "In fact, I'd say to you all, if a sailor or marine, or an officer takes a liking to you, then forget your pride and be nice to him."

"I couldn't bear that. I have someone I love," said Katherine.

The woman laughed. "He'll soon forget you, missy. Do ya think he's gonna wait fourteen years for you to come back? That's if you do come back! No, we're on our own now and we have to do anything to survive. I've heard tell that the women that get to Port Jackson often have to turn their hand to whoring just to get by."

It was a terrible prospect. Katherine huddled against the wood slats of the hold and hugged her knees. She wondered where Conrad was. Would he really follow her? She wanted him to and yet she feared for him. The place they were going would draw on all her resources to survive and until then she had eight months at sea. It seemed an eternity. It was now April and they would not arrive in New South Wales until December. Although it would be winter in England, she had been told that the seasons were reversed on that side of the world and December would be summertime. The thought overwhelmed her. But worse, much worse than

313

that was leaving her family. They had not reached the Atlantic Ocean yet and already she felt their loss deeply. And when she arrived in Port Jackson, she would endure the desperate struggle to survive.

Her thoughts turned to the sergeant. He was a rough, ugly man and there was no question of her being 'nice' to him. He was of the servant class and he had no right to touch her. Perhaps she ought to complain to the captain? She was a lady and...she looked down at the gown that Betsy had brought her two days before. She already felt dirty and as she ran her fingers through golden hair that was escaping its pins and starting to tumble about her shoulders, she knew she did not look like a lady. No, she looked like a convict. She was a prisoner of His Majesty and the sooner she accepted it, the better it would be for her.

Their first walk on deck was wonderful. The fresh sea air tasted like wine and for a moment, the women felt happier. The captain had instructed that they must be shackled while on deck, but otherwise they were free to move about the hold as they wished. Katherine stared across the bleak, grey water and sighed.

"Enjoying your stroll, my lady?"

Katherine turned to see the sergeant at her side.

"It's good to be out of the hold for a time."

She surveyed the man standing in front of her in a red and yellow uniform. Sergeant Ned Crowther was a bully; she knew that by now. He dominated the younger, less experienced soldiers in his company and she had heard that he wasn't shy of using his fists on anyone who got in his way.

He looked her up and down. "I have a gown in my trunk. Thought it might come in handy for a lady like you."

"You brought a gown on board with you?"

"Well, when I heard that we were to be honoured by the presence of Lady Fox, I thought you might appreciate something fresh to wear."

She turned her head away. "No, thank you. I'm happy as I am."

He sniffed with disdain. "You won't be so hoity-toity in a week or so." He smiled showing yellow teeth. "But there's plenty of time and I can wait. When you change your mind, let me know."

Life aboard HMS Guardian took on a precarious routine. There was nothing else to do but wait for the meagre rations to arrive and look forward to the hour on deck each day. Katherine knew she was getting thinner, the gown she was wearing hung loosely on her. She tied her hair back and tried to wash in the little water allocated to the women, often sacrificing drinking it for washing with it. Her dreams where turbulent and disturbing, but sometimes she would dream that she was lying in a tub of hot scented water and Betsy was fussing round her. At other times she was dining at a table covered with plates of delicious food. But when she reached out to taste it, it would dissolve before her eyes. And then she would wake up in the dankness of the hold and hear the other prisoners crying out in their sleep.

They crossed the Bay of Biscay with a severe gale blowing. The chain pumps were put into operation as the vessel was taking on water and eventually they heard that the main topsails had been blown to pieces. Those were a terrible two days for the prisoners in the hold. Chilled to the bone on soaking bedding, they huddled together, listening to the wind howling and trying not to lose their stomach contents as the ship rolled and lurched around them.

Captain Philips had already planned to put into port at Cadiz in Spain, but now it was imperative to make repairs. The prisoners remained below and although they could see the bright blue sky when the hatch was opened, they were not allowed to go on deck.

Once repairs were completed and fresh water taken on board, they were on their way once more. A feeling of apathy had descended on the prisoners and many did not want to rise from the floor and go on deck. Katherine began to nurse them, trying her best to cheer them along, wiping vomit away from their mouths with a rag dipped in water. She had very little nursing experience, but even she realised that some of the prisoners had given up, had lost their will to live. It frightened her. Could this be her condition in another week or month? She looked around at the gloomy and unsanitary conditions and knew that starvation and disease were staring them in the face. If only she could speak to the captain, surely he would understand and move the sick prisoners to more comfortable quarters?

Katherine had spied him standing high up, surveying his kingdom and he looked a kindly man. If she could get word to him, perhaps he would bow to her request and then the idea of using an intermediary came to her. Yes, someone in authority might speak on her behalf.

A young naval officer was standing near the rail and she remembered his name. Lieutenant Wadman. Watching the marines carefully and trying to look as nonchalant as possible, Katherine manoeuvred herself closer to him.

"Good afternoon, lieutenant," she smiled.

He turned surprised that a prisoner should address him. And then he realised who she was.

"Good afternoon, my lady."

She sighed. "I haven't been called that for quite a while." She ran her fingers through hair that was lank and dirty.

"Nevertheless, you are still high-born despite your crime."

She swallowed hard. "Yes, I suppose I am. And because of that, I wondered if I could speak to the captain?"

"You wish to speak with Captain Philips?" he said, smiling slightly.

She nodded. "I want to ask if the sick prisoners might be taken out of the hold. They need drier and warmer conditions or they are going to die."

He seemed stunned at her request. "Is that so," he chuckled. "I really thought you were going to demand better conditions for yourself. That's what I would do in your situation."

"I'm more concerned for the sick than myself."

"That's noble of you." He gave a sigh. "Unfortunately, the captain won't agree to your request so there's no point in troubling him."

"Can nothing be done?"

"The prisoners are being dealt with as prisoners ought." He gave a slight bow that seemed to be mocking her. "Good day, my lady."

She watched his retreating back with loathing. Making her way along the rail she stopped by the side of a longboat and looked out to sea. They were nearing the southern tip of Portugal and would put in at Gibraltar, before reaching the coast of Africa.

"Had a nice chin-wag with the lieutenant, did you, my lady?" She turned to see Sergeant Crowther bearing down on her. "I guess that's normal, since he's of your class."

She backed away from him. "I wanted to see Captain Philips. To ask for better conditions for the sick prisoners." She studied his large moon face. "They'll die if they stay in the hold."

"Will they now? That would be a pity. I don't like to see prisoners die on a voyage. Too much paperwork."

She wondered if she could appeal to his better nature. "Could you do something? The children are terribly ill with the fever."

He smiled. "That depends on you." His eyes swept down her body. "You've grown a mite grubby for my taste. But a bit of soap and water and a fresh gown would make you look more your old self." She opened her mouth to speak, but nothing came out. "Well, my lady, do you want to help the other prisoners or not? It's entirely up to you."

"I c...can't."

"What a shame. And here's me thinking you'd be more reasonable. But there's plenty of time yet."

Desperately, she looked about her. The crew was busy with their tasks and then her eyes strayed to the main sails billowing in the strong wind. Some sailors were up the rigging and as she shielded her eyes from the glare of the sun, she noticed one looking down at her. He wore a striped woollen hat pulled over his ears, his face in shadow. He looked away when he saw her staring at him.

The hour was up and Katherine was pushed and shoved back into the hold. The gloom from coming from bright sunshine appalled her. The sick were stretched out on the straw, some groaning, the children crying. Then she saw Mary holding Joshua.

She sat down next to her.

"Dear Lord, don't tell me Joshua is sick too?"

Mary nodded. "Fever like the others. Strikes me that he'll not make it to Port Jackson after all."

Katherine dipped a rag in a bucket of water and washed his face. "Sergeant Crowther says he'll help the sick prisoners if I...treat him well."

Mary gave a low chuckle. "No, he won't, Kate. He might help you, but not others. If you do decide to go with him, then do it for yourself. It's the only way you'll survive." She gestured towards the widow of the sailor. "She's with the corporal. And he's already found her fresh clothes and more food." She grimaced. "They do it in one of the longboats."

Katherine gritted her teeth. "If I do take up with that odious man, it will be for myself, yes, but for you and Joshua too. I will get us more food and hopefully some medicine."

Mary looked at her quizzically. "That would be a rare treat and as for physic for my Joshua, well, you can't imagine how grateful I would be." Tears poured down her wrinkled face as she held her grandson to her. "But what about your man?"

"We've been at sea for two months and there's still six months ahead of us. I hope he understands that I needed to survive."

"Then God have mercy on us."

Katherine couldn't bear to watch her pain. Tomorrow she would speak to the sergeant and agree to his demands. As she closed her eyes in sleep, she thought of Conrad and prayed that he would forgive her and still love her when she saw him again.

CHAPTER SIXTEEN

Conrad had to steel every nerve in his body as he watched Katherine struggle aboard HMS Guardian. The line of convicts was a terrible sight to see, chained together, many already looking exhausted and very ill.

"Dear Lord, it's inhuman," he said to Katherine's Uncle George.

"We can only pray that she is strong enough to withstand the voyage. She's young and in good health and that will be to her advantage." George gestured towards the children and elderly, shackled in the same manner. "But how they will survive, I cannot imagine. But now you must be on your way."

"I'll not go until I see her in the hold." And he did not. Standing on the quayside, he waited until Katherine had gone from his sight and then he shook the hand of the man next to him. "Thank you for your help and wish me luck."

"God speed, sir. The yacht is smaller and lighter and will travel fast. You should be in Spain well ahead of the frigate. And when you see Katherine again, as I'm sure you will, please tell her…well, you know what to tell her."

Conrad smiled and left him, striding down the pier to the Countess of Croston, moored by a warehouse. A sailor was waiting to cast off as soon as he was aboard. Conrad went immediately below deck into the main saloon and gestured for the footman to pour him a brandy. He drank it back in one gulp and placed the glass back on the tray.

"How was it?" said Geraldine. "Did you see Katherine?"

Conrad nodded. "Yes, I did and how we can treat human beings like that is beyond me."

"But they're not regarded as human beings. They're convicts," Richard sighed.

"So I noticed," said Conrad, taking a seat next to him. His gaze travelled round the sumptuous surroundings that were his yacht. Mahogany furniture gave the saloon a warm and cosy feel and the gleaming brass fittings and luxurious seating made it comfortable for the passengers. On board there was a chef, maids and footmen, always on call should they be needed. These conditions were very different from those experienced by Katherine at that moment. Conrad sat back in his seat. "It's going to be a frightful journey for Kate from the first day, but it will get worse once out in the Atlantic. But if she can just make it through the first half of the voyage then she'll have a chance."

"So, we need to put our plan into operation as soon as possible?" asked Richard.

"Indeed we do. We cannot leave her on board any later than Cape Town and if we can achieve our objective sooner, all the better. Our next port of call is Cadiz and we should be just ahead of the frigate. That's where Patrick and I will disembark and wait out the time at an inn. When Guardian docks, we will sign up as crewmen."

A sailor appeared and saluted. "Begging your pardon, my lord, but Master has put you on Middle Watch," he said briskly, before turning on his heel and resuming his tasks. The crew was experienced and under the stern command of Master Hughes, but for the last four months they had had a raw recruit amongst their number.

Richard chuckled. "And what the blazes is Middle Watch?"

"It's the watch between midnight and four in the morning," said Conrad, raising his eyebrows. "Obviously, Master Hughes is starting me with the toughest duties on this voyage." He passed a weary hand over his face.

Geraldine noticed. "You should take more rest. Are you sure you should do this? You're not used to working all hours in such harsh conditions."

"It's been difficult, I'll give you that," said Conrad, grinning. "But having no sailing skills whatsoever, I needed to become part of the crew in order to learn what I needed to know." He gave a tired smile. "Only I can do what needs to be done and I'm sure with Patrick's help we will prevail."

She decided not to argue the point.

"How will you contact Katherine?" asked Geraldine, after a moment of silence.

"That might be difficult, since I believe the convicts are kept in the hold for most of the time. But no doubt I'll find a way."

Geraldine pondered on this. "Even if you can't speak to her, she needs to know that you're on board. You need a sign that means something to both of you. A token that she will recognise." She tapped her finger on her lips. "And I think I know what." She stood and left the saloon, Conrad and Richard watching her in bewilderment. Moments later she reappeared. "Why don't you take this. It's not a happy memory, but at least it's one that means something to both of you and especially Katherine."

She held out her hand and revealed a red, silk handkerchief.

Prisoners started dying throughout the night. First a small child and then an old man. Some died unnoticed until one or other of the prisoners realised that they had gone and their bodies would be moved to one side. By dawn there were six shrouded bodies to be buried at sea, although none of the prisoners were permitted to attend the hasty funerals. To Katherine's relief, Joshua survived the night although it was obvious that without medicine he wouldn't recover.

When Katherine went out on deck for air, she saw the sergeant talking to one of his men. She studied him, knowing that being in his proximity would fill her with disgust. But he was a means to an end. Perhaps she could bear it if she thought of Conrad, but even that idea filled her with shame. How could a person keep their dignity, their humanity in the conditions they were suffering?

When she saw that the sergeant was free, she approached him. "I'll do as you want, providing you give me extra rations."

He smiled smugly. "Is that so? I thought you'd come round eventually, though you'll need fattening up. Can't bear a woman with bones sticking through her clothes."

"It's not for me," she said angrily. She was determined to wring everything she could out of him. "I want more food for my friends. And I want some medicine for the prisoners with fever."

"Medicine!"

"I've heard that the surgeon has preparations of quinine on board. I want some."

He rubbed his chin. "That will be difficult to get. Especially to treat all the prisoners who are sick."

She relented, her expression becoming softer. "Then just get me enough for one child. That's all I ask."

He smiled and reached out to stroke her cheek, feeling excited. She knocked him away and that made

323

him harden even more. A woman who resisted him always gave him more pleasure than a compliant one.

"You drive a hard bargain, my lady."

"Then so be it. It's the medicine or nothing," she said, her chin in the air.

Katherine was amazed when the sergeant brought the extra food and the medicine that evening and although she knew that many other prisoners needed it, she closed her mind and concentrated on Joshua, feeding the spoonfuls of quinine into his cracked and bleeding mouth.

"He's a goner," said the sergeant impatiently. "You're wasting your time on that one."

She ignored him.

It was two days later when Sergeant Crowther found her a place to wash. She had no idea where he had taken her but it looked like an ante-room just behind the supply hold. Stripping off her dirty clothes, she stood in a basin and poured water over herself, lathered her skin with a small piece of soap and then poured more water over her hair, washing it until the true colour shone through. The gown he had given her was quite pretty, in pastel pink with a flower design and braiding sewn round the sleeves and bodice. It felt wonderful to be clean again and by the time the sergeant appeared, she looked more presentable.

"Yes, quite pleasing, if I say so myself." He bent to kiss her neck, but she shied away from him. "Now that's no way to thank me, my lady." She looked at him in defiance. "Hope you're not going to welch on our deal? That would make me very angry and things won't go well for you or your friends."

"I don't intend welching."

He raised his eyebrows. "Good." He looked around. "It's too hot below deck. Come with me."

"Where are we going?"

He only grinned and taking her arm led her back through the ship and out onto the deck. It was cloudy and the heat oppressive. They were off the coast of Africa and sometimes the peppery aroma of that dark continent wafted towards them, but beyond the ship's lanterns was a black void with only the sound of the waves against the hull to give them an idea that they were still on the ocean. He stopped at one of the longboats and pushed her round the side. She felt shocked, bewildered, as he turned her to face him and then his hands were everywhere, on her breasts and lifting up her gown to fondle between her legs. She was his now and he was determined to enjoy her to the hilt.

Katherine gasped at his strength and her lack of it, as he pressed her up against the boat, imprisoning her with his hefty body. She was not prepared for the smell of his breath or the way he slobbered over her face and neck. The terrible indignity became unbearable and tears trickled down her cheeks.

"I've always wanted a woman of noble birth," he said, hooking her leg over his arm. He grunted, fumbling with himself. "In you go." He was prevented from penetrating her by the sound of someone close by calling his name. He let go of her and she shrank back into the shadows, hoping she wouldn't be seen. "Bloody hell, what is it now?" he said, buttoning up his breeches. "Below decks for you, my girl, but I'll be back for due payment. Now I've had a taste of you, I want the rest of the meal."

A sailor appeared and saluted. "Sorry to disturb you, sir. But Lieutenant Wadman wishes to see you immediately," he said in a strong German accent.

"What does he want now?"

"Don't know sir, he didn't say."

"Escort this prisoner to the hold," the sergeant ordered, as he strode across the deck to see the lieutenant.

The sailor took her arm and guided her across the deck. Just as they reached the hatch, he pulled her to one side.

"That was lucky. I saw him take you from the hold but then lost sight of you," he said in King's English. "He didn't hurt you? I thought I might have been too late."

"Who are you?" she asked, shrinking away from him, surprised at his sudden change in accent. He stepped closer so that the light from the lantern lit up his features. "Conrad! Is it really you?"

"Yes, Kate, it's me," he smiled. He gestured towards the sergeant talking to the lieutenant. "I heard him bragging about an assignation with a lady and I realised I must act quickly. Patrick is here too. We've been on board since Cadiz."

She couldn't help laughing at his simple sailor's clothes with a hat pulled over his ears and she reached out to touch him, expecting him to dissolve away like the plates of food in her dreams.

"Patrick? But how?"

"He's signed on as ship's carpenter."

She remembered how he had found her and tears stung her eyes. "I didn't want to go with him. But he brought extra food and medicine for Joshua."

"I know why you did it, Kate. You don't have to explain."

"Please forgive me."

"There's nothing to forgive." He pulled her closer. "Dear Lord, you've lost so much weight." He looked around. "I must get you below before you're missed.

Explanations will have to come later." He caressed her cheek. "Oh, my Kate. Remember that I love you."

Katherine went back to the hold feeling dazed. She lay down next to Mary and turned her back on her, trying to get her thoughts straight. Everything had happened so quickly, she couldn't believe it was true.

Mary stroked her shoulder. "There now," she said. "It's all done."

Biting her lip she decided she would go along with the pretence that she had been with the sergeant.

"Yes, it's done now."

"Why don't you tell him that you're finished with him? You don't need to carry on," said Mary. "I don't want you to suffer on my account. We'll get by on the rations we have."

Katherine rolled over to face her. "We won't survive on such little food." She looked across at Joshua. "I must carry on for your grandson's sake."

As Katherine lay there, she couldn't stop smiling. The thought that Conrad was on the ship, going about his duties as an ordinary seaman, filled her with warmth. But her smile faded as she wondered if he was in danger. What would happen if he were discovered? She groaned inwardly, praying that he would come to no harm. And yet, for the first time in months, she looked forward to the following day, filled with hope and expectation.

Waking the following morning was difficult. Katherine ached in every joint and could hardly rise from the straw that was her bed. She felt her cheek, hoping that she too had not contracted the fever that had taken so many of them. It would be ironic if she became ill and died now, when Conrad was only a short distance away.

More prisoners had perished in the night and she helped carry their bodies to the ladder for removal. It was a grim thought how many would be left by the time they reached Port Jackson.

A week passed and it started getting uncomfortably hot in the hold. The captain ordered that the hatch be left open, with a marine guarding it at all times. Katherine looked forward to her hour on deck even more, standing at the rail, hoping to see Conrad. And sometimes she would and the effort not to acknowledge his presence caused her pain.

Joshua improved in health each day and his mischievous nature was more apparent, much to the delight of his grandmother. His ankles were too small for the shackles and he found he could slip his feet through easily. His blue eyes twinkling, he would scamper about the deck, the marines finding it difficult to contain him since he would evade them to go to areas forbidden to prisoners. And then he would be brought back by the ear by the sergeant or corporal. It seemed the sailors found it amusing to watch this cat and mouse game and often cheered him on as he dived under the outstretched arms of his captors. If he could hide any bits of food under his shirt, then he would do so, even though his grandmother would admonish him for stealing and Katherine would warn him of the danger of being flogged.

For some strange reason Sergeant Crowther had not pressed his demands since the aborted first time. And then one afternoon he sent the corporal down with a cooked chicken and a small cask of ale. Katherine tore the chicken into pieces and shared it amongst the others.

An hour later they went out on deck and she met the sergeant.

"Did you enjoy the chicken?" he asked. She didn't look at him but only nodded. "Then I'll be wanting payment tonight. You've had enough from me and I've had nowt in return." The surgeon called him and he left, striding across the deck towards the sickbay.

"I hate that man," said Katherine, turning to Mary.

"Perhaps he might get sick and die," said Mary. "If anyone deserves to die, he does."

Katherine looked about her, hoping to see Conrad. But he was nowhere in sight. Despondently, she went back to the hold. The hours ticked by and she waited for the sergeant, her mind spinning with plans of escape, some ludicrous and some desperate.

The hatch opened and Katherine waited, her heart throbbing in her throat. The corporal came down and looked about him. "I'm searching for the sarge. Has he been here?"

Everyone stared at Katherine and she felt obliged to answer. "No, I haven't seen him since this afternoon."

The corporal shrugged and climbed the steps.

It was about an hour later that shouts and running feet alerted the prisoners that something had happened. One of the men plucked up the courage to climb the ladder and peep over the edge of the hatch. After a while he came down and took his place amongst the others.

"There's a bit of a hue and cry up there. Marines and sailors running hither and thither. There's no one guarding us, so if you want to escape now's the time."

"Escape! Where to? There's only the bloody sea," snapped another man.

"What do you think has happened?" asked Katherine, ignoring their altercation.

The man pulled a face. "Could be pirates. Or the Frogs deciding to attack us. Won't make any difference to us. We're dead meat anyway."

Katherine turned her head away. She didn't intend giving up now, not after Conrad had made himself known to her. Even if they were attacked by pirates or the French and were sunk, they would be together. In the dark waters of the sea, they would find each other, just as she believed her mother and father had done. She knew that they were only weeks away from going round the Cape of Good Hope and the name itself gave her a feeling of optimism. But her heart ached to see Conrad again. Just a glimpse of him satisfied her for the rest of the day.

The corporal descended the stairs once more and came straight to Katherine.

"Captain wants to see you," he said, shackling her feet in irons. "Come on, don't keep him waiting."

He helped her climb the ladder and holding her arm, pulled her across the deck to the stern, up some steps and then she was through a door and in the captain's presence. She looked about her, stunned that a cabin could be so beautiful. Highly polished oak seemed to be everywhere, the panelling, the large table, the floor. A huge window dominated the end of the room and through this there was a wonderful view of the sea. After living in squalor for over three months, this apartment seemed like one a person would find on a royal yacht. Lieutenant Wadman and another man she recognised as Mr Simons, the ship's surgeon, stood either side of the captain.

"Prisoner as requested, sir," said the corporal, saluting.

Captain Philips was sitting behind the table and raised his eyes as she came through the door. Katherine saw a man in his later years with greying hair and an expression that showed he was a weathered sailor and experienced captain.

"I've called you here...my lady," he started hesitantly. She tried not to smile knowing that he didn't know how to address her, "because Sergeant Crowther cannot be found and we firmly believe that he has come to an unfortunate end."

She frowned. "What has this to do with me?"

His eyes narrowed. "The corporal has told me that you were having a... liaison with the sergeant and I want to know when last you met him."

Colour flooded her cheeks. "The last time I saw him was when I walked on deck this afternoon," she said in a low voice.

"Did he speak with you?"

"Briefly."

"What did he say?"

"Nothing of significance."

Captain Philips studied her carefully. "On the deck, by the side of one of the boats, we found a substantial amount of blood. I believe that Sergeant Crowther met his end there, probably knifed and then his body thrown overboard."

Katherine felt shock and then relief that she would not have to suffer at his hands again.

"I'm sorry about that," she lied. "But it still has nothing to do with me. When last I saw the sergeant he was alive and well."

"Did you fix up a liaison with the sergeant for this evening?"

"No."

The captain turned to the corporal. "Tell her what you told me."

The corporal grinned. "I heard the sarge say how he was looking forward to this evening on account he was dipping his wick with a lady."

The captain blinked hard. "Yes, all right corporal. I didn't mean you to repeat the exact words."

"Sorry, sir."

Captain Philips turned to Katherine. "So, you were meeting the sergeant this evening?"

Katherine looked down at her manacled feet. "I admit it. He spoke of wanting to see me, but I felt too ashamed to say so."

"Then you told a lie?"

"Yes."

He turned to Lieutenant Wadman who surveyed her with cold eyes. "I gave you orders to stop this fraternisation with the prisoners."

"I've tried stopping it, sir. But there's a lot of men on this ship and men without women…"

The captain held up his hand. "Yes, yes." He opened a drawer in the table and took something out. He threw it in front of her and she stared at it in horror. "I would accept your story, except we found this near the pool of blood. I've questioned my officers and it doesn't seem to belong to any of them. So, Lady Fox, my thoughts turned to you, since there is only one other person on this ship that could own an expensive red, silk handkerchief like that. And that person is you." The room became deathly quiet as everyone watched her. "Examine it carefully and tell me if you've seen it before. And, my lady, I would prefer it if you didn't waste my time with lies."

She picked it up with shaking hands. "This is not mine," said Katherine. "It's a gentleman's handkerchief."

The captain nodded. "Indeed it is, my lady. However, I thought that someone might have given it to you as a farewell gift."

"No, I received no such gift."

He leaned back in his chair. "You're sure about that?"

"Yes." Katherine started to panic. "I did get a few gifts before I came on board, mostly fruit that I ate very quickly and toilet items…But they were stolen."

Captain Philips sighed as though he was tired of listening. "My lady, as captain of this vessel, I am the law. If I find you guilty of this crime then I have the authority to have you hanged."

Katherine felt her mouth drying. "Why do you think I might have killed Sergeant Crowther?"

"Vengeance or hatred. Who can say?" He studied her pale face. "You've already been convicted of murder, madam! Who's to say that you didn't choose a second victim?"

"I did not kill the sergeant," she cried angrily. "The other…crime I admitted to."

"Yes, but many months later, when someone else was to take the blame."

"Even so, I owned up to it, but I will not admit to something I did not do." Something occurred to her. "You say he was stabbed to death? Where did I get the knife?"

He shrugged. "You could have stolen that from anywhere. My crew can be very careless at times about leaving their possessions about."

"But I'm locked in the hold. I'm watched at all times."

"We should search her, sir," said the lieutenant. "She might have stowed the knife away for further use."

Desperation made her want to scream at them, but she kept her voice steady. "I only have two items on my person. A locket with a portrait of my parents inside and a Claddagh pin. I own nothing else."

"Show me," said the captain, holding out his hand.

Colour flooded her face once more. "They're hidden in my clothes."

"I still want to see them." She lifted the bottom of her gown and put her fingers into the hem that she had ripped slightly to keep the valuables that were so precious to her. She passed the locket and pin to the captain. He looked at the Claddagh pin for a few seconds and then opened the locket. He studied the portraits and raised his eyebrows. "The daughter of a sea captain indeed." He turned back to the three men. "I would like to talk to the prisoner alone."

"It might not be…" the lieutenant began but the captain dismissed them with a look that made it clear he would brook no dissent.

Katherine stood alone in front of the table. The room seemed to weigh down on her and she took in shuddering breaths. She watched the captain like a mongoose watches a snake, knowing she had every reason to fear this man. On this ship he had the power over life and death and if he considered her guilty, then he could order her immediate execution. Dear Lord, she thought in horror, had she escaped the hangman's noose in England, only to suffer it thousands of miles from home under an unfriendly sky? And with Conrad there as witness. How did the handkerchief come to be on board? It was one of Geraldine's, she was sure about that and the only person who must have brought it, was Conrad himself.

The captain rose slowly to his feet. "I should have you thrown in the brig." Katherine stared down at the floor feeling numb. He perched himself on the edge of the table and looked towards the window. "But in truth, I've felt uncomfortable since you came aboard. You're not the usual type of prisoner I've come to expect." Katherine felt her heart jump in her chest and was surprised how quickly she had learnt that any intonation of sympathy from anyone always brought hope. But hope died very quickly when he added, "You will be put under close guard pending an investigation and if you're found guilty you will hang, lady or not."

It was all getting too much for her. Large tears coursed down her face. "I did a terrible thing...ending my husband's life...and if I could undo it then I would...but I did not kill Sergeant Crowther. I swear I did not."

He pulled a chair from under the table and made her sit down. And then he poured a small amount of brandy into a glass goblet and gave it to her.

"Drink this. It will calm you." Captain Philips watched her sip the contents. "Is it true what they say, that your husband kidnapped you when you were a girl?" Katherine nodded. "Sir Herbert Fox had a reputation for suspicious business practices. I knew about his investment in the seedier side of life, but I didn't agree with his financial interests in the slave trade, for all I'm captain of a convict ship."

Katherine nearly dropped her glass with shock. "My husband had dealings in the slave trade? But that's impossible, he deplored slavery. He supported William Wilberforce."

The captain's expression softened. "No, my lady. Your husband was an advocate of the slave trade, that I am sure about."

Katherine put down her glass, a feeling of helplessness washing over her.

"I believed him, but it was all lies. My marriage was a charade right from the start."

The captain clicked his tongue in sympathy. "No good dwelling on the past. I think you've enough troubles to deal with in the present." He handed back the locket and pin. Katherine took them and held them tightly against her, hoping she had time to convince him that she was innocent and by doing so, claw back something of the pride she had lost. "Until an investigation can take place you will be removed from the hold and placed in a secure place." He moved round the table, took his seat and called for the corporal to take her away.

She was escorted to a small supply hold that seemed to have been cleared of sacks, since a tidy pile of empty ones were stacked in the corner. A hammock had been strung up and to her surprise, she was given water to wash with and clean clothes. Although she was locked in, the air was a lot fresher, since a draught blew under the door.

She had hardly got used to her surroundings when the key turned in the lock and the door opened. Standing on the threshold was Lieutenant Wadman, his expression severe.

"Good evening, my lady," he said. "I trust you find the accommodation to your liking?"

"It's excellent. Thank you," she smiled, hoping she didn't sound facetious.

"I've assigned a man to attend to food and water for you."

"That's very kind."

"Step forward," he said to the crewman who had stayed in the passageway behind him.

Conrad did as he was ordered and smiled as he touched his forehead in a salute. "My name is Schmidt," he said in a German accent. "I'm at your service, my lady."

CHAPTER SEVENTEEN

Katherine had a fever. She fell ill late in the afternoon and couldn't eat the food that Conrad had brought. Feeling listless with pains in her head and back, she brushed off his concerns and told him that she was just tired. But the following morning it was obvious that she had been stricken by the same malady that had taken many of the other prisoners. Realising that she needed nursing care, Conrad had suggested that Mary Tunny act as nurse and Captain Philips had reluctantly agreed. And where Mary went, Joshua would follow.

"But they'd better be on their best behaviour," said the captain. "Any infraction of the rules and they will go straight back to the hold."

Although Katherine seemed to be fighting her illness, Mary was concerned.

"I've done all I can," she said, wiping her face with a cold, wet flannel. "Thank the Lord she's here and not in the hold. I doubt she would survive if she were."

Joshua stood beside the hammock, staring down at the patient.

"Is she going to die, Gran?"

"Hush, now," she admonished him. "Of course not. We'll get her better in no time."

Conrad placed the pitcher on a small table and carried the tin can over to Mary. She held Katherine's head, encouraging her to take a sip of water.

He bit his lip anxiously. "Everything is set for leaving the ship as we approach Cape Town. But we'll be making our escape at night. We can't leave with Kate in this condition. Unless we carry her."

Mary knew all about Lord Croston and had marvelled that an earl could take the guise of an ordinary seaman in order to save the woman he loves. But to be included in their plans had stunned and delighted her, even though it meant a perilous journey. She and her grandson would have the opportunity of living a different life, a safer life and far away from New South Wales.

"It will kill her, if we move her," Mary sighed. "You spoke of being in a longboat for a while?"

Conrad nodded. "My yacht is meeting us at Saint Helena Bay, but that's about fifty miles from Cape Town."

Mary glanced back at Katherine. She was restless and her face flushed with the fever. "Then let's just pray she gets better."

Conrad left them to continue his duties. He had become used to life aboard ship and often he would forget that he had title and wealth. Croston Court seemed a long way away, in a previous life. On board the Guardian he was called 'Fritzy' and his fake German accent was becoming a habit, using it when he had no need. But this illness of Katherine's worried him. They were to rendezvous with the Countess of Croston in two weeks' time and God knows what would happen if they did not make the rendezvous. Of course, Haighton and Frobisher would wait for them, but for how long would they wait? However, that problem would have to be left for another day, since first, Katherine needed to be in better health.

He saw Lieutenant Wadman standing on the quarterdeck and approached him. "I've come to report on the condition of Lady Fox, sir."

"Do you mean the prisoner?"

"Yes, sir. She's ill and needs quinine. I would like permission to see the surgeon and fetch her some."

"How ill is she?"

"She has a high fever and is very restless."

"In danger of dying?"

"Yes, sir."

Lieutenant Wadman sniffed in contempt. "Can't understand why the captain didn't lock her in the brig. She's starting to get privileges she's not entitled to."

Conrad stood quietly. How many times had he wanted to speak his mind to this arrogant young fool? In normal circumstances he would have, being an earl gave him many privileges. But for now, he was a lowly seaman with no rights and he had to keep silent.

"The quinine, sir?"

"Certainly not. If she dies, she dies." Conrad turned to go but the lieutenant had had second thoughts. "Wait! See the surgeon and get her some. Tell him I sent you."

"Thank you, sir."

"No, thank the Earl of Croston when I return to England. I'm sure he'll be delighted that I showed kindness to his ladylove. And hopefully, his gratitude will extend to pulling a few strings in getting me promoted to lieutenant commander."

Conrad tried not to smile as he made his way to the sickbay.

Mr Simons was a kindly man, who had become dismayed over the rates of fever amongst the prisoners. But quinine was in short supply and when Conrad appeared he shook his head.

"I can't afford to give any more to the prisoners. I must keep my reserves for the crew and officials in my care."

"Lieutenant Wadman has given permission," said Conrad, feeling alarmed.

"That's as maybe, but it's impossible and I shall tell him so when I see him."

Conrad went back to Katherine's cabin and told Mary what had happened.

"Then she's sure to die and there's not a thing we can do about it."

She continued wiping Katherine's face and didn't see Joshua's rigid expression.

As usual, Mary stayed with her patient when Joshua went on deck for some fresh air. He had stopped dashing about since being moved from the hold and would often spend the hour watching the sailors at work. This time, he wandered over to the rail and spent some minutes looking over the side of the ship. The sea shimmered below a cloudless sky and the sun blazed down as if it was intent on roasting them alive. He made his way along the rail, unconcerned, interested only in the waves foaming against the hull. The door to the sickbay was nearby and when he saw the marines were more preoccupied in the other prisoners than with him, he darted through and jumped down the companion-way.

He hid behind the stairs while he assessed the situation. Mr Simons was bent over a crewman lying on a berth and then he realised that the cupboard containing the medicines was just a few feet away. Sprinting nimbly across the floor, he hid once more beside the table and then took the last few steps to the cupboard. He opened it and looked for quinine.

"K..K..Kwin...een," he mouthed, as he searched along the bottles.

And then he found the bottle and pushed it inside his shirt. His return journey was trouble free; the surgeon still occupied with his patient and the way clear for his escape. When he reached the hatch at the top of the companion-way, he saw that the marines were at the far end of the deck. He patted the bottle to make sure it was still there and slipped out, resuming his interest in the waves crashing against the ship's side.

Mary frowned as she stared at the bottle. "How do we know it's the right medicine?" she asked her grandson.

He pointed to the label. "It says so don't it?"

She wasn't convinced. "I think I'll wait until his…Schmidt arrives. He can tell us if it's the right stuff."

"That's no good. Kate could be dead before then. Give her some, it can't do her no harm."

Mary opened the stopper and sniffed the contents. "Don't smell the same as Sergeant Crowther's physic." She poured a little on the palm of her hand. "And it's white and thicker." She stared at her grandson. "Oh, Joshua, I'm afeard to give her this. We might kill her."

Joshua stared at Katherine, sleeping but restless. "She might die anyway."

Reluctantly, Mary held the vial to Katherine's lips and encouraged her to drink some. The patient pulled a face and her eyelids flickered open.

"That tastes horrible. What is it?"

"Medicine. To make you better," said Joshua, his blue eyes sparkling with delight.

"It's quinine," said Mary.

"Are you sure?"

Mary grimaced. "If truth were known, we ain't sure. Neither of us can read."

Conrad came in carrying their dinner. "Salt meat and dry bread," he said. "Same as yesterday. But I managed to find an orange for you." He saw that Katherine was awake. "Oh, my goodness. Are you feeling better?" He felt her head and then put his arms round her, oblivious that he had an audience. "Your fever has broken, thank God."

"We gave her quinine," said Mary. "At least, we think it's quinine."

Anxiously, Conrad took the bottle out of Mary's hand.

"I looked for the right medicine," said Joshua, now doubting his bravery. "See, on the bottle. It starts with a 'k' for quinine."

"Quinine starts with a 'q'. And this is kaolin," smiled Conrad.

"Is that poisonous?" asked Joshua, his eyes wide with fright.

Conrad shook his head. "I believe this is for someone with an ailing stomach."

Mary burst into laughter. "To stop them being forever on the piss pot. We must learn to read when we leave this damned ship."

Katherine had been told that their departure would be soon and she couldn't wait to go, so desperate was she to put her feet on dry land. She had been on the Guardian for four months and yet it seemed like four years.

"I will never believe you're a sailor," said Katherine, two days later, when she had grown a little stronger, but still confined to the hammock. "You never mentioned you had experience."

Conrad laughed. "That's because I hadn't. I had to learn everything from the beginning. But fortunately I knew enough to sign up with this crew."

Katherine struggled with her thoughts. "As an ordinary seaman? Wouldn't you seem out of place?"

He grinned. "It's convenient being just an ordinary crewmember. And they signed us on without any trouble since volunteers are thin on the ground when it comes to a convict ship." He shook his head. "The pay is appalling. I never realised what little a seaman earned. And as for who I am?" He bowed and clicked his heels. In a thick German accent he said, "I am no longer the Earl of Croston, but Andreas Schmidt at your service, my lady." He chuckled. "If anything, it allows me to swear in German and no one understands a word I'm saying."

She shuffled her aching body into a more comfortable position.

"Well, you're here," she said, resting a hand on his chest. "And that's what really matters."

He took her hand and kissed it. "I told you I would never leave you."

"Please tell me about the sergeant and the handkerchief."

He glanced towards the door, knowing that Mary and Joshua would be returning soon from their hour on deck.

"Patrick and I decided that Crowther was becoming a threat," he said, keeping his voice low. "Both a threat to you and our plans."

"So you killed him?" asked Katherine.

Conrad nodded. "We had no choice but to…remove him."

"What about the handkerchief?"

He pulled a face. "I stupidly dropped that in the scuffle with him."

"But why did you have it on you in the first place?"

Conrad told her of Geraldine's idea and Katherine felt stunned that such an object should be used as a means of communication. If she had received it as planned, she would have immediately guessed that either Conrad or Richard was on board.

Conrad smiled. "However, it wasn't needed, since fate intervened to bring us together in a completely different way." He kissed her lips. "Now you must sleep while I return to my other duties."

He was just about to leave when Mary returned, colliding with him at the door and almost knocking him over.

"It's Joshua," she said, trying to catch her breath. "He's been arrested for stealing that blessed medicine. Lieutenant Wadman says he's to be flogged. A nine-year-old boy, would you believe."

"He will not be flogged," said Conrad. "Where is he?"

"Locked up somewhere." She gestured over her shoulder. "That bastard marine outside says I can't see him and brought me straight back here."

Conrad left immediately and went to see the captain. Captain Philips listened to his arguments in amazement that this ordinary seaman, and a foreigner at that, could be so articulate in the English language. Conrad told the truth, saying that the boy had meant well and only wanted to save Lady Fox's life by finding some quinine for her.

"It was quinine he was intent on stealing, was it? If I'd known he meant to steal quinine, then it would have been a much severe punishment." Conrad could have bitten his tongue out and made to protest, but the captain silenced him. "Why didn't you come to me when Lady Fox was ill?"

"I went to see Lieutenant Wadman and he gave his permission for the medicine. It was Mr Simons who refused to give it to me."

Captain Philips sighed. "That's his prerogative. He's responsible for the distribution of medicines." He rose from the table and walked over to the window. "I told you that any infraction of the rules would mean curtailment of privileges and Tunny would join the other prisoners in the hold."

"Lady Fox is still very ill. She needs Mary Tunny to nurse her."

"Mary Tunny will return to the hold."

Conrad hesitated before saying, "Yes, sir."

"As for the boy. He'll receive half a dozen lashes tomorrow afternoon."

"He's only a child, sir."

"Then it will teach him to grow into an adult."

Conrad went in search of Patrick and found him mending a wooden support on the chain pump.

"We're going tonight," said Conrad through his teeth. "We can't afford to wait any longer."

"But my lord..." Conrad raised his hand warning him to keep his voice down, but looking around, there was no one in earshot. "We are still a hundred miles from Saint Helena Bay. It's too far away. We need to be closer."

Conrad shook his head. "The boy is to be flogged tomorrow afternoon and I must prevent it."

"How many lashes?"

"Half a dozen, the captain says."

"Then let him take them."

"Are you insane!"

"He's a strong boy and better that he takes the punishment than we launch a small boat miles from our destination. We could all die."

"You would let a child be flogged to save our plan?"

"I would if it was necessary." He picked up the small hammer and tapped a nail into the handle of the pump.

Conrad turned from him in bewilderment and looked across at a young midshipman giving orders to let out more sail. Two sailors started climbing the rigging.

Conrad had relied on Patrick's support for the last two months and now, his opposition startled him.

He turned back to the man fitting a piece of wood into place.

"Don't you understand? If Joshua is whipped and goes back to the hold then his wounds will fester and he'll die from infection. I promised his grandmother that they could come to safety with us and I mean to keep that promise."

Patrick nodded. "I do understand, but when I came on this mission, it was to save her ladyship only. Now we have a further two passengers that were not accounted for."

"There is room enough in the boat for them and provisions too."

"Only if we get closer to Saint Helena Bay. We might meet a storm and be pushed off course. It must be within fifty miles or we'll not survive."

Conrad rubbed his brow in exasperation. "Patrick, I know how you feel and your sentiments are correct. I included the extra two people in the plan and I must bear the responsibility. But Mary Tunny and her grandson have helped keep Kate alive these last months and I have a great deal to thank them for." He thought for a few seconds. "We leave tonight but I will remain behind. Without me, it means there will be enough rations to last the longer journey. I will try and get away in Cape Town."

Patrick stared at him for a few seconds before giving a rueful laugh. "Sir, they'll suspect you had a hand in the escape and you'll be arrested. And do you believe Lady Fox will go without you? No, my lord, she will not."

"And neither will she allow you to stay behind."

Patrick agreed. "The decision has to be yours."

Conrad struggled with his conscience. "Then Joshua must suffer the flogging and may God forgive me."

Conrad told Katherine when he brought her rations. Her eyes opened wide in shock that Joshua was to receive half a dozen lashes.

"They can't do it, surely? Not to a child?"

"The captain said he should have hanged for attempting to steal the quinine."

"It's so cruel. Oh, Conrad, can't you do something?"

He stared at her, feeling helpless. Although still very weak, she had managed to pull herself out of the hammock, knowing that the longer she lay there, the worse she would feel and she had made a seat for herself out of the pile of sacks. Now Conrad was sitting next to her.

"I'm so sorry, Kate. I know that you're fond of the boy." He shook his head. "God damn it, I've grown fond of him. But it will jeopardise our plan to help him." He caressed her cheek. "Have faith, darling girl, Joshua will come through this and we'll make our escape as planned."

He pulled her close and kissed her. They sat quietly for a while, in each other's arms, lost in thought.

After Conrad had left her, she looked around the small room, so empty now that Mary had been removed to the hold and Joshua was locked in the brig.

"I want to go home," she whispered, hugging her knees.

And those words echoing down through the years, so familiar, so poignant, seemed more terrible than ever.

That evening, at five minutes to eight o'clock, Conrad made his way on deck to take First Watch.

The sailor he was relieving gave a huge yawn. "Nothing's happened, but there's been a bank of fog drifting towards us for the last hour. Young Wadman up there," he gestured to the quarterdeck, "has asked us to keep a look out for Frogs."

Conrad felt startled. "Why should the French bother us?"

The sailor grinned. "Haven't you heard? Oh, no, you wouldn't have since you're too preoccupied with that 'special' prisoner of yours. News came from a passing ship. Bony's been beat in Egypt at a place called Alexandria. Him and his rag-tag army will be scurrying back to France no doubt." He tapped a nose that was far too long for his features. "My guess it's the end for old Bonaparte. Anyway, Wadman thinks that the Frenchies will be so mad, that they'll attack any ship flying the Union Jack. Well, I'm off. Keep an eye on the fog...and Frogs." He left, chuckling at his own quip.

Conrad took up position. Staring out into the darkness of the night, he thought about what he had heard. His crewmate was right, the French couldn't withstand another defeat and Bonaparte would make a hasty retreat back to Paris before the winter. It seemed that the war was all but over. He looked up at the sails barely moving in the slight breeze. The fog bank would take a while to get to them and when it did, they would be shrouded in a thick mist that would make his watch more difficult if not impossible.

His mind wandered to Joshua and the inevitable punishment the following day. He grimaced as he thought of the boy being bound to a grating and his back lashed with the cat o'nine tails. But there was nothing he could do for him. He must keep to the plan. They would leave the ship when they were within fifty miles of Cape Town and row towards Saint Helena Bay to rendezvous with the Countess of Croston. With Kate safe and cared for, her health should improve quickly. That's all he wanted, to see her well and happy again.

"Anything to report?"

He was surprised that Lieutenant Wadman had come down from the quarterdeck.

"No, sir. Everything's quiet."

"You know about the Frogs?"

"Yes, sir."

The lieutenant looked him up and down before asking, "Whereabouts in Germany do you hail from?"

"Hamburg," said Conrad quickly, wary that he must watch what he said. Wadman was not only arrogant but also cunning and it would be a tragedy if his false identity was discovered so close to their escape.

"Never been there. Been to Munich, though." Conrad didn't reply, knowing that a mere crewman didn't become familiar with an officer. Suddenly, he looked down and although the lanterns only gave minimal light, he saw something shiny peeping out of the lieutenant's pocket. Lieutenant Wadman noticed his interest and gave a smirk. With a flourish he pulled out the handkerchief and threaded it through his fingers. "Captain pushed this in a drawer so I thought I would appropriate it, since I knew he would forget its existence in due course."

"It's pretty."

"Of course, my initial isn't 'R'," he mused. He gave Conrad a sidelong glance. "I'm sure it's hers, you know. Lady Fox. And I'm certain she's guilty of murdering Sergeant Crowther. Oh, she vehemently denied it, but she's already killed once so a second time should be easy enough."

"Yes, sir."

Wadman pursed his mouth and turned on him angrily. "Are you just agreeing with me or do you really believe she did it?"

Conrad clenched his fist to stem his irritation. "I don't agree or disagree, sir."

"You're a peculiar one, Schmidt," he said, frowning. "You have a certain style, an elegance about you that runs contrary to any other crewman I've met. And your hands are not those of a sailor. Too soft by half. If I didn't know better I would say you had aristocratic blood running through your veins."

Conrad smiled. "I hardly think so."

Wadman nodded. "Perhaps your father was a nobleman and your mother…" Conrad gave him a sharp look. "Well, no more said, eh?" Conrad was finding him annoying and wished he would go back to the quarterdeck. "You seem to have grown quite attached to Lady Fox?"

"I do my duty, sir."

He clicked his tongue. "I'm sure it's more than that. I've heard you give up half your rations for her."

"She's been ill and needs more nourishment."

"Do you have designs on her, Schmidt? Are you thinking that she might take up with you when we arrive at Port Jackson?"

"Certainly not, sir."

"If she takes up with anyone, no doubt it will be someone with status. Captain of the guard, perhaps, or even the governor. Certainly not a mere sailor."

"Yes, sir," said Conrad, paying no heed to his prattle. He had been keeping his attention on the fog slowly drifting towards them. The grey mass was like a wall, seemingly impenetrable and yet, once they were engulfed in it, they would not be able to see their hand in front of their faces. He narrowed his eyes. Was that a glint of light he had seen in the mist? It was probably the moon reflecting off the moisture droplets, he thought, but then it happened again. A reddish, yellow spark just visible in the fog. In horror, he saw the dark shape loom towards them. "It's a man o' war, sir! I can't see their colours, but I don't think it's one of ours."

Lieutenant Wadman raised his telescope. "Dear God, it's the French! All hands to quarters!"

Conrad ran to the bell and sounded the alarm. Within seconds, the deck was covered with running sailors and marines, all going to their designated positions.

"What is it, Mr Wadman?" shouted the captain who had just appeared from the forecastle.

"The French, sir. They're on our starboard side and I believe their gun ports are open."

The heart-stopping boom of the guns sounded and then the shrill whistle as the cannon balls came their way. The Guardian was hit below the waterline on the stern; smashing the rudder and creating a gaping hole in the hold.

She was equipped with only sufficient guns to ward off a minor assault and was no match for a man-of-war with over sixty guns. Bewildered that a convict ship should be under attack, the gunners ran frantically to their positions in order to return fire. Within minutes, a barrage of cannon shell was heading towards the French.

Conrad's duty was to put out fires and for ten minutes he was absorbed in pouring seawater over the flames that licked at the sails and scorched the deck, stepping over the broken bodies of two sailors and a marine who had been blown from their positions at the first bombardment.

He looked about him. The hatch to the prisoner's hold was still open, the marine guarding it now lying dead nearby, his arm blown off from the shoulder. Conrad lowered himself down and what he saw made him groan. Some of the prisoners were standing ankle deep in water, their eyes filled with fear. Others were lying about, listless and looking ill, oblivious that the hold was flooding. A volley of questions came his way, from the able prisoners. He tried to pacify them.

He quickly climbed the ladder and immediately saw the lieutenant directing two sailors in lifting the mangled debris of the main topsails off the captain's leg.

"The hold is flooding, sir. Shall I get the prisoners on deck?"

"Damn the prisoners! Let them drown. The rudder's gone and the main keel damaged. The ship is full of holes so we're all going to the bottom of the sea anyway."

Conrad opened his mouth to reply, when a cannon ball smashed through the rail, blasting the lieutenant, sailors and Captain Philips across the deck. Conrad was knocked off his feet and flung against the main mast. It was a full two minutes before he could pick himself up and bending over, he spent another minute trying to catch his breath, before wiping the blood from his face and staring down at the mutilated remains of Captain Philips and his men.

He saw the red, silk handkerchief poking out of the lieutenant's pocket and stooping quickly, pulled it out.

"You won't be needing this, sir," he said, pushing it into his shirt and striding towards the small storeroom where Katherine was confined. The marine guarding her was young, very young and his face showed his terror. "Go on deck. The corporal has need of you."

"What's happening?" said the marine, handing the key to Conrad.

"We're engaged in battle with a French man o' war, so you had better get in a longboat and row away from the ship."

The marine ran to the companion-way while Conrad turned the key and swung open the door. Katherine was standing near the hammock and ran to him. He caught her in his arms.

"Are we being attacked?"

Conrad nodded. "Yes, the Guardian won't survive so I think it's time to abandon ship."

"What about Mary and Joshua?"

"We'll have to leave them."

She pulled away from him. "No, Conrad, I won't go without them."

"Kate, there isn't time to fetch them. We must get to a boat immediately."

She shook her head. "Grandmama always said there's time for the important things in life and Mary and Joshua are important."

He let out a sigh. "Oh, my Kate, you will always be my conscience. All right, do you remember the boat where I first found you?" She nodded. "Meet me there and I'll bring them to you."

Finding Mary was easy, since the prisoners who were able, had climbed the ladder and were wandering about on deck in a daze.

"We're leaving the ship," said Conrad, gripping her arm. "Kate is already waiting for us near the end boat. Go and join her."

"Joshua?"

"I'll get him out of the brig. Go, now, while everyone is busy, but don't let anyone see you."

He left her, striding towards the brig and Mary looked about her. Her sight and hearing were assailed at the horror that seemed to be everywhere, at the broken and bloodied bodies, the cries of the remaining officers as they tried to take command, their yells mingling with the screams of the injured and dying.

On the way to the brig, Conrad met Patrick and sent him in the direction of the boat to start lowering it into the water, while Conrad carried on with his quest to fetch Joshua.

As Conrad climbed down the ladder, he saw the boy sitting on a barrel in what looked like a metal cage. The marine guarding him was a more experienced man and raised his musket when he heard someone coming down the ladder.

"Who goes there?"

Conrad identified himself. "I've come for the prisoner. We must abandon ship."

"I've received no orders. Where's the captain?"

"Dead. Now, if you want to live, then I suggest you do as I say."

The marine listened to the booming guns overhead. "Sounds pretty unpleasant up there," he said, lowering his weapon.

"Not as unpleasant as being down here when we sink." He held out his hand. "Give me the key and I'll release the boy."

The marine shook his head. "The prisoner is my responsibility."

"Then you unlock the door."

"I think not." They stared at each other. The marine raised his musket once more. "Never liked you, Fritzy. Can't stand the French, but I've always been suspicious of Germans. Wouldn't surprise me if you brought the man o' war down on us. Sent them a signal did you?"

Conrad gave a half-smile. "No I didn't. And I'm an Englishman," he said, dropping the German accent.

"What?"

"I'm English. Born and bred in the county of Gloucestershire within sight of the Cotswolds." Another cannon ball hit the ship, shaking the hull and flinging Conrad into the marine, knocking him off balance. He grabbed the musket and pointed it at the marine's head. "Now, unlock the door and release the boy or I'll blow off your bloody head!" The marine took the key from his belt and put it in the lock. Joshua had been watching, his small hands wrapped round the bars of his cell and when the door opened he ran straight to Conrad. "I still advise you to get on deck," said Conrad to the marine. He placed an arm round the boy's shoulders. "Come on, there isn't much time."

Still holding the musket, he urged Joshua in front of him and followed him up the ladder, keeping his eyes on the marine. He only turned for a moment to push Joshua through the open hatch, when movement behind him made him turn his head. The marine was at his back and then a sharp pain shot through him making him gasp. Sinking against the ladder, Conrad slipped slowly to the bottom of the steps, losing his grip on the musket and unaware that the ivory handle of a knife was protruding from his right shoulder. The marine pulled the blade out and made ready for a second strike.

CHAPTER EIGHTEEN

Conrad tried to fight the waves of nausea. The shock of the attack paralysed him for a few seconds, but when he saw the marine, his face full of rage and the glint of the blade ready for a second blow, he summoned the strength to raise his hands to protect himself and kick out at his assailant, making him stagger backwards. Conrad rolled across the floor out of his way and then heard the blast of musket fire and saw the marine slamming into the iron cage that had previously held Joshua. The marine stayed still for a moment and then slipped silently to the floor. Looking up, Conrad saw Joshua, the musket held tightly in his hands.

"He kept telling me about the flogging I was going to get and how the blood would cover my back and run down my legs and I would have red marks on me forever."

Conrad looked at the bleeding form lying against the metal bars, his body twisted. "Well, he won't be saying anything more. You did well, boy. Now give me your arm. We must get on deck."

Joshua helped him up and they climbed the steps together. Once out on deck, they skirted round the fallen debris and numerous fires that engulfed the Guardian until they reached the longboat at the end. Patrick was lowering it into the water, Katherine and Mary watching him.

Katherine let out a cry of fright when she saw Conrad leaning heavily on Joshua's shoulder.

"Oh, God, you're hurt."

"Knife wound in my back," he gasped. "I'll be all right, Kate."

She put her arm round him.

Some ammunition exploded close to them, causing the rope to be pulled out of Patrick's hands and the boat plunged into the sea.

Patrick looked over the side. "It's still in one piece, thank goodness, but we'll have to jump. I'll go first then I can retrieve the boat. Then Mary and the boy and finally you, my lord and Lady Fox."

Conrad nodded and they watched as Patrick climbed over the rail and disappeared from sight. And then Mary and Joshua held hands and followed him over the side.

Katherine held on tightly to Conrad. "Are you ready? I will count to three."

She looked down into the dark void that was the Atlantic Ocean. It was a long way to jump, the height of Croston Court. She remembered the day they had stood on the battlements and smiled. Counting to three, she closed her eyes and they jumped together.

The air whistled past them as they fell and then coldness enveloped them. Katherine had hit the water with a smack that hurt her arms and legs and then they seemed to be underwater for a long time. She opened her eyes. All was blackness although she was aware of holding onto Conrad's jacket and feeling his body close to hers. Thoughts of her parents drifted through her mind. Had they done this? Had they jumped into the water, clinging onto each other, never to be parted? Had they tried to swim to survive, but ultimately been claimed by the cruel sea?

Katherine's head bobbed on the surface and she looked around. Above her she could see the Guardian in flames. Crew, prisoners, marines and anyone else who could, were jumping into the water. The boat had drifted a little way from the ship but Patrick had been able to swim to it and after locating Joshua, pulled him aboard. And then Katherine could hear him shouting their names.

Holding onto a heavy and unconscious Conrad, she saw Mary just a little way ahead and called to her.

"Mary! Are you all right?"

"I live, my lady. Though an old body like me can't be jumping off ships too often."

Patrick heard their voices and rowed the boat towards them. With Katherine pushing from behind he managed to pull Conrad into the boat and then he helped the women to safety. Katherine sat with her arms round Conrad as Patrick took the oars and tried to get them as far away from the sinking ship as possible. In the distance, on the edge of the fog bank, they could see the French man-of-war, its guns now silent.

"What are they doing?" asked Katherine.

"They know the frigate is doomed and are picking up survivors," said Patrick.

"So people will be saved," she said, smiling.

"Aye, but only to become prisoners of war."

Katherine thought about this and decided that for the convicts, it might be a better situation. But not for the others. She watched as the noise and lights of the frigate and man-of-war got fainter and then they were surrounded by darkness.

"Where are we going?"

"I need to row east, my lady," said Patrick, looking at the compass.

She looked up at the brilliant Southern Cross in the night sky and realised that they had crossed the equator long ago and the North Star was beyond their vision. She also knew that the fog would soon obliterate the stars' spectacular splendour.

"Towards Saint Helena Bay?"

"Yes, my lady," he smiled.

The longboat was equipped with two pairs of oars and seeing the second pair lying idle, Joshua changed his position.

"I shall help you," he said, taking an oar.

Katherine kneeled by the side of Conrad and rolled him over. He moaned with pain. She removed his jacket and ripped his shirtsleeve to reveal a blood-red gash in his shoulder.

"I should bind this, but I've nothing clean to use."

Moving him had made him regain consciousness and he pulled himself up into a sitting position, holding his injured shoulder and grimacing slightly.

"Where are we?"

"Rowing east, but we're a long way from our destination," said Patrick.

"Let me get my strength and I'll row with you."

"Nonsense," said Mary. "I'll join my grandson and take the other oar. We'll be moving along at a fine pace in no time."

Katherine put her hand on Conrad's arm. "I must deal with your wound, or it won't stop bleeding. But I have nothing to use."

Conrad smiled and pulled the handkerchief from out of his shirt. "Use this."

Katherine took it, her expression unreadable and tied it round the gash, pulling it tight. "Where did you get it?"

"Took it from Lieutenant Wadman after he was killed."

She pulled a face. "Seems to me that this damned handkerchief is never going to leave me in peace."

Conrad took her hand and kissed it.

Everyone took turns to row. Conrad refused to be excused and Katherine, although still weak, insisted on sitting beside him while they took an oar each. The boat had been loaded with food and water over the last few days, hidden under the canvas that covered the boat while on deck. And now this cover, stowed away in the bow, became their refuge.

Throughout that first night they stayed under it for warmth and then it gave them shade the following day from the fierce sun.

A second night was spent under the stars and while the others slept, Katherine and Conrad lay side by side, talking of England and home, of Philippa and the family and friends they had left behind and yet, hoped to see very soon.

The second day was greeted with squally showers and the canvas cover gave them shelter while they bailed out water that washed over the side.

Conrad's wound started healing and to Katherine's relief did not fester. A sextant and telescope had also been put aboard along with the compass and Conrad used them regularly, plotting their course and looking out for land, ever grateful for the rapid but detailed tutoring of Master Hughes.

But the continual spray of seawater made their clothes unbearably salty and the fabric started to chafe their raw skin causing salt sores. They decided to remove what clothing was decent and continued rowing, their efforts reinforced by wind and current.

On the morning of their fifth day, Katherine awoke to a cobalt-blue ocean and a shimmering sky with just a few wispy clouds. She looked about her but all she could see was the vastness of the Atlantic, until two dolphins suddenly appeared, their noses nudging the boat. Laughing, Katherine reached out and stroked them and cried out with delight when they responded with strange clicking sounds.

"Perhaps they're telling us that land is close," smiled Conrad.

Patrick raised the telescope. "You could be right, my lord."

He passed the telescope to Conrad. "I don't think that's Saint Helena Bay. If it is then where is the Countess of Croston?"

They shielded their eyes, eager to get a view. In the distance they could see wide, sandy beaches and a small village.

Conrad pointed. "Can you see over there? There are people on the beach waiting for us. Dear Lord, I hope they're friendly."

There must have been two dozen people jumping about on the sand, men, women and children, all waving in a frantic manner.

"Could be them canny...bulls, my lord," said Mary, drawing Joshua close to her. "Them what eat folk like us."

Katherine studied the beach and small, mud huts built just to one side. She was sure she could see fishing nets hanging up to dry and if she was right, then surely fishermen must be friendly? Her body ached to stand on dry land and she watched the golden sand with longing.

"I don't think they're cannibals," said Conrad. "But I think we had better be cautious." They manoeuvred the boat nearer to land and it was as they got closer that Conrad gave a cry of surprise. He had been scrutinising the crowd on the beach through the telescope and had thought he had seen someone he recognised. "No, it can't be. Surely not." He brought the figure into focus. "Dear Lord, it's Frobisher. Standing there amongst the natives."

They pulled for shore and when they reached the breakers, the people from the village ran into the water

361

and helped bring the boat in, their black faces aglow with delight, their language incomprehensible and yet, full of bubbling laughter. Without ceremony, many pairs of arms lifted them out of the boat.

Frobisher came across to Conrad and they shook hands. "You're a sight for sore eyes," said Conrad.

"We decided to enlist the help of all the villages along the coast, to look out for you." smiled Frobisher. "This place is called Paternoster, but Saint Helena Bay is just on the other side of the headland and the yacht is waiting for us there."

Their stay in the village was brief, just long enough to take a drink and a small bite of food. And then they climbed into a cart pulled by an ox, travelling at a leisurely pace round the headland, spending most of the time in silence, lost in thought. Under the brilliant blue sky of the West Coast of Africa and now safe on land, it was as if each of them had to come to terms with their ordeal. But the sight of the Countess of Croston brought them back to the present. Beautiful and shining brilliant white in the morning sun, she bobbed on the water, her sails furled.

"What do you think of her?" whispered Conrad, pulling Katherine close to him.

She nodded in delight. "I'm so pleased you named her after Philippa."

He didn't answer, only smiled.

The cart rumbled along the makeshift pier and then stopped. They climbed out and suddenly, there seemed to be people everywhere, kissing and hugging them. Richard took Katherine's hand and kissed it, Geraldine threw her arms round her, telling her how thin she looked.

And then Katherine saw Betsy. "What are you doing here?" She noticed the wedding ring on Betsy's finger and smiled.

"Eeh, me and my Harry had to come," said the maid in her wonderful Durham lilt that was a joy to hear. "I knew you would need me." She scrutinised Katherine's tangled locks. "Have you been brushing your hair every morning and night, my lady?"

The reprimand was so ordinary that Katherine felt a lump come to her throat. "I'm sorry, Betsy. I seemed to have lost my hairbrush."

Everyone burst into laughter and Betsy blushed, unaware that she had said anything amusing. And then they all went on board.

It felt wonderful to bathe properly and change into clean underwear. Betsy had been surprised that her lady had remained in the tub for well over an hour and had insisted on having her hair washed three times.

When everything was done, Katherine opened the cupboard and, in absolute amazement, saw her gowns displayed like flowers in a beautiful garden.

"His lordship requested that I bring everything you need, my lady," said Betsy. "And your aunt insisted that I bring this gown. I wondered if it was for a special occasion?"

She pointed to the end of the rail and Katherine gasped. For there in all its loveliness was the gown she had ordered when Conrad had been away in Worcester and which her aunt must have collected from the dressmakers on completion. The pale blue taffeta shimmered in the sunlight, the silver thread sparkled and as she caressed it and traced her fingers along the blue, silk ribbon beneath the bodice, she thought of how long ago it seemed that she had ordered it. She could hardly believe that she had once lived that privileged life. Even the visits she used to make to her Aunt Sybil's humble cottage in Bristol seemed a time of comfort compared to her terrible experience on the Guardian.

"You've brought my wedding gown, Betsy," she murmured.

"You'll need to put on a little weight, but you'll look a fair treat when you do wear it." And then she helped her onto the bunk. "Now, you need to rest, my lady."

After she had left, Katherine lay quietly, staring through the porthole, her eyelids heavy and her body trembling with the need to sleep. As she started drifting away, she heard Conrad's laughter in the passageway and she smiled. She was safe. Sinking into the softness of the covers, she slept away the rest of the morning and all of the afternoon.

By the time Betsy came to wake her for an early supper, the sun was a golden ball low in the sky. Katherine opened her eyes expecting to be aboard the convict ship and when she realised that she was safe, she laughed out loud to hide the happy tears that kept trickling down her cheeks.

Betsy helped her dress, a task that the maid thought so commonplace and yet for Katherine, an absolute wonder since she thought dressing for supper was something she would never do again.

They sat on deck to eat a simple, plain meal, since their stomachs were not used to rich food, but it was a wonderful meal, their first proper meal together. Mary and Joshua sat with them and Joshua, who had hardly said a dozen words since coming on board, was filled with excitement.

"This boat is a beauty, sir," he said, his blue eyes sparkling.

Conrad nodded. "Yes, she is. Would you like to have a turn at managing her? I'm sure Master Hughes would instruct you."

Joshua's face broke into a wide grin.

"What's to become of us, my lord?" asked Mary.

"What would you like to do?"

"As you wish, my lord. I washed and mended clothes to earn a living, but I'm willing to turn my hand to anything, as will Joshua."

"The authorities will believe you were lost when the Guardian went down." He gestured to Katherine and Patrick. "In effect, we have all perished at sea."

"What a terrible thought," said Katherine. "To be regarded as dead."

Conrad reached across and took Katherine's hand. His eyes drank in her appearance and he marvelled how a good sleep and her happiness had dissolved the look of absolute fatigue. Now, sitting opposite him wearing a pretty gown of cream muslin, with a ribbon in her hair, he knew exactly how their future would be.

"I want to sail to Madeira. We'll be safe there and I'm in the process of buying a villa. In fact, the sale should be completed by now."

He looked across at Frobisher who nodded. "Yes, my lord, the renovations should be finished and Mrs Craddock was in the process of hiring staff when I left. Also all necessary vehicles are purchased."

Conrad gripped Katherine's hand tighter. "A home for you and me. Unfortunately, you cannot return to England. You're too well known and I don't want to take the risk of you being arrested and sent away on another convict ship."

"I can't bear that thought," said Katherine.

"If we stay in Madeira, then the Countess of Croston can sail back to England and collect your family.

They're all waiting to hear of the success of our mission. I'd like Frobisher to inform them that we are safe before they hear of the Guardian's sinking. Otherwise, they might think we are lost." He winked at his secretary. "Also, I'm sure your wife will require your company at this special time."

Katherine's mouth fell open realising the implication of his words. "Anne is with child?"

"Yes indeed, my lady," smiled Frobisher. "We'll have a new addition to the Frobisher family in October."

"That's wonderful." Katherine smiled with him and then turned to Conrad. "And my family will spend time with us in Madeira?"

Conrad nodded. "I'm sure their trunks are already packed," he chuckled.

"And my mother is also waiting for news," said Patrick.

Katherine almost clapped her hands in delight. Her thoughts overwhelmed her at life's strange twists and turns. "Madeira," she whispered. "That's where my father was going on his last voyage with my mother."

Mary had her own thoughts to deal with. "Then could we go with you, my lord? Me and Joshua? We can serve you in your villa in anyway you wish."

Conrad frowned. "You don't want to return to England?"

"No, my lord. We want to stay with Kate...I mean Lady Fox. We've been through a lot together and I'm sure we'll be happy with her."

"Then you will come with us," smiled Conrad. He turned to Katherine. "There is the slight problem of Westcroft?"

Katherine shook her head. "Westcroft is not mine. I don't care if I never see it again." She gave Geraldine a sidelong glance. "Mr Newton has my will. I left Westcroft to you."

Geraldine protested. "It doesn't seem right, to take Westcroft from you."

"The estate will be yours if I marry." She addressed her next comments to Conrad. "If you remember, I was told that I would lose it all if I wed within twenty years. And I want to be your wife."

"Are you certain, my darling?" Conrad whispered, his heart thudding in his throat. "You're giving up quite a fortune."

She took a sip of wine, licking her lips at the sweet, unaccustomed taste. "I couldn't be more certain."

Betsy appeared and after giving a slight curtsey she handed the red, silk handkerchief to Lord Croston.

"I've washed it, my lord. I thought you would want it back."

"Thank you, Betsy," he said, taking it from her.

As he did so, a pain shot through his shoulder and it slipped from his hand. It fluttered to the ground like a dying butterfly to land at Katherine's feet.

Patrick threw back his head and laughed.

"What are you laughing at?" said Conrad, wincing at the pain and rubbing his shoulder.

"It's something I heard the sailors talking about on board the Guardian. That once in Port Jackson, if a man wants a woman as his wife, then he drops a handkerchief at her feet. It acts as a proposal and marriage ceremony all at the same time."

Conrad winked at Katherine. "Then it seems you are already my wife."

She leaned over and caressed his cheek. "Yes, but I will expect a proper ceremony when we reach Madeira." She smiled and looked out at the setting sun, so big and beautiful against the darkening sky and then looked down at the handkerchief lying at her feet. "I have a wonderful gown to wear and I mean to wear it."

That night, Conrad and Katherine took a short walk and then stood together on the beach, looking out to sea. The moon was bright and reflected a shimmering glow on the surface of the water.

"We shall set sail for Madeira in the morning," he said. "Wait until you see your new home. It's a beautiful villa set in the hillside and looking over the bay. There you'll be able to rest and get your strength back"

"Oh, Conrad, could we not leave the day after tomorrow?"

"Why do you want to wait? Everything will be prepared for you when we arrive. It will be fully furnished and well staffed. You need the voyage behind you as soon as possible for your health's sake."

She threw back her head, her laughter like a tinkling bell and looked about her. "It's so beautiful here and tomorrow I want us to take another walk on the beach, just like this and I want to feel the sand between my toes. I want to sit under a tree and watch the leaves fluttering in the breeze. I just want to enjoy...being alive."

"Then that's what we'll do," he smiled, pulling her close.

Katherine took in a breath and leaned her head against his shoulder. "One day we will return to England to visit Widcombe Hall and Croston Court won't we?"

"Of course," he said and then added softly, "I promise you, my Kate, that these will be our golden years and I'll do everything to make you happy."

And then she heard the call of the dolphins and saw them swimming round the yacht.

She slipped her hand through his arm. "Shall we go back and say goodnight to the dolphins?"

Taking her by the shoulders, he drew her down onto the sand. "The dolphins can wait," he whispered. "According to Patrick we were married today, so this must be our wedding night. Don't you agree, my darling wife?"

* * * * * *

ALSO BY JULIA BELL

If Birds Fly Low
To Guide Her Home
The Wild Poppy
When Lucy Ceased to Be
A Pearl Comb for a Lady
Nyssa's Promise
Songbird: (The Songbird Story – Book One)
A Tangle of Echoes: (The Songbird Story – Book Two)
Deceit of Angels

These novels are available as ebooks on Amazon, but are currently in the process of being published in paperback

IF BIRDS FLY LOW

Since her mother's death, Charlotte Scott has been reared by her Aunt Faith. But her childhood has been plagued by strange knockings on her bedroom door in the dead of night. A summons she never answers since she fears what might be waiting for her behind the door. Meeting Noel Chandler, a tutor at the university in Cambridge causes tension, since Charlotte thinks him prejudiced against women. Noel is actually Squire Chandler and lives at Martlesham Manor a Tudor house in Suffolk.

It is while visiting Martlesham Manor with her cousin, Adele, that Charlotte learns the story of Prudence Chandler who, in the seventeenth century, was denounced as a witch by her husband and mother-in-law and consequently hanged.

Charlotte becomes absorbed with the story of Prudence and realises there are many mysteries at the Manor. Who is the woman who moves silently around the house at night? Why is there a terrible feeling of dread that permeates the old building? And why do the birds fly low since there is always a threat of rain hanging over the Manor? As their love grows, Charlotte and Noel start to uncover the truth of his ancestral home.

But the truth will involve Charlotte more intimately than she could possibly imagine.

TO GUIDE HER HOME

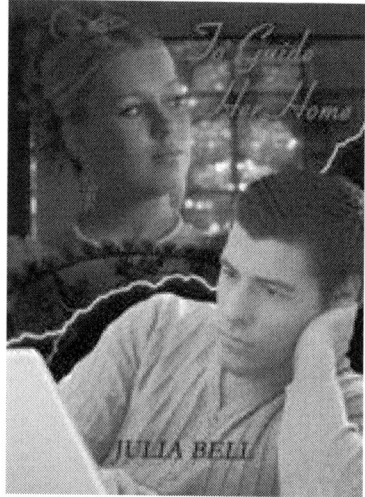

In the late nineteenth century Lydia Prescott has no ambition to settle down to marriage until she has travelled and seen the world. But her life and emotions are shaken up when she meets Doctor Russell Brooks. Unknown to Lydia, Russ is actually an electronics engineer and living in 1998. They are linked by Lydia's home, Prescott Grange on the outskirts of Worcester. In Russ's time, this has been converted into stylish apartments and he has discovered a winding staircase that leads him into the Victorian era.

Russ finds he's attracted to the beautiful fair-haired young woman; a woman very different from those he knows in the twentieth century. But is their love possible when it spans over one hundred years? Russ endeavours to turn himself into a nineteenth century gentleman hoping to win Lydia's heart by playing to her rules. A rival in the person of Doctor Aiden Kinkard spoils his endeavours since Kinkard is determined that Lydia will become his wife.

Russ hopes that one day he will persuade Lydia to live with him in his time, but this has terrible consequences for Lydia and will put her life in danger. As Russ learns more about Doctor Kinkard and begins to question the man's motives and identity, he comes to realise he has met pure evil.

THE WILD POPPY

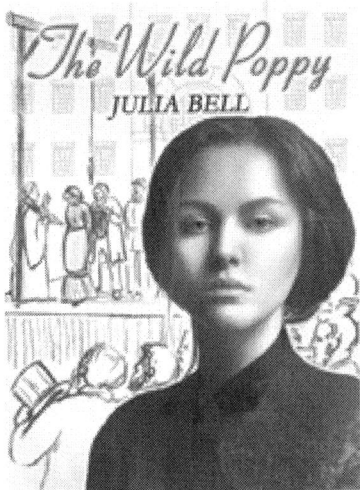

Living during the time of Florence Nightingale and the first woman doctor, Elizabeth Garrett, **Melody Kinsman** is determined to succeed as a newspaper reporter. But in 1864, a female reporter is unheard of and because of the prejudice of the male establishment Melody finds it difficult to persuade an editor to buy her articles.

When she accompanies her friend, **The Hon. Celia Sinclair** to London, she uses it as an opportunity to report the news and events in the capital. She finally confronts the attractive but enigmatic owner of the Cork Street Journal, **Guy Wyngate** who reluctantly gives her the opportunity to prove herself. But first she must face the difficult challenges thrown at her, since Guy wants to test her commitment to the newspaper business.

This commitment will have consequences on her future happiness with the man she gave her heart to when a young girl and to another who is waiting to win her love.

WHEN LUCY CEASED TO BE

Having lost her mother the previous year, twelve-year-old Lucy Paget tries to make a contented life with her father on their farm in Ilkley, Yorkshire. But her father, Sid, would rather spend his time and money in the public house. One day in a fit of pique, Sid sets her up on a chair and tries to sell her to the men in the public house. There are no buyers until a certain gentleman shows an interest and decides to take up the offer. Edwin Beaumont has plans for poor Lucy and for the next eight years, she is trapped in a life of secrets and deceit as she adopts the guise of Edwin's daughter. Meeting her 'cousin' Theo Keeton brings some consolation and over time, his friend Matthew Raynor wins her heart. But Edwin's deception will not only lead to heartbreak, but also Lucy has to face the truth that Matthew might not be the man she thought he was when he is suspected of murder.

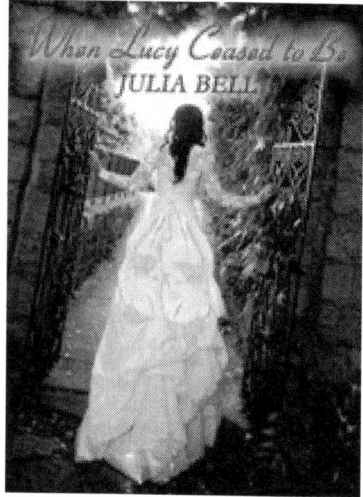

A PEARL COMB FOR A LADY

This is a romance through time.

A pearl comb weaves its way through the centuries, falling into the hands of three very remarkable but determined women. Their stories encompass courage, betrayal, survival and romance, as they find the path that will lead them to true love.

Christabel is feisty with an overactive imagination. Aged 18 and living during the Battle of Waterloo, she's in love with a soldier who only wants to use her to advance his military career.

Victoria, living in the mid-nineteenth century is sweet-natured but haunted by the loss of her child.

Finally there's Jenny, a 21st Century career woman who's unable to sacrifice her pride and forgive the man she loves.

NYSSA'S PROMISE

Since childhood Nyssa Wheeler has lived with her stepsister Gwen in a small house in Fulham, London. But Nyssa possesses the ability of a psychic empath and can read people's emotions through touch. This 'gift' has enabled her to pursue the work of a private investigator.

In the year 1904, she decides to take the position of companion to the Dowager Lady Kirby, living at Kirby House near Bodmin in Cornwall. Here she meets the dowager's two sons, Sir Howel, the sixth baronet and Captain Daveth Kirby, newly home from fighting the Boers in South Africa.

Although seeking a quieter life, Nyssa is drawn into the mystery of the disappearance of Lady Marie Kirby, Sir Howel's new wife. Her investigation involves her in the legend of the Beast of Bodmin Moor, a creature that supposedly prowls the moor. As the deaths mount up, Nyssa and Daveth must find the murderer before Nyssa, herself, becomes the next victim.

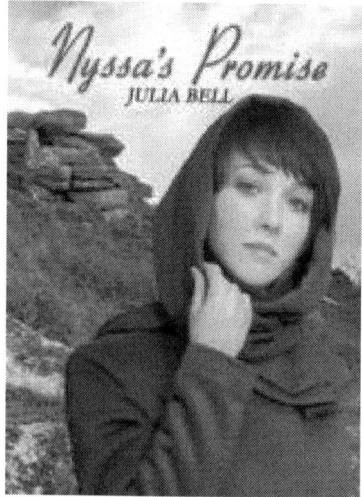

SONGBIRD
THE SONGBIRD STORY – BOOK ONE

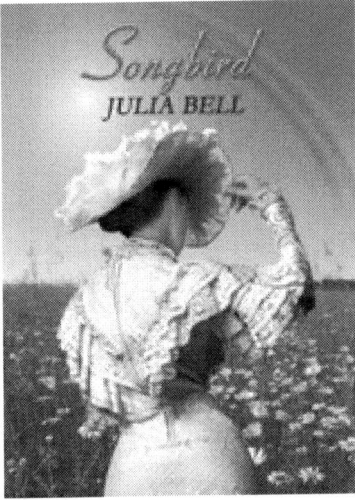

Isabelle Asquith has only one ambition in life and that is to become an opera singer. To do this she must attend The Royal Academy of Music in London and become classically trained. Isabelle is a widow and has a young son to support and the fees for the academy are beyond her means as a music teacher. Her only recourse is to apply for the annual scholarship.

In the summer of 1885 after losing the scholarship for a second time and eager to earn more money, she decides to answer an advertisement. This simple act and the meeting of a mysterious man called 'Karl' will change her life forever.

In the coming years, Isabelle is destined to discover not only her true potential, but also the lengths she is willing to go to realise her ambition.

A TANGLE OF ECHOES
THE SONGBIRD STORY – BOOK TWO

Venice Asquith is the granddaughter of both an earl and a viscount, but this has not prevented her from wanting to train as a doctor. In the London of the 1920's, women physicians are not completely accepted by the medical establishment and Venice has an uphill struggle to realise her ambition.

Meeting the mysterious Tristan Cavell throws her into turmoil. She is not only physically attracted to him, but also intrigued by the secrets he seems to keep. Tristan comes from the poverty of the East End of London and is a veteran of the Great War. He has done well for himself and owns a lucrative hotel and nightclub. But he also owns a casino, an activity that is on the fringes of the law. He believes Venice is out of his league and that her family would never accept him.

However, Venice disagrees and she decides that she must either become his wife or his mistress. Throwing caution to the wind, this decision is made on the toss of the dice and it's a decision she soon comes to regret. When Venice becomes involved in a tragic incident concerning Tristan's business partner Larry Johnson and Larry's girlfriend Martha, she discovers another side to Tristan's nature; a side that alarms her. Although Tristan

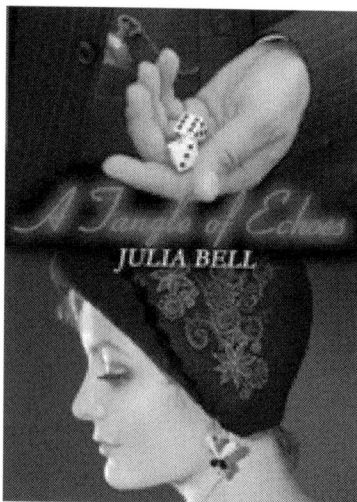

only wants to protect her, she finds his behaviour controlling and suffocating.

Venice is unaware that her grandmother's secret is waiting in the wings to bring terrifying consequences. She and Tristan will have to face these consequences together and this will test their love for each other. The tangle of echoes from the past will change their lives even though the events occurred many years before they were born.

A Special Note from the Author

This story is the sequel to my novel **Songbird**, but I firmly believe that you don't need to read **Songbird** to enjoy **A Tangle of Echoes**. In **Songbird**, I told the story of Isabelle Asquith, but in **A Tangle of Echoes**, it is Venice's story (Isabelle's granddaughter) that takes centre stage.

If you've already read **Songbird** then I know you'll enjoy **A Tangle of Echoes**, but if you haven't then perhaps you'll feel intrigued enough to give Isabelle's story a try and discover how her secret came about all those years ago.

DECEIT OF ANGELS

For nineteen years, Anna Stevens perseveres with a faithless husband in a marriage that destroys her plans to go to university and follow a career.

When Anna escapes to Bristol to work for Jason Harrington, the attractive and wealthy owner of Harrington Rhodes Shipping Agents, she has finally made the decision to leave her husband and make a new life for herself. But Anna has told Jason that she is a widow and when she and Jason fall in love, Anna finds herself trapped in her lies. When her estranged husband finds her, Anna must pay a devastating price for her deceit - a price that would have lasting consequences for her and the man she loves.

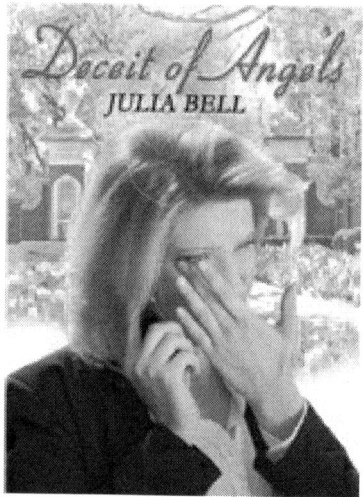

A LETTER FROM THE AUTHOR

Dear Reader,

Thank you so much for choosing to read **Broken Blossoms**. I love writing but having my books read makes them come alive. Until they are read, the characters are only in my imagination and they need to live and be enjoyed. So, I hope you enjoy reading all my novels and you're able to spare a little time in telling me about it.

You can do this via my website.

Julia Bell
www.JuliaBellRomanticFiction.co.uk

39272727R00226

Printed in Poland
by Amazon Fulfillment
Poland Sp. z o.o., Wrocław